MW01599124

蔡志忠／**编绘**

中国对外翻译有限公司
萧潇／**译**

智慧的呢喃

达摩禅

Zen of Bodhidharma

Whispers of Wisdom

中国出版集团
现代出版社

图书在版编目(CIP)数据

达摩禅：汉英对照 / 蔡志忠编绘；萧潇译. —北京：现代出版社，2016.1

(蔡志忠漫画中国传统文化经典)

ISBN 978-7-5143-4299-4

Ⅰ.①达… Ⅱ.①蔡… ②萧… Ⅲ.①漫画－连环画－作品集－中国－现代 Ⅳ.①J228.2

中国版本图书馆CIP数据核字(2015)第277015号

蔡志忠漫画中国传统文化经典：中英文对照版

达摩禅

作　　者　蔡志忠　编绘

　　　　　中国对外翻译有限公司　萧　潇　译

责任编辑　曾雪梅

出版发行　现代出版社

地　　址　北京市安定门外安华里504号

邮政编码　100011

电　　话　010-64267325　64245264（传真）

网　　址　www.1980xd.com

电子邮箱　xiandai@vip.sina.com

印　　刷　三河市南阳印刷有限公司

开　　本　710mm×1000mm　1/16

印　　张　20.5

版　　次　2016年1月第1版　2016年1月第1次印刷

书　　号　ISBN 978-7-5143-4299-4

定　　价　42.00元

目录
contents

序：禅是什么？

Preface: What is Zen?

图文 / 蔡志忠
Text & Illustrations by Tsai Chih Chung

禪

打坐的起源

大概由于古时候没有报纸、杂志、电视，很多古人没事时便独自静坐。

而在无意中发现静坐会引发身心细微的神妙作用，因此发展出坐禅的独门学问。

从欧洲古代遗留下来的图画中便可发现，早在两千多年前，北欧便有静虑禅坐的历史了。

虽然早在2300多年前，庄子的著作便有一篇“颜回忘坐”描述颜回的打坐境界，但中国的禅起源于印度的禅那，于公元527年由达摩祖师带来中土。

The Origin of Meditation

Ancient people would often sit alone as there were no such things as newspaper, magazines and television for them to while away their time.

They happened to find subtle yet amazing changes they would experience in body and mind when they sat in meditation. Meditation then became a spiritual practice.

As shown by some drawings from ancient Europe, Nordic people began to practice meditation as early as over 2,000 years ago.

Over 2,300 years ago, Zhuangzi or Master Zhuang wrote in his work Zhuangzi an essay titled “Yan Hui Deep in Meditation”, describing how the famous disciple of Confucius benefited from the meditative process. However, meditation in association with Zen or Chan Buddhism did not emerge until 527 when Bodhidharma introduced Indian dhyana to China.

禅来自美丽的传说

2,500年前，印度的圣人佛陀在灵鹫山

An Amazing Tale of Zen

The Buddha, the Indian sage, gave

为大众说法，他拿出一朵莲花示众，一言不发。众人皆困惑不解，只有迦叶尊者会心微笑。

a lecture on the Buddhist teachings on Rajagaha or the Vulture's Peak 2,500 years ago. On the lecture, the Buddha remained silent, holding a lotus in his hand.The audience felt confused, except for Mahakasyapa who smiled a knowing smile.

佛陀于是对众人说："我悟道的方法是：看透一切、包容一切，以喜悦的心看清事物的本来面目。这种微妙法门超越语言、文字、数理，不能用逻辑思考，而是要用体会才能领悟的。刚才迦叶尊者已经领悟而起共鸣，所以我将禅心传给他。"

The Buddha then said："I came to my enlightenment by seeing into things, tolerating things, and discovering with joy their true nature. This is a subtle approach beyond language, beyond mathematics, and even beyond logic. It can be understood and grasped only through personal experience. Mahakasyapa has understood it and made a knowing response. That's why I would pass on the essence of Zen to him."

于是迦叶成为禅宗的初祖，拈花微笑便是禅宗的起源。禅宗在一花一笑间诞生了。

Mahakasyapa later became the First Patriarch of Zen.

This is the story of the flower sermon, To which the origin of Zen was ascribed.

无有功德

No Karmic Merit

菩提达摩来到中国，梁武帝请他到金陵问道。

Bodhidharma visited Emperor Wu of Liang in Jinling (present-day Nanjing).

梁武帝问达摩说："我造寺庙、抄佛

Emperor Wu："How much karmic

经、度和尚无数，请问我有多少功德？”

merit have I earned for building monasteries, having sutras copied and ordaining Buddhist monks?”

达摩回答说：“没有功德。”

Bodhidharma: “None.”

梁武帝又问：“佛法圣教的第一义谛是什么？”

Emperor Wu: “So what is the highest meaning of noble truth?”

达摩回答说：“廓然无圣。”

Bodhidharma: “There is no noble truth. There is only emptiness.”

梁武帝又问：“在我面前者是谁？”

Emperor Wu: “Then, who is standing before me?”

达摩说：“不识。”

Bodhidharma: “I know not.”

由于与梁武帝话不投机，达摩就离开梁，到北方的魏国，隐居于少林寺。

The two couldn't see eye to eye. Bodhidharma then left Liang for the northern state of Wei. He lived in seclusion in the Shaolin Temple there.

参禅学佛的目的不是预购天堂入场券，期待死后自己能进入西方净土。

The point of learning Zen is not to secure you a place in the Paradise, nor in the Western Land of Bliss after your death.

悟道为的是此生能成为身心的真正主人，而不是为来世的生意投资。

Enlightenment helps you become the true master of your own body and mind, instead of investing in your future life.

禅是什么？

禅不是宗教，不是哲学，不是科学，不是心理学。

禅不是知识，是悟性；禅不是巧辩，是灵慧。

禅即是融入当下，而不是思维空想。举心即错，拟议即乖。

What is Zen?

Zen is not religion, nor philosophy, Nor science, nor psychology.

It offers not knowledge, but power of enlightenment. It is not about clever talk, but about true wisdom.

Zen is profound contemplation of the present moment. It is not daydreaming, nor applying your mind to erroneous or misleading ideas.

禅是生命的态度

禅是看清世间之后，真正认识自己。

禅是体悟生命实相之后的生活态度。

禅存在于无涯的时空之中，世间随时随处都能见到禅，问题在于我们能不能体会。

Zen is an Attitude toward Life

Zen leads you to the truth about the world, then to your true self.

Zen is an attitude toward life by finding its nature.

In the timeless and boundless universe, Zen is omnipresent. The question is whether we can perceive it or not.

参禅不只是打坐

有位名叫薛简的官员问六祖惠能说："京城参禅的大德们都说，觉悟必须要坐禅习定。请问大师有什么高见？"

Zen Meditation is More Than Sitting

An official called Xue Jian asked Huineng the Sixth Patriarch, "The great meditation practitioners in the capital city all agree that sitting in meditation is a must-take way to enlightenment. What do you think?"

六祖惠能回答说："道由心悟，岂在坐也？"

Huineng answered, "The way of enlightenment lies in one's mind. What does it have to do with sitting?"

参禅悟道不是经由打坐便可获得成果。

Sitting doesn't necessarily mean Zen meditation or enlightenment.

六祖惠能说："生来坐不卧，死去卧不坐；原是臭骨头，何为立功过？"

Huineng the Sixth Patriarch said, "When alive, one keeps sitting without lying down. When dead, one lies without sitting up. In both cases, a set of stinking bones! What has it to do with the great lesson of life?"

磨砖不能成镜，枯坐也不能成佛，参禅悟道要能觉悟出真心本性，才能进入禅的境界里。

A brick will never be ground into a mirror. One never comes to Buddhaship by sitting idly.

One goes into the realm of Zen only when he sees into his own nature through meditation and enlightenment.

禅即是离一切相

Zen Means Getting Rid of All Appearances

习禅并不是要向外求取，而是对内心的自我省察。

Practicing Zen is not a process of searching the outside. Instead, it is a process of introspection.

法海问六祖惠能说："什么是即心即佛？"

Fahai asked Huineng the Six Patriarch, "What is the Buddha in the mind?"

六祖惠能回答说："前念不生即心，

To this, Huineng replied, "Don't

后念不灭即佛。成一切相即心，离一切相即禅。”

stick to your previous thoughts. That's mind. Don't waver at your thoughts. That's Buddha. All signs are generated from mind. Getting rid of appearances leads you to Buddhahood.”

借教悟宗

Enlightenment via Buddha's Teachings

禅是通过佛陀的教导，悟出禅宗的根本精髓。

禅是直接实践佛陀言教的方式，抵达最终的寂静无苦智慧彼岸。

禅宗的传道方法也非常特殊：不立文字，教外别传。直指人心，见性成佛。

Zen is a way to attain the essence of Zen, Via the Buddha's teachings.

Zen is to put the Buddha's teachings into practice, To reach the Other Shore of Enlightenment.

Zen is passed down in a particular way：A special transmission outside the scriptures, Not founded upon words and letters. By pointing directly to [one's] mind, It lets one see into [one's own true] nature and [thus] attain Buddhahood.

不立文字

Not Founded Upon Words and Letters

六祖惠能说：“迷人口念，智者心行。”

禅宗重视自力、自度、自救。

Huineng the Sixth Patriarch said, “The ignorant simply pays lip service. The wise puts it into practice.”

Zen attaches great importance to self-reliance, self-liberation and self-salvation.

培养特立独行的坚强人格，以达到禅悟的境地，欲想成就得道，就必须亲自经历种种艰苦磨炼。

One attains enlightenment by developing strength of character and experiencing hardships.

承言者丧，逐句者迷。

One sticking to speech is unable to attain enlightenment. One sticking to text gets lost.

禅宗极少使用佛教的术语，重视体证、经验、实践，而不是言说、论析、理论。

The teachings of Zen seldom use Buddhist terms; rather, they focus on personal experience and practice, instead of words, analysis or theories.

重要的是做，而不是讲。

Action speaks louder than words.

语言文字只是媒介，而不是真理。

The latter are only a vehicle, instead of the ultimate truth.

禅是活生生的体验，不存在任何的言语文字中。

Zen is hands-on experience, rather than textbook learning.

禅宗讲求实践而不重视言说，

It values practice over speech.

禅并不依据固定的佛教经论。

It never relies upon established Buddhist scriptures.

教外别传

A Special Transmission outside the Scriptures

禅宗是经论言教以外的另一支传承，

Zen is an original school of

禅宗是创造性的宗派，它不依据固定的经论，没有复杂的思想体系，没有神秘的宗教仪式。

Buddhism, independent of established scriptures.

Zen is a Buddhist school full of originality and creativity, relying upon no established scriptures. Without complicated ideological system or mysterious rituals.

禅以一跃而入直截了当的方式直接传承佛陀的心髓，达至开悟。

Zen believes in “sudden” englightenment, To attain the essence of Buddhism and Buddhahood.

直指人心

Pointing Directly to [one's] Mind

内见自性不动，名为禅。

见则直下便见，拟思即差。

Zen is to see into one's nature.

One sees it by instinct, without any thought. With a single thought, it's not Zen.

禅宗是直指人心、明心见性。

Zen helps one see into one's nature and points directly to one's mind.

向外寻求解脱之道，便是骑驴觅驴。

To search the way of liberation from the outside is no different from looking for a donkey on its very back.

禅，不是依样画葫芦的鹦鹉学嘴。

禅，是用自己的心勇敢面对生命。

Zen is not to mechanically imitate.

Zen is to face one's life with one's true mind.

见性成佛

Seeing into One's Nature and Attaining Buddhahood

心性本净，佛性本有，直指人心，见

One's mind and nature is originally

性成佛。

pure. Buddha is originally in one's mind. One sees into his nature and attains Buddhahood.

心即是佛，佛原本即是众生，众生的问题在于他的心。

One's mind is the Buddha. The Buddha is in every ordinary person. The only problem lies with one's heart and mind.

心、佛、众生本是一体，三者无所差别。

There's no difference between one's mind, the Buddha and the ordinary.

长沙景岑禅师说："学道之人不识真，只为从来认识神，无始劫来生死本，痴人唤作本来人。"

Master Jingcen from Changsha put it, "The practioners never know the Buddha, as they've kept pursuing the so-called consciousness. There's actually no start or end, no life or death. Only the ignorant tries to seize hold of that 'self'."

人生的种种痛苦烦恼，缘起于我们的自心。

Sufferings and pains are generated from one's mind.

未悟通生命实相的凡夫，即是红尘此岸的众生。

The ordinary unable to see into the truth of life are all flesh on This Shore of the Mortal World.

佛是调御丈夫，降伏自己的心而达至无苦境界，即是抵达寂静彼岸的佛。

The Buddha is the Master of Adjusting who manages to vanquish his own mind. In this way, the Buddha reached the Other Shore of Enlightenment.

生命即是无穷当下的积累

Life is an Assemblage of Innumerable Present Moments

禅：不说生之前；不说死之后。不说

Zen talks of neither time before

过去；不说将来。

birth，Nor after death. It heeds neither the past，Nor the future.

它最重要的法门是观察此时、此地、此刻、当下、刹那、瞬间！

Its greatest wisdom lies in the observation of the present moment. Now and here!

禅定

Meditation

弟子问：“何名为坐禅？”

A disciple asked，“What's sitting in meditation indeed?”

禅师说：“对一切好坏境界，心念不起名为坐，内见自性不动名为禅。”

The Master replied，“Keeping calm to any outside condition，be it good or bad，is sitting. Seeing into your original nature is Zen.”

六祖惠能说：“外离相为禅，内不乱为定。外禅内定，是为禅定。外若着相，内心即乱。外若离相，心即不乱。”

Huineng the Sixth Patriarch said，“Getting rid of all external signs is Zen. Keeping internal calmness is stability. Meditation means keep your inner peace without disturbance from outside signs. One's inner peace is disturbed，once one is under the influence of signs. One keeps his inner peace，if he gets rid of external signs.”

无上菩提者，被于身为律，说于口为法，行于心为禅。

The Supreme Bodhi means disciplines for actions，Dharmas for teaching and Zen for mind.

为学日增、为道日损

To Learn More and to Give Up More

老子说：“为学日增，为道日损，损

As Laozi put it，“Accumulate day

之又损，以至于无为，无为则无不为。”

by day, to learn more knowledge. Give up day by day, to learn more about the Way and finally to reach the realm of inaction, letting things take their own course.”

习禅并不是使人有所得，而是为了舍弃!

Practicing Zen isn't to gain more. Instead, Zen aims to teach people how to give up.

舍去心中种种习性：

偏爱、憎恶、贪婪、仇恨、嫉妒、虚荣、自卑、自大、骄傲。

One gives up all sorts of evil practices: Partiality, loathing, greed, hatred, jealous, vanity, self-abasement, arrogance and pride.

坐禅

Sitting in Meditation

弟子问禅师说：“禅是什么？”

A disciple asked his master, “What is Zen?”

禅师回答说：“今天的月亮特别圆。”

The master answered, “The moon today is full.”

对弟子的疑惑，禅师总是回答以最终的情境。

The master always described the scene, Whatever the disciple asked.

虽然一生看起来很长，但每天的月亮不一样，每一段时间都不相同，每个当下都独一无二。

A life seems quite long. The moon keeps changing every day.No two periods of time are identical. Every moment is unique.

禅，即是珍视每一时、每一物、每一刹那当下。

Zen is to cherish every second, every thing, every moment.

禅者的心像一面镜子，永远只反映当下现前。

A Zen practitioner focuses only on the present moment and reflects it like a mirror.

禅说了什么？

如果你问“禅说了什么”，表面上它什么都没有说。

如果你认为“禅什么都没说”，开悟者会说：“实质上它什么都说了。”

禅是看到生命的真实：满目青山一任看，云在青天水在瓶。

一切天下万物，都以自己的本来面目，处于自己的位置，展现该有的样子。

凡夫妄想世界能依自己的期待化现，开悟者没有一个期待的自己，他只是无我地融入变化。

What does Zen Tell?

“What does Zen tell?” It seems to say nothing at all.

“Zen tells nothing at all,” if you say like this, An enlightened man will tell you, “Zen tells everything actually.”

Zen is to see into the truth of life: The green mountain stands there as it is. Clouds float in the azure sky and water is in the vase.

Everything in the world sits as it originally is At the place it originally is.

The ordinary harbor the vain hope that the world goes as they'd wish. The enlightened forget themselves and harbor no anticipation, only immersing themselves wholeheartedly into the changes in the world.

不受世间污染

佛陀说：“莲花生于水、长于水，但高出水面，纯洁不受污染。人生于俗世、长于俗世，但借着心灵的升华而高出俗世，不受俗世污染。”

Keeping Untainted and Pure

The Buddha said, “Lotus grows in and out of the water and keeps untainted and pure. One lives in the secular world and keeps untainted from the secular trifles, thanks to his pure mind."

禅即是生存于红尘，而不受红尘的一切所污染。开悟的禅者，永远活在于当下！不为过去、不为将来。

Zen lives in the secular world, untainted and pure. The enlightened always live the very moment. They think about neither the past nor the future.

因为开悟者们知道生命的实相是："时间是由所有无穷多数的当下所积累而成的，任何刹那当下才是生命的真实。"

As the enlightened have seen into the truth of life: "The length of life is added up by innumerable moments. The life thus lies in every moment of the present."

在没有马的国度里，驴子被当成马。现今世上谈禅说道鹦鹉学舌的假禅者很多。如何分辨真假禅者？真正开悟的禅者不是用口说，他们真确地生活于禅境界里如实而行。

Donkeys are taken as horses in a country there are no horses. There are simply too many fakes who keep talking about Zen. How to tell the fake from the genuine Zen practitioner then? The enlightened never pay lip service. Instead, they live Zen.

禅是体悟生命实相之后的生活态度！

Zen is an attitude toward life after having seen into the truth of life.

自己当家做主，活在每一刹那当下。

Be yourself and live every present moment.

楔　子

Introduction

祖师西来
Bodhidharma from the west
佛教由东汉便传入中国，
而禅宗则是由南印度修行者
菩提达摩传到中国的。
Buddhism was introduced into China in the Eastern Han Dynasty, while Zen was brought to China by a South Indian practitioner called Bodhidharma.
公元五二七年（梁大通元年），
九月二十一日，达摩由广州上岸。
Bodhidharma landed on China in Guangzhou on 21 September 527 (the first year of the Datong era of the Liang Dynasty).

十月一日，
达摩受梁武帝之邀
到达首都南京。
He arrived in the capital city Nanjing on October 1st by the invitation of Emperor Wu of Liang.

这时南朝的梁武帝非常喜欢佛法，
平时经常穿着佛衣，长期吃斋念佛。
Emperor Wu of Liang, a dynastic regime of the Southern Dynasties, was a Buddhist follower. Usually clad in a Buddhist monk's costume, the emperor practiced abstinence from meat and prayed to Buddha.

梁武帝问达摩说：
“朕一生弘扬佛法，造寺、度僧、
抄经无数，到底有多少功德？”
Emperor Wu asked Bodhidharma, "How much karmic merit have I earned for building monasteries, having sutras copied and ordaining Buddhist monks?"

没有功德。
None.

为何没有功德?
Why's that?

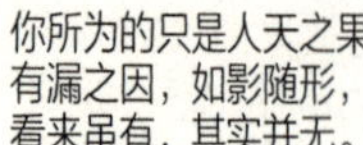
你所为的只是人天之果
有漏之因，如影随形，
看来虽有，其实并无。

What you've done is only quite common result from an imperfect cause. Those seemingly substantial things are actually nothing at all.

什么才是真功德?
What's the authentic karmic merit?

清净智慧，微妙圆融，
本体空寂，无法可得。
Wisdom of purity. Subtle harmony. No established dharmas for the void.

这种功德，绝非世间
有为法所能求得的。
This karmic merit cannot be achieved via the way of this secular world.

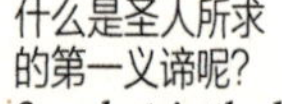
什么是圣人所求
的第一义谛呢?
So what is the highest meaning of noble truth?

廓然浩荡，
本无圣贤。
There is no noble truth. There is only emptiness.

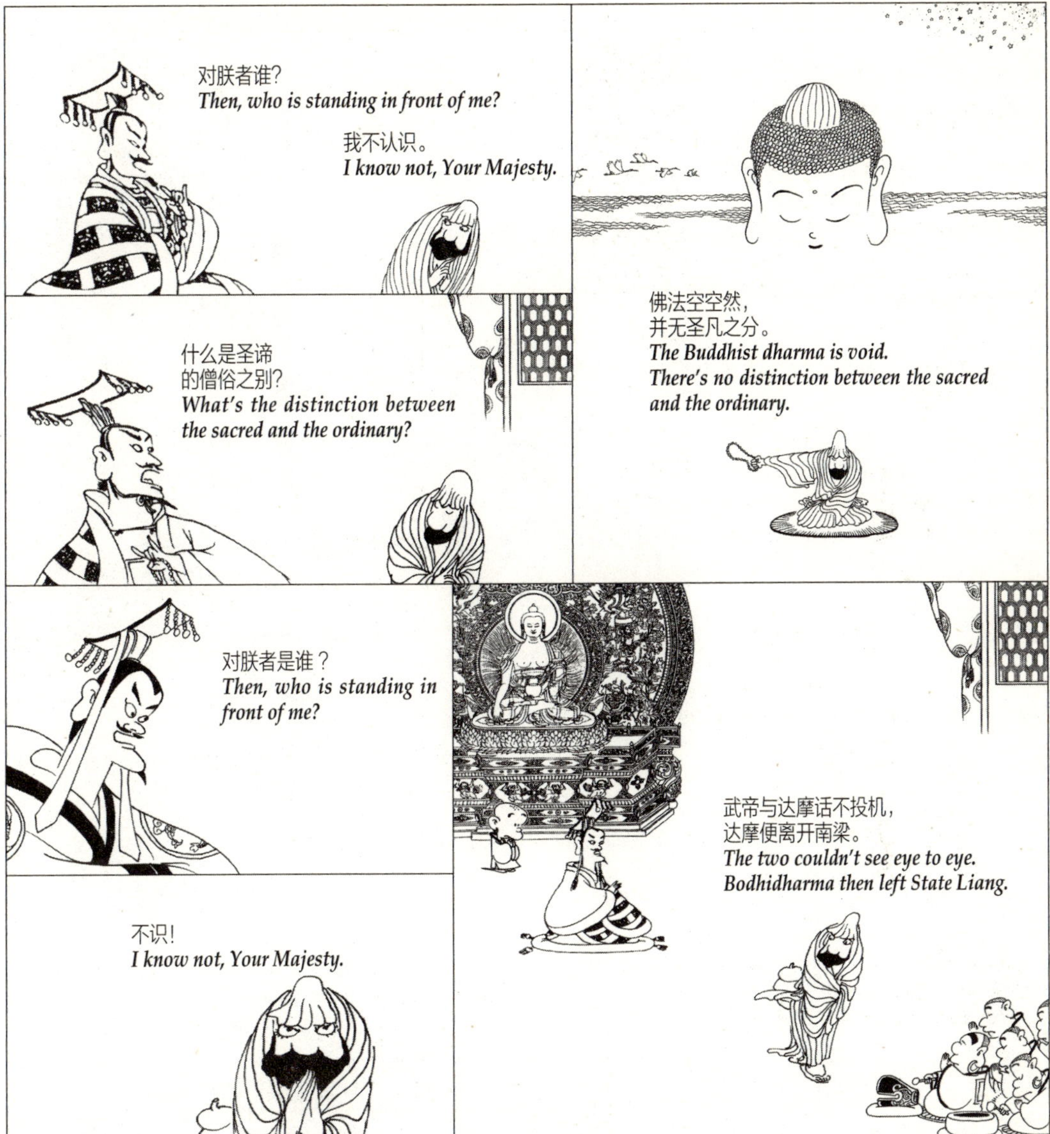
对朕者谁?
Then, who is standing in front of me?
我不认识。
I know not, Your Majesty.
什么是圣谛
的僧俗之别?
What's the distinction between
the sacred and the ordinary?
佛法空空然,
并无圣凡之分。
The Buddhist dharma is void.
There's no distinction between the sacred
and the ordinary.
对朕者是谁?
Then, who is standing in
front of me?
不识!
I know not, Your Majesty.
武帝与达摩话不投机,
达摩便离开南梁。
The two couldn't see eye to eye.
Bodhidharma then left State Liang.

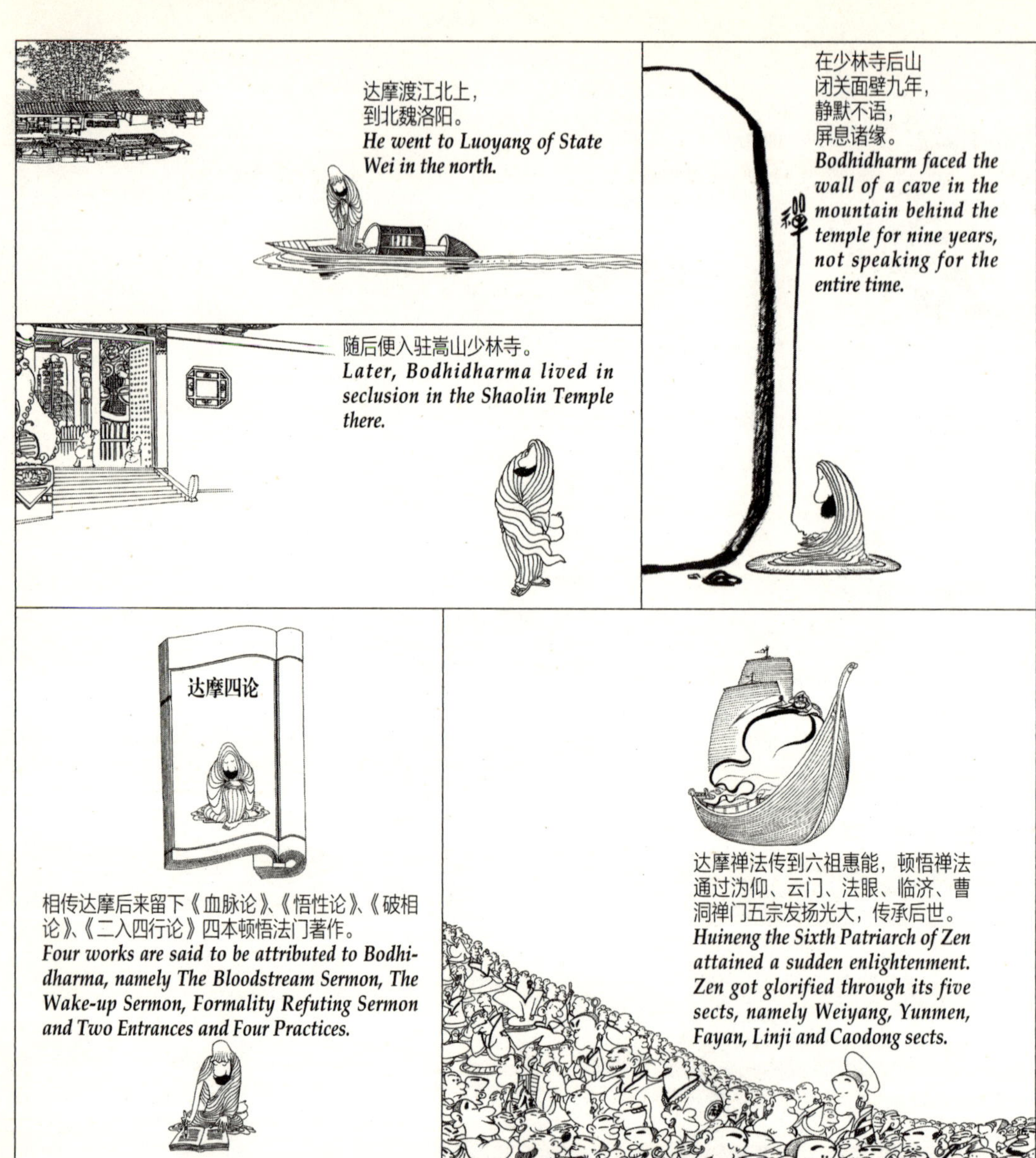
达摩渡江北上，
到北魏洛阳。
He went to Luoyang of State Wei in the north.
在少林寺后山
闭关面壁九年，
静默不语，
屏息诸缘。
Bodhidharm faced the wall of a cave in the mountain behind the temple for nine years, not speaking for the entire time.
随后便入驻嵩山少林寺。
Later, Bodhidharma lived in seclusion in the Shaolin Temple there.
达摩四论
相传达摩后来留下《血脉论》、《悟性论》、《破相论》、《二入四行论》四本顿悟法门著作。
Four works are said to be attributed to Bodhidharma, namely The Bloodstream Sermon, The Wake-up Sermon, Formality Refuting Sermon and Two Entrances and Four Practices.
达摩禅法传到六祖惠能，顿悟禅法通过沩仰、云门、法眼、临济、曹洞禅门五宗发扬光大，传承后世。
Huineng the Sixth Patriarch of Zen attained a sudden enlightenment. Zen got glorified through its five sects, namely Weiyang, Yunmen, Fayan, Linji and Caodong sects.

达摩血脉论

Bloodstream Sermon

第一章　心是什么

Chapter I What is Mind?

佛是什么？
佛就是我们的本心！
What is Buddha?
Buddha is our mind!
我们的心就是佛！
佛即是我们自己的心！
Our mind is Buddha!
Buddha is our mind!
心就是佛，
佛就是心！
Mind is Buddha.
Buddha is mind!
以下，本书所呈现的佛陀都代表我们的本心，并非在指金光闪闪、能施福护佑众生的神祇。
The Buddhas in the following part represent our mind, instead of being the glorious gods who may bless the living creatures.
佛即是本心！
Buddha is our mind!

宇宙时空久远宽广，
天地万物的真如实相只有一个。
In the timeless and boundless universe there is only one truth.
过去、现在、未来的所有开悟者们，
无法通过语言文字表达悟境，
Buddhas of the past, present and future cannot put what enlightenment is like in words.
WISDOM
都是以心传心的方式，
传达他们的觉悟心得。
Thus they teach mind to mind without bothering about definitions.
因此达摩禅法的宗旨便是：
教外别传；
不立文字；
直指人心；
见性成佛。
The essence of Bodhidharma's Zen lies as:
A special transmission outside the scriptures,
Not founded upon words and letters,
By pointing directly to [one's] mind,
It lets one see into [one's own true] nature and [thus] attain Buddhahood.

1　三界混起，同归一心，前佛后佛，以心传心，不立文字。

十界三千只依一心
Everything that appears in the three realms comes from the mind.
弟子问达摩：
“不借由文字，什么是心呢？”
A disciple asked Bodhidharma,
“But if they don't define it, what do they mean by mind?”
达摩回答说：
“问我的就是你的心，
回答你的就是我的心。”
Bodhidharma answered,
“You ask. That's your mind. I answer. That's my mind.”
如果我没有心，
怎么来回答你？
If I had no mind, how could I answer?
如果你没有心，
又如何来问我？
If you had no mind, how could you ask?

2 问曰：“若不立文字，以何为心？”答曰：“汝问吾即是汝心，吾答汝即是吾心。吾若无心因何解答汝？汝若无心因何解问吾？问吾即是汝心。”

为何即心是佛？
Why is this mind the buddha?
佛就是自己的心。
This mind is the Buddha.
从无始以来，
在任何时空的一切运动，
都是你本心所发出来的作用，
Through endless kalpas, without beginning, whatever you do, wherever you are, that's your real mind;
这个心就是你的本佛，
即心是佛就是这个意思。
That's your real Buddha.
That's what "This mind is the Buddha" means.
除此心外，
再也没有别的佛可得。
Beyond this mind you'll never find another Buddha.
离开此心，
往外觅寻菩提涅槃，
是不可能的事。
To search for enlightenment or nirvana beyond this mind is impossible.

3　从无始旷大劫以来，乃至施为运动一切时中，一切处所，皆是汝本心，皆是汝本佛。即心是佛，亦复如是。

4　除此心外，终无别佛可得；离此心外觅菩提涅槃，无有是处。

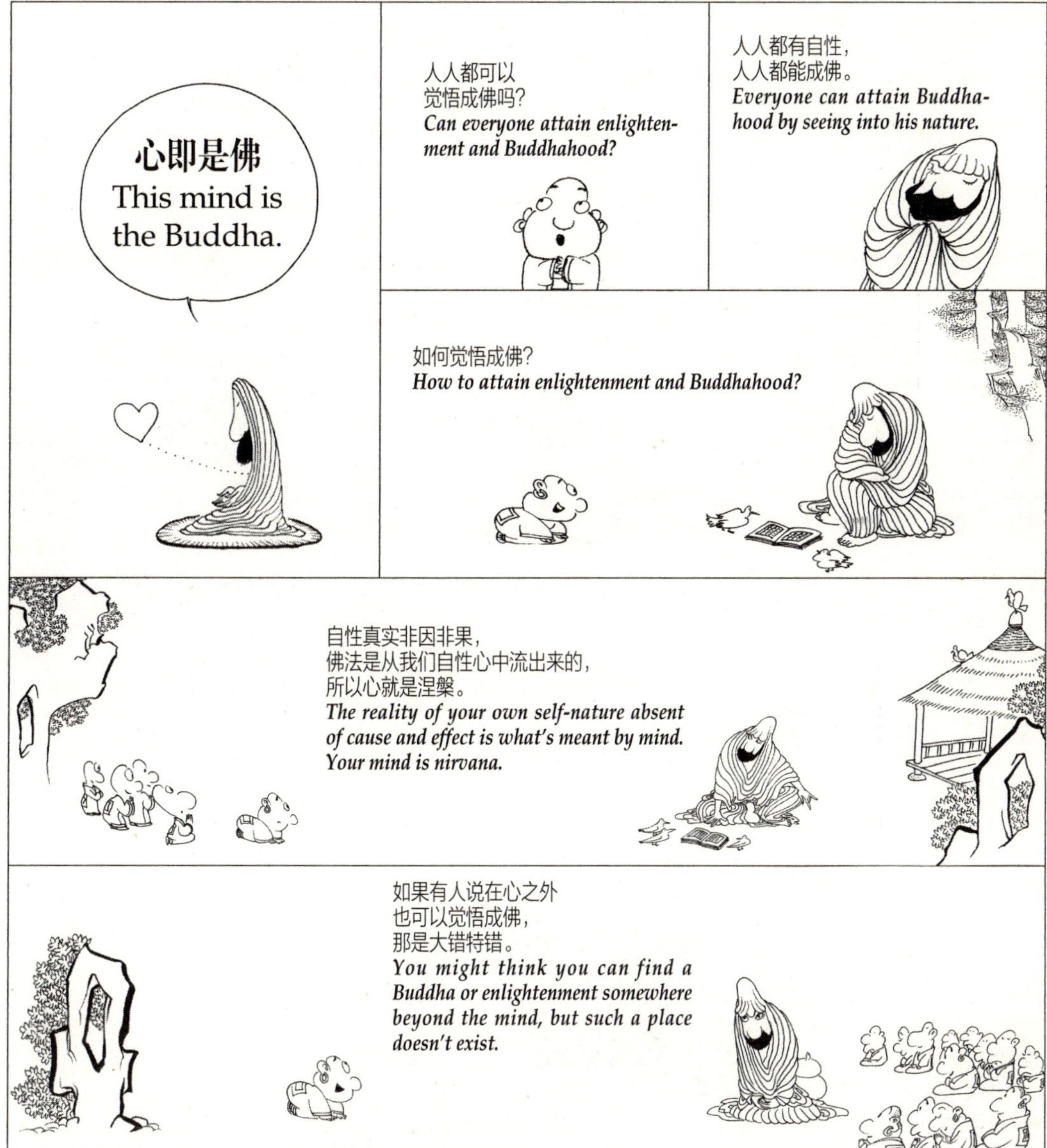
心即是佛
This mind is the Buddha.
人人都可以
觉悟成佛吗?
Can everyone attain enlightenment and Buddhahood?
人人都有自性,
人人都能成佛。
Everyone can attain Buddhahood by seeing into his nature.
如何觉悟成佛?
How to attain enlightenment and Buddhahood?
自性真实非因非果,
佛法是从我们自性心中流出来的,
所以心就是涅槃。
The reality of your own self-nature absent of cause and effect is what's meant by mind. Your mind is nirvana.
如果有人说在心之外
也可以觉悟成佛,
那是大错特错。
You might think you can find a Buddha or enlightenment somewhere beyond the mind, but such a place doesn't exist.

5 自性真实非因非果。法即是心义，自心是涅槃。若言心外有佛及菩提可得，无有是处。

佛即菩提
The Buddha is enlighten-ment.
佛与觉悟在哪里?
Where are the Buddha and enlightenment?
佛与觉悟就在你的心里。
The Buddha and enlighten-ment are in your mind.
例如有人想要用手提起虚空，办得到吗?
Trying to find a Buddha or enlighten-ment is like trying to grab the void.
虚空只是有名字，没有实体相貌。
The void has a name but no form.

6　佛及菩提皆在何处?

7　譬如有人以手提虚空得否? 虚空但有名，亦无相貌。

虚空拿不到丢不掉，
用手抓不着。
It's not something you can pick up or put down. And you certainly can't grab if.
佛即是觉悟！
除了此心之外，
见佛终究不可得。
The Buddha is enlightenment!
Beyond the mind there's no Buddha.
佛是由自心所成就的，
如何能离开此心往外觅佛呢？
The Buddha is a product of the mind. Why look for a Buddha beyond this mind?
过去、现在的开悟者们，
都只谈其心。
Buddhas of the past and future only talk about this mind.

8 取不得舍不得，是捉空不得。

9 除此心外，见佛终不得也。佛是自心作得，因何离此心外觅佛？

10 前佛后佛只言其心。

第二章　自心即是佛

Chapter II The Mind is the Buddha

心外无佛
Beyond the mind there's no Buddha.
佛就在此心。
心即是佛，佛即是心；
心外无佛，佛外无心。
The Buddha is in your mind.
The mind is the Buddha and the Buddha is the mind. Beyond the mind there's no Buddha and beyond the Buddha there's no mind.
心中有佛，
就是这个意思吗？
That's what we say to have the Buddha in your mind, isn't it?
你的心就是佛，
The Buddha is your mind.
而不是心中有一位 2500 年前
在菩提树下开悟的释迦佛陀。
It doesn't refer to Sakyamuni the Buddha who came to enlightenment under the bodhi tree 2,500 years ago.

11 心即是佛，佛即是心；心外无佛，佛外无心。

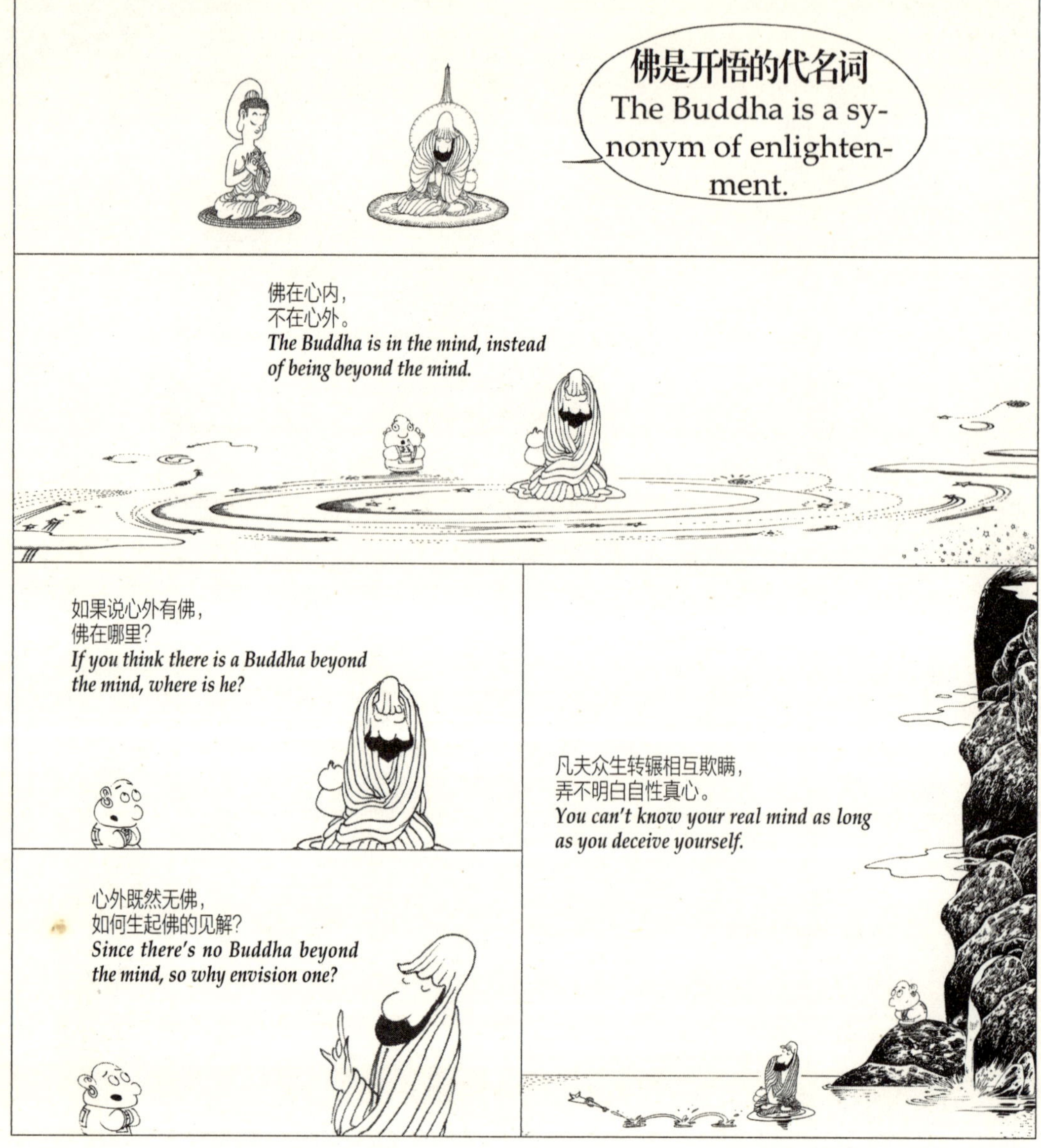
佛是开悟的代名词
The Buddha is a synonym of enlightenment.
佛在心内，
不在心外。
The Buddha is in the mind, instead of being beyond the mind.
如果说心外有佛，
佛在哪里？
If you think there is a Buddha beyond the mind, where is he?
凡夫众生转辗相互欺瞒，
弄不明白自性真心。
You can't know your real mind as long as you deceive yourself.
心外既然无佛，
如何生起佛的见解？
Since there's no Buddha beyond the mind, so why envision one?

12 若言心外有佛，佛在何处？心外既无佛，何起佛见？

13 递相诳惑，不能了本心。

众生迷惑，
被没有生命之物
所吸引而不能自拔，
As long as you're enthralled by
a lifeless form, you're not free.
众生不信佛说，
自我欺骗没好处。
If you don't believe me, deceiving
yourself won't help.
众生颠倒真相，
不是佛的过错。
It's not the Buddha's fault.
People, though, are deluded.
众生不知道自心是佛，
还往外寻求。
They're unaware that their own
mind is the Buddha. Otherwise
they wouldn't look for a Buddha
outside the mind.

14 被它无情物摄，无自由。

15 若也不信，自诳无益。佛无过患，众生颠倒，不觉不知自心是佛。

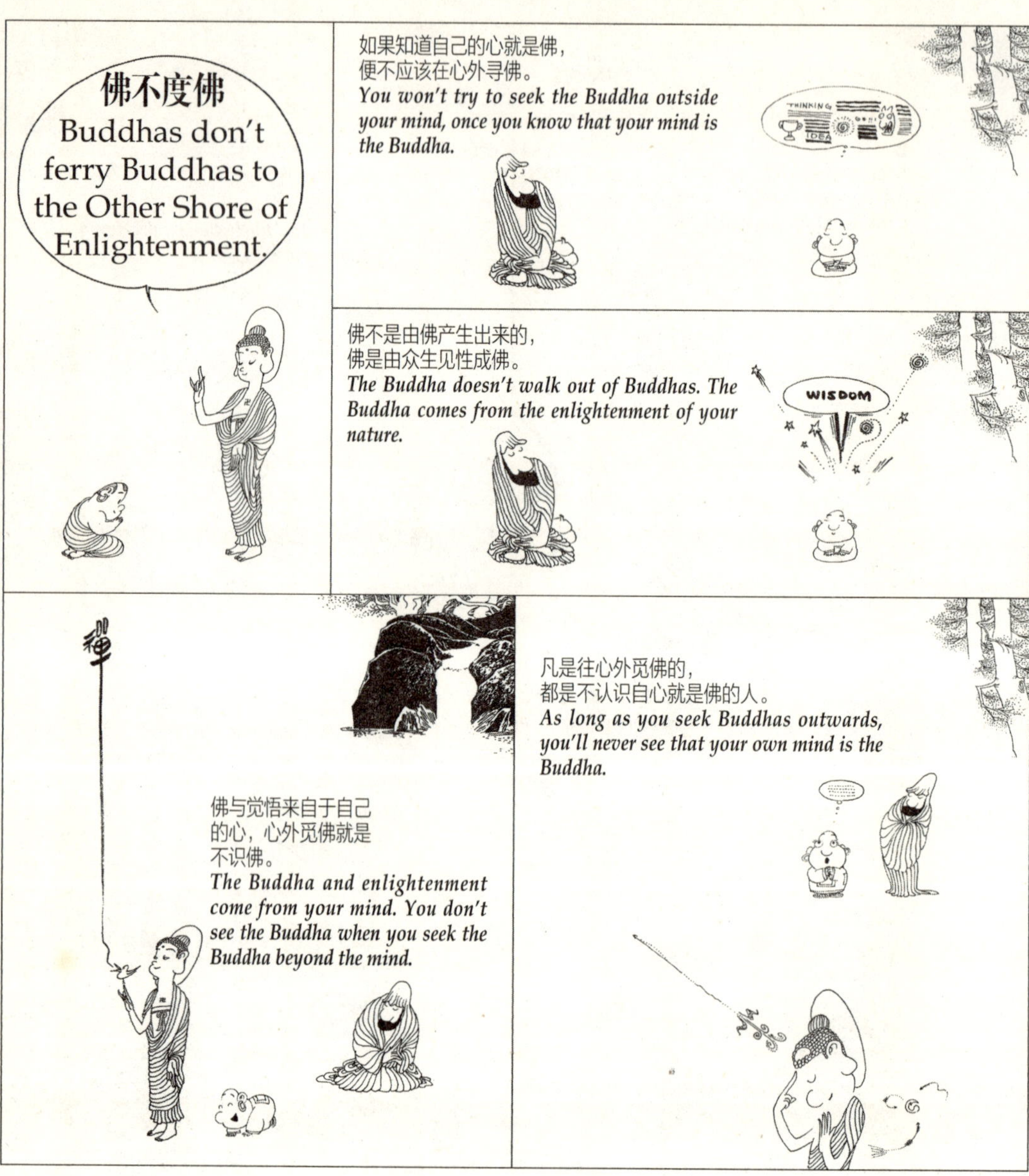
佛不度佛
Buddhas don't ferry Buddhas to the Other Shore of Enlightenment.
如果知道自己的心就是佛，
便不应该在心外寻佛。
You won't try to seek the Buddha outside your mind, once you know that your mind is the Buddha.
THINKING
IDEA
佛不是由佛产生出来的，
佛是由众生见性成佛。
The Buddha doesn't walk out of Buddhas. The Buddha comes from the enlightenment of your nature.
WISDOM
禪
佛与觉悟来自于自己
的心，心外觅佛就是
不识佛。
The Buddha and enlightenment come from your mind. You don't see the Buddha when you seek the Buddha beyond the mind.
凡是往心外觅佛的，
都是不认识自心就是佛的人。
As long as you seek Buddhas outwards, you'll never see that your own mind is the Buddha.

16 若知自心是佛，不应心外觅佛。佛不度佛，将心觅佛不识佛。

17 但是外觅佛者，尽是不识自心是佛。

不能用自心佛
去礼拜外佛，
Don't use a Buddha to worship a Buddha.
也不能用自己的心去念佛。
Don't use the mind to invoke a Buddha.
南无阿弥陀佛！
佛陀慈悲保佑！
Namo Amitabha!
May the Buddha bless me!
佛不诵经，
佛不持戒，
佛不犯戒，
佛无持犯，
Buddhas don't recite sutras.
Buddhas don't keep precepts. Buddhas don't break precepts.
Buddhas don't keep or break anything.
佛也不造善恶。
Buddhas don't do good or evil.

18 亦不得将佛礼佛，不得将心念佛。

19 佛不诵经，佛不持戒，佛不犯戒，佛无持犯，亦不造善恶。

见性即佛
Whoever sees his nature is a Buddha.
清净的自性就是佛！
Your pure nature is the Buddha!
想要见到自心的真佛，
必须先看见自性。
To find a Buddha, you have to see your nature.
如果看不见自己本来面目，
念佛、诵经、持斋、持戒
没有任何好处。
If you don't see your nature, it leads to no good by being mindful of Buddhas, chanting sutras, keeping vegetarian fast or keeping precepts.
为什么呢？
Why?
念佛得因果，诵经得聪明，
持戒得升天，布施得福报。
Being mindful of Buddhas results in good karma. Chanting sutras results in good intelligence. Keeping precepts results in a good rebirth in heaven. Making offerings results in future blessings.

20 若欲觅佛，须是见性，见性即是佛。若不见性，念佛、诵经、持斋、持戒亦无益处。

21 念佛得因果，诵经得聪明，持戒得生天，布施得福报。

但光靠这些方法，
终究不可以成佛。
But no Buddhas, despite all these.
如果自己不能明白，
可以去请教见性的善知识，
解除心中的疑惑，
If you don't understand it by yourself, you'll
have to find a teacher to clear your doubts.
但是只有见性的人才配称
善知识，不见性的人不能
称为善知识。
But unless he sees his nature, such a
person isn't a good teacher.
如果不能见性，
就算他能讲十二部经律论，
Unable to see his nature, he can't escape
samsara or the Wheel of Birth and Death,
也不能脱离痛苦烦恼轮回，
仍然在世间受苦不能开悟。
And he suffers in the three realms
without hope of release, even if he
can recite the 12 divisions of the
Buddhist canons.

22 觅佛终不得也。

23 若自己不明了，须参善知识，了却生死根本。若不见性，即不名善知识。

24 若不如此，纵说得十二部经，亦不免生死轮回，三界受苦，无出期时。

过去有一位善星比丘，
能够背诵十二部佛经，
Sunasatra was able to recite all the 12 divisions of the Buddhist canons.
但仍然无法脱离轮回之苦，
因为他没有见性。
But he didn't escape the Wheel, because he didn't see his nature.
THINKING
IDEA
善星都如此，而今天的人能讲得三五本佛经，
If this was the case with Sunasatra, then people nowadays, who recite a few sutras or shastras
就自以为得佛法真谛，
这样的人其实都是愚人。
And take them as the Dharma, are fools.
不认识自己的心，
即使经书背得再熟，
都没有用处。
Unless you see your own mind, it is useless, how many sutras you're able to recite.

25　昔有善星比丘，诵得十二部经，犹自不免轮回，缘为不见性。善星既如此，今时人讲得三五本经论以为佛法者，愚人也。若不识得自心，诵得闲文书，都无用处。

第三章　见性才能成佛
Chapter III To Attain Buddhahood by Seeing Your Nature

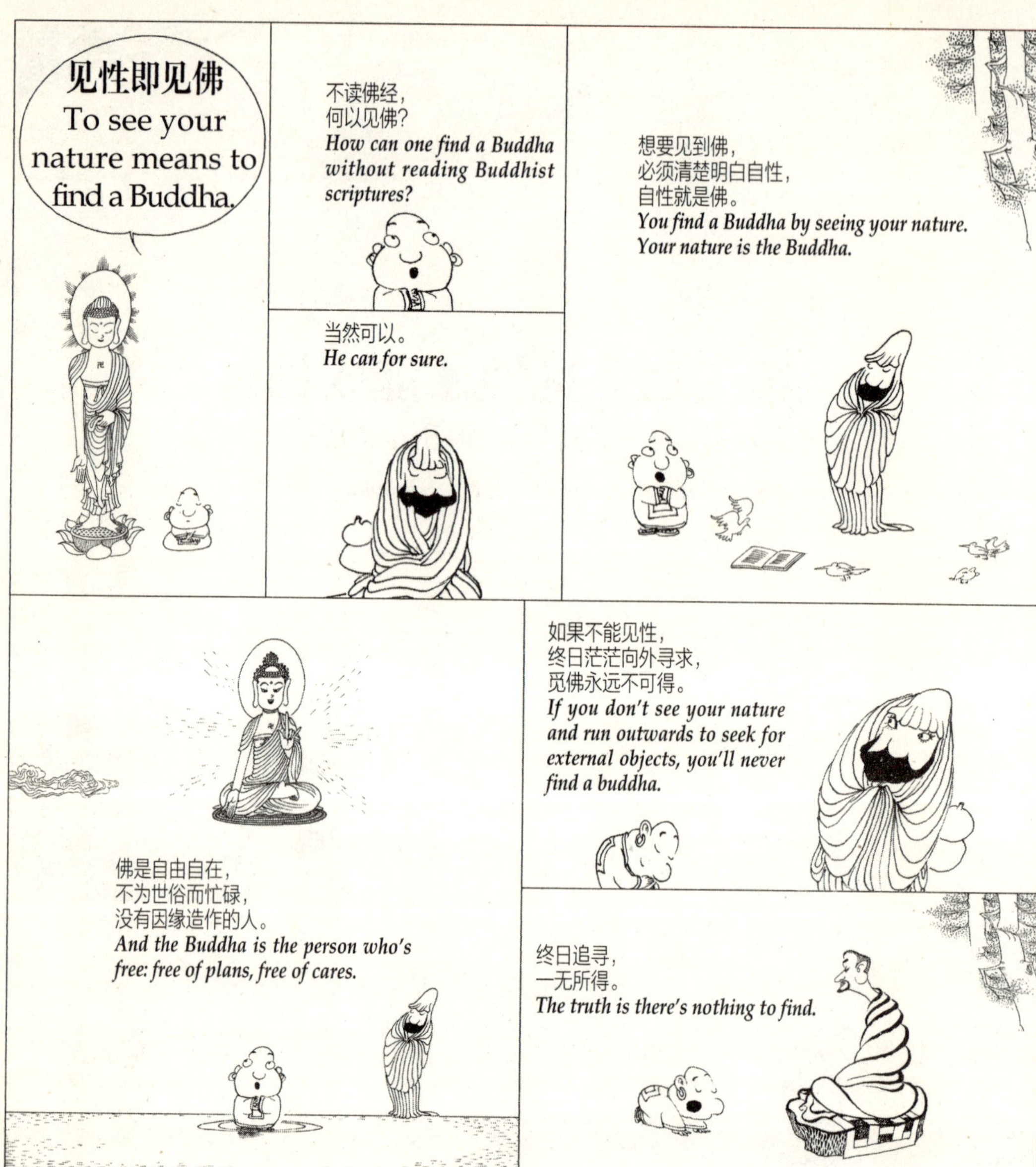
见性即见佛
To see your nature means to find a Buddha.
不读佛经，
何以见佛？
How can one find a Buddha without reading Buddhist scriptures?
当然可以。
He can for sure.
想要见到佛，
必须清楚明白自性，
自性就是佛。
You find a Buddha by seeing your nature. Your nature is the Buddha.
佛是自由自在，
不为世俗而忙碌，
没有因缘造作的人。
And the Buddha is the person who's free: free of plans, free of cares.
如果不能见性，
终日茫茫向外寻求，
觅佛永远不可得。
If you don't see your nature and run outwards to seek for external objects, you'll never find a buddha.
终日追寻，
一无所得。
The truth is there's nothing to find.

26 若要觅佛，直须见性。性即是佛。

27 佛即是自在人，无事无作人。若不见性，终日茫茫，向外驰求，觅佛元来不得。

28 虽无一物可得。

想要真会，
必须向善知识求教，
并且要恳切苦求，
才能令自心会解。
But to reach such an understanding you need a good teacher and you need to struggle to make yourself understand.
善知识，求您
收我为弟子。
Master, please take me as your disciple.
人生事大，不要白白虚度，
自我欺骗一点好处也没有。
Life and death are important. Don't suffer them in vain. It's no good to deceiving yourself.
纵有珍馐美味如山，
眷属多如恒河沙数。
What's use to indulge yourself in delicacies and beautiful women?
眼前看得到的东西，
死后还能见吗？
Would you still see them after death?
世间所拥有的一切，
有如梦幻泡影。
The things you have in this world are as illusionary as a dream.
若不马上寻找明师，
很快就会空过一生。
Your life would soon pass by in vain, if you couldn't find a good teacher as soon as possible.

29 若求会亦须参善知识，切须苦求，令心会解。

30 生死事大，不得空过，自诳无益。纵有珍馐如山，眷属如恒河沙，开眼即见，合眼还见吗？故知有为之法，如梦幻等。若不急寻师，空过一生。

即使人人都有佛性，
但不经由明师开导，
终究还是很难明白。
It's hard to see your nature without a good teacher to guide you along, even if everyone has the potential for Buddhahood.
善知识，求求您收
我为弟子吧。
Master, please take me as your disciple.
没有老师而能自行
开悟，万中稀有。
There're few who could get enlightened without a good teacher to guide them.
如果自己因缘际会，
悟通见性真理，
即不用参善知识。
Some may see into the truth of life and attain enlightenment by themselves, without consulting with good teachers.
WISDOM
这种生而知之的人，
是非常特殊的。
There're truly few of such people who were born with knowledge.
哈！是我自己
悟出真理的！
Aha! I got enlightened all by myself!

31 然即佛性自有，若不因师，终不明了。不因师悟者，万中稀有。

32 若自己以缘会合，得圣人意，即不用参善知识。此即是生而知之，胜学也。

如果还没悟通自性，
就必须努力勤苦参学，
因为教导才能开悟。
You must practice hard, to see your true nature. Only teaching leads to enlightenment, in this case.

如果还没开悟，
自认为不学也行。
An unenlightened person may, however, hold it unnessary to learn or practice.

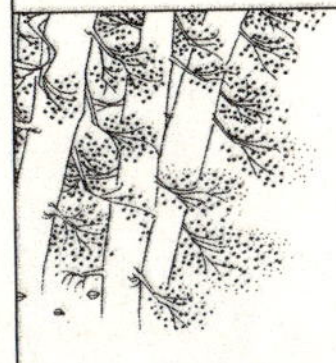

这种迷中之人，自己还分不出青红皂白，
便随意宣说佛法，就是诽谤佛法。
Such a blinded person cannot tell right and wrong. He actually slanders the Buddhist teachings when giving a lecture on them.

这类人就算说法如雨，
但全部是魔说，而非佛说。
He in fact speaks the devil's crooked ways, instead of the Buddha's teachings, however beautiful his words sound.

这种老师是魔王，
弟子是魔民。
A teacher like this is rather a devil king and his disciples the devil's followers.

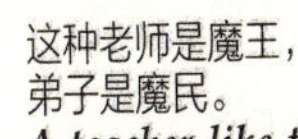

迷者无知，任由他所欺骗，
不知不觉中堕落生死大海。
The ignorant followers are deceived and fall into the dark sea of life and death.

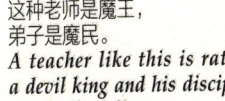

33 若未悟解，须勤苦参学，因教方得悟。若未悟了，不学亦得。不同迷人，不能分别皂白，妄言宣佛敕，谤佛忌法。

34 如斯等类，说法如雨，尽是魔说，即非佛说。师是魔王，弟子是魔民，迷人任它指挥，不觉堕生死海。

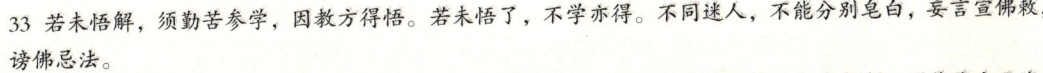

如果还没有见性，纵然能说得
十二部经教，也只是魔说。
A person unable to see his nature can only
speak of the devil's crooked ways, even if he
chants the 12 divisions of the Buddhist canons.
无法分别是非黑白，
又如何能脱离生死？
How can one who is unable to tell
right and wrong get free from the
Wheel of Birth and Death?
魔王的子民，
不是佛家弟子。
The devil king's followers are
never the Buddhist followers.

35 若不见性，说得十二部经教，尽是魔说。魔家眷属，不是佛家弟子。既不辨皂白，凭何免生死？

佛在何处?
Where's the Buddha?
见性即是佛，
不见性就是众生?
Whoever sees his nature is a Buddha; whoever doesn't is a mortal. It is true?
没错！如果认为离开众生性，
还有别的佛可得，
That's right! But if you can find your Buddha-nature apart from your mortal nature,
那么，佛现在在哪里?
where is it?
!
众生性就是佛性。
性外无佛，佛即是性；
除此性外，无佛可得，
Our mortal nature is our Buddha nature. Beyond this nature there's no Buddha. The Buddha is our nature. There's no Buddha beyond this nature.
除了本性觉悟，
此外再没有觉悟的由来。
No enlightenment lies beyond seeing your nature.

36 若见性即是佛，不见性即是众生。若离众生性，别有佛性可得者，佛今在何处?

37 即众生性，即是佛性也。性外无佛，佛即是性；除此性外，无佛可得，佛外无性可得。

不免生死
Unable to escape the Wheel of Birth and Death
如果不见性，念佛、诵经、布施、持戒、精进，做各种善事，能成佛吗？
But suppose I don't see my nature, can't I still attain Buddha by invoking Buddhas, reciting sutras, making offerings, observing precepts, practicing devotions or doing good things?
不能成佛。
No, you can't.
为何不能成佛？
Why not?
这些全都是因缘法，只是因果受报的轮回法，跟见性觉悟无关。
If you attain anything at all, it's conditional and karmic. It has nothing to do with getting enlightened by seeing your nature.
何时才能修成佛道呢？
When can I attain enlightenment and Buddhahood?
必须见性，才能成佛。
To attain enlightenment and Buddhahood, you have to see your nature.

38 问曰："若不见性，念佛、诵经、布施、持戒、精进，广兴福利，得成佛否？"答曰："不得。"

39 又问："因何不得？"答曰："有少法可得，是有为法，是因果、是受报、是轮回法，不免生死。"

40 何时得成佛道？成佛须是见性。

如果不说见性，
而说因果能成佛，
这非佛法，而是外道法。
Unless you see your nature, all the talks about cause and effect, are the dharmas of the Exterior Path.
众生是佛，不修外道法。
As the ordinary have the potential for Buddhahood, they don't follow the Exterior Path dharmas.
如果内心存有丝毫妄念，
想要成佛都是不可能的。
You cannot attain Buddhahood, with any single delusion.
佛不持戒，
心性本空，
非垢非净。
A Buddha does not keep or break anything
His mind is free of anything in nature.
It is neither pure nor impure.
因为诸法
无修无证，
无因无果。
He is free of practice and realization.
He is free of cause and effect.

41 若不见性，因果等语，是外道法。若是佛不习外道法。

42 但有住着一心一能一解一见，佛都不许。佛无持犯，心性本空，亦非垢净。诸法无修无证，无因无果。

佛不持戒，佛不修善，
佛不造恶，佛不精进，
A Buddha doesn't observe precepts.
A Buddha does neither good nor evil.
A Buddha doesn't practice devotions.
佛不懈怠，
佛是不造因果的人。
A Buddha isn't energetic or lazy.
A Buddha is someone without cause or effect.
如果心中有任何执着，
就无法见到自性佛。
Caught up with anything, one cannot see his Nature-Buddha.
自性真佛与妄想中金光闪闪、
能施福报的神祇是不同的。
The Nature-Buddha is never a shining god in your imagination who can bless the ordinary.
佛不是佛，
不要作佛解。
A Buddha isn't a Buddha.
Don't see him as a Buddha.

43 佛不持戒，佛不修善，佛不造恶，佛不精进，佛不懈怠，佛是无作人。

44 但有住着心，见佛即不许也。佛不是佛，莫作佛解。

如果不明白这个意思，
那么他一生中都无法
明白本心。
If you dont see what I'm talking about, at any times and anywhere, you just don't see your true nature.
本心即是佛！
The nature if the Buddha!
如果不明白本心，
那么在他一生中便
无法达成无作无想。
People who don't see their nature never reach the realm of emptiness.
他是个大罪人，
是个学佛的大笨人。
They are sinful poeple and fools.
我最懂佛法！
I know best about the Buddhist dharma!
他只会落入无意义
的空谈，昏沉如醉
不能分辨好坏是非。
They will fall into the insignificant lip serives and are too muddle-headed to tell good from evil.
我会背很多部佛经。
I can recite many Buddhist scriptures.

45 若不见此义，一切时中，一切处处，皆是不了本心。若不见性，一切时中拟作无作想，是大罪人，是痴人。

46 落无记空中，昏昏如醉人，不辨好恶。

息缘止虑
Giving up your delusions
不见性便可修成佛道，
这是绝对不可能的。
You never attain Buddhahood without seeing your nature.
如果想达成无作无想，
必须先要见性，
他的心才能息缘绝虑。
If you intend to reach the realm of emptiness, you have to see your nature before you can put an end to all states and conditions and delusions.
如果有人认为并没有
因果报应，毫无忌惮
地造作一切恶业。
Some may commit all sorts of evil deeds, claiming karma doesn't exist.
诸法空相，万法皆空！
Dharmas are emptiness in nature. All of them are emptiness.
口出妄言说：
“既然一切皆空，
造恶也无所谓。”
They erroneously maintain that since everything is empty, committing evil makes no difference.
既然诸法皆空，
干坏事也无所谓！
It's okay to do what you like, as all dharmas are emptiness.
!

47 若拟修无作法，先须见性，然后息缘虑。

48 若不见性得成佛道，无有是处。有人拨无因果，炽然作恶业，妄言本空，作恶无过。

这种人，将堕入无间
黑暗地狱，永无出期。
Those people fall into the endless darkness of Avichi, with no hope of release.
!
如果他有智慧，
就不应该有这种想法。
The wise should hold no such idea.
是啊！
Yes!

49 如此之人，堕无间黑暗地狱，永无出期。若是智人，不应作如是见解。

不见本心
Unable to see the nature
人的身体活动，不都是我们自己的心在作用吗？
One has all his bodily movements controlled by his mind. Doesn't he?
为何平时我们看不见自己的心呢？
But we don't see our mind. Why's that?
本心常在现前，是你自己没发现。
The mind is always present. You just don't see it.
既然心就在现前，为何我看不见？
But if the mind is present, why don't I see it?
你做过梦吗？
Do you ever dream?
做过梦。
Of course.

50　问曰："既若施为运动，一切时中皆是本心；色身无常之时，云何不见本心？"答曰："本心常现前，汝自不见？"

51　问曰："心既见在，何故不见？"师反问曰："汝曾做梦否？"答："曾做梦。"

做梦时，是你
自己在做梦吗？
When you dream, is that you?
是我自己在做梦。
Yes, it's me.
你说话运动与你
自己有分别吗？
And are there any distinctions between your movements and you yourself?
没有分别。
No, there aren't.
既然没有分别，那么此身就是你的
法身，而这个法身就是你的本心。
If there aren't, then this body is your real body.
And this real body is your mind.
这个心会变吗？
Does this mind change?
从无始以来此心
就未曾改变！
This mind, through endless
kalpas, has never changed.
此心不曾有生死，
此心也不生不灭。
It has never lived or died, nor arisen or ceased.

52 问曰："汝做梦之时，是汝本身否？" 答："是本身。"

53 又问："汝言语施为运动与汝别不别？" 答曰："不别。" 师曰："既若不别，即此身是汝本法身；即此法身是汝本心。"

54 此心从无始旷大劫来，与如今不别；未曾有生死，不生不灭。

此心，
不增不减，不垢不净，
不好不恶，不来不去。
It has never increased or decreased.
It's been not pure or impure, neither good nor evil.
It has come from nowhere or gone nowhere.
无是非，无男女相，
无僧俗老少，无圣无凡。
It's been not true or false.
It's appeared neither male nor female.
It's been neither a monk nor a layman, neither old nor young, neither a sage nor an ordinary.
无佛，无众生，
无修证，无因果，
无筋力，无相貌。
It's never been a Buddha or a mortal.
It's strived for no realization and suffered no karma. It has had no physical strength or form.
本心宛如虚空，
抓不到，丢不掉，
山河石壁都不能阻挡。
Your true nature is like void. You can neither grasp it nor get rid of it. It can't be stopped by mountains, rivers or cliffs.

55　不增不减，不垢不净，不好不恶，不来不去。亦无是非、亦无男女相、亦无僧俗老少、无圣无凡；亦无佛、亦无众生、亦无修证、亦无因果、亦无筋力、亦无相貌。

56　犹如虚空，取不得、舍不得，山河石壁不能为碍。

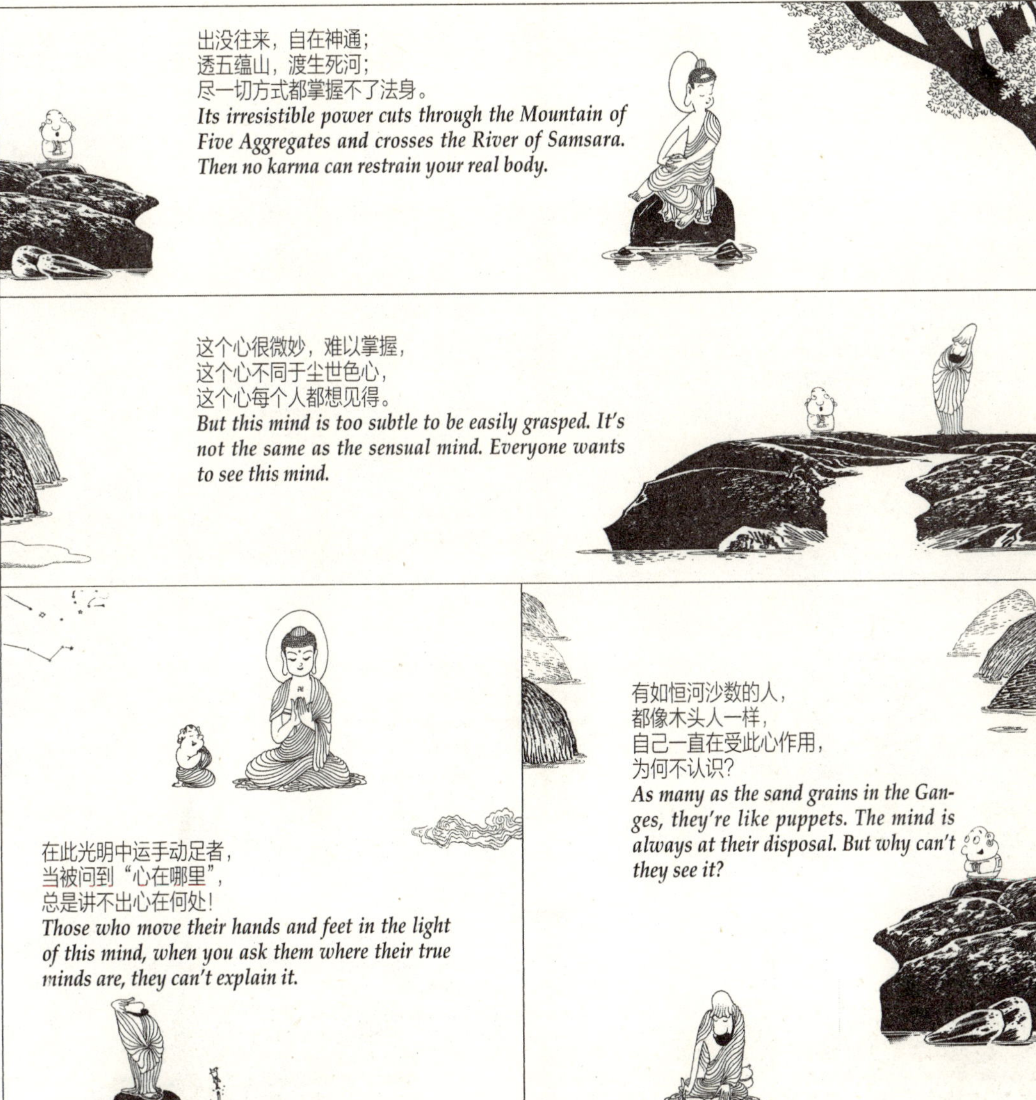
出没往来，自在神通；
透五蕴山，渡生死河；
尽一切方式都掌握不了法身。
Its irresistible power cuts through the Mountain of Five Aggregates and crosses the River of Samsara. Then no karma can restrain your real body.
这个心很微妙，难以掌握，
这个心不同于尘世色心，
这个心每个人都想见得。
But this mind is too subtle to be easily grasped. It's not the same as the sensual mind. Everyone wants to see this mind.
在此光明中运手动足者，
当被问到"心在哪里"，
总是讲不出心在何处！
Those who move their hands and feet in the light of this mind, when you ask them where their true minds are, they can't explain it.
有如恒河沙数的人，
都像木头人一样，
自己一直在受此心作用，
为何不认识？
As many as the sand grains in the Ganges, they're like puppets. The mind is always at their disposal. But why can't they see it?

57 出没往来，自在神通；透五蕴山，渡生死河；一切业拘此法身不得。

58 此心微妙难见，此心不同色心，此心是人皆欲得见。

59 于此光明中运手动足者，如恒河沙，及乎问着，总道不得，犹如木人相似，总是自己受用，因何不识？

佛说：
“一切众生都是迷中之人，
因此造业。”
The Buddha said,
“All the living creatures are deluded. This
is why they are caught up by karma.”
堕落生死河中逃脱不出来，
只因为众生不见性。
That's why they cannot pull themselves
out of the River of Samsara. It's all because
they don't see their nature.
如果众生不迷，
为何没有人答得出来？
If people weren't deluded, why would they ask about
something right in front of them?
连让自己运手动足
的本心也不认识？
And why would none of them see
the nature that controls the the
movement of their hands and feet?

60 佛言一切众生，尽是迷人，因此作业，堕生死河，欲出还没，只为不见性。

61 众生若不迷，因何问着其中事，无有一人得会者，自家运手动足因何不识？

圣人说的话是对的，
只是迷人自己不明白。
自家本心难以明白，
唯有佛陀一人会此法。
The Buddha has come to the point.
Deluded people don't know who they are.
Nobody except the Buddha has grasped the essence of the mind.
其他的人、天及众生们，
全都不知道自己的心。
Neither the heaven nor the ordinary see their mind and nature.
!
禅
开悟的智者知道，
这个心称为法性，
也名为解脱。
Only the enlightened knows that this mind is the dharma-nature or moksha (liberation).
一切生死奈它不了，
一切法也拘它不得。
Neither life nor death can restrain this mind. Nothing can.

62 故知圣人语不错，迷人自不会晓。故知此难明，惟佛一人能会此法；余人天及众生等，尽不明了。

63 若智慧明了，此心号名法性，亦名解脱。生死不拘，一切法拘它不得。

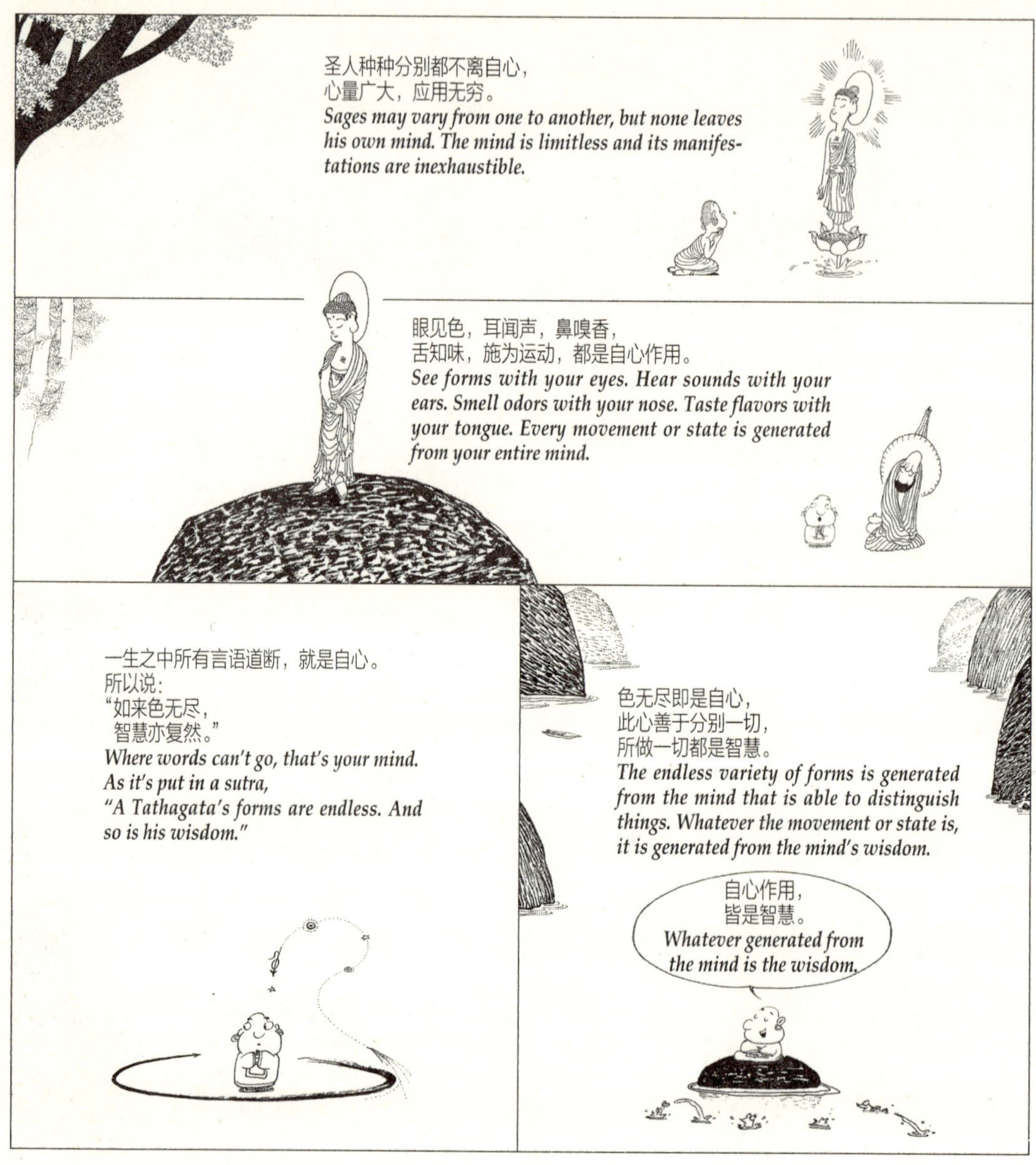
圣人种种分别都不离自心，
心量广大，应用无穷。
Sages may vary from one to another, but none leaves his own mind. The mind is limitless and its manifestations are inexhaustible.
眼见色，耳闻声，鼻嗅香，
舌知味，施为运动，都是自心作用。
See forms with your eyes. Hear sounds with your ears. Smell odors with your nose. Taste flavors with your tongue. Every movement or state is generated from your entire mind.
一生之中所有言语道断，就是自心。
所以说：
“如来色无尽，
智慧亦复然。”
Where words can't go, that's your mind.
As it's put in a sutra,
"A Tathagata's forms are endless. And so is his wisdom."
色无尽即是自心，
此心善于分别一切，
所做一切都是智慧。
The endless variety of forms is generated from the mind that is able to distinguish things. Whatever the movement or state is, it is generated from the mind's wisdom.
自心作用，
皆是智慧。
Whatever generated from the mind is the wisdom.

64　圣人种种分别，皆不离自心。心量广大，应用无穷，应眼见色，应耳闻声，应鼻嗅香，应舌知味，乃至施为运动，皆是自心。一切时中但有语言道断，即是自心。

65　故云：“如来色无尽，智慧亦复然。”色无尽是自心，心识善能分别一切，乃至施为运用，皆是智慧。

我们的色身就是烦恼，
有色身存在就有生灭。
A physical body of the four elements
is troublesome. A physical body is
subject to birth and death.
生
住
异
灭
法身常住于无所住处，
因为如来法身不变异。
But the real body exists without existing,
as a Tathagata's real body never changes.
佛经
佛经说：
"众生应知，
佛性本自有之。"
The sutra says,
"People should realize that the Buddha-nature
is something they have been born with."
灵山法会佛陀拈花，
迦叶微笑悟得本性。
Mahakasyapa only realized his own nature,
so he smiled an understanding smile at what
the Buddha who held a lotus in his hand.

66 故云如来色无尽，智慧亦复然。四大色身，即是烦恼，色身即有生灭，法身常住无所住，如来法身常不变异故。

67 经云："众生应知，佛性本自有之。"迦叶只是悟得本性。

本性就是心，心就是本性，
这个本性与诸佛的心相同。
Our nature is the mind. And the mind is our nature. This nature is the same as the mind of all Buddhas.
前佛后佛所传的就是此心，
除了此心之外，再也无佛可得。
Buddhas of the past and future only transmit this mind. Beyond this mind there's no Buddha anywhere.
颠倒众生不知道心就是佛，
到处求佛，终日忙忙碌碌，
But deluded people don't realize that their own mind is the Buddha. They keep searching outside.
念佛礼佛，然而佛在何处？
所以不应该有这样的想法。
They never stop invoking or worshipping Buddhas, wondering where the Buddha is. Don't indulge yourself in such illusions.

68 本性即是心，心即是性，性即此同诸佛心。前佛后佛只传此心，除此心外，无佛可得。

69 颠倒众生不知自心是佛，向外驰求，终日忙忙；念佛礼佛，佛在何处？不应作如是等见。

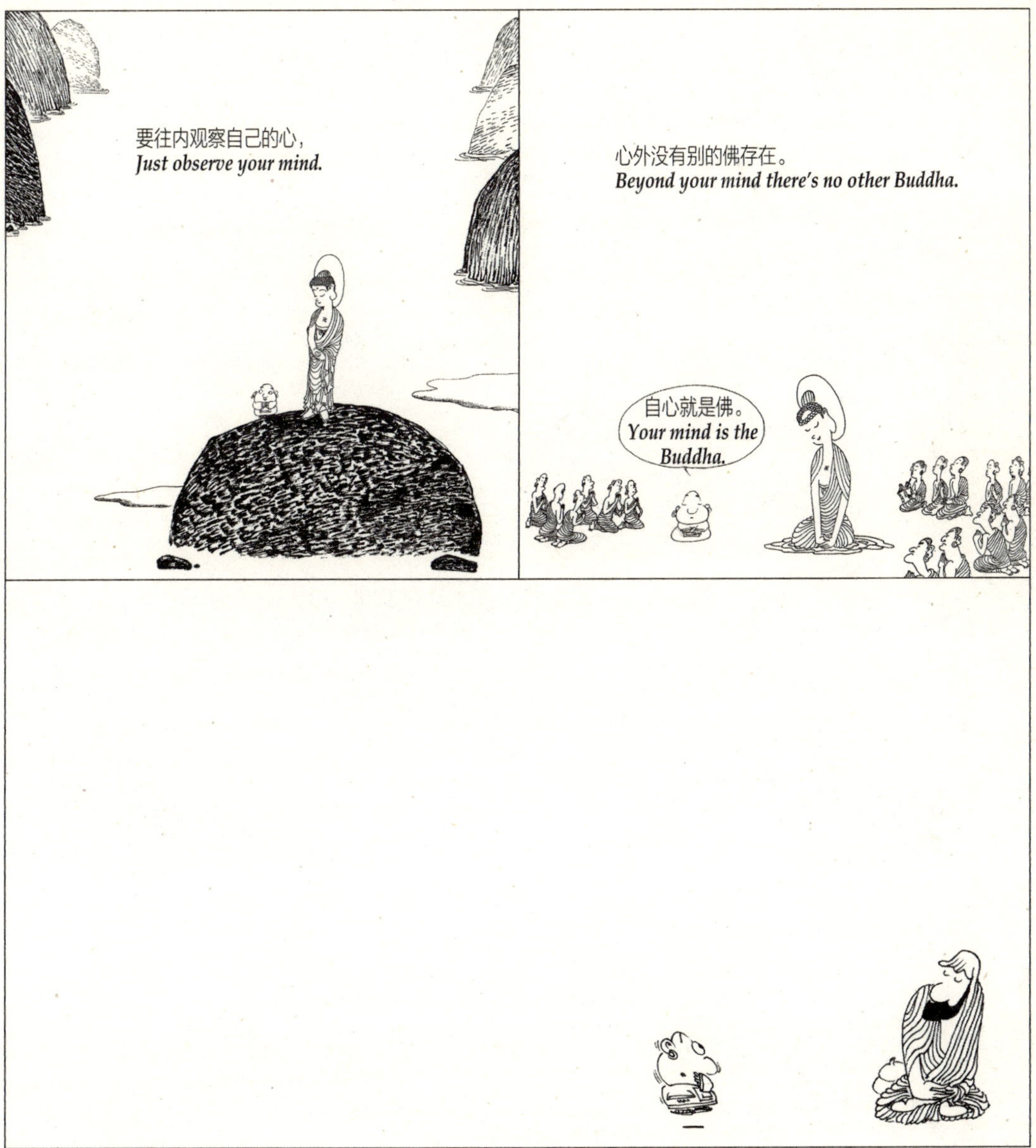
要往内观察自己的心，
Just observe your mind.
心外没有别的佛存在。
Beyond your mind there's no other Buddha.
自心就是佛。
Your mind is the Buddha.

70 但知自心，心外更无别佛。

心取相即是魔
Devil is generated from forms.
金刚经
《金刚经》又说：
“所在之处，即为有佛。”
The sutra also says,
“Wherever you are, there's a Buddha.”
《金刚经》说：
“凡所有相，
皆是虚妄。”
Diamond Sutra says,
“Everything that has form is an illusion.”
自心就是佛，不应当以
自己的佛去礼拜别的佛。
Your mind is the Buddha. Don't worship another Buddha as a Buddha yourself.
如果有佛和菩萨的相貌
忽然出现在我们眼前，
切记不要礼拜。
Even if a Buddha or bodhisattva should suddenly appear before you, there's no need for reverence.

71 经云：“凡所有相，皆是虚妄。”又云：“所在之处，即为有佛。”

72 自心是佛，不应将佛礼佛，但是有佛及菩萨相貌，忽尔见前，切不用礼敬。

为什么?
But why?
我们的心原本空寂，
本无相貌。
This mind of ours is empty and contains no such form.
如果取相即是魔，
尽落入邪道。
Those who hold onto appearances are devils. They fall from the Path.

73 我心空寂，本无如是相貌，若取相即是魔，尽落邪道。

心无相即是空
Emptiness is generated from a form-free mind.
理会幻境者无智，
智者不理会幻境。
理会幻境者，被魔所控制。
我怕学人不会，特此说明。
Those who worship don't know and those who know don't worship.
By worshipping you come under the spell of devils. I point this out, in case you're unaware of it.
如果幻象由心生起，
无视心所生的幻境。
If worship illusions born of the mind, Ignore it.
真正的开悟者，
心不会产生幻象。
The enlightened don't hold onto illusions.
你们必须注意：心产生奇异情境时，
不要理会，也不要害怕、恐惧、疑惑。
Keep this in mind: Even if something unusual should appear, take no notice of it. Don't fear it and don't doubt your mind.

74 若是幻从心起，即不用礼。礼者不知，知者不礼，礼被魔摄。恐学人不知，故作是辨。

75 诸佛如来本性体上，都无如是相貌，切须在意。但有异境界切不用采括，亦莫生怕怖，不要疑惑。

我心本来清净，
无论心生任何相貌。
Where could there be room for any such form, as our mind is empty and pure in essence?
甚至是天龙、夜叉、鬼神、帝释、梵王等相，都不必心生敬重，也不要惊怕恐惧。
Also, at the appearance of Divine Guardians, yakshas, spirits and demons, Sakra or Brahmans, conceive neither respect nor fear.
我心本来空寂，
一切相貌皆是妄见，
因此千万别取相。
Your mind is basically empty. All appearances are illusions. Don't hold on to appearances.
如果心生佛见、法见
以及见到佛菩萨相貌，
心生敬重时，便堕落到
众生果位，不能自由。
If you envision a Buddha, a dharma or a bodhisattva and conceive respect for them, you relegate yourself to the realm of mortals and get caught up there.

76 我心本来清净，何处有如许相貌。乃至天龙、夜叉、鬼神、帝释、梵王等相，亦不用心生敬重，亦莫怕惧。

77 我心本来空寂，一切相貌皆是妄见，但莫取相。若起佛见法见及佛菩萨等相貌，而生敬重，自堕众生位中。

最直接的要领是：
“心不取一切相！”
此外更无别语。
The essential thing:
"Don't hold on to any appearance whatsoever!"
I have no other advice.
金刚经
《金刚经》说：
“凡所有相，
皆是虚妄。”
Diamond Sutra says,
"Everything that has form is an illusion."
境随心转，
幻无定相。
不以自我立场去看眼前情境，
就是不取相，离相合于圣意。
What you see gets changed with your mind. The illusions have no fixed existence or constant forms.
Don't see what you see from your angle and you'll be of one mind with the Buddha.
因此《金刚经》说：
“离一切相，即名诸佛。”
Diamond Sutra says,
"That which is free of all form is the Buddha."

78 若欲直会，但莫取一切相即得，更无别语。

79 故经云：“凡所有相，皆是虚妄。”都无定实，幻无定相。是无常法，但不取相，合它圣意。故经云：“离一切相，即名诸佛。”

佛是自心
The Buddha is your mind.
天魔波旬与阿修罗都能神通。
变成佛菩萨相，能行种种变化
是外道，一定不是佛。
Mara and Asura both possess the power of manifestation. They can take the forms of Buddhas and bodhisattvas in all sorts of guises. But they're false. None of them are Buddhas.
为何不能礼拜佛菩萨呢？
But why shouldn't we worship Buddhas and bodhisattvas?
自心就是佛，
不要拜错对象。
佛是印度语，
中文称为觉性。
The Buddha is your own mind. Don't misdirect your worship. Buddha is Sanskrit for what you call awareness in Chinese.
佛就是觉性。
Buddhahood is awareness.
觉者灵觉，应机接物，
扬眉瞬目，运手动足，
都是自己的灵觉之性。
It's all your born nature of awareness that guides your responding, brow arching, eye blinking and the movement of your hands and feet.

80 问曰："因何不得礼佛菩萨等？"答曰："天魔波旬、阿修罗示见神通，皆作得菩萨相貌。种种变化，是外道，总不是佛。"

81 佛是自心，莫错礼拜。佛是西国语，此土云觉性。觉者灵觉，应机接物，扬眉瞬目，运手动足，皆是自己灵觉之性。

禪
性就是心，心就是佛，
佛就是道，道就是禅。
禅这个字不是一般人
所能明了的。
And this nature is the mind. And the mind is the Buddha. And the Buddha is the path.
And the path is Zen. But the word Zen is one that remains a puzzle to both mortals.
!
禅是什么意思?
What is Zen at all?
见本性为禅，
若不见性就不是禅。
Seeing your nature is Zen. Unless you see your nature, it's not Zen.

82 性即是心，心即是佛，佛即是道，道即是禅。禅之一字，非凡圣所测。

83 又云："见本性为禅。若不见本性，即非禅也。"

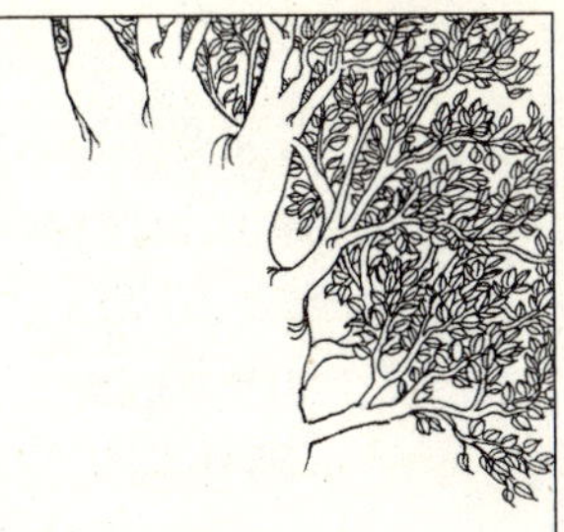

第四章　至道不可言说
Chapter IV The Ultimate Way is Indescribable

本来清净
The mind is tranquil and pure in essence.
什么是真正的佛法?
What's the true Buddha-dharma?
纵算说得千经万论，如果不见本性，
只是凡夫说凡法，而不是真正佛法。
Even if you can explain thousands of sutras and shastras, unless you see your own nature, what your talk about is the teaching of a mortal, instead of being Buddha-dharma.
至道幽深，
难以通过文字说明清楚。
The Ultimate Way is too sublime to be elaborated in words.
佛经又如何说明清楚
其中的境界呢?
Of what use are the Buddhist scriptures?
佛

84 假使说得千经万论，若不见本性，只是凡夫，非是佛法。至道幽深，不可话会，典教凭何所及。

自见本性无关文字，
即使不认识字也能见性成佛。
Someone who sees his own nature finds the Way, even if he can't read a single word.
见性即是佛，圣体本来清净，没有杂秽。
所有言说，都是开悟者们自心见性经验。
Someone who sees his nature is a Buddha. And since a Buddha's body is intrinsically pure and unsullied and everything he says is an expression of his mind.
用体本空，
悟境无法透过文字表达，
十二部经如何能转述佛理？
The mind is basically empty. The way to realm of enlightenment can't be elaborated in words. Then how can the 12 divisions of the Buddhist Canons paraphrase Buddha-dharma?
道本圆成，
不用修证。
道非声色，
微妙难见。
如人饮水，
冷暖自知。
The Way is basically perfect.
It requires no perfecting.
The Way has no form or sound.
It's too subtle to be perceived.
It's like drinking water,
only the drinker can tell the water temperature.

85 但见本性，一字不识亦得。见性即是佛，圣体本来清净，无有杂秽。

86 所有言说，皆是圣人从心起用。用体本来空，名言犹不及，十二部经凭何得及。

87 道本圆成，不用修证。道非声色，微妙难见。如人饮水，冷暖自知。

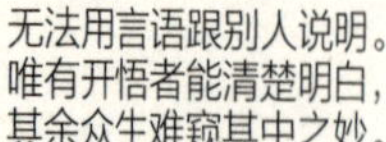

无法用言语跟别人说明。
唯有开悟者能清楚明白，
其余众生难窥其中之妙。
Only the enlightened knows the indescribable essence of the Ultimate Way. It remains veiled to the ordinary.

凡夫无智慧，所以执相，
The wisdom of the ordinary falls short and they hold onto signs, forms or appearances.

不明白自心本来空寂，
执着一切法即堕外道。
They're unaware that their minds are intrinsically empty. And by mistakenly clinging to the appearance of things, they lose the Way.

如果知道诸法从心生，
一切不可以执着，
执着即不能见性。
If you know that everything comes from the mind, then don't become attached. Once attached, you're unable to see your nature.

88 不可向人说也。唯有如来能知，余人天等类，都不觉知。

89 凡夫智不及，所以有执相。不了自心本来空寂，妄执相及一切法即堕外道。若知诸法从心生，不应有执，执即不知。

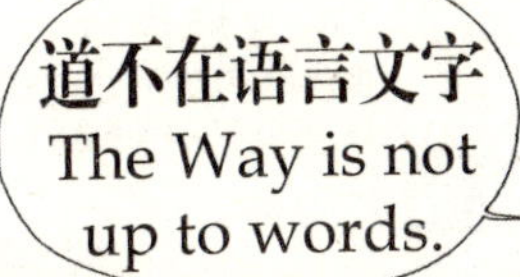
道不在语言文字
The Way is not up to words.

如果能见本性，佛学十二部经典只不过是闲暇时的读物。
But once you see your own nature, the entire 12 divisions of the Buddhist Canons become so much prose.

千经万论都是在教导明心见性，言下契会，文字言语有何用处？
Its thousands of sutras and shastras only amount to a clear mind. Understanding comes in midsentence. What good are doctrines?

最高的真理离开语言文字，教导佛经名词文句不是道。
The ultimate truth is beyond words. Doctrines are words, instead of the Way.

90 若见本性，十二部经总是闲文字。千经万论只是明心，言下契会，教将何用？

91 至理绝言；教是语词，实不是道。

道本无法用语言说明清楚，
能通过言语表达的即非道。
The Way is indescribable. Words are illusions.
道无法用语言表达。
The Way is indescribable.
如果夜晚梦见
楼阁、宫殿、象马，
They're no different from things that appear in your dreams at night, be they palaces or carriages,
或者树木、丛林、水池、亭院，
心中不能生起丝毫贪念。
Forested parks or lakeside pavilions. Don't conceive any delight for such things.
所梦见情境都是
未来的投生之处。
They're all cradles of rebirth.
临终时不取相，业障便消除。
如果心生怀疑，即遭魔所摄。
Keep this in mind when you approach death. Don't cling to appearances, and you'll break through all barriers. A moment's hesitation and you'll be under the spell of devils.

92 道本无言，言说是妄。

93 若夜梦见楼阁宫殿象马之属，及树木丛林池亭如是等相；不得起一念乐着，尽是托生之处，切须在意。临终之时，不得取相，即得除障。疑心瞥起，即魔摄。

自性法身，
本来清净，
不受污染。
Your real body is intrinsically pure and impervious.
只因迷惘无知，
才在不知不觉造业报。
But because of delusions, you're unaware of it. And because of this, you suffer karma in vain.

94 法身本来清净无受，只缘迷故，不觉不知，因兹故妄受报。

第五章　修行的要领
Chapter V Key Points to Self-cultivation

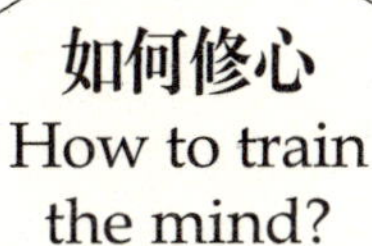
如何修心
How to train the mind?

要如何修心?
How to train the mind?

修心要先改变自己的习性。
You must first change your habits.

心有所乐便执着于乐，
而无法自在。
如果能明白自心本来空寂，
就不会沾染恶习。
Wherever you find delight, you find bondage. But once you awaken to your intrinsically-empty mind, you're no longer bound by vices.

开悟者面对世间的各种情境时，
不以自己立场评断际遇的好坏。
An enlightened person sees the world as it is, without mingling into it his own judgments.

95 所以有乐着，不得自在。只今若悟得本来身心，即不染习。

96 若从圣入凡，示见种种杂类，自为众生。

他的心没有好坏顺逆，
在任何当下都很自在，
He finds freedom in good fortune and bad.
世间一切都奈何他不得。
Such is his power that karma can't hold him.
凡夫神志昏昧，
But the awareness of an ordinary man is dim,
酒
无法像开悟者
一样内外明彻。
Compared to that of an enlightened person who penetrates everything inside and out.
若有疑惑就不做，
只要一做即流浪生死轮回，
If you're not sure, don't act. Once you act, you wander through birth and death.
事后虽然也后悔，
但也没有相救之处。
And regret having no refuge.
对不起啊……我又喝酒啦！
I'm so sorry. I drank again.

97 故圣人逆顺皆得自在，一切业拘它不得。

98 凡夫神识昏昧，不同圣人，内外明彻。若有疑即不作，作即流浪生死，后悔无相救处。

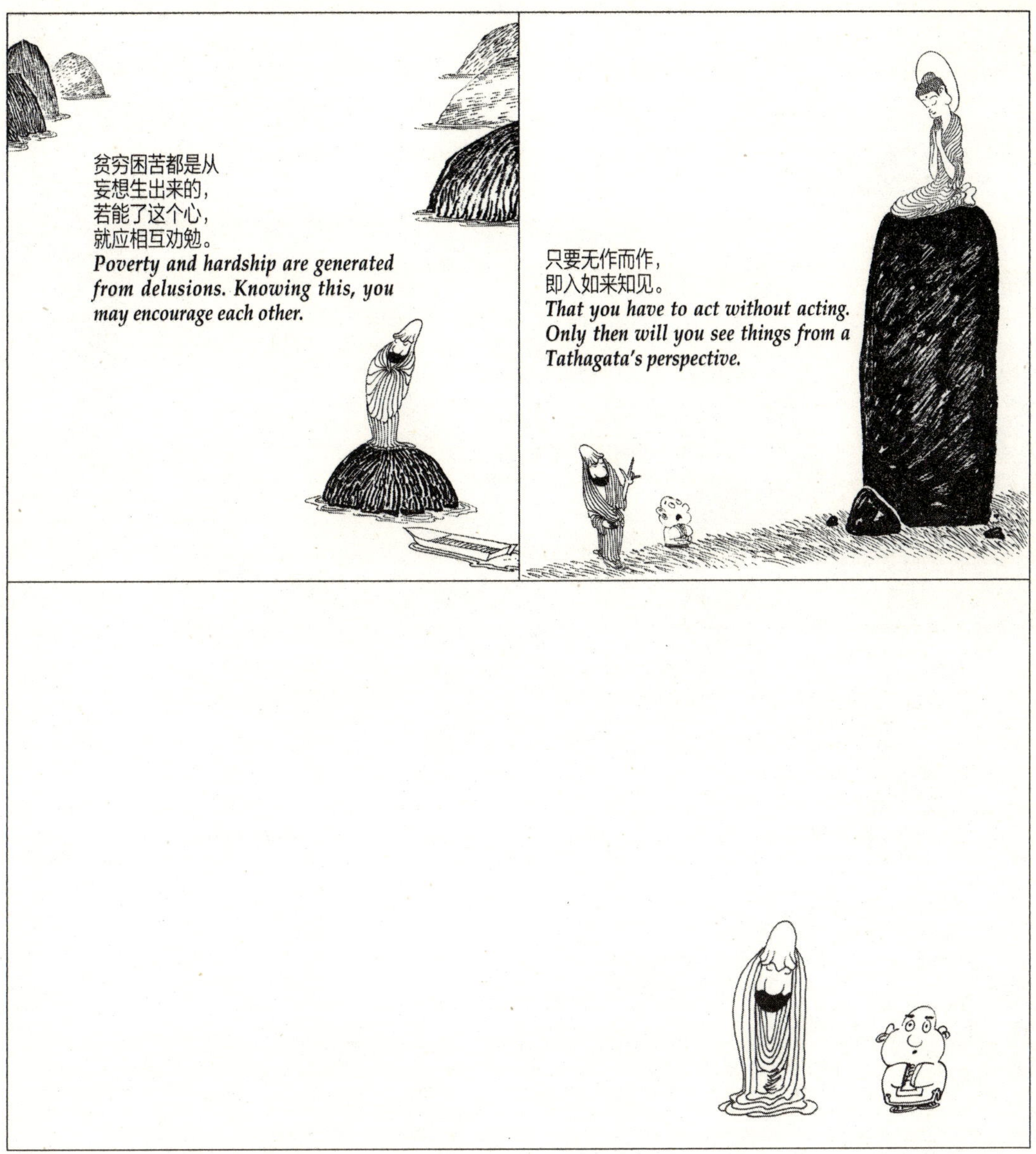
贫穷困苦都是从
妄想生出来的，
若能了这个心，
就应相互劝勉。
Poverty and hardship are generated from delusions. Knowing this, you may encourage each other.
只要无作而作，
即入如来知见。
That you have to act without acting. Only then will you see things from a Tathagata's perspective.

99 贫穷困苦皆从妄想生，若了是心，递相劝勉，但无作而作，即入如来知见。

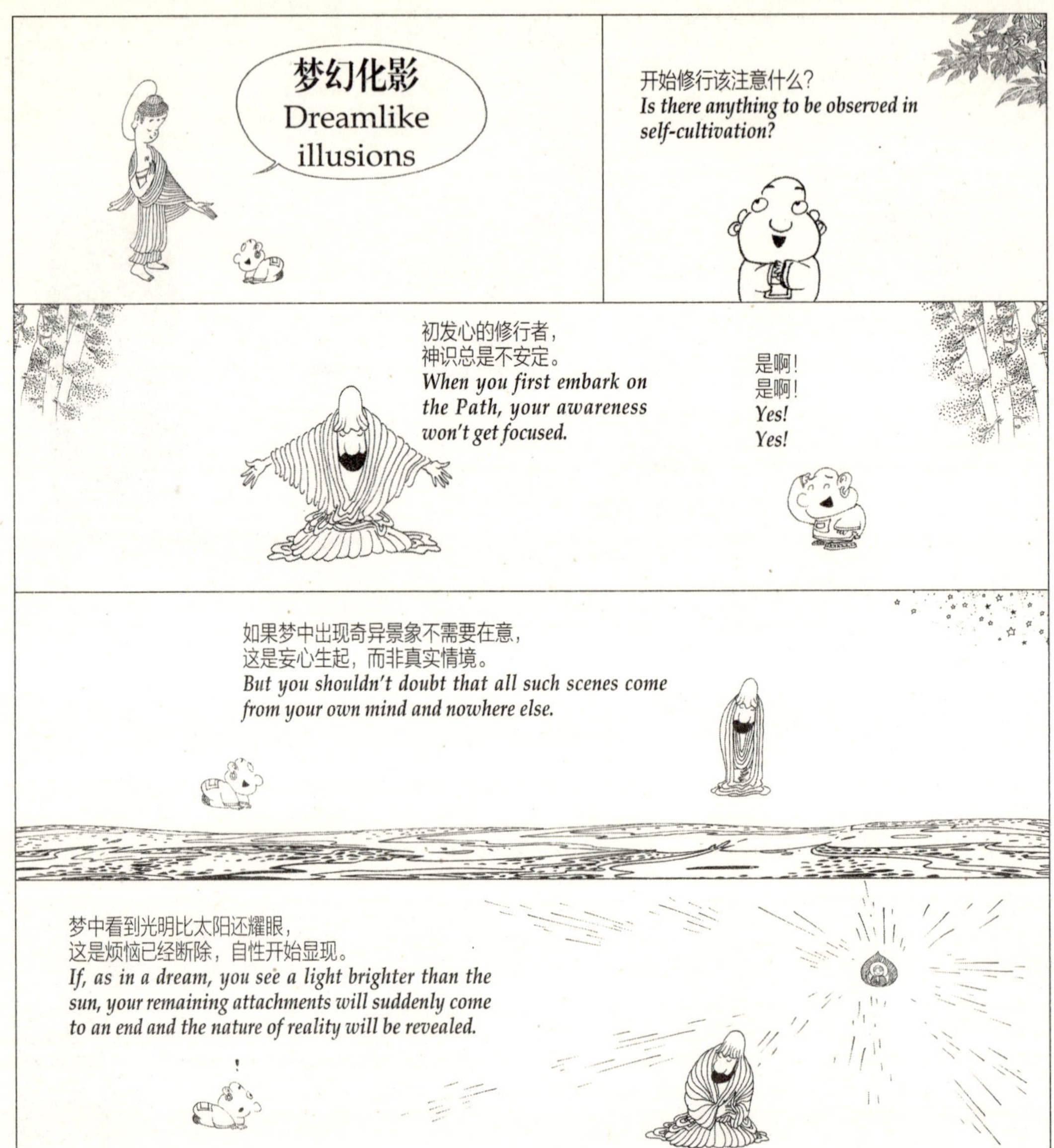
梦幻化影
Dreamlike illusions
开始修行该注意什么?
Is there anything to be observed in self-cultivation?
初发心的修行者，
神识总是不安定。
When you first embark on the Path, your awareness won't get focused.
是啊!
是啊!
Yes!
Yes!
如果梦中出现奇异景象不需要在意，
这是妄心生起，而非真实情境。
But you shouldn't doubt that all such scenes come from your own mind and nowhere else.
梦中看到光明比太阳还耀眼，
这是烦恼已经断除，自性开始显现。
If, as in a dream, you see a light brighter than the sun, your remaining attachments will suddenly come to an end and the nature of reality will be revealed.
!

100 初发心人，神识总不定；

101 若梦中频见异境，辄不用疑，皆是自心起故，不从外来。

102 梦若见光明出现，过于日轮，即余习顿尽，法界性见。

发生这种事就是成道因，
这种经验只有自己清楚，
无法用言语跟别人说明白。
Such an occurrence serves as the basis for enlightenment. But this is something only you know. You can't explain it to others.

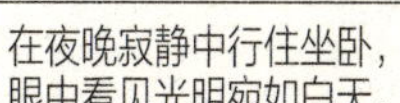

在静园林中行住坐卧时，
眼见大小光明，不必在意，
这是自性所发出的光明。
Or if, while you're walking, standing, sitting or lying in a quiet grove, you see a light, regardless of whether it's bright or dim. Don't tell others and don't focus on it. It's the light of your own nature.

这种经验只有自己清楚，
无法用言语跟别人说明白。
But this is something only you know. You can't explain it to others.

在夜晚寂静中行住坐卧，
眼中看见光明宛如白天。
Or if, while you're walking, standing, sitting or lying in the stillness and darkness of night, everything appears as though in daylight.

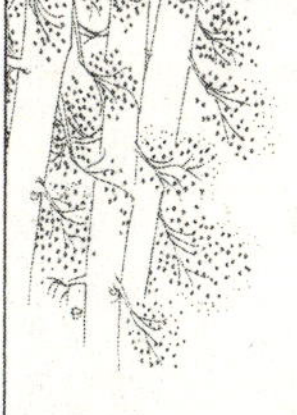

这种经验只有自己清楚，
无法用言语跟别人说明白。
But this is something only you know. You can't explain it to others.

不要疑惑，这是真心将要显露。
梦中看见星月分明，
是由于心中妄想将要熄灭。
Don't doubt your eyes. It's your own mind about to reveal itself. Or if, you see in your dream the moon and stars in all their clarity, it means the delusions you've held are about to end.

103 若有此事，即是成道之因。唯自知，不可向人说。

104 或静园林中行住坐卧，眼见光明，或大或小，莫与人说，亦不得取，亦是自性光明。

105 或夜静暗中行住坐卧，眼睹光明，与昼无异，不得怪，并是自心欲明显。或夜梦中见星月分明，亦自心诸缘欲息，亦不得向人说。

如果梦中昏沉，有如在黑暗道路行走，要知道这是自己的烦恼业障还很深重。
And if your dreams aren't clear, as if you were walking in the dark, it's because your mind is masked by cares.
若然见到本性，不用读经念佛，广学多知无益，反使神识转昏。
If you see your nature, you don't need to chant sutras or invoke Buddhas. Erudition and knowledge may be not only useless, but also cloud your awareness.
佛学教导只是为了让我们明白自心，
Doctrines are only for guiding you to see your mind.
如果已经看清自己本来面目，
Once you've seen your mind,
何必借用佛经帮助你看见自性？
Why bother with doctrines any more?
!

106 梦若昏昏，犹如阴暗中行，亦是自心烦恼障重，亦自知。

107 若见本性，不用读经念佛，广学多知无益，神识转昏。设教只为标心；若识心，何用看教？

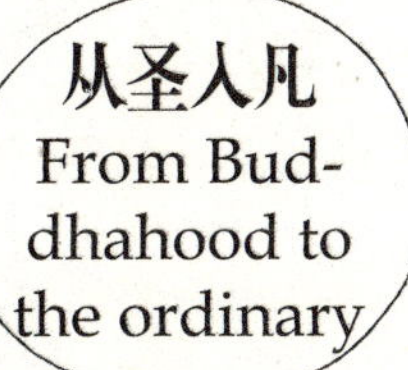
从圣入凡
From Buddhahood to the ordinary

要如何修心？
How to train the mind?

要改变自己的习性，
心有所乐便执着于乐，
而无法自在。
You must first change your habits. Wherever you find delight, you find bondage.

如果能明白自心本来空寂，
就不会沾染恶习。
But once you awaken to your intrinsically-empty mind, you're no longer bound by vices.

生气发怒情绪与道相违背，
对修行没有好处。
If you're always getting angry, you'll turn your nature against the Way. It does no good to your self-cultivation.

圣人出入生死，
随意自在，隐显不定。
一切好坏顺逆，
都无法动摇他的心。
Buddhas move freely through birth and death, appearing and disappearing at will.
They can't be restrained by karma.

108 所以有乐着，不得自在。只今若悟得本来身心，即不染习。

109 若多嗔恚，令性转与道相违，自赚无益。

110 圣人于生死中，自在出没，隐显不定，一切业拘它不得。

圣人破除邪魔，
任谁对他无可奈何。
Buddhas can't be overcome by devils.
一切众生但见本性，余习气顿灭。
神识不昧，不用思考便领会，
只在当下。
Once the ordinary see their nature, all attachments end. Even if awareness is clear, you can only find it right at the very present.
过去的习气瞬间消灭，神识清楚。
要是见性必须是当下就见，
All attachments come to an end. Your awareness gets clear. But it's only now at the present you see your nature.
想要得道，
不可执着任何一切法。
息业养神，余习亦尽。
自然明白，不假用功。
If you really want to find the Way, don't hold on to anything.
Once you put an end to karma and nurture your awareness, any attachments that remain will come to an end. Understanding comes naturally. You don't have to make any effort.

111 圣人破邪魔。

112 一切众生但见本性，余习顿灭。神识不昧，须是直下便会，只在如今。

113 欲真会道，莫执一切法；息业养神，余习亦尽。自然明白，不假用功。

往外求道的人，
不了解佛意，
却用功最多。
Those who seek the Way beyond their nature don't understand what the Buddha meant. However, they work hardest.

他们违背见性真谛，
整天念佛读经不断，
妄念烦恼不曾停息，
终究无法逃脱轮回。
And the harder they try, the farther they get from the Buddha-nature. All day long they invoke Buddhas and chant sutras. But they remain blind to their own divine nature and they don't escape the Wheel.

佛是安逸的清闲人，
何必四处追求名利，
最后有何用处？
A Buddha is an idle person. He doesn't run around after fortune and fame. What good are such things in the end?

不见性人，读经念佛，
长学精进，日夜不懈。
Those who don't see their nature chant sutras, invoke Buddhas and study long and hard, day and night.

114 外道不会佛意，用功最多。

115 违背圣意，终日驱驱，念佛转经，昏于神性，不免轮回。

116 佛是闲人，何用驱驱，广求名利，后时何用？

117 但不见性人，读经念佛，长学精进；六时行道。

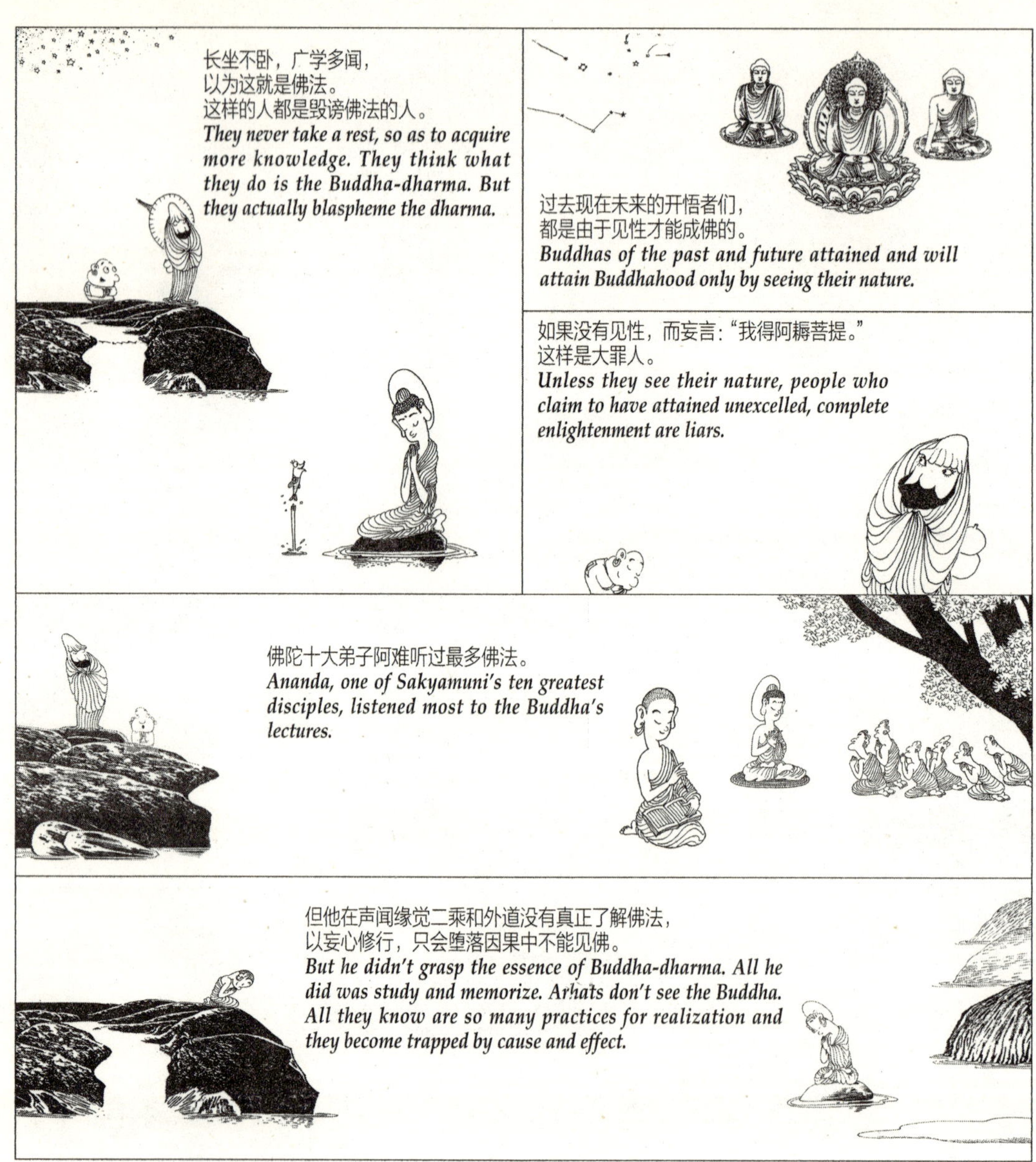
长坐不卧，广学多闻，
以为这就是佛法。
这样的人都是毁谤佛法的人。
They never take a rest, so as to acquire more knowledge. They think what they do is the Buddha-dharma. But they actually blaspheme the dharma.
过去现在未来的开悟者们，
都是由于见性才能成佛的。
Buddhas of the past and future attained and will attain Buddhahood only by seeing their nature.
如果没有见性，而妄言："我得阿耨菩提。"
这样是大罪人。
Unless they see their nature, people who claim to have attained unexcelled, complete enlightenment are liars.
佛陀十大弟子阿难听过最多佛法。
Ananda, one of Sakyamuni's ten greatest disciples, listened most to the Buddha's lectures.
但他在声闻缘觉二乘和外道没有真正了解佛法，
以妄心修行，只会堕落因果中不能见佛。
But he didn't grasp the essence of Buddha-dharma. All he did was study and memorize. Arhats don't see the Buddha. All they know are so many practices for realization and they become trapped by cause and effect.

118 长坐不卧；广学多闻，以为佛法。此等众生，尽是谤佛法人。

119 前佛后佛，只言见性。诸行无常。若不见性，妄言我得阿耨菩提，此是大罪人。

120 十大弟子阿难多闻中得第一，于佛无识只学多闻，二乘外道皆无识佛，识数修证，堕在因果中。

如果说：
“众生的业报，永远无法逃脱生死轮回。”
Such is the ordinary's karma:
No escape from the Wheel of Birth and Death.
这是违背佛陀的本意。
毁谤佛众生，把他们杀了也没有罪过。
By doing the opposite of what lies intended,
they blaspheme the Buddha. Killing them
would not be wrong.
大般涅槃经
《大般涅槃经》说：
“阐提人不相信佛法，杀了他也无罪。”
Nirvana Sutra says,
“Since icchantikas are incapable of belief, killing them would be blameless”.
对佛法有信心者，
就是将来会成佛的人。
对于不见性的人，
也不用毁谤他的过错，
自讨没趣。
Whereas those who believe in Buddha-dharma
attain Buddhahood some day.
Just ignore those who are blinded to their nature,
as that would only invite a snub.

121 是众生业报，不免生死，远背佛意，即是谤佛众生，杀却无罪过。

122 经云：“阐提人不生信心，杀却无罪过。”若有信心，此人是佛位人。若不见性，即不用取次谤它良善，自赚无益。

第六章　当下即是天堂
Chapter VI Heaven is in the Very Moment

WISDOM

天堂地狱
就在现前
Heaven or hell is right
before your eyes
弟子问达摩:
“有天堂与地狱吗?”
A disciple asked Bodhidharma:
“Are there heaven and hell?”
达摩回答:“有。”
Bodhidharma answered, “Of course.”
在哪里?
Where are they?
天堂与地狱
就在现前!
Heaven and hell are
right before your eyes!
!
为何我看不到?
But why can't I see them?
因为你有自我。
Because you're caught in the idea of self.
你看到了吗?
Do you see them?

123 天堂地狱只在眼前。

有我有你之时，
便看不到天堂。
You can't see heaven, once you're caught in the ideas of self and others.
无我无你，
还有谁需要见天堂？
Without those ideas, is there any need to see heaven?
无我无你，便能看到天堂？
Can I see heaven by getting rid of those ideas?
善恶因果报
应历历在现！
愚人不信，
当下堕黑暗地狱，
自己也无所觉知，
Good and bad are distinct,
Cause and effect are clear.
But fools don't believe and fall straight into a hell of endless darkness without even knowing it.
这是由于业障深重的原因，
所以不相信有天堂和地狱。
Their heavy karma keeps them from believing.

124 善恶历然，因果分明。愚人不信，现堕黑暗地狱中；亦不觉不知，只缘业重故，所以不信。

有如瞎子不信世间有光明，
无论怎么说明他也不相信。
They're like blind people who don't believe there's such a thing as light, no matter how hard you try to explain.
由于瞎子看不见，
如何分辨黑暗与光明?
How do you expect the blind who never see the light to distinguish dark and light?
愚痴的人也是如此，
如今堕落畜生道众生。
The same holds true for fools who end up among the lower orders of existence.
出生于贫穷下贱家庭，
求生不能，求死不得。
Or among the poor and despised. They can't live and they can't die.
虽然看起来在受苦，
如果问他生活得如何……
Suffering as they are, if you ask them how they feel about their life...

125 譬如无目人，不通道有光明，纵向伊说亦不信，只缘盲故，凭何辨得日光；愚人亦复如是。

126 现今堕畜生杂类，诞在贫穷下贱，求生不得，求死不得。虽受是苦，直问着亦言我今快乐，不异天堂。

你日子过得如何？
How's your life?
我快乐得如同住在天堂。
I'm as happy as if I were in heaven.
为什么会这样呢？
How's that?
一切众生，以出生处自得其乐，而不感到痛苦。
All living creatures, even those who think themselves wellborn, are likewise unaware.
造恶的人也是如此，由于过去处在恶业中。
So it is true for those who commit evil deeds.
我来为各位说佛法！
Allow me to explain the dharma!
造恶者不相信佛法，也是无可奈何。
Because of the heaviness of their karma, those who commit evil deeds can't believe and can't get free.
佛法本空，空就是没有因缘果报！
Dharma is empty in essence. Emptiness means without any cause and effect or any karma!

127 故知一切众生，生处为乐，亦不觉不知。

128 如斯恶人，只缘业障重故，所以不能发信心者，不自由它也。

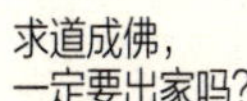

求道成佛，
一定要出家吗？
Do those who want to follow the Way to Buddhahood have to become a Buddhist monk?

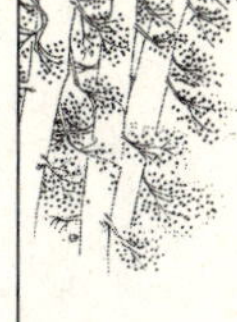

如果见自心是佛，
即使没有出家，
在家居士也是佛。
People who see that their mind is the Buddha don't necessarily become a Buddhist monk. Lay Buddhists are Buddhas, too.

如果不能洞察自心是佛，
即使出家，也是心外求法的外道。
Unless they see their nature, people who become Buddhist monks are simply laymen pursuing the Way beyond their mind in vain.

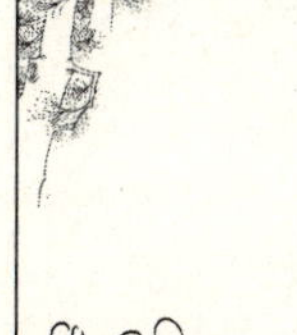
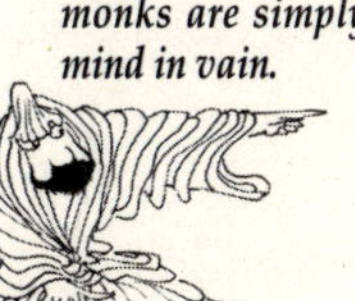

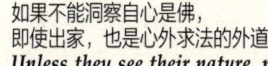

129 若见自心是佛，不在剃除须发，白衣亦是佛。

130 若不见性，剃除须发，亦是外道。

性本清净
Your nature is essentially pure
在家居士有妻子，
淫欲未除怎能成佛？
But since married laymen don't give up sex, how can they attain Buddhahood?
成佛关键只在见性，
而不在淫欲。
It's only about seeing your nature. It has nothing to do with sex.
能不能成佛在于有没有见性；
如果能见性，淫欲也是空寂。
Once you see your nature, sex is basically immaterial.
若能断除淫欲，
不以淫欲为乐，
就不会影响开悟。
It ends along with your delight in it. Even if some habits may remain, they have no impacts on your attaining enlightenment.

131 问曰："白衣有妻子，淫欲不除，凭何得成佛？"答曰："只言见性不言淫欲。"
132 只为不见性，但得见性，淫欲本来空寂，自尔断除，亦不乐着，纵有余习，不能为害。

是什么原因呢?
Why's that?
因为自性本清净。
Because your nature is essentially pure.
自性虽处在五蕴色身中,
但其性本来清净无污染。
Despite dwelling in a material body of Five Aggregates, your nature is basically pure. It can't be corrupted.
清净法身!
本来无受、无饥、无渴。
Your real body is basically pure. It feels essentially no sensation, no hunger or thirst.
无寒热、无病、
无恩爱、无眷属、
无苦乐、无好恶、
无短长、无强弱。
It feels basically no warmth or cold, no sickness, no love or attachment, no pleasure or pain, no good or bad, no disavantages or advantages, no weakness or strength.

133 问:“何以故?”答:“性本清净故。”

134 虽处在五蕴色身中,其性本来清净,染污不得。法身本来无受,无饥无渴,无寒热,无病,无恩爱,无眷属,无苦乐,无好恶,无短长,无强弱。

本来无一物可得；
只因为执着于此色身，
因此才有饥渴、寒热、疾病、痛苦等相。
Actually, there's nothing here. It's only because you cling to this material body that things like hunger and thirst, warmth and cold, sickness and pain appear.
如果没有执着，
便能脱离生死，清净自在。
Once you stop clinging and let things be, you'll be free, even of birth and death, and enjoy purity and tranquility.
相由心生，境随心转。
一切法从心想生。
What you see are generated from you mind. What you feel depends upon what you think. All dharmas come from your mind.
转一切法便与圣人一样，
神通自在无碍。
You'll possess spiritual powers that can't be obstructed. And you'll be at peace wherever you are.

135 本来无有一物可得；只缘执有此色身。因即有饥渴、寒热、瘴病等相。

136 若不执，即一任作。若于生死中得自在，转一切法，与圣人神通自在无碍，无处不安。

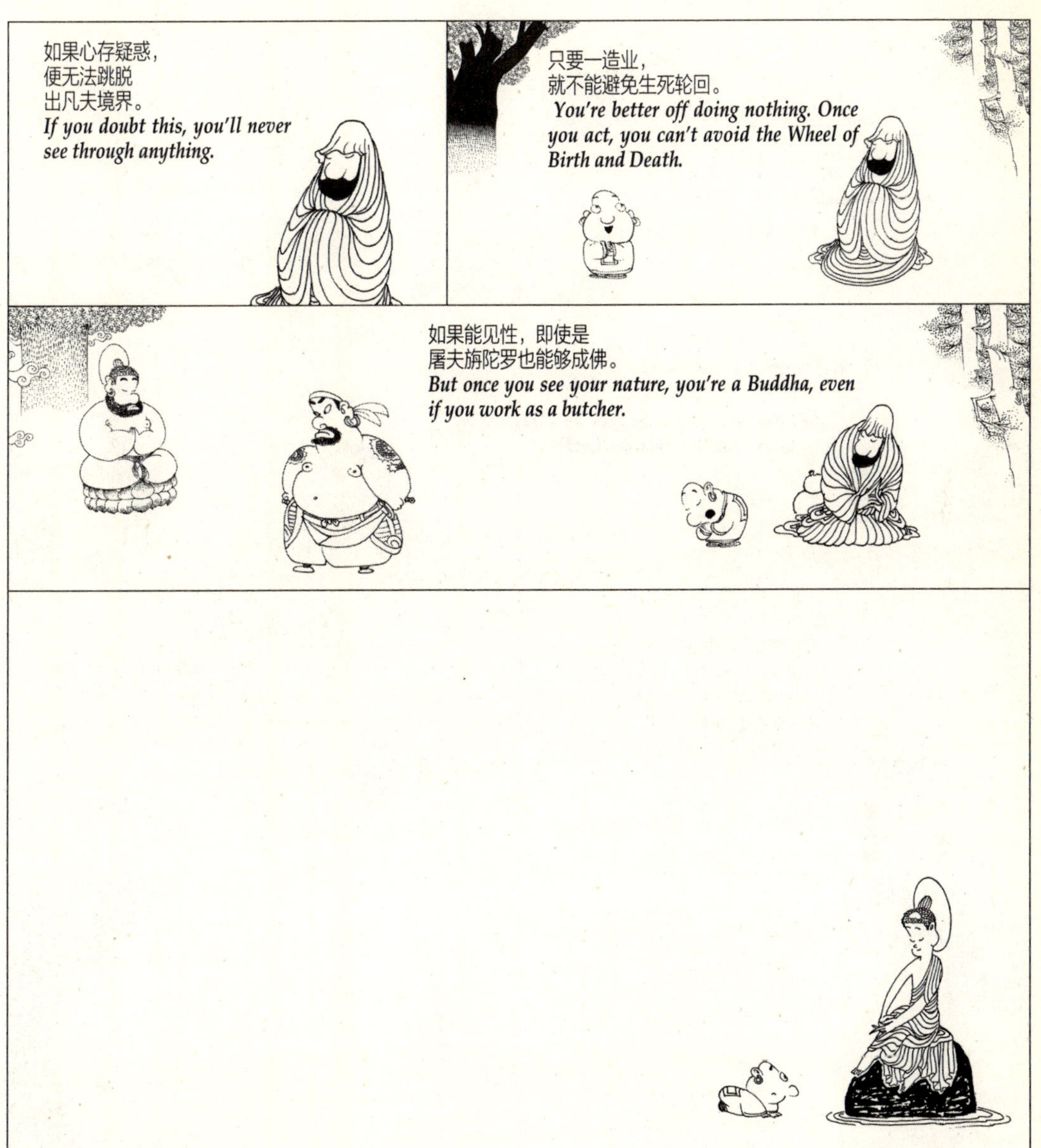
如果心存疑惑，
便无法跳脱
出凡夫境界。
If you doubt this, you'll never see through anything.
只要一造业，
就不能避免生死轮回。
You're better off doing nothing. Once you act, you can't avoid the Wheel of Birth and Death.
如果能见性，即使是
屠夫旃陀罗也能够成佛。
But once you see your nature, you're a Buddha, even if you work as a butcher.

137 若心有疑，决定透一切境界不过。不作最好，作了不免轮回生死。若见性，旃陀罗亦得成佛。

业报有无只在一心
It's only about your mind, instead of karma
旃陀罗门从事屠夫和刽子手的杀生工作，如何能成佛？
But butchers create karma by slaughtering animals. How can they be Buddhas?
成佛在于见不见性，跟修行者所从事的行业无关。
It's only about seeing your nature. It has nothing to do with creating karma. Regardless of what we do, our karma has no hold on us.
从无始以来，众生迷失本性，造业堕入地狱。
Through endless kalpas without beginning, it's only because people don't see their nature that they end up in hell.
如果众生悟得本性，将不会再造作一切恶业。
Once a person realizes his original nature, he stops creating karma.

138 问曰："旃陀罗杀生作业，如何得成佛？"答曰："只言见性不言作业。纵作业不同，一切业拘不得。"

139 从无始旷大劫来，只为不见性，堕地狱中，所以作业轮回生死。从悟得本性，终不作业。

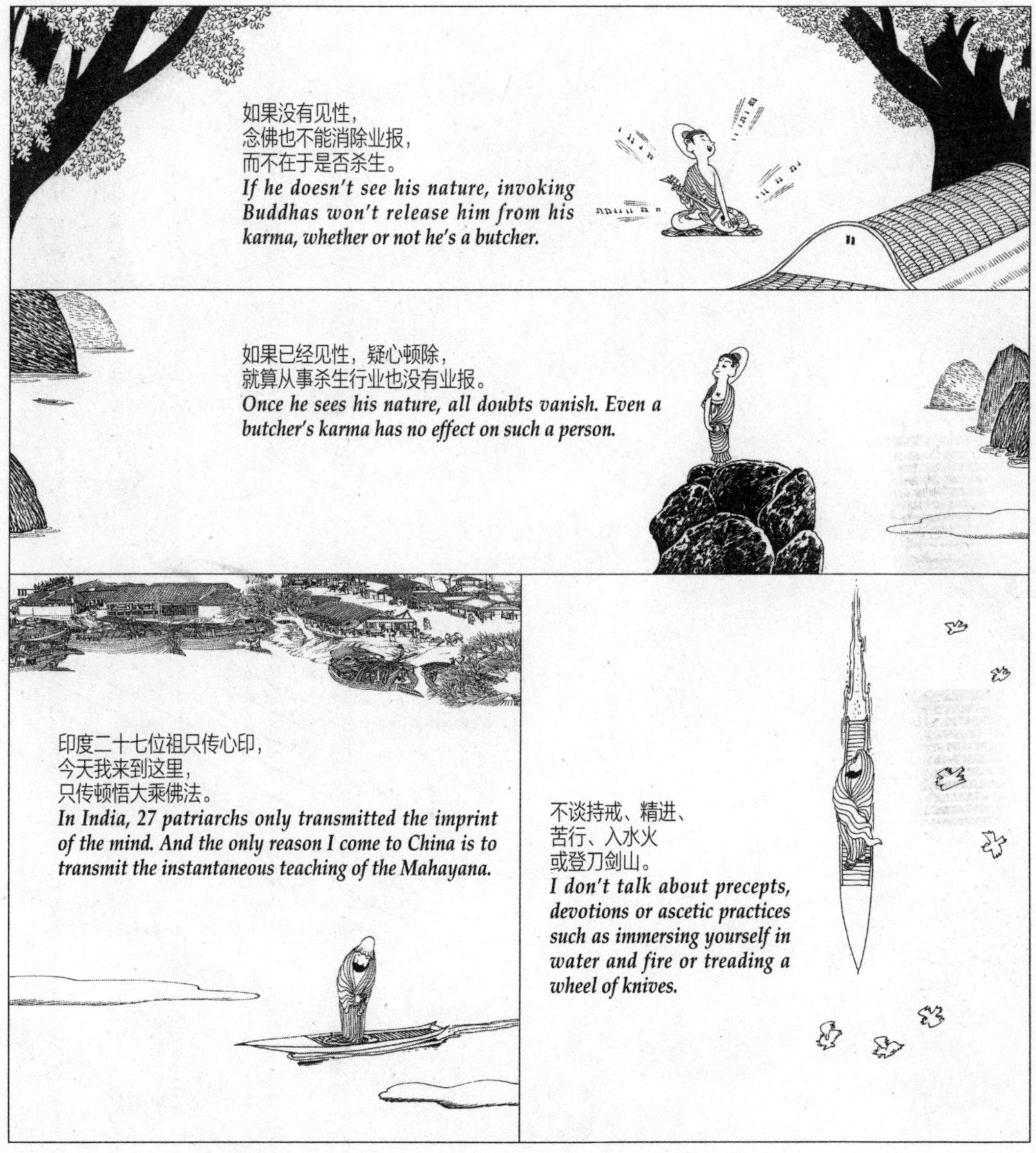
如果没有见性，
念佛也不能消除业报，
而不在于是否杀生。
If he doesn't see his nature, invoking Buddhas won't release him from his karma, whether or not he's a butcher.
如果已经见性，疑心顿除，
就算从事杀生行业也没有业报。
Once he sees his nature, all doubts vanish. Even a butcher's karma has no effect on such a person.
印度二十七位祖只传心印，
今天我来到这里，
只传顿悟大乘佛法。
In India, 27 patriarchs only transmitted the imprint of the mind. And the only reason I come to China is to transmit the instantaneous teaching of the Mahayana.
不谈持戒、精进、
苦行、入水火
或登刀剑山。
I don't talk about precepts, devotions or ascetic practices such as immersing yourself in water and fire or treading a wheel of knives.

140 若不见性，念佛免报不得，非论杀生命。若见性疑心顿除，杀生命亦不奈它何。

141 自西天二十七祖，只是递传心印。吾今来此土，唯传顿教大乘，即心是佛，不言持戒精进苦行。乃至入水火，登于剑轮。

苦行是外道法
Ascetic practices are provisional
持戒苦行不能成佛吗？
Can I attain Buddhahood by observing precepts and following ascetic practices?
苦行是外道法，不能成佛。
Ascetic practices are only provisional. You can't attain Buddhahood through them.
为什么？
Why?
成佛只在见心性，不在身行。
You can only attain Buddhahood by seeing your mind and nature. It has nothing to do with what you do with your physical body.
每日一食、长坐不卧，都是心外求法的外道法。
Things such as having one meal a day or never lying down are fanatical, provisional teachings.
若识得施为身心运作的那颗本心，你就是诸佛心。
Once you see your mind behind all your thoughts and movements, yours is the mind of all Buddhas.
是的，师父！
I see, Master!

142 一食长坐不卧，尽是外道有为法。若识得施为运动灵觉之性，汝即诸佛心。

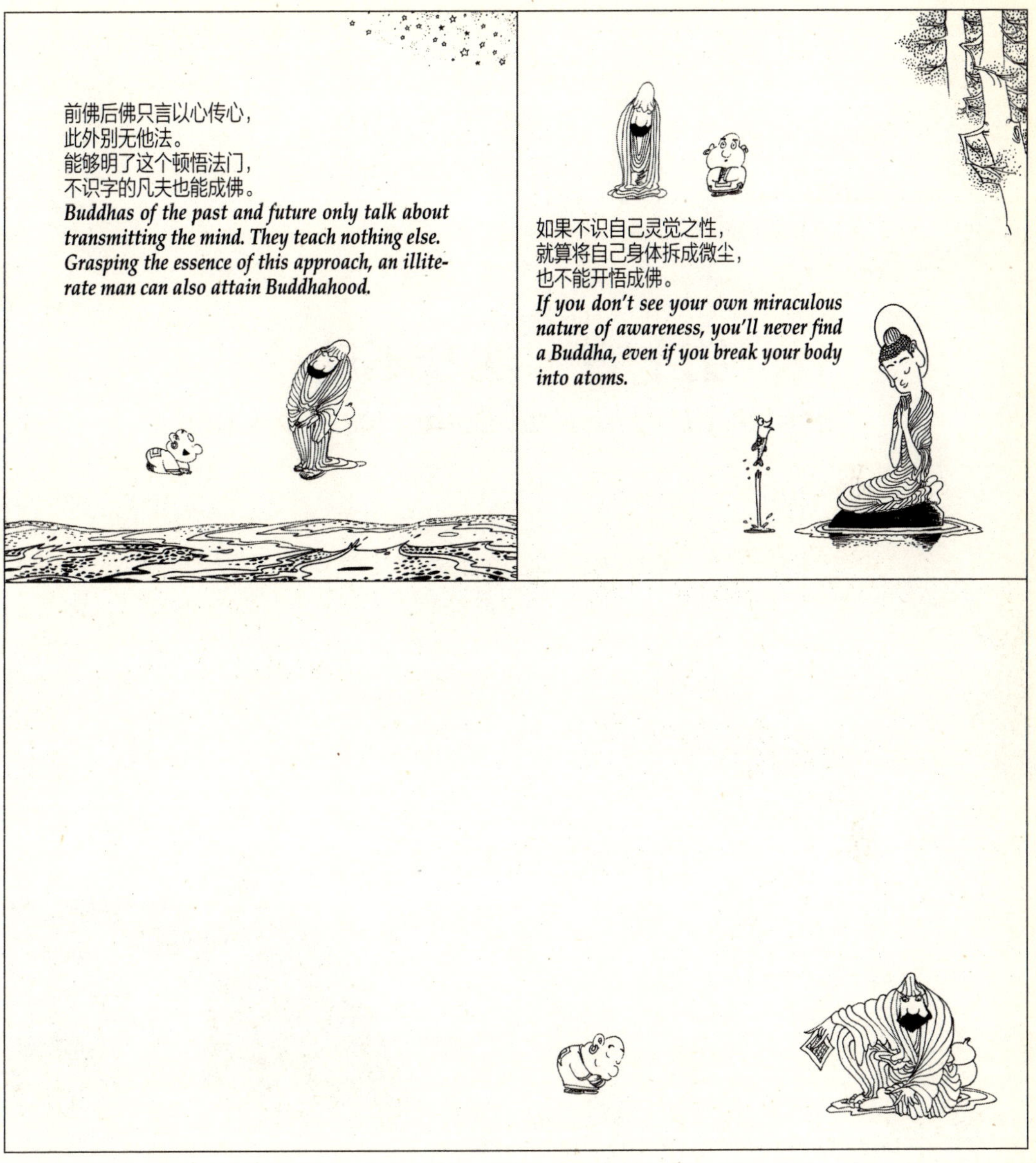

前佛后佛只言以心传心，
此外别无他法。
能够明了这个顿悟法门，
不识字的凡夫也能成佛。
Buddhas of the past and future only talk about transmitting the mind. They teach nothing else. Grasping the essence of this approach, an illiterate man can also attain Buddhahood.
如果不识自己灵觉之性，
就算将自己身体拆成微尘，
也不能开悟成佛。
If you don't see your own miraculous nature of awareness, you'll never find a Buddha, even if you break your body into atoms.

143 前佛后佛只言传心，更无别法。若识此法，凡夫一字不识亦是佛。若不识自己灵觉之性，假使身破如微尘，觅佛终不得也。

第七章　法身不动
Chapter VII The Real Body Doesn't Move

空心不动
The mind of emptiness doesn't move
动是心动，
动即其用。
All motion is the mind's motion. Motion is its function.
自心如何能动？
So how does the mind move?
动外无心，
心外无动。
动不是心，
心不是动。
Apart from motion there's no mind, and apart from the mind there's no motion. But motion isn't the mind. And the mind isn't motion.
动本无心，
心本无动。
动不离心，
心不离动。
Motion is basically mindless. And the mind is basically motionless. But motion doesn't exist without the mind. And the mind doesn't exist without motion.

144 动是心动，动即其用。

145 动外无心，心外无动。动不是心，心不是动。动本无心，心本无动。动不离心，心不离动。

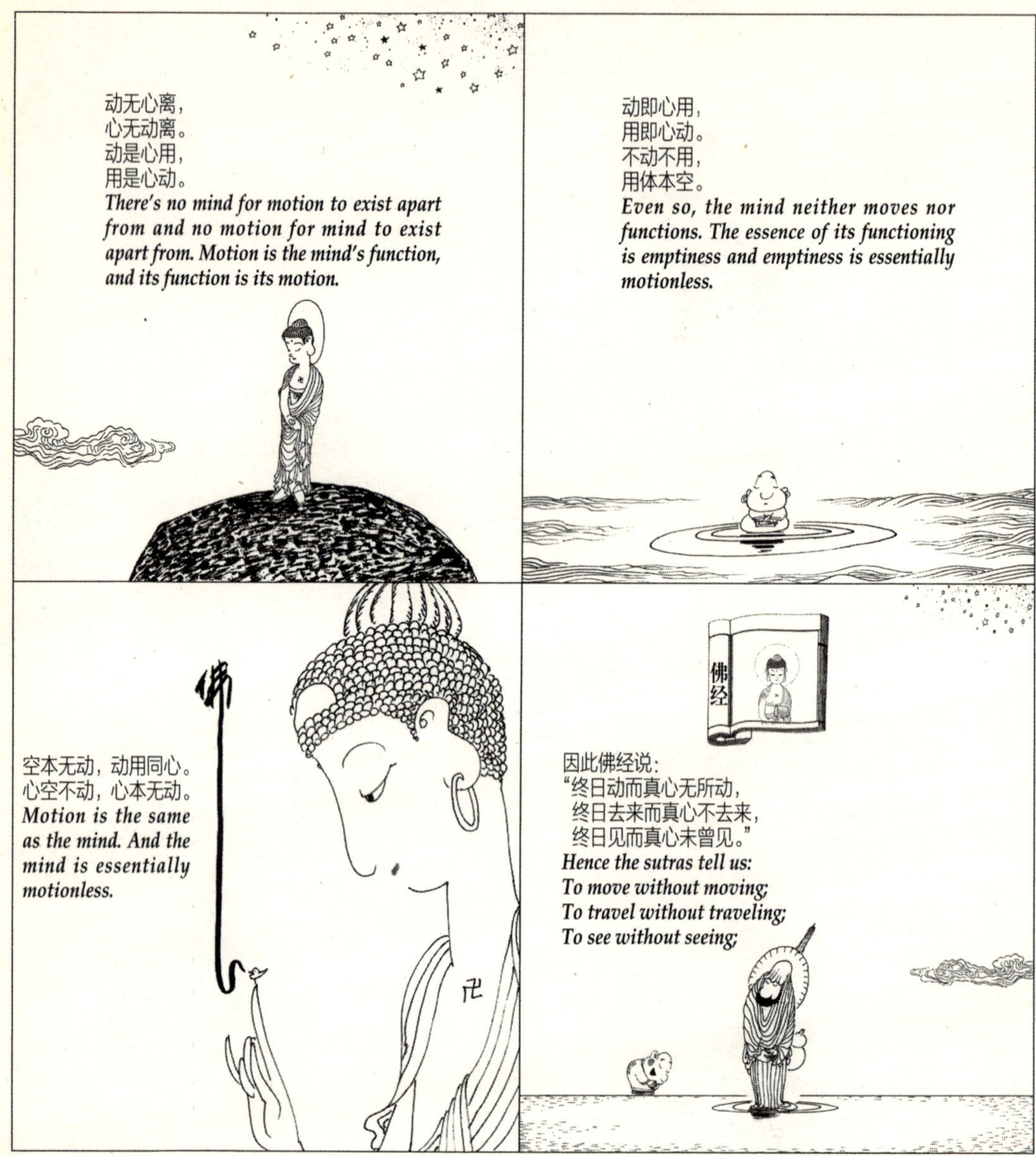
动无心离，
心无动离。
动是心用，
用是心动。
There's no mind for motion to exist apart from and no motion for mind to exist apart from. Motion is the mind's function, and its function is its motion.
动即心用，
用即心动。
不动不用，
用体本空。
Even so, the mind neither moves nor functions. The essence of its functioning is emptiness and emptiness is essentially motionless.
佛
空本无动，动用同心。
心空不动，心本无动。
Motion is the same as the mind. And the mind is essentially motionless.
佛经
因此佛经说：
“终日动而真心无所动，
终日去来而真心不去来，
终日见而真心未曾见。”
Hence the sutras tell us:
To move without moving;
To travel without traveling;
To see without seeing;

146 动无心离，心无动离，动是心用，用是心动。动即心用，用即心动。不动不用，用体本空。空本无动，动用同心，心本无动。

147 故经云：“动而无所动，终日去来而未曾去，终日见而未曾见。”

终日笑而真心未曾笑，
终日闻而真心未曾闻，
终日知而真心未曾知。
To laugh without laughing;
To hear without hearing;
To know without knowing;
终日喜而真心未曾喜，
终日行而真心未曾行，
终日住而真心无所住。
To be happy without being happy;
To walk without walking;
And to stand without standing.
佛经
佛经说：
“言语道断，心行处灭，
见闻觉知，本自圆寂。”
And the sutras say,
“The Ultimate Way goes beyond words and thought. Basically, seeing, hearing, perceiving and knowing are completely empty.”
乃至嗔、喜、痛、痒，
何异木人，
只缘推寻痛痒不可得。
Your anger, joy or pain is like that of a puppet's. You search but you won't find a thing.

148 终日笑而未曾笑，终日闻而未曾闻，终日知而未曾知，终日喜而未曾喜，终日行而未曾行，终日住而未曾住。

149 故经云：“言语道断，心行处灭，见闻觉知，本自圆寂。乃至嗔喜痛痒何异木人，只缘推寻痛痒不可得。”

佛经

佛经说：
"恶得苦报，善有善报，
嗔恨堕入地狱，欢喜会升天堂。"
According to the sutras,
"evil deeds result in hardships and good deeds result in blessings. Ill-will people fall into hell and joyful people go to heaven."

心性本空没有偏见，心无所执着，便无际遇的好坏顺逆。如果自己没有开悟，讲经便无根据，无法说清楚要领。
But once you know that the nature of anger and joy is empty and you let them go, you free yourself from karma. If you don't see your nature, quoting sutras is of no help.

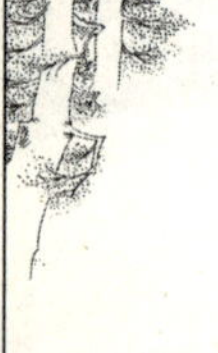

以上老师所说，
都是开悟见解？
Sir, are those all your opinions on enlightenment?

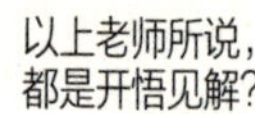

这只是略说邪正，
距离真正的佛法，
何止一二而已？
Those are only my personal opinions and you may explore further more. How dare we say we're approaching the true Buddharma?

这时达摩唱了一首佛偈：
心心心难可寻，
宽时遍法界，
窄也不容针。
Bodhidharma then chanted a gatha:
The true mind is hard to be traced.
It may be widespread in the universe.
It may be too narrow to allow a needle in.

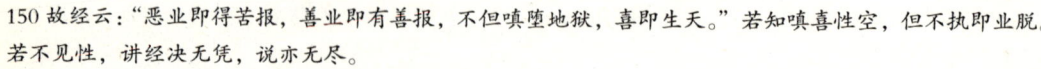

150 故经云："恶业即得苦报，善业即有善报，不但嗔堕地狱，喜即生天。"若知嗔喜性空，但不执即业脱。若不见性，讲经决无凭，说亦无尽。

151 略标邪正如是，不及一二也。

152 颂曰："心心心难可寻，宽时遍法界，窄也不容针。"

我本求心不求佛，
了知三界空无物。
What I'm trying to find is my true mind, instead of a Buddha,
As I know that there's nothing in this universe.
若欲求佛但求心，
只这心心心是佛。
To attain Buddhahood, you just turn to your mind,
Which is the only way to the Buddha.
我本求心心自持，
求心不得待心知。
The mind may keep you outside,
So that you can do nothing but to wait.
佛性不从心外得，
心生便是罪生时。
Your Buddha-nature is never beyond your mind.

153 我本求心不求佛，了知三界空无物。若欲求佛但求心，只这心心心是佛。我本求心心自持，求心不得待心知。佛性不从心外得，心生便是罪生时。

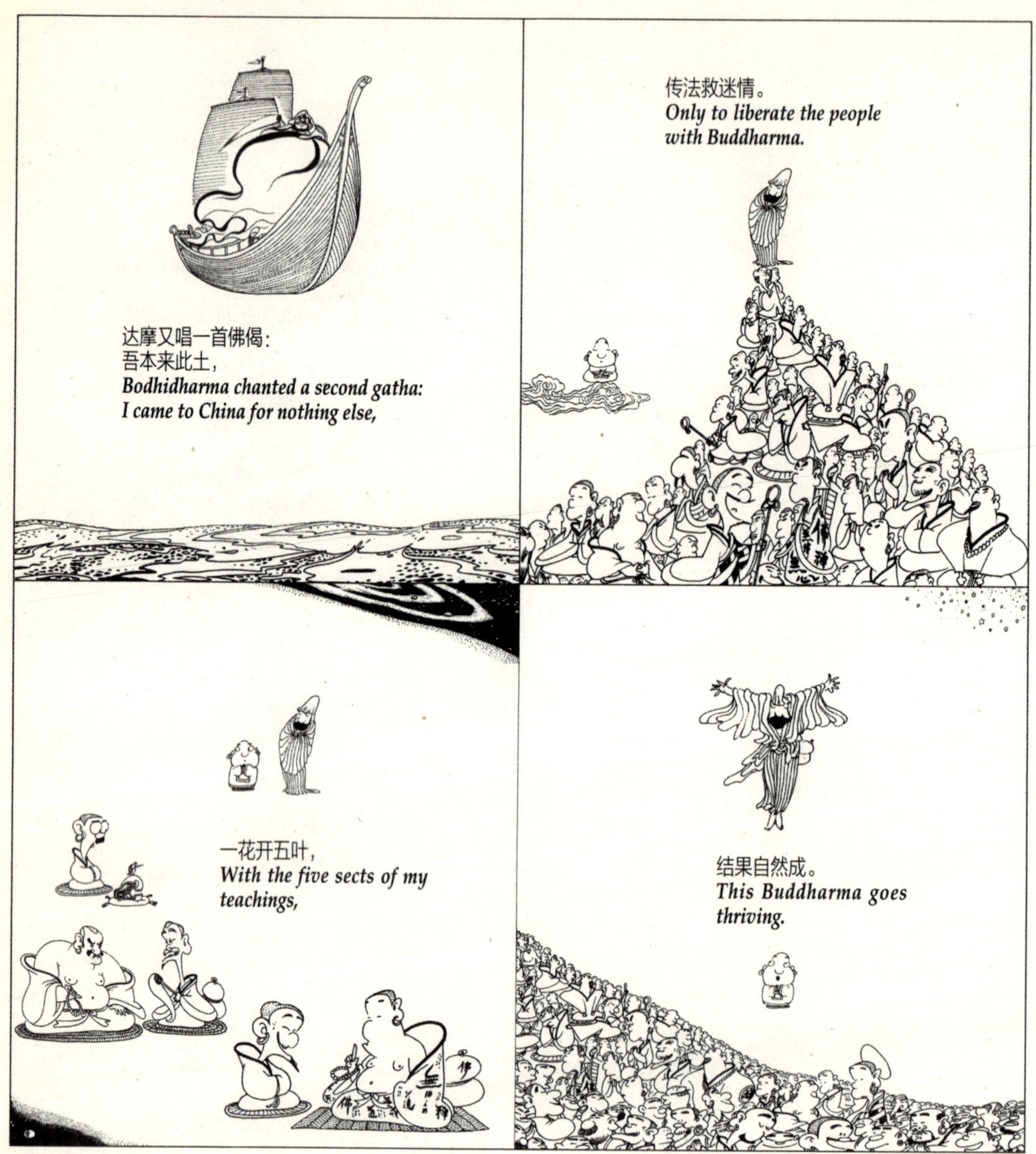
达摩又唱一首佛偈：
吾本来此土，
Bodhidharma chanted a second gatha:
I came to China for nothing else,
传法救迷情。
Only to liberate the people
with Buddharma.
一花开五叶，
With the five sects of my
teachings,
结果自然成。
This Buddharma goes
thriving.

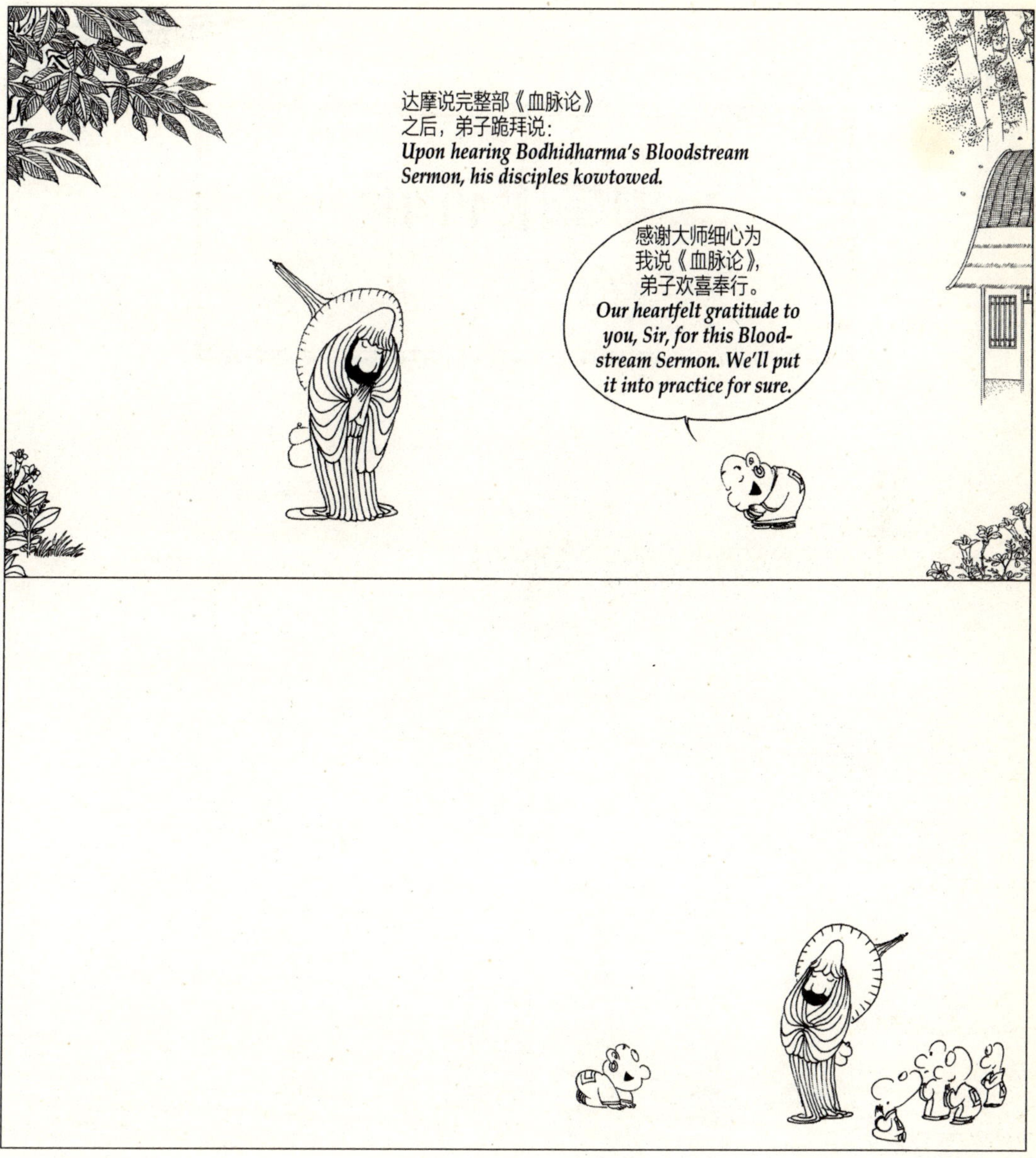
达摩说完整部《血脉论》
之后，弟子跪拜说：
Upon hearing Bodhidharma's Bloodstream Sermon, his disciples kowtowed.
感谢大师细心为我说《血脉论》，弟子欢喜奉行。
Our heartfelt gratitude to you, Sir, for this Bloodstream Sermon. We'll put it into practice for sure.

达摩悟性论

Wake-up Sermon

第一章　寂灭是道

Chapter I　The Essence of the Way is Detachment

寂灭为体
Detachment is the essence
弟子问达摩：
A disciple asked Bodhidharma,
“什么是道？”
“What is the Way?”
达摩回答：
“令心寂灭，即是道！”
Bodhidharma answered,
“The essence of the Way is detachment.”
什么是修行？
What is practice for?
离一切相，
即是修行！
The goal of those who practice
is freedom from appearances.
佛经说：
The sutras say,
“寂灭是菩提，
灭诸相故。”
“Detachment is enlightenment,
because it negates appearances.”

1　夫道者；以寂灭为体。

2　修者；以离相为宗。故经云：“寂灭是菩提，灭诸相故。”

什么是佛?
What is Buddhahood?
佛即是觉悟!
人人都有一颗觉悟的心,
人人都能开悟抵达智慧
彼岸,故名为佛。
Buddhahood means enlightenment.
Everyone has a Buddha-nature and is able
to reach the Other Shore of Enlightenment.
Those who achieve this goal are Buddhas.
佛
经
佛经说:
"离一切诸相,即名诸佛。"
The sutras say,
"Those who free themselves from all appearances
are called Buddhas."
什么是相?
What is appearences.
眼前所见的情境即是相。
What you see is all appearances,
signs and forms.

3 佛者觉也;人有觉心,得菩提道,故名为佛。经云:"离一切诸相,即名诸佛。"

4 相由心生。

什么是无相？
What is non-appearance?

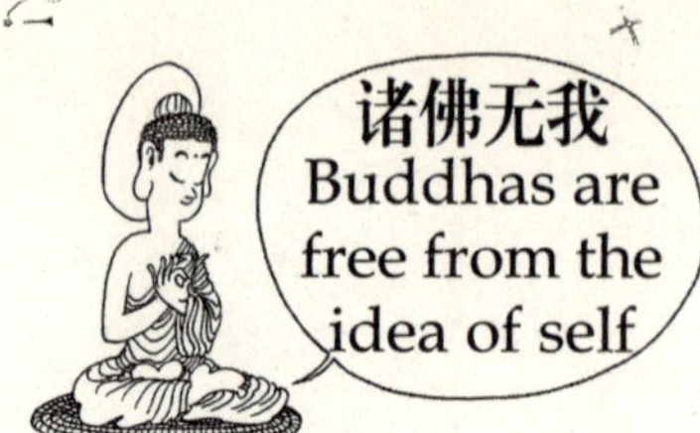
诸佛无我
Buddhas are free from the idea of self

有相也是无相之相，
不可以眼见，唯有智慧能知。
The appearance of appearances as non-appearance can't be seen. It can only be known through wisdom.

当我们不以自我立场看事物时，
现前情境便是无相。
Once a person sees the world without standing on his own point, what he sees is non-appearance.

如果听闻此法能生出信心，
这个人就能发大乘超三界。
Whoever hears and believes this teaching embarks on the Great Vehicle and leaves the three realms.

什么是三界？
What are the three realms?

贪、嗔、痴，
就是三界。
The three realms are greed, anger and delusion.

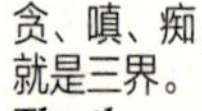

什么是超三界？
What is to leave the three realms?

化贪、嗔、痴为戒、定、慧，
就叫超三界。
To leave the three realms means to go from greed, anger and delusion to morality, meditation and wisdom.

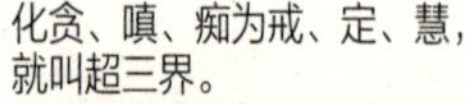

5 是知有相，是无相之相。不可以眼见，唯可以智知。

6 若闻此法者，生一念信心，此人以发大乘超三界。

7 三界者：贪、嗔、痴是。返贪、嗔、痴为戒、定、慧，即名超三界。

有心才有
贪、嗔、痴
Greed, anger and delusion are generated from your mind
贪、嗔、痴从哪来?
Where are greed, anger and delusion from?
贪、嗔、痴
来自众生心,
Greed, anger and delusion are generated from living creatures' mind.
无我，便没有贪、嗔、痴。
Getting released from the idea of self, one is free from greed, anger and delusion.
如何开悟成佛?
How to attain enlightenment and Buddhahood?
内观自心,
察觉三毒的来处，就是佛性。
Anyone capable of reflection is bound to see that the nature of greed, anger and delusion is the Buddha-nature.
除此之外
再也没有别的佛性。
Beyond greed, anger and delusion there is no other buddha-natures.

8 然贪、嗔、痴亦无实性，但据众生而言矣。

9 若能返照，了了见贪、嗔、痴性即是佛性，贪、嗔、痴外更无别有佛性。

佛经

经文说：
“开悟的关键，是自心常处于三毒，
能令自心不生三毒，而成为世尊。”
The sutras say,
“Buddhas have only become buddhas while living with the three poisons and nourishing themselves on the pure Dharma.”

三毒就是：贪、嗔、痴。
The three poisons are referred to greed, anger and delusion.

什么是佛乘？
What is Buddha-vehicle?

大乘是最上乘，
是一切大乘菩萨所行之处，
所以大乘无所不乘，也无所乘。
The Great Vehicle is the greatest of all Buddha-vehicles. It's the conveyance of bodhisattvas who use everything without using anything

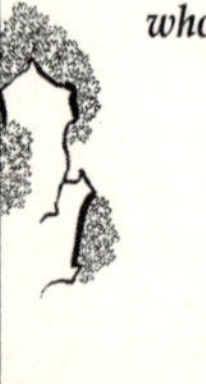

佛经

终日乘，又未曾乘，
这就是佛乘。
因此佛经说：
“无乘，就是佛乘。”
And who travel all day without traveling.
Such is Buddha-vehicle.
The sutras say,
“No vehicle is the Buddha-vehicle.”

10　经云：“诸佛从本来，常处于三毒，长养于白法，而成于世尊。”

11　三毒者：贪、嗔、痴也。

12　言大乘最上乘者，皆是菩萨所行之处，无所不乘，亦无所乘，终日乘未尝乘，此为佛乘。经云：“无乘为佛乘也。”

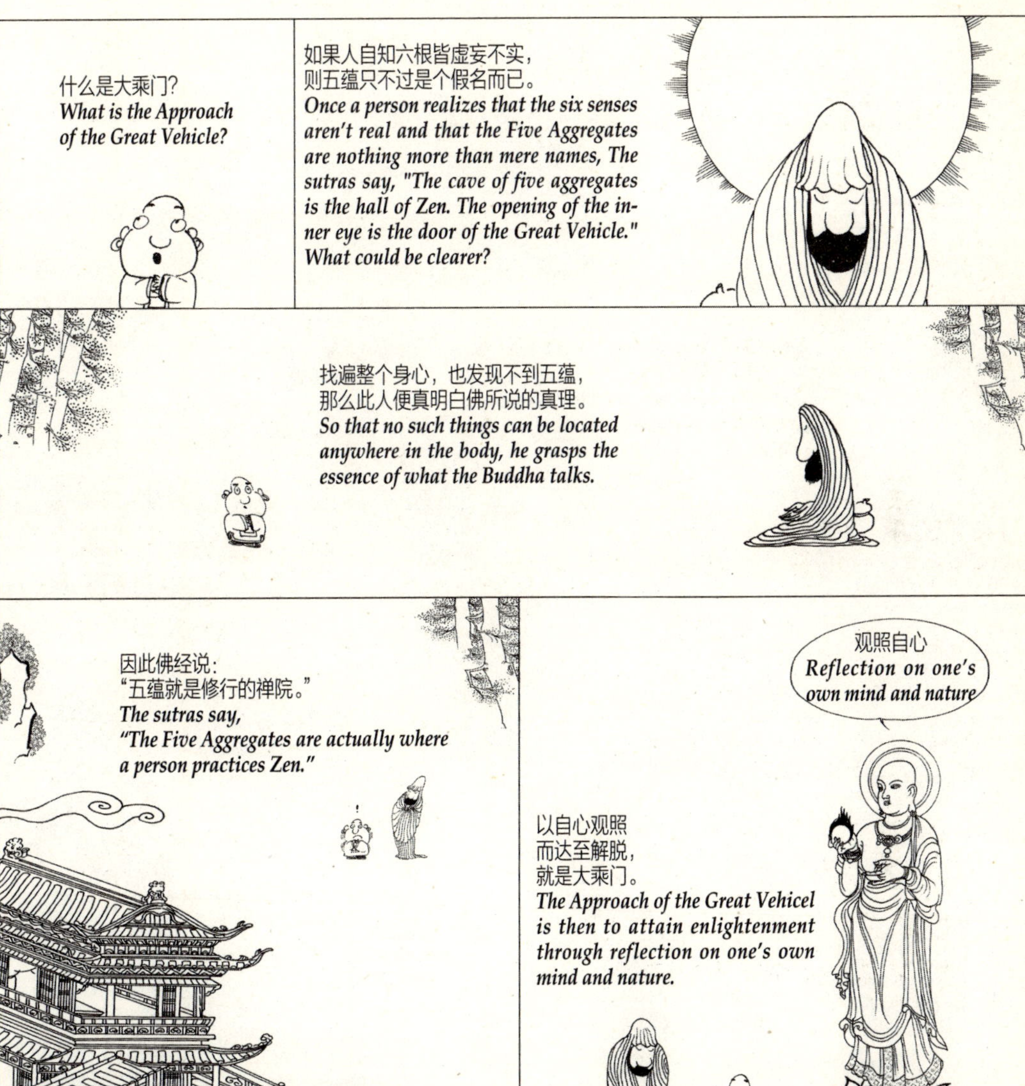
什么是大乘门?
What is the Approach of the Great Vehicle?
如果人自知六根皆虚妄不实，则五蕴只不过是个假名而已。
Once a person realizes that the six senses aren't real and that the Five Aggregates are nothing more than mere names, The sutras say, "The cave of five aggregates is the hall of Zen. The opening of the inner eye is the door of the Great Vehicle." What could be clearer?
找遍整个身心，也发现不到五蕴，那么此人便真明白佛所说的真理。
So that no such things can be located anywhere in the body, he grasps the essence of what the Buddha talks.
因此佛经说：“五蕴就是修行的禅院。”
The sutras say, "The Five Aggregates are actually where a person practices Zen."
观照自心
Reflection on one's own mind and nature
以自心观照而达至解脱，就是大乘门。
The Approach of the Great Vehicel is then to attain enlightenment through reflection on one's own mind and nature.

13 若人知六根不实，五蕴假名，遍体求之，必无定处，当知此人解佛语。

14 经云：“五蕴窟宅名禅院。”内照开解即大乘门。

什么是禅定?
What is Zen?
内心不忆一切法,
就是禅定。
Thinking about no dharmas is Zen.
如能了解这句话,
那么行住坐卧都是禅定。
Once you know this, walking, standing, sitting or lying down, everything you do is Zen.
知道心即是空,
名为见佛。
know that the mind is empty is to see the Buddha.
什么是大坐禅?
What is the Great Meditation?
觉者无心
The enlightened have no mind
不见于心,
称之为见佛。
To see no mind is to see the Buddha.
无心即是见佛
To see no mind is to see the Buddha.
十方诸佛
视心为无心。
Buddhas of the ten directions see mind as no mind.

15 可不明哉。不忆一切法，乃名为禅定。

16 若了此言者，行住坐卧皆禅定。知心是空，名为见佛。

17 何以故？十方诸佛皆以无心，不见于心，名为见佛。

连身都舍弃了，
称之为大布施。
To give up your body without regret is the Great Charity.
离一切动，
离一切定，
就是大坐禅。
To transcend motion and stillness is the Great Meditation.
怎么说?
What does that mean?
凡夫无时无刻求动，
小乘修行者无时无刻求静，
The ordinary keep moving and Hinayana practitioners stay still.
不求动也不求静的坐禅，
就是大坐禅。
But the Great Meditation pursues neither moving nor stillness.

18 舍身不吝，名大布施。离诸动定，名大坐禅。

19 何以故？凡夫一向动，小乘一向定，谓出过凡夫小乘之坐禅，名大坐禅。

能这样体会的人，
面对一切情境不求自解，
一切诸病不治便能自愈，
这就是大禅定力。
Those who reach such an understanding free themselves from all appearances without effort and cure all illnesses without treatment. Such is the power of Great Zen.
凡是以心求法者为迷，
不以心求法者即是悟。
It's a wrong way to pursue the dharma by using the mind. The enlightened follow the dharma without delusions from the mind.
如何才算解脱？
What is liberation?
不执着佛经文字，
即是解脱。
Freeing oneself from texts is liberation.
什么是护法？
How to guard the Buddharma?
六尘不染，
名为护法。
Remaining unblemished by the dust of sensation is guarding the Buddharma.
什么叫作出家？
How to give up one's home?

20　若作此会者，一切诸相不求自解，一切诸病不治自瘥，此皆大禅定力。凡将心求法者为迷，不将心求法者为悟。

21　不着文字名解脱。

22　不染六尘名护法。

23　出离生死名出家。

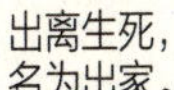

出离生死，
名为出家。
Transcending birth and death
is giving up one's home.

如何才能得道？
How to reach the Way?

不受后有，
才能得道。
Not suffering another existence
is reaching the Way.

什么是涅槃？
What is nirvana?

不生妄想，
名为涅槃。
Living without delusions
is nirvana.

什么是大智慧？
What is the Great Wisdom?

不处无明，
名为大智慧。
Living without ignorance is
the Great Wisdom.

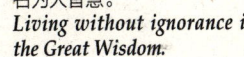

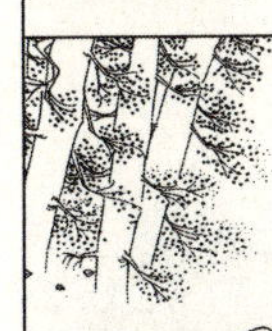

什么是般涅槃？
What is parinirvana?

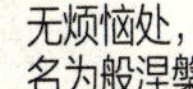

无烦恼处，
名为般涅槃。
Nirvana without affliction is
parinirvana.

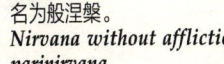

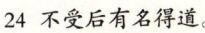

24 不受后有名得道。

25 不生妄想名涅槃。

26 不处无明为大智慧。

27 无烦恼处名般涅槃。

什么是彼岸?
What is the Other Shore?
无心相之处,
称为彼岸。
The place of non-appearance is the Other Shore.
彼岸
此岸
什么是此岸?
What is This Shore?
众生执迷时,
有此岸与彼岸的分别,
This Shore only exists in people's delusion.
开悟之后,
就没有此岸彼岸分别。
There's no distinction between This Shore and the Other Shore in enlightenment.
觉悟者的心
不在此岸,也不在彼岸,
因此能跳脱此岸、彼岸。
The minds of the enlightened dwell on neither This Shore nor the Other Shore. The enlightened thus are able to get released from the boundaries of both shores.
为什么?
Why?
凡夫一直身在此岸。
The ordinary are confined on This Shore.

28 无心相处名为彼岸。

29 迷时有此岸,若悟时无此岸。

30 何以故?为凡夫一向住此。若觉最上乘者,心不住此,亦不住彼,故能离于此彼岸也。

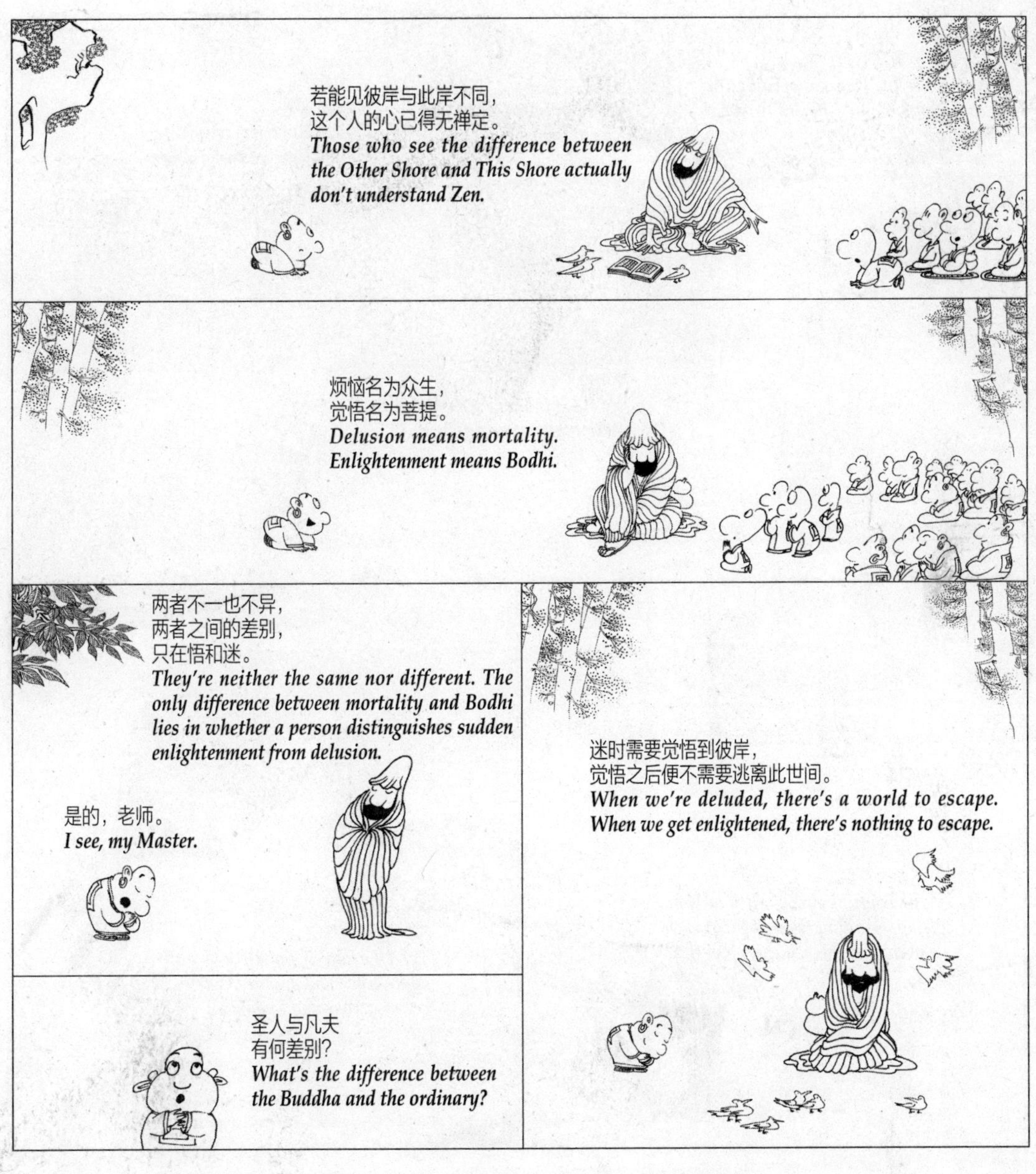
若能见彼岸与此岸不同，
这个人的心已得无禅定。
Those who see the difference between the Other Shore and This Shore actually don't understand Zen.
烦恼名为众生，
觉悟名为菩提。
Delusion means mortality. Enlightenment means Bodhi.
两者不一也不异，
两者之间的差别，
只在悟和迷。
They're neither the same nor different. The only difference between mortality and Bodhi lies in whether a person distinguishes sudden enlightenment from delusion.
是的，老师。
I see, my Master.
圣人与凡夫
有何差别？
What's the difference between the Buddha and the ordinary?
迷时需要觉悟到彼岸，
觉悟之后便不需要逃离此世间。
When we're deluded, there's a world to escape. When we get enlightened, there's nothing to escape.

31 若见彼岸异于此岸，此人之心，已得无禅定。烦恼名众生，悟解名菩提，亦不一不异，只隔具迷悟耳。

32 迷时有世间可出，悟时无世间可出。

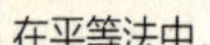

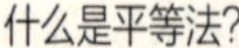
在平等法中，
凡夫与圣人没有区别。
In the light of the Dharma of Equality, the ordinary look no different from the enlightened.
什么是平等法?
What does the Dharma of Equality mean?

没有差别，
即是平等。
Equality refers to no discrimination between things.

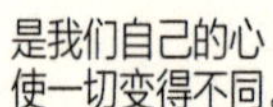
是我们自己的心
使一切变得不同。
It's the mind and standpoint that make things seem different.

平等法
佛经说:
The sutras say,
“平等法者，
凡夫不能入门，
圣人达不到。”
“The Dharma of Equality is something the ordinary can't comprehend and the enlightened can't practice.”

唯有大菩萨和诸佛如来，
才能达到平等法。
The Dharma of Equality is only approached and practiced by great bodhisattvas and Buddhas.

33 平等法中，不见凡夫异于圣人。

34 无有差别即是平等。

35 经云:“平等法者，凡夫不能入，圣人不能行。”

36 平等法者，唯有大菩萨与诸佛如来行也。

若见生异于死
动异于静，
皆名不平等。
Inequality sheds its shadow over those who draw lines between life and death or between motion and stillness.
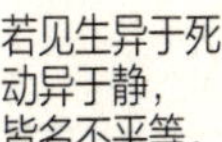

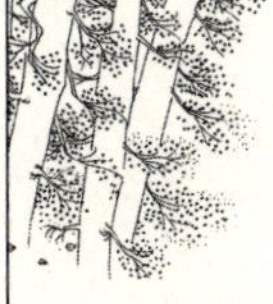

视烦恼与涅槃相同，
是名平等没有不同。
Those who see no discrimination between things find no difference between sufferings and nirvana.

为什么？
Why?

因为烦恼、涅槃
都来自空，
因此没有不同。
Because the nature of both sufferings and nirvana is emptiness. Thus, there's no difference between them from the standpoint of emptiness.

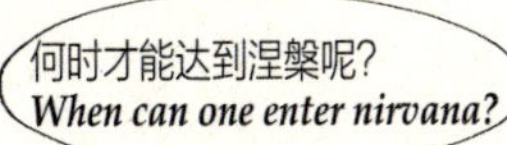
何时才能达到涅槃呢？
When can one enter nirvana?
小乘修行者妄想了断烦恼，
一心想进入涅槃，反被涅槃纠缠。
Hinayana practitioners end up with being trapped by nirvana, as they hold a vain hope of putting an end to sufferings and of entering nirvana.

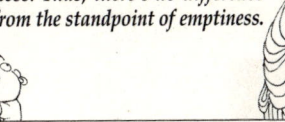

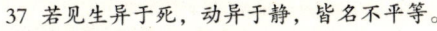

37 若见生异于死，动异于静，皆名不平等。

38 不见烦恼异于涅槃，是名平等。

39 何以故？烦恼与涅槃，同一性空故。

40 是以小乘人妄断烦恼，妄入涅槃为涅槃所滞。

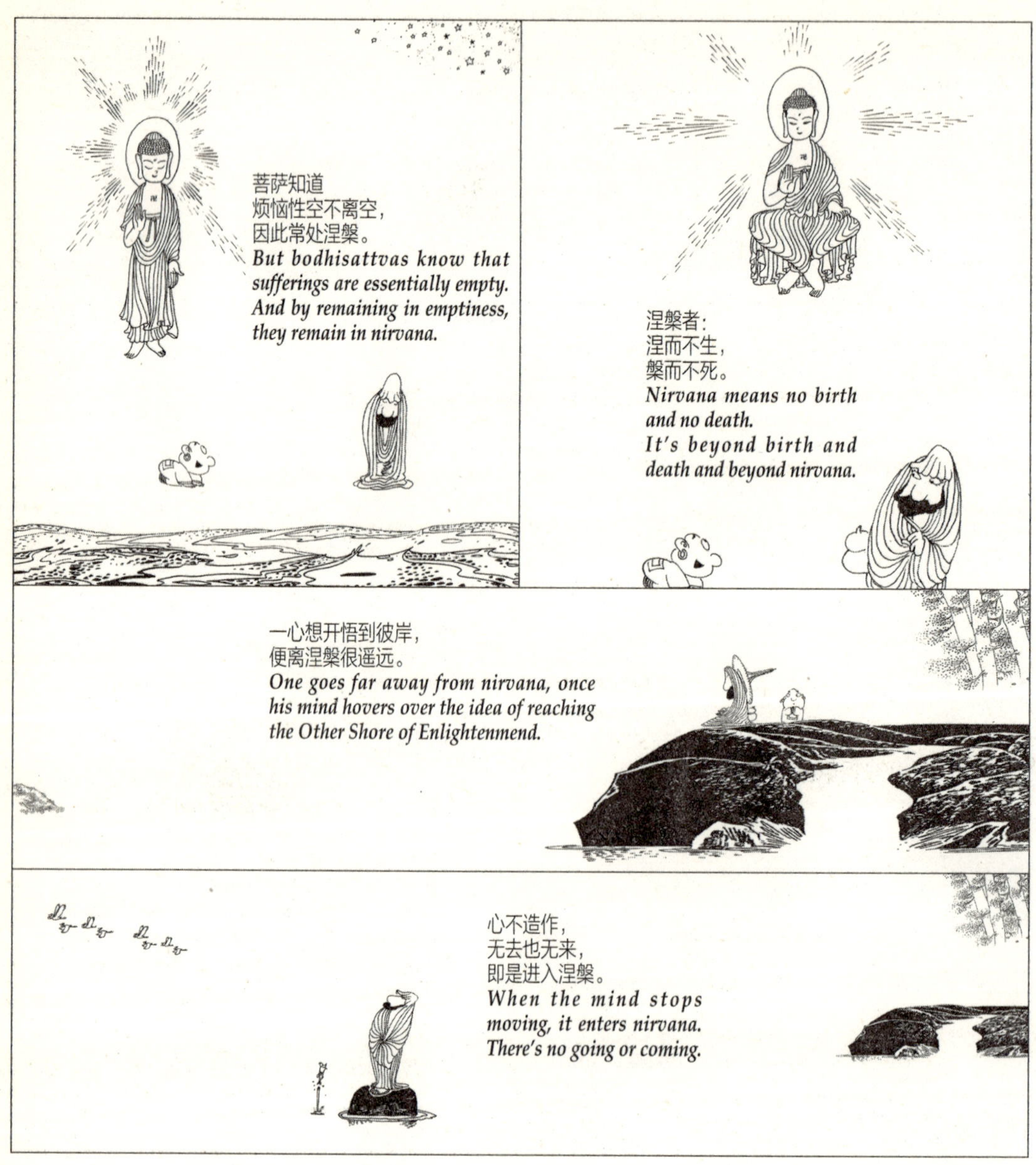
菩萨知道
烦恼性空不离空，
因此常处涅槃。
But bodhisattvas know that sufferings are essentially empty. And by remaining in emptiness, they remain in nirvana.
涅槃者：
涅而不生，
槃而不死。
Nirvana means no birth and no death.
It's beyond birth and death and beyond nirvana.
一心想开悟到彼岸，
便离涅槃很遥远。
One goes far away from nirvana, once his mind hovers over the idea of reaching the Other Shore of Enlightenmend.
心不造作，
无去也无来，
即是进入涅槃。
When the mind stops moving, it enters nirvana.
There's no going or coming.

41 菩萨知烦恼性空，即不离空，故常在涅槃。

42 涅槃者：涅而不生，槃而不死，出离生死，出般涅槃。心无去来，即入涅槃。

什么是涅槃?
What is nirvana?
涅槃就是
心空无想。
Nirvana is an empty mind.
如何达到涅槃?
How to reach nirvana?
开悟者能得涅槃,
在于无妄想处。
The enlightened reach nirvana by freeing themselves from delusions.
菩萨修行道场,
在于无烦恼处。
Bodhisattvas find their bodhimandas at the places free of afflictions.
心无念无想之处,
没有贪、嗔、痴。
A place of non-perception is one without greed, anger or delusion.
贪
嗔
痴

43 是知涅槃即是空心。

44 诸佛入涅槃者,为在无妄想处。菩萨入道场者,即是无烦恼处。空闲处者,即是无贪、嗔、痴也。

贪为欲界，
嗔为色界，
痴为无色界。
Greed is the Desire Realm, anger the Form Realm and delusion the Formless Realm.
一念心生即入三界；
一念心灭即出三界。
You fall into the three realms, once you're caught up in a perception. You leave the three realms, once you give up perceptions.
三界的生灭，
万法的有无，
都来自于心。
Be it the beginning or end of the three realms, or the existence or nonexistence of anything, it depends on the mind.
凡是说一法，便有如
破瓦石竹木等无情之物。
This applies to everything, even to such inanimate objects as rubbles, rocks, bamboos and trees.

45 贪为欲界、嗔为色界、痴为无色界，若一念心生，即入三界；一念心灭，即出三界。是知三界生灭，万法有无，皆由一心。

46 凡言一法者：似破瓦石竹木无情之物。

如果知道心只是个假名，
并无实体存在，那么便
知道自己的心也如此，
Whoever that knows that the mind is a mere name and devoid of anything knows that it is also true for his mind.
心既非有，
心也非无。
The mind is neither in existance nor in non-existance.
什么是有?
What is being in existence?
凡夫无时无刻生心，
就是有。
The ordinary are caught up in perceptions, claiming it is in existence.
什么是无?
What is being in non-existence?
小乘修行者无时无刻
除灭心念，就是无。
Hinayana practitioners keep negating the mind, claiming it is in non-existance.

47 若知心是假名，无有实体，即知自家之心亦是非有，亦是非无。

48 何以故？凡夫一向生心，名为有。

49 小乘一向灭心，名为无；菩萨与佛未曾生心，未曾灭心，名为非有非无心；非有非无心，此名为中道。

什么是
非有心
非无心？
What is being neither
in existence nor in
non-existance?
就是非有心
也非无心。
This is being neither in
existence nor in non-existance.
菩萨与佛
不曾生心，
也不灭心。
But bodhisattvas and
Buddhas are neither caught
up in nor negate the mind.
什么是中道？
What is the Middle Way?
非有心
非无心，
就是中道。
Being neither in existence
nor in non-existance is
called the Middle Way.
什么是迷？
What is delusion?
持执着心学法，
就是心法俱迷。
If you use your mind to
pursue the Buddharma, you
won't understand either your
mind or the dharma.

50 菩萨与佛未曾生心，未曾灭心，名为非有非无心；

51 非有非无心，此名为中道。

52 是知持心学法，则心法俱迷；不持心学法，则心法俱悟。

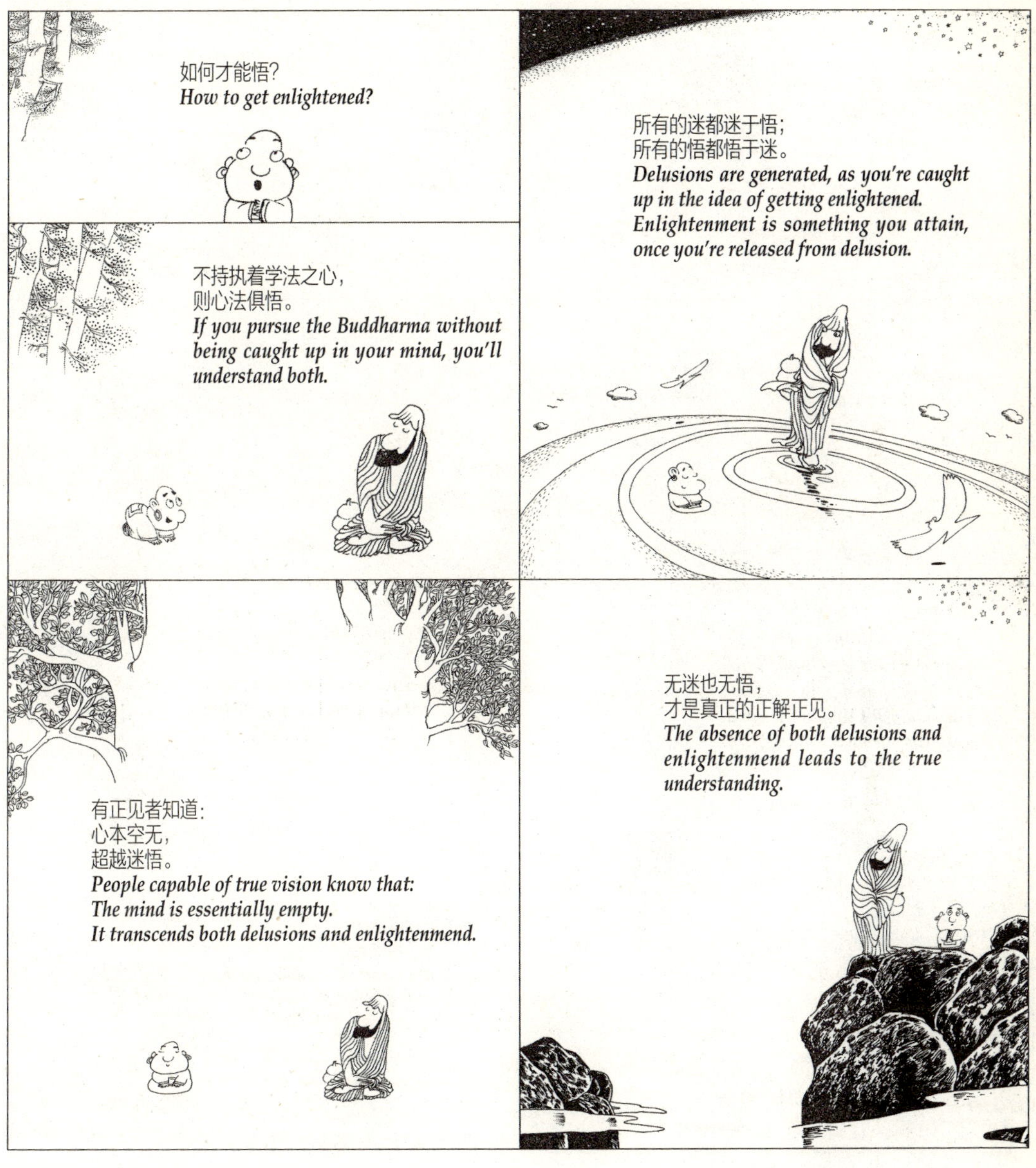
如何才能悟?
How to get enlightened?
不持执着学法之心,
则心法俱悟。
If you pursue the Buddharma without being caught up in your mind, you'll understand both.
所有的迷都迷于悟;
所有的悟都悟于迷。
Delusions are generated, as you're caught up in the idea of getting enlightened.
Enlightenment is something you attain, once you're released from delusion.
有正见者知道:
心本空无,
超越迷悟。
People capable of true vision know that:
The mind is essentially empty.
It transcends both delusions and enlightenmend.
无迷也无悟,
才是真正的正解正见。
The absence of both delusions and enlightenmend leads to the true understanding.

53 不持心学法，则心法俱悟。

54 凡迷者：迷于悟，悟者：悟于迷。

55 正见之人，知心空无，即超迷悟。无有迷悟，始名正解、正见。

什么是色？
What is the form?
眼前情境，
即是色。
What you see is the form.
什么是心？
What is the mind?
现在问我的，
即是心。
What is placing questions to me is the mind.
面对色时，
心应该如何？
What does the mind do in the face of the form?
色不自色，由心故色；
心不自心，由色故心。
The form isn't simply the form, as it is generated from the mind. The mind isn't simply the mind, as it depends on the form.
怎么说呢？
What does that mean?
外在情境只是纯然情境，
原无净垢分别。
Scenes are simply scenes, without being pure or dirty.
是由于我们的内心，
才产生情境的善恶。
It is the mind that labels scenes as being good or bad.

56 色不自色，由心故色；心不自心，由色故心。

内心受外在情境影响，
心不思维算计，
便无际遇顺逆差别，
也没有心境好坏。
The mind is then under the influence of scenes.
Scenes are neither good nor bad and there are no good or bad feelings, so long as the mind doesn't discriminate.
于是心色两相生相灭，
没有心，也没有色。
The mind and the form generate and negate each other. There's neither the mind nor the form.
!

57 是知心色两相俱生灭。

第二章　见无所见

Chapter II To See by Seeing Nothing

真见不生心
No biased opinions are generated from a true view.
如何才算真见？
What is a true view?
明白有则有于无，
无则无于有，是名真见。
Those who have a clear understanding of the interrelationship between existence and non-existance hold a true view.
真见者无所不见，
也无所见。
With such a true view, one sees everything, while nothing is seen.
看遍了宇宙十方，
也视之为未曾有见，
就是真见。
Such a view reaches throughout all the ten directions of the universe without seeing, as nothing is seen.
为什么？
Why?

58 有者有于无，无者无于有，是名真见。

59 夫真见者，无所不见，亦无所见，见满十方，未曾有见。

60 何以故？

开悟者使用
他的心像镜子一样，
完全反映当下现前。
The enlightened's mind is like a mirror, faithfully reflecting what he sees.
只是随着变化而变化，
而没有一个自己存在。
An enlightened person fully adapts to all changes, without being caught in the idea of self.
他能达到无所见、
见无见、见非见，
Such a person is thus able to see nothing, see the invisible and know what he sees is actually non-existance.
面对现前情境时不生心，
这种境界才称为真见。
A true view doesn't stir any biased opinions.
WISDOM

61 无所见故，见无见故，见非见故。

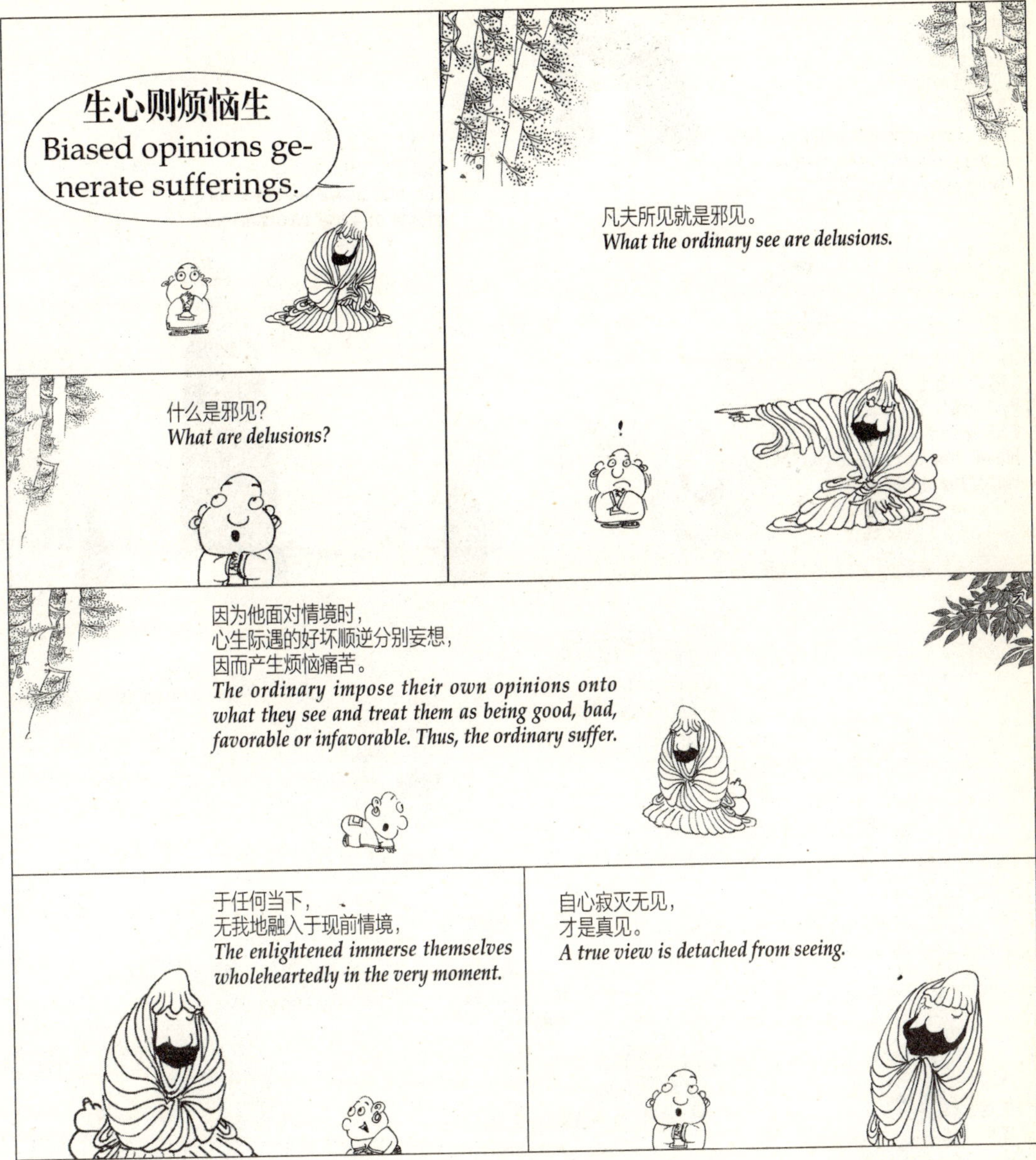
生心则烦恼生
Biased opinions generate sufferings.
凡夫所见就是邪见。
What the ordinary see are delusions.
什么是邪见?
What are delusions?
因为他面对情境时，
心生际遇的好坏顺逆分别妄想，
因而产生烦恼痛苦。
The ordinary impose their own opinions onto what they see and treat them as being good, bad, favorable or infavorable. Thus, the ordinary suffer.
于任何当下，
无我地融入于现前情境，
The enlightened immerse themselves wholeheartedly in the very moment.
自心寂灭无见，
才是真见。
A true view is detached from seeing.

62 凡夫所见，皆名妄想。若寂灭无见，始名真见。

心境相对情境，
内心计算外缘，
于是便产生了
际遇的好坏。
The mind responses to the outside world and treats conditions as being good or bad.
外境、内心俱净，
能够这样才叫作真见。
When the world and the mind are both pure, a true view emerges.
如果内不起心，
则外无情境顺逆净垢，
The mind untainted with biased opinions sees no good or bad of the outside world.
什么是正见？
What is a right view?
纯洁没有自我的立场
所生的见，才是正见。
A view untainted with the idea of self is a right view.
如何才能得道？
How to reach the Way?
面对当下眼前情境时
不生心，称之为得道。
Someone who's reached the Way sees the world as it is, without any biased opinions.

63 心境相对，见生于中，若内不起心，则外不生境，境心俱净，乃名为真见。

64 作此解时，乃名正见。不见一切法，乃名得道。

见与不见
To see or not to see
什么叫作解法?
What is an understanding?
无我地融入于当下，不评断算计一切际遇的好坏，叫作解法。
An understanding means to immerse oneself wholeheartedly in the very moment he is in, without making any personal judgement of it.
为什么?
Why?
见与不见都没有成见，
解与不解不生自我见解。
To see or not to see, neither is a preoccupied view. To understand or not to understand, neither is a personally-biased understanding.
无成见之见才是真见;
没有成解之解才是大解。
A true view is never biased. A true understanding is never a ready-made.
正见不只是直观所见，
还包括没有看到的那一面。
A true view includes both the seen and the unseen.

65 不解一切法，乃名解法。

66 何以故？见与不见，俱不见故；解与不解，俱不解故。无见之见，乃名真见；无解之解，乃名大解。夫正见者：非直见于见，亦乃见于不见。

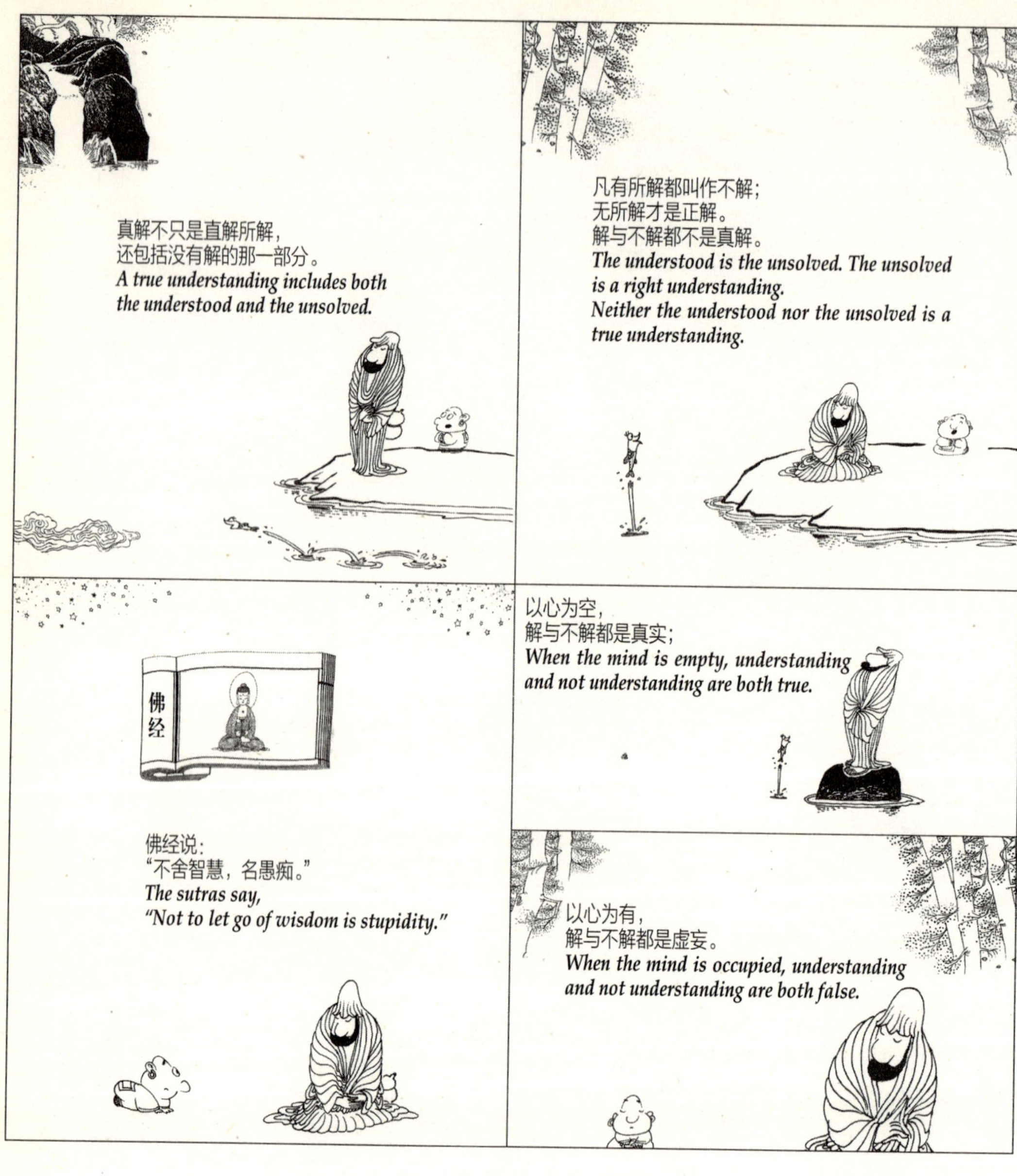
真解不只是直解所解，
还包括没有解的那一部分。
A true understanding includes both the understood and the unsolved.
凡有所解都叫作不解；
无所解才是正解。
解与不解都不是真解。
The understood is the unsolved. The unsolved is a right understanding.
Neither the understood nor the unsolved is a true understanding.
佛经
佛经说：
“不舍智慧，名愚痴。”
The sutras say,
“Not to let go of wisdom is stupidity.”
以心为空，
解与不解都是真实；
When the mind is empty, understanding and not understanding are both true.
以心为有，
解与不解都是虚妄。
When the mind is occupied, understanding and not understanding are both false.

67 真解者：非直解于解，亦乃解于无解。凡有所解，皆名不解；无所解者，始名正解；解与不解，俱非解也。

68 经云：“不舍智慧，名愚痴。”

69 以心为空，解与不解俱是真；以心为有，解与不解俱是妄。

圣人不逐法
The enlightened never pursue the dharma on purpose.
悟时法逐人；
迷时人逐法。
The dharma depends on the enlightened.
The deluded depend on the dharam.
如果法随着人走，
那么没有法也成为法；
The dharma grows out of nothing, when it depends on the enlightened.
如果人追着法走，
那么正法也成为非法。
But the dharma becomes corrupted and false, once the deluded depend on it.
法
Dharma
如果我们的心认为世界怎么样，
世界就呈现出我们所想的样子。
The world appears as it is seen by your mind.

70 若解时法逐人，若不解时人逐法。若法逐于人，则非法成法；若人逐于法，则法成非法。

法
Dharma
如果人追逐法，
则真法也成为妄法。
The true dharma becomes corrupted and false, once the deluded depend on it.
如果法逐于人，
则无法也成为真法。
The true dharma grows out of nothing, when it depends on the enlightened.
因此圣人不以心求法，
也不以法求心，
Thus, the enlightened never pursue the dharma by using the mind or try to see the mind by applying the dharma.
不以心求心，
也不以法求法。
The enlightened never try to see the mind by using the mind or pursue the dharma by applying the dharma.

71 若人逐于法，则法皆妄；若法逐于人，则法皆真。

72 是以圣人亦不将心求法，亦不将法求心，亦不将心求心，亦不将法求法。

法由何处生？
Where is the dharma generated?
法生于心吗？
Is the dharma generated from the mind?
不！
心不生法，
法也不生心。
No. The dharma isn't generated from the mind. Nor the mind from the dharma.
心法寂然不动，
常在定境中。
Both the mind and the dharma remain skill, and the enlightened are always in samadhi.
际遇不好之时，
应该如何？
What should we do in adversity?
面对现前情境时，
不要以自我的立场生心，
便无际遇好坏。
Impose no personal judgement onto the situation and you'll be free from feeling good or bad of the situation.
众生心生则佛法灭；
众生心灭则佛法生。
When the mind takes control, the Buddharma disappears. When the mind recedes, the Buddharma appears.
生心就不能见道吗？
Can't we reach the Way when the mind takes control?

73 所以心不生法，法不生心，心法两寂，故常为在定。

74 众生心生，则佛法灭；众生心灭，则佛法生。

心念生则真法灭，
心念灭则真法生。
When the mind takes control, the true dharma disappears. When the mind recedes, the true dharma appears.
能看清所有情境，
都只是变化的一刹那，各不相属，
便是得道人。
Whoever knows that nothing depends on anything else has found the Way.
明白心不住于情境，
便是道上之人。
And whoever knows that the mind depends on nothing attains enlightenment.
迷时所作造罪业，
开悟之后所行不生罪业。
Karma only plagues the deluded with karma.
The enlightened are released from karma.

75 心生则真法灭，心灭则真法生。

76 已知一切法，各各不相属，是名得道人。知心不属一切法，此人常在道场。迷时有罪，解时无罪。

罪无处所
There's no room for karma.
为何不生罪业？
How to get released from karma?
无我便无造罪者，
罪无从生起。
心灭罪亡两俱空。
No karma is created, as there's no karma-creator when there's no idea of self. There is thus no cradle for karma. Karma disappears when the mind recedes.
迷时无心造罪也造出罪业，
开悟之后无心则无罪。
The karma unintentionally created by the deluded is karma after all. The enlightened's mind is empty and there's no room for karma.
为何无罪？
How's that?
佛经
佛经说：
"诸法无性，
真用莫疑，
疑即成罪。"
The sutras say,
"Nothing has a nature of its own. Just act. Don't doubt it. Caught by doubt, you fall into karma."
无我无心，
则没有生罪之处。
Those who are not caught in the idea of self have the empty mind, so that there's no room for karma.

77 何以故？罪性空故。若迷时无罪见罪，若解时即罪非罪。

78 何以故？罪无处所故。经云："诸法无性，真用莫疑，疑即成罪。"

为什么？
Why?
执迷之时，六识五蕴
都是痛苦烦恼之源。
When you're deluded, the Six Senses and
Five Aggregates lead to suffering.
罪因疑惑而生，
如果觉悟无惑，
从前的罪业即被消灭。
Karma is generated from doubts. The enlightened
are released from the past karma.
开悟之后，六识五蕴
皆为涅槃的入口处。
When you're enlightened, the Six Senses and
Five Aggregates lead to nirvana.
修道者只向一心，
不往外求道。
Anyone who seeks the Way doesn't
look beyond the mind.

79 何以故？罪因疑惑而生。若作此解者，前世罪业即为消灭。

80 迷时六识五阴皆是烦恼生死法，悟时六识五阴皆是涅槃无生死法。修道人不外求道。

为什么?
Why?
因为知心,
即是道!
He knows that the mind is the Way.
得心之时，无心可得，
得道之时，无道可得。
But when he finds the mind, he finds nothing. And when he finds the Way, he finds nothing.
如果有人说以心求道，
即是邪见。
If you think you can use the mind to find the Way, you're wrong.
为何不能
以心求道?
Why can't we do that?
迷时，有佛也有法;
悟时，无佛也无法。
When you're deluded, there's no dharma, even though you may see the Buddha. When you're enlightened, there's neither the Buddha nor the dharma.

81 何以故？知心是道。

82 若得心时，无心可得；若得道时，无道可得。

83 若言将心求道得者，皆名邪见。

84 迷时有佛有法，悟无佛无法。

悟即是佛
Enlightenmet is Buddhahood.
因为觉悟
就是佛法。
This is because enlightenment is the Buddharma.
为什么无佛也无法?
Why's there neither the Buddha nor the dharma?
修道者身灭则道成，
如同树脱掉树皮。
If you're looking for the Way, the Way won't appear until your body disappears. It's like stripping bark from a tree.
生此业报之身，
一念一念之间
变化无常，
没有不变的法。
This karmic body undergoes constant change. It has no fixed dharma.
禅

85 何以故？悟即是佛法。夫修道者：身灭道成。亦如甲折树。生此业报身，念念无常，无一定法。

随心念修行便是，
不必刻意舍离生死，
不贪爱生死；
Practice by following your mind. Don't hold hatred or love for life and death.
在念念中不妄想，
则能达至智慧彼岸，
得无生法忍。
Keep your mind free of delusion. And you'll reach the Other Shore of Enlightenmend and after death, you'll be blessed with the assurance of no rebirth.
何谓生死？
What are birth and death?
缘起名生，
识灭名死。
Causes rise and generate birth. Senses die and it is death.
外缘内识俱灭，
即是无生死。
External causes and internal senses die and there's neither birth nor death.

86 但随念修之；亦不得厌生死，亦不得爱生死；但念念之中，不得妄想；则生证有余涅槃，死入无生法忍。

眼见情境时，
心不染情境；
耳闻音声时，
心不染音声；
便能得解脱。
The mind is untainted with what you see or hear.
You'll attain liberation.
眼不执着情境，
眼就是禅入口；
耳不执着音声，
耳即是禅大门。
Eyes that aren't attached to the form are the gate of Zen.
Ears that aren't attached to the sound are the gate of Zen.
不执着眼前所见情境，
就能常处于解脱之中，
执着所见受所见系缚。
In short, those who perceive the existence and nature of phenomena and remain unattached are liberated. Those who perceive the external appearance of phenomena are at their mercy.
不被烦恼所系缚者，即名解脱，
除此之外再没有别的解脱了。
Not to be subject to afflictions is what's meant by liberation. There's no other liberation.

87 眼见色时，不染于色；耳闻声时，不染于声；皆解脱也。

88 眼不着色，眼为禅门；耳不着声，耳为禅门。

89 总而言，见色有见色性，不着常解脱；见色相者常系缚。不为烦恼所系缚者，即名解脱，更无别解脱。

色不生心，
心不生色。
When you know how to look at the form, it doesn't give rise to mind and the mind doesn't give rise to the form.
善观察色的修行者，
不从眼前情境生妄心。
The practitioners who know how to deal with the form are never plagued with delusions.
不令心自造苦乐境，
于是色心内外俱清净。
They allow no room for the mind to fabricate joy or suffering. In this way, they attain the inner peace.

90 善观色者，色不生心，心不生色，即色与心俱清净。

天堂与地狱
Heaven and hell
可以说有天堂地狱，
也可以说无天堂地狱。
You may say there're heaven and hell. And you may say there's neither heaven nor hell.
有天堂吗？
有地狱吗？
Is there heaven?
Is there hell?
为何天堂地狱
可说有，也可说无？
How can we put it that way?
天堂地狱就在你的六尺之躯，
关键在于你的心。
Heaven or hell, it right dwells in your physical body and mind.
“心无妄想时，一心一天堂；
心有妄想时，一心一地狱。”
"Without delusions, the mind is heaven. With delusions, the mind is hell."

91 天堂地狱的有无。

92 无妄想时，一心是一佛国，有妄想时，一心一是地狱。

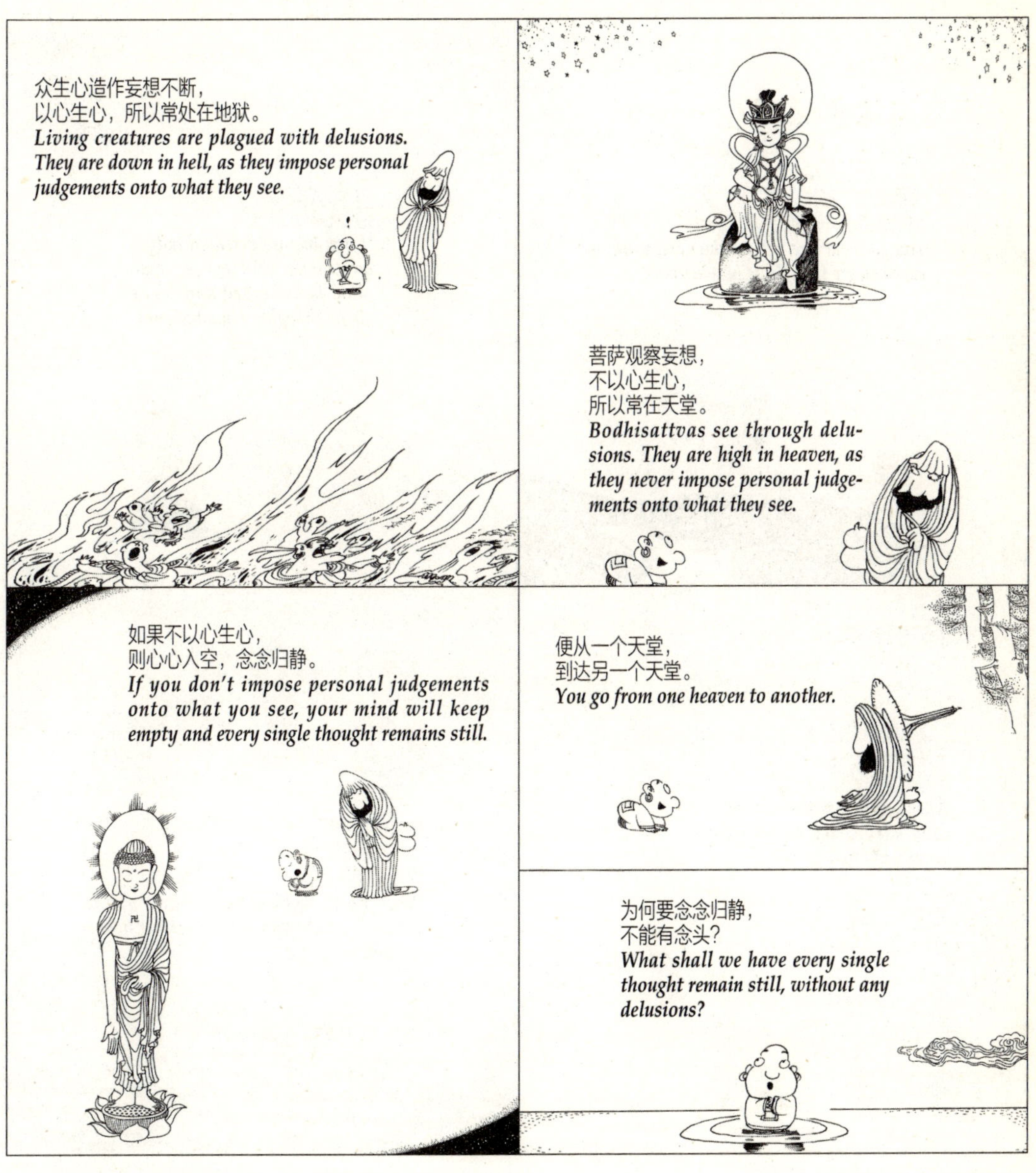
众生心造作妄想不断，
以心生心，所以常处在地狱。
Living creatures are plagued with delusions. They are down in hell, as they impose personal judgements onto what they see.
!
菩萨观察妄想，
不以心生心，
所以常在天堂。
Bodhisattvas see through delusions. They are high in heaven, as they never impose personal judgements onto what they see.
如果不以心生心，
则心心入空，念念归静。
If you don't impose personal judgements onto what you see, your mind will keep empty and every single thought remains still.
便从一个天堂，
到达另一个天堂。
You go from one heaven to another.
为何要念念归静，
不能有念头？
What shall we have every single thought remain still, without any delusions?

93 众生造作妄想，以心生心，故常在地狱。菩萨观察妄想，不以心生心，常在佛国。

94 若不以心生心，则心心入空，念念归静，从一佛国至一佛国。

如果以心生心，
则心心不入静地。
If you impose personal judgements onto what you see, your mind is disturbed and every single thought is in whirlpool.
念念归动，便从一个
地狱转到另一个地狱。
You go from one hell to the next, with every single thought is in whirlpool.
如果一念心不起，
便没有善恶二业，
也无天堂与地狱。
When no thought arises, there's neither good karma nor bad karma, neither heaven nor hell.
如果一念心兴起，
于是有善恶二业，
便有天堂与地狱；
When a thought arises, there're good karma and bad karma, heaven and hell.

95 若以心生心，则心心不静，念念归动，从一地狱历一地狱。

96 若一念心起，则有善恶二业，有天堂地狱。若一念心不起，即无善恶二业，亦无天堂地狱。

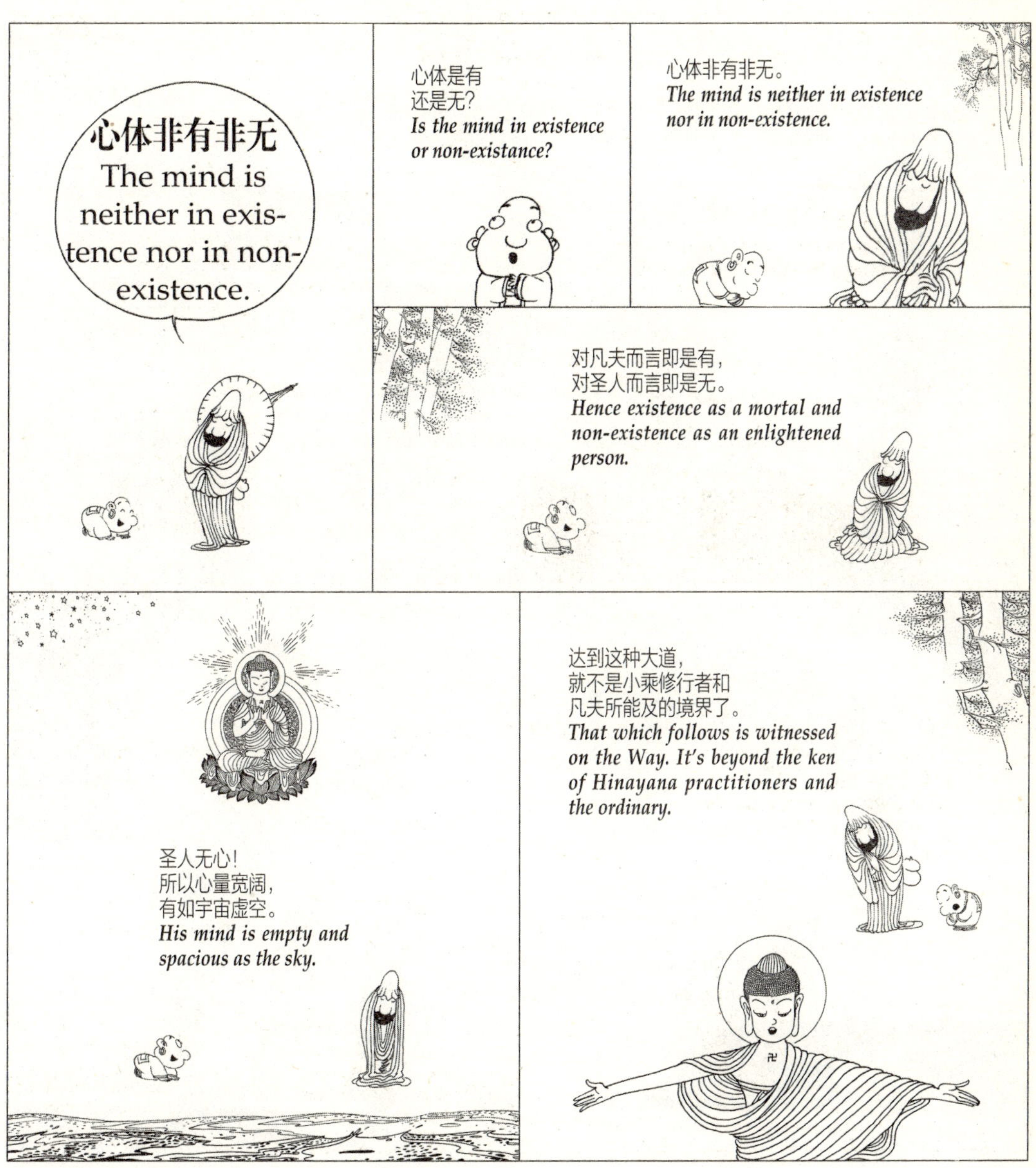
心体非有非无
The mind is neither in existence nor in non-existence.
心体是有
还是无？
Is the mind in existence or non-existance?
心体非有非无。
The mind is neither in existence nor in non-existence.
对凡夫而言即是有，
对圣人而言即是无。
Hence existence as a mortal and non-existence as an enlightened person.
圣人无心！
所以心量宽阔，
有如宇宙虚空。
His mind is empty and spacious as the sky.
达到这种大道，
就不是小乘修行者和
凡夫所能及的境界了。
That which follows is witnessed on the Way. It's beyond the ken of Hinayana practitioners and the ordinary.

97　为体非有非无，在凡即有，在圣即无。圣人无其心，故胸臆空洞，与天同量。此已下并是大道中证，非小乘及凡夫境界也。

心得涅槃时
会怎么样？
What will happen when
the mind reaches nirvana?

得涅槃，
即不见有涅槃。
When the mind reaches nirvana,
you don't see nirvana.

为何不见涅槃？
Why's that?

心就是涅槃。如果说心外
有另外的涅槃，就是邪见。
For the mind is itself nirvana. If you
see nirvana somewhere outside the
mind, you're deceiving yourself.

一切烦恼都是成佛种子，
通过烦恼才能得到智慧。
Every suffering is a seed of Buddhahood,
because suffering impels the ordinary to
seek wisdom.

可以说由烦恼生如来，
但不能说烦恼是如来。
But you can only say that suffering
gives rise to Buddhahood. You can't
say that suffering is Buddhahood.

98 心得涅槃时，即不见有涅槃。

99 何以故？心是涅槃。若心外更见涅槃，此名着邪见也。

100 一切烦恼都是成佛种子，通过烦恼才能得到智慧。

101 只可道烦恼生如来，不可得道烦恼是如来。

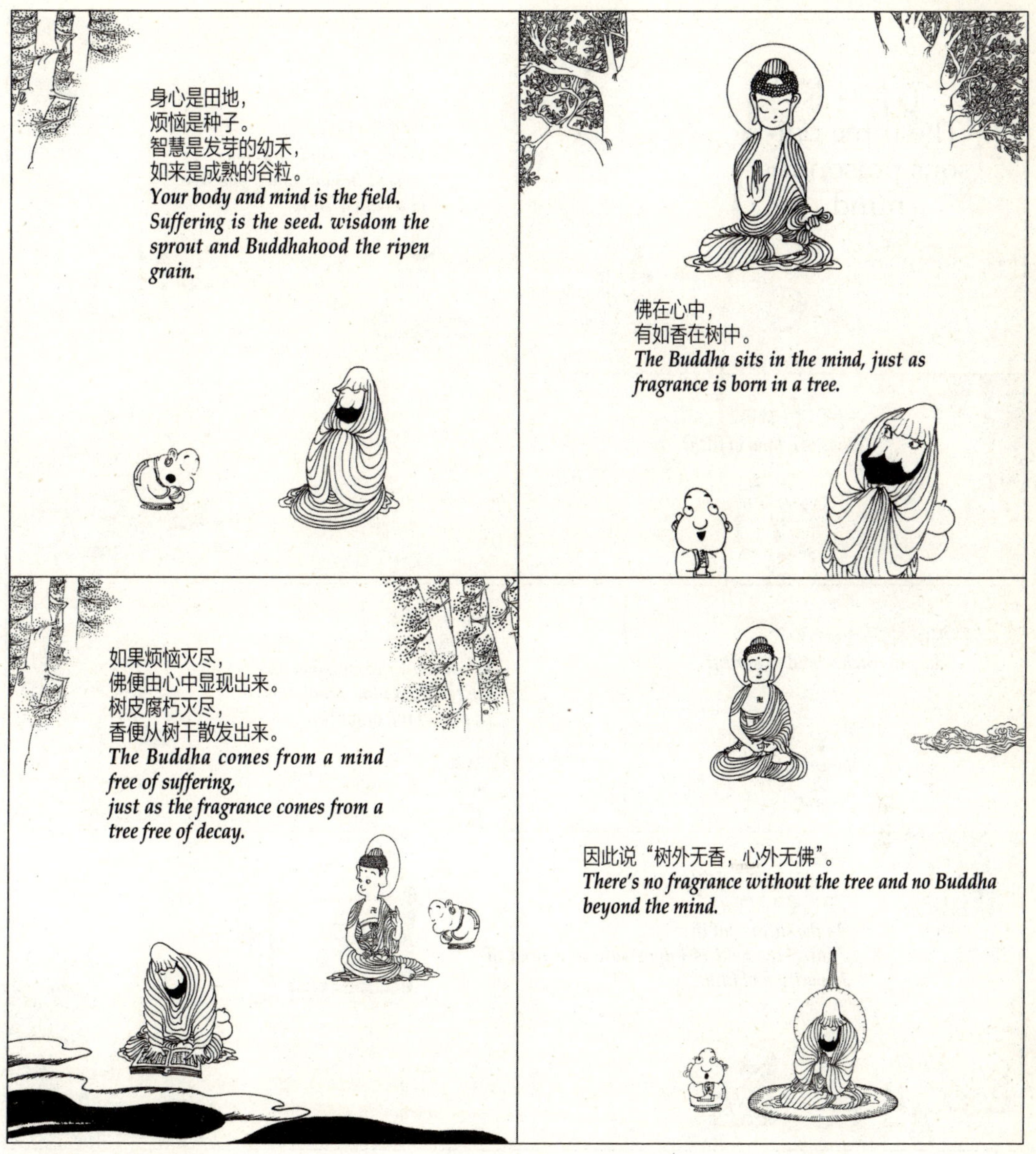
身心是田地，
烦恼是种子。
智慧是发芽的幼禾，
如来是成熟的谷粒。
Your body and mind is the field.
Suffering is the seed. wisdom the sprout and Buddhahood the ripen grain.
佛在心中，
有如香在树中。
The Buddha sits in the mind, just as fragrance is born in a tree.
如果烦恼灭尽，
佛便由心中显现出来。
树皮腐朽灭尽，
香便从树干散发出来。
The Buddha comes from a mind free of suffering,
just as the fragrance comes from a tree free of decay.
因此说“树外无香，心外无佛”。
There's no fragrance without the tree and no Buddha beyond the mind.

102 故身心为田畴，烦恼为种子，智慧为萌芽，如来喻于谷也。

103 佛在心中，如香在树中；烦恼若尽，佛从心出；朽腐若尽，香从树出。即知树外无香，心外无佛。

心有三毒
The three poisons poison the mind.
心中有三毒者，
是名国土秽恶。
When the three poisons are present in your mind, you live in a land of filth.
什么是国土秽恶？
What is a land of filth?
如何才能国土清净？
How to reach a land of purity?
心中无三毒者，
是名国土清净。
When the three poisons are absent from your mind, you live in a land of purity.
佛经说：
"充满污秽的不净之地，
开悟是不可能的。"
As the sutras put it,
"Enlightenment is impossible in a land of impurity and filth."
佛经

104 心中有三毒者，是名国土秽恶。

105 心中无三毒者，是名国土清净。

106 经云："若使国土不净，秽恶充满，诸佛世尊于中出者，无有此事。"

不净污秽
就是无明三毒；
Impurity and filth refer
to the three poisons.
开悟就是
清净觉悟的心。
Enlightenment brings purity
and tranquil to your mind.
!

107 不净秽恶者，即无明三毒是；诸佛世尊者，即清净觉悟心是。

第三章　言说与不说

Chapter III Saying and Not Saying

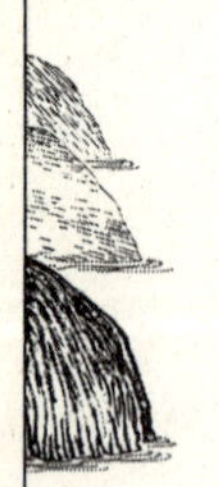

言与默
Words and silence
佛经所记载的言语文字，尽是佛法。
There's no language that isn't the dharma.
如果把言语当成无，
整天言说也是道；
To talk all day is the Way, once you see into words' nature of emptiness.
如果把言语当成有，
终日默然不语也非道。
To remain silent all day isn't the Way, if you don't see into words' nature of emptiness.
如何掌握言和默？
How to deal with words and silence?
时而以默然代替言说，
时而以言述说默。
Remain silent at some time and talk abou silence at other time.

因此如来说法，
有时说而不默，
有时默而不言。
Thus, the Buddha sometimes talks and sometimes remains silent when he gives a lecture on Buddharma.
能悟通言说默然交互应用，
就是深懂说法三昧。
Those who understand both words and silence are in samadhi.
如果明白时而言说，言便得解脱。
如果不明白时而默，默便受束缚。
If you speak when you know, your words are free. If you remain silent when you don't know, your silence is fettered.
因此言若离相，
言语便是解脱。
If words are not attached to appearances, they are free.
如果默若着相，
默而不语即是束缚。
If silence is attached to appearances, it's fettered.
!

108 是故如来言不乘默，默不乘言，言不离默；悟此言默者，皆在三昧。

109 若知时而言，言亦解脱；若不知时而默，默亦系缚。

110 是故言若离相，言亦名解脱；默若着相，默即是系缚。

佛经
佛经文字是用来解脱，
不要被文字所束缚。
Words are essentially free. They have nothing to do with attachment.
佛经
其实束缚来自于自己，
而不是佛经的文字。
And attachment has nothing to do with words. It's you who set fetters on yourself.

111 夫文字者：本性解脱。文字不能就系缚，系缚自本来未就文字。

道无贵贱
The Way is neither high nor low.
法有高低
之分吗?
Is the dharma high or low?
道无贵贱,
法无高低。
The Way is neither high nor low. So is the dharma.
若法有高低,
即是非法。
It is not the dharma, once it is set as being high or low.
若以非法为筏,
人乘非法之筏时,
A person may take a raft of non-dharma.
能分辨出非法,
那么非法也算是法。
The non-dharma becomes dharma, once the person on that raft of non-dharma tells non-dharma from dharma.

112 法无高下，若见高下非法也。

113 非法为筏，是法为人筏者。人乘其筏者即得渡于非法，则是法也。

男女有贵贱之分吗？
Is a man nobler than a woman?
如果依世俗说法，
人有男女贵贱之别；
According to common views, there're male and female and the rich and the poor.
如果以道的角度，
便无男女贵贱分别。
But according to the Way, there's no difference between male and female or between the rich and the poor.
因此天女悟道后，
还是保持女性形象。
That's why a goddess keeps her female body after she got enlightened.
车匿开悟得道后，
也不改自己的贱称。
And that's why Channa keeps his name after he got enlightened.

114 若世俗言，即有男女贵贱；以道言之，即无男女贵贱。

115 以是天女悟道，不变女形；车匿解真，宁移贱称乎。

天女在十二年中，
欲求女相而不可得。
也知道在十二年中，
求男相也不可得。
The goddess searched for twelve years for her womanhood without success.
Thus she knew that to search in these twelve years for the manhood would likewise be fruitless.

十二年者就是眼、耳、鼻、舌、身、意、色、声、香、味、触、法十二入。
The twelve years refer to the twelve entrances,namely eyes, ears, nose, tongue, body, mind, form, sound, smell, taste, tactile sensation and dharma.

眼
耳
鼻
舌

116 此盖非男女贵贱，皆由一相也。天女于十二年中，求女相了不可得，即知于十二年中，求男相亦不可得。十二年者，即十二入是也。

第四章　心佛不二
Chapter IV The Mind and the Buddha are the Same

不着心相
No disturbance from the mind

心与佛相同
或不相同?
Are the mind and the Buddha
the same or different?

离心无佛，
离佛无心。
Without the mind, there is no Buddha.
Without the Buddha, there is no mind.

心跟佛如同冰跟水的关系，
离开水无冰，离开冰无水。
Likewise, without water, there is no ice.
And without ice, there is no water.

佛
经

佛经说:
“不见相，
名为见佛。”
As the sutras put it,
“When you see no appearance,
you see the Buddha.”

心不着相，
离佛则无心。
佛从心生，但是心
不是从佛产生的。
Don't become attached to appearances of the mind.
Without the Buddha, there is not mind.
The mind gives birth to the Buddha. But the mind
doesn't come from the Buddha.

117 离心无佛，离佛无心。亦如离水无冰，亦如离冰无水。凡言离心者，非是远离于心，但使不着心相。

118 经云:“不见相，名为见佛。”

119 即是离心相也。离佛无心者；言佛从心出，心能生佛。然佛从心生，而心未尝生于佛。

如同鱼生于水，
而水不生于鱼。
要想观鱼，
未见鱼之前
先见到水。
Just as fish comes from water, but water doesn't come from fish. Whoever wants to see fish sees the water first.
要想观佛，
未见佛之前
先见到心。
And whoever wants to see a Buddha sees the mind first.
心
但应切记：
见到鱼之后，要忘记水的存在；
见到佛之后，要忘记心的存在。
But keep this in your mind:
Once you've seen the fish, forget about the water.
And once you've seen the Buddha, forget about the mind.
如果不忘于心，为心所惑；
如果不忘于水，被水所迷。
If you don't forget about the mind, you get confused at the mind, just as you get confused at the water, if you don't forget about it.

120 亦如鱼生于水，水不生于鱼。欲观于鱼，未见鱼，而先见水。欲观佛者，未见佛，而先见心。

121 即知已见鱼者，忘于水；已见佛者，忘于心。若不忘于心，尚为心所惑；若不忘于水，尚被水所迷。

第五章　众生与菩提

Chapter V　Mortality and Buddhahood

冰和水
Ice and water
众生与菩提之间，
如同冰和水的关系。
Mortality and Buddhahood
are like water and ice.
被三毒烈火所烧，就是众生；
被三解脱所清净，就是菩提。
To be afflicted by the three poisons is mortality. To be purified by the three releases is Buddhahood.
水被寒冬冻结，
就是冰。
Water freezes into ice in harsh winter.
冰被夏日消融，就是水。
Ice melts into water in scorching summer.
如果舍弃冰，就没有水；
如舍弃众生，则无菩提。
Without ice, there's no more water.
Without mortality, there's no more Buddhahood.

122 众生与菩提，亦如冰之与水；为三毒所烧，即名众生；为三解脱所净，即名菩提。

123 为三冬所冻，即名为冰；为三夏所消，即名为水。

124 若舍却冰，即无别水；若弃却众生，则无别菩提。

被世尘泯昧，
就是色心。
Anyone who is blinded with secular trifles is caught up in the mind forms and appearances.
见性开悟之后，就是佛。
Anyone who sees his mind attains enlightenment and Buddhahood.
所以心佛本质相同?
That is to say, the mind and the Buddha are the same in essence?
心的本体就是佛，
佛的本体就是心。
The mind is in essence the Buddha and the Buddha in essence the mind.
冰的本质就是水，
水的本质就是冰。
Ice is in essence water and water in essence ice.

125 明知冰性即是水性，水性即是冰性。

迷者为众生
悟者为菩提
The decluded is mortality and the enlightened the Buddha.
众生与菩提
本质相同。
Mortality and Buddhahood are the same in essence.
什么是菩提?
What is Buddhahood?
众生与菩提来自相同本性，
有如乌头与附子同根一样。
Mortality and Buddhahood share the same nature, just as rhizome of Chinese monkshood and monkshood share the same root.
!
只因为时间不同，迷与悟境界不同，
才有众生、菩提两个不同称号。
Mortality and Buddhahood are only terms for the same thing in delusion and enlightenment.

126 众生性者，即菩提性也。

127 众生与菩提同一性，亦如乌头与附子共根耳。

128 但时节不同，迷异境故，有众生菩提二名矣。

心是内在的智慧，
防范身外的色尘。
The mind is the internal wisdom to protect the body from the delusion of forms and appearances.
是众生自度成佛，
或是佛度化众生，
平等而没有差别。
Mortals liberate Buddhas and Buddhas liberate mortals. This is what's meant by equality.
求人不如求己，
众生自己就是佛。
God helps those who help themselves. Mortals are essentially Buddhas themselves.
众生自度成佛，
即是通过烦恼而开悟解脱；
Mortals liberate Buddhas when affliction creates enlightenment.
佛度一切众生，即是
由觉悟灭除一切烦恼。
And Buddhas liberate mortals, as enlightenment negates affliction.

129 但知心者智内，照身者戒外。真众生度佛，佛度众生，是名平等。

130 众生度佛者，烦恼生悟解。佛度众生者，悟解灭烦恼。

开悟者知道，
不是无烦恼无觉悟，
而是知道没有烦恼，
便没有觉悟。
The enlightened know that there're always affliction and enlightment and enlightment is right generated from affliction.
迷时佛度众生，
悟时众生度佛。
Buddhas liberate mortals who are in delusion. Mortals who are enlightened liberate Buddhas.
为什么？
Why?
佛不是来自于佛，
佛是从众生开悟成佛的。
Buddhahood isn't endowed by Buddhas. Buddhahood is attained by mortals who are enlightened.
无明、贪爱都是众生的别名。
众生与无明，有如左掌与
右掌，没有区别。
Delusion and greed are different names for mortality. Delusion and mortality are like the left hand and the right hand. There's no difference.
诸佛以无明为父，
以贪爱为母，
Buddhas regard delusion as their father and greed as their mother.

131 是知非无烦恼，非无悟解；是知非烦恼无以生悟解，

132 若迷时佛度众生，若悟时众生度佛。

133 何以故？佛不自成，皆由众生度故。诸佛以无明为父，贪爱为母，无明贪爱皆是众生别名也。众生与无明，亦如左掌与右掌，更无别也。

开悟无彼岸
There's no the Other Shore in enlightenmend

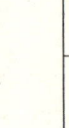

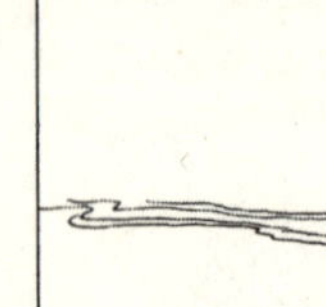

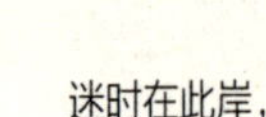

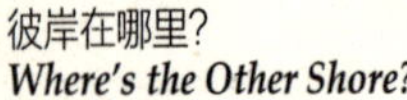

彼岸在哪里?
Where's the Other Shore?

彼岸在开悟的地方。
It is in enlightenment.

迷时在此岸,
悟时在彼岸。
When you're deluded, you're on This Shore. When you're enlightened, you're on the Other Shore.

如何才能悟?
How to get enlightened?

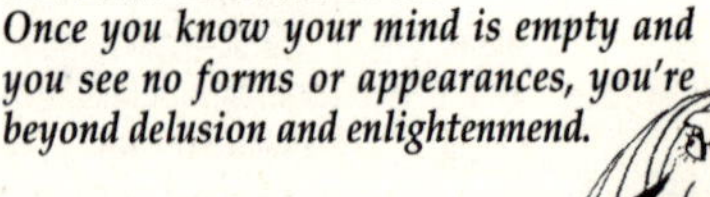
如果知道心性本空,
也不见相,这时离迷也离悟。
Once you know your mind is empty and you see no forms or appearances, you're beyond delusion and enlightenmend.

这时便到达
彼岸了吗?
Am I on the Other Shore in that case?

心中无迷也无悟,
便无彼岸。
And once you're beyond delusion and enlightenment, the Other Shore doesn't exist.

如来不在此岸,
也不在彼岸,
也不在两岸之间。
The Tathagata is neither on This Shore nor the Other Shore. And he isn't in midstream.

134 迷时在此岸,悟时在彼岸。

135 若知心空不见相,则离迷悟。

136 既离迷悟,亦无彼岸。如来不在此岸,亦不在彼岸,不在中流。

两岸之间
In the midstream
什么是
小乘修行者?
What are Hinayana practitioners?
身在两岸之间,
是小乘修行者。
Hinayana practitioners are in the midstream
什么是
凡夫众生?
What are mortals?
身在此岸,
是凡夫众生。
Mortals are on This Shore.
酒
什么是
开悟菩提?
What are Buddhas?
身在彼岸,
是开悟菩提。
Buddhas are on the Other Shore.

137 中流者，小乘人也。

138 此岸者，凡夫也。

139 彼岸者，菩提也。

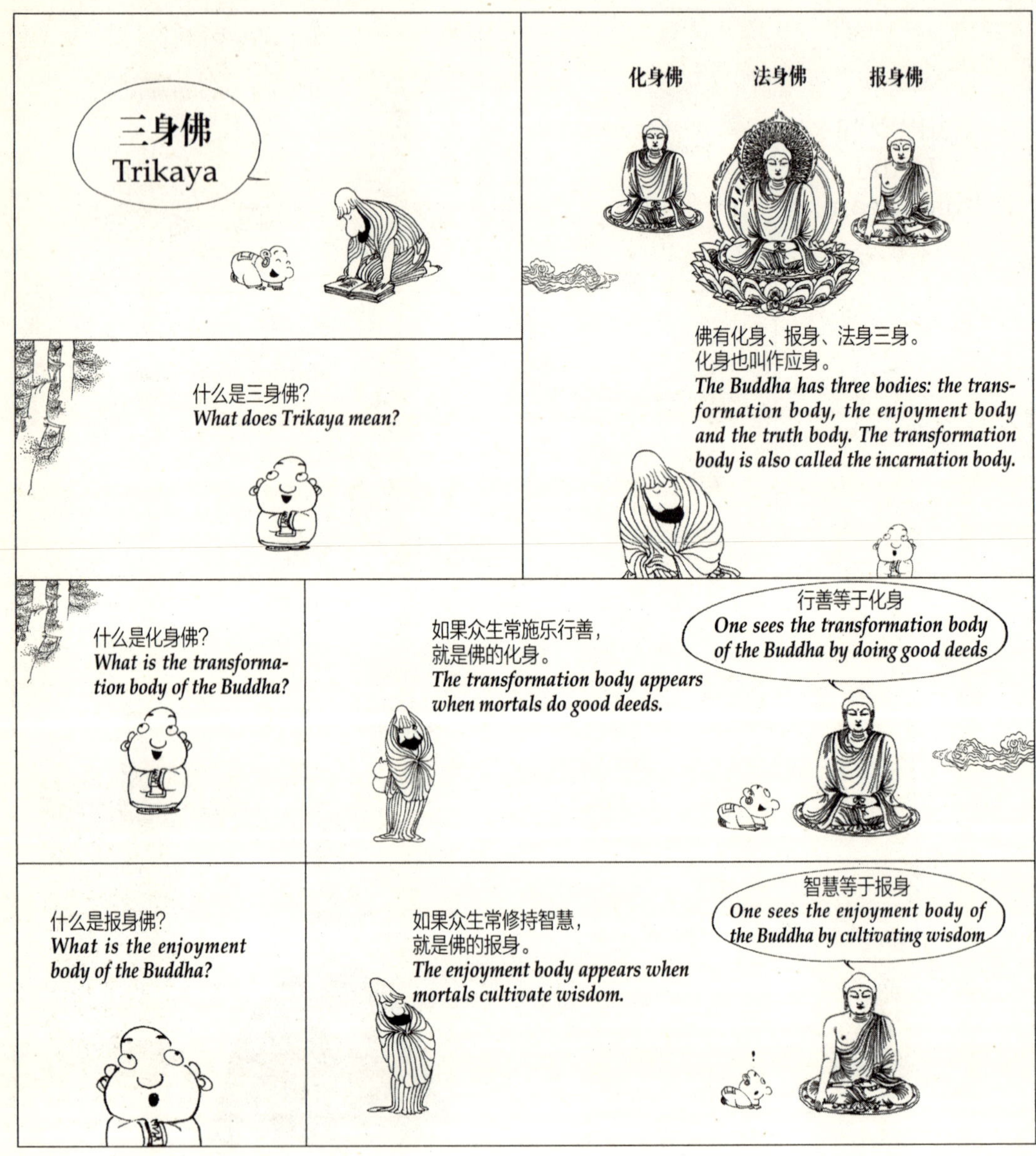
三身佛
Trikaya
化身佛
法身佛
报身佛
什么是三身佛?
What does Trikaya mean?
佛有化身、报身、法身三身。
化身也叫作应身。
The Buddha has three bodies: the transformation body, the enjoyment body and the truth body. The transformation body is also called the incarnation body.
什么是化身佛?
What is the transformation body of the Buddha?
如果众生常施乐行善，
就是佛的化身。
The transformation body appears when mortals do good deeds.
行善等于化身
One sees the transformation body of the Buddha by doing good deeds
什么是报身佛?
What is the enjoyment body of the Buddha?
如果众生常修持智慧，
就是佛的报身。
The enjoyment body appears when mortals cultivate wisdom.
智慧等于报身
One sees the enjoyment body of the Buddha by cultivating wisdom

140 佛有三身者；化身报身法身；化身亦云应身。

141 若众生常作善时即化身。

142 现修智慧时即报身。

什么是法身佛?
What is the truth body of the Buddha?
如果众生常觉悟无为，就是佛的法身。
The truth body appears when mortals become aware of the sublime.
觉悟无为等于法身!
One sees the truth body of the Buddha by attaining enlightenment!
老师，三身佛隐喻什么境界?
Master, what does Trikaya mean?
悟
众生飞腾十方随宜救济，就是化身佛。
The transformation body is the one you see flying in all directions to rescue others wherever it can.
众生断惑有如雪山大士，就是报身佛。
The enjoyment body puts an end to delusions. The Great Enlightenment occurred in the Himalayas suddenly becomes true.

143 现觉无为即法身。

144 常现飞腾十方随宜救济者，化身佛也。若断惑即是雪山成道，报身佛也。

众生无言、无说、无作、无得，就是法身佛。
The truth body says nothing, does nothing and gains nothing.
佛就是众生自己，没有所谓三身佛？
Buddhahood is in mortality. Is there nothing like Trikaya?
若以最高真理的角度看，连一佛也无，哪来三佛？
As the Ultimate Truth puts it, there's not a single Buddha, let alone Trikaya.
!
所谓三佛，只是针对上、中、下智慧不同的众生所作的说法而已。
The so-called three bodies of the Buddha are merely a talk based on the levels of human understanding, which can be shallow, moderate or deep.
下智者迷失于善有善报，妄见化身佛；
People of shallow understanding imagine they're piling up blessings and see the transformation body of the Buddha.

145 无言无说，无作无得，湛然常住，法身佛也。

146 若论至理，一佛尚无，何得有三？此谓三身者，但据人智也。人有上中下说，

147 下智之人妄兴福力也，妄见化身佛。

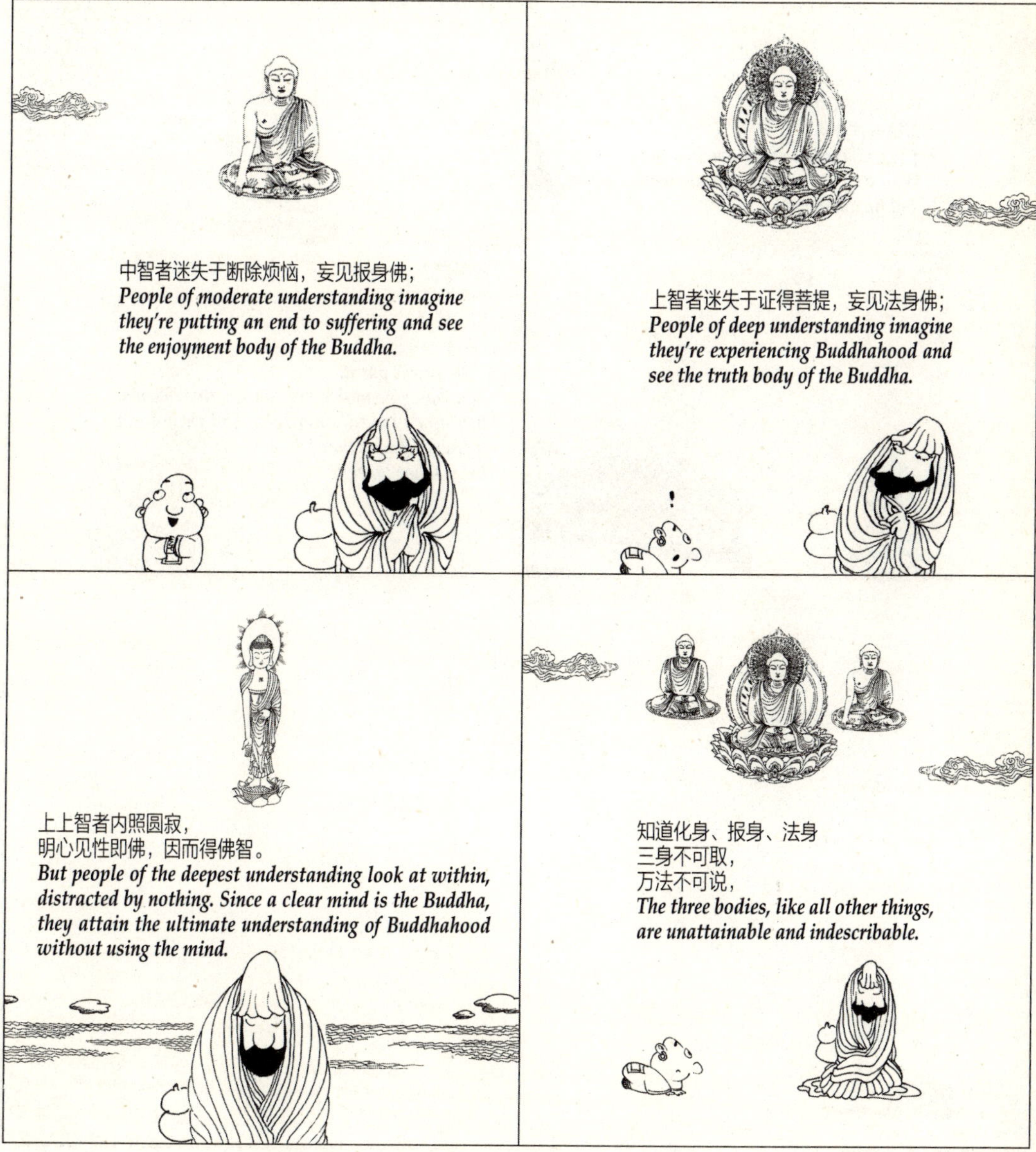
中智者迷失于断除烦恼，妄见报身佛；
People of moderate understanding imagine they're putting an end to suffering and see the enjoyment body of the Buddha.
上智者迷失于证得菩提，妄见法身佛；
People of deep understanding imagine they're experiencing Buddhahood and see the truth body of the Buddha.
!
上上智者内照圆寂，
明心见性即佛，因而得佛智。
But people of the deepest understanding look at within, distracted by nothing. Since a clear mind is the Buddha, they attain the ultimate understanding of Buddhahood without using the mind.
知道化身、报身、法身
三身不可取，
万法不可说，
The three bodies, like all other things, are unattainable and indescribable.

148 中智之人妄断烦恼，妄见报身佛；上智之人妄证菩提，妄见法身佛；上上智之人内照圆寂，明心即佛不待心而得佛智。

149 知三身与万法皆不可取不可说。

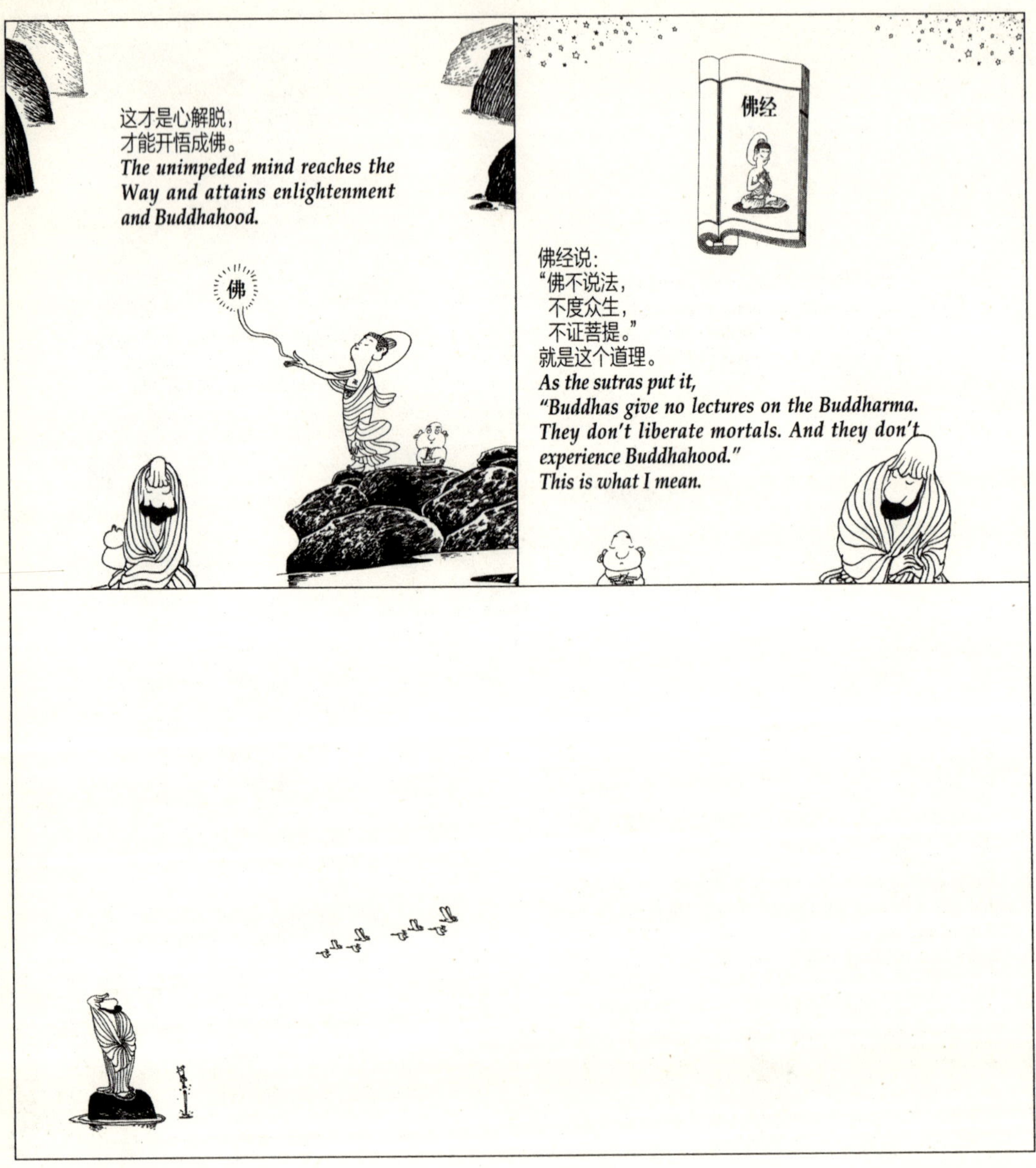
这才是心解脱，
才能开悟成佛。
The unimpeded mind reaches the Way and attains enlightenment and Buddhahood.
佛
佛经
佛经说：
“佛不说法，
不度众生，
不证菩提。”
就是这个道理。
As the sutras put it,
“Buddhas give no lectures on the Buddharma. They don't liberate mortals. And they don't experience Buddhahood.”
This is what I mean.

150 此即解脱心，成于大道。

151 经云：“佛不说法，不度众生，不证菩提。”此之谓矣！

第六章　造因生业果

Chapter VI Karma

众生造业
Individuals create karma.
什么是造业？
What is karma?
有意的行为造成因果，
就是造业。
The cause and effect intentionally made is karma.
造业会有何后果？
What will happen then?
造业必产生业报，善得善果，
恶得恶果。乃生出痛苦伤悲。
There's the karmic cycle. Good deeds result in good results and evil deeds lead to evil consequences. Thus suffering and sadness are generated.
如何能不造业？
How to avoid karma?
无心便无业报，
众生造业，业不造众生。
Once your mind remains empty, there's no karma. Individuals create karma. Karma doesn't create individuals.

152 众生造业，业不造众生。

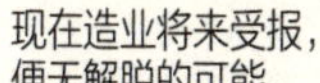

现在造业将来受报，
便无解脱的可能。
They create karma in this life and receive what they deserve in the next. They never escape.

至人一生都不造业，
因此不受业报。
Only perfect men create no karma in this life and receive no reward or punishment.

佛经

佛经说：
“诸业不造，自然得道。”
此言不虚！
As the sutras put it, "Who creates no karma obtains the Dharma." That's absolutely true.

人能造业，业不能造人；
人若造业，业与人俱生；
人若不造业，业与人俱灭。
Individuals generate instead of being generated from karma. When you create karma, you're reborn along with your karma. When you create no karma, you vanish along with your karma.

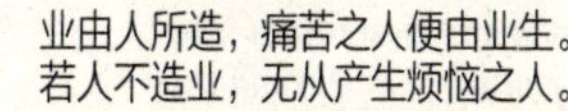

业由人所造，痛苦之人便由业生。
若人不造业，无从产生烦恼之人。
Once an individual creates karma, there may be one more person suffering from his karma. If an individual creates no karma, karma has no hold on him.

WISDOM

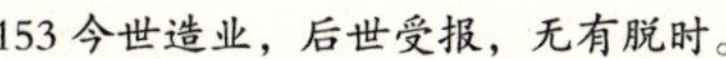

153 今世造业，后世受报，无有脱时。

154 唯有至人，于此身中，不造诸业，故不受报。

155 经云：“诸业不造，自然得道。”岂虚言哉！岂虚言哉！人能造业，业不能造人；人若造业，业与人俱生；人若不造业，业与人俱灭。

156 是知业由人造，人由业生。人若不造业，即业无由生人也。

道不能弘人
The Way is what your mind is.
人能弘道，
道不能弘人。
The Way is what your mind is, be it great or trivial.
误以为没有报应，难道没有遭受苦果吗？
Mortals keep creating karma and mistakenly insist that there's no reward or punishment. But can they deny suffering?
过去心造业，未来心得业报。
因果相报何时了？
Can they deny that what the present state of mind sows the next state of mind reaps? How can they escape?
如果过去心不造业，
未来心不会得业报，
哪里还看得到业报？
But if the present state of mind sows nothing, the next state of mind reaps nothing. Don't misconceive karma.

157 亦如人能弘道，道不能弘人。今之凡夫，往往造业，妄说无报，岂至少不苦哉？

158 若以至少而理前心，造后心报，何有脱时？若前心不造，即后心无报，复安妄见业报？

佛不造业！
佛无自我，
无我便无造业者。
The Buddha creates no karma, as
he is caught up in no idea of self.
No self, no karma creator.

佛不生心，无心便没有业报。
佛不造因，无因便没有果报。
The Buddha's mind is empty. An empty
mind creates no karma. The Buddha creates
no cause. No cause, no effect.

苦行才能成佛吗？
Are austerities indispensable to attain
Buddhahood?

佛经说：
“虽信有佛，但认为苦行
才能成佛，就是邪见。”
As the sutras put is,
“Despite believing in Buddhas, people who imagine
that Buddhas practice austerities aren't Buddhists.”

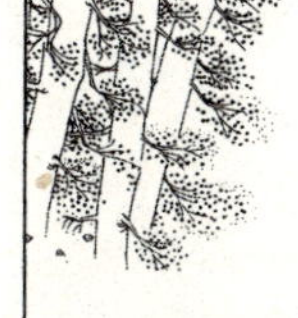
虽然相信有佛存在，但认为受辱
才能成佛，这是邪见。
是人信心不足，称作没有善根的人。
The same holds for those who imagine that Buddhas are
subject to humiliations. They're icchantikas incapable
of belief.

159 经云：“虽信有佛，言佛苦行，是名邪见。”

160 虽信有佛，言佛有金锵马麦之报，是名信不具足，是名一阐提。

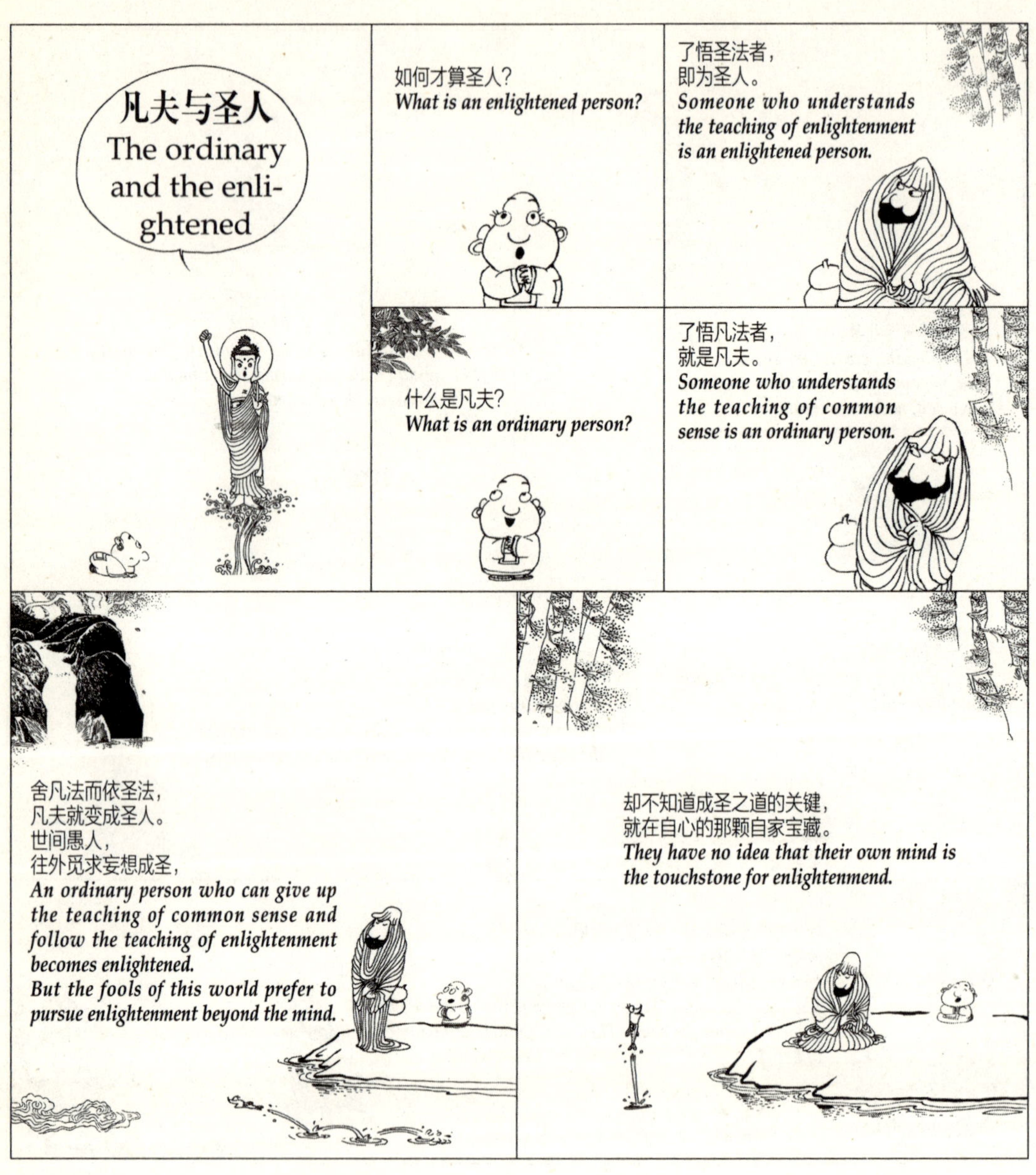
凡夫与圣人
The ordinary and the enlightened
如何才算圣人？
What is an enlightened person?
了悟圣法者，
即为圣人。
Someone who understands the teaching of enlightenment is an enlightened person.
什么是凡夫？
What is an ordinary person?
了悟凡法者，
就是凡夫。
Someone who understands the teaching of common sense is an ordinary person.
舍凡法而依圣法，
凡夫就变成圣人。
世间愚人，
往外觅求妄想成圣，
An ordinary person who can give up the teaching of common sense and follow the teaching of enlightenment becomes enlightened.
But the fools of this world prefer to pursue enlightenment beyond the mind.
却不知道成圣之道的关键，
就在自心的那颗自家宝藏。
They have no idea that their own mind is the touchstone for enlightenmend.

161 解圣法名为圣人，

162 解凡法者名为凡夫。

163 但能舍凡法就圣法，即凡夫成圣人矣。世间愚人，但欲远求圣人，不信慧解之心为圣人也。

佛经

佛经说：
“别在无智者面前
说这些经文。”
As the sutras put it,
"No mention these scriptures to the unworthy."

佛经

佛经说：
“人心就是法，
无智者不信此心。”
Also,
"The mind is the Buddharma. But the unworthy has no faith in the mind."

圣人自我开悟才获得解脱，
凡是往外求法或向佛求福报，
都是错误的邪见，
The enlightened attained enlightenment by consulting their minds. The unworthy pursue enlightenment beyong the mind or ask the Buddha for blessings.

金刚经

《金刚经》说：
“若见诸相非相，
即见如来。”
As the sutras put it,
"When you see that all forms and appearances are non-forms and non-appearances, you see the Buddha."

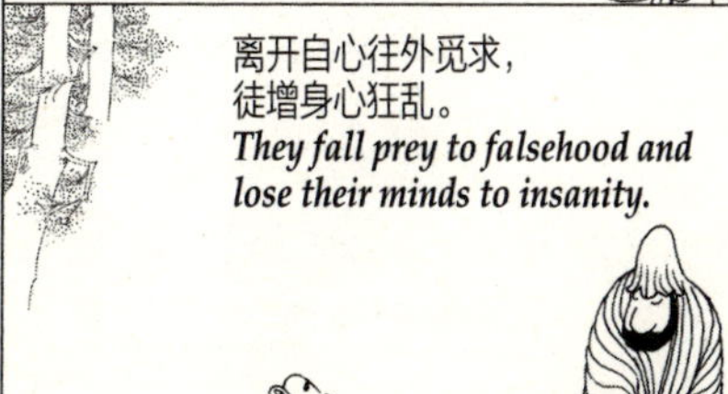

离开自心往外觅求，
徒增身心狂乱。
They fall prey to falsehood and lose their minds to insanity.

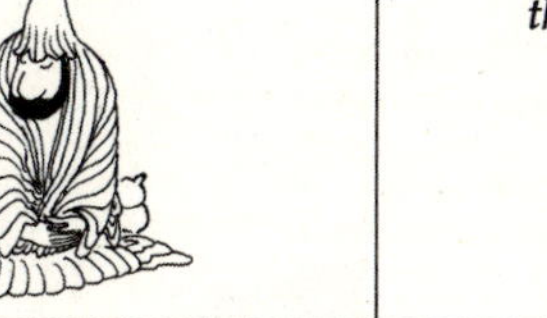

164 经云：“无智人中，莫说此经。”
165 经云：“心也法也，无智之人，不信此心。”
166 解法成于圣人，但欲远外求学，爱慕空中佛像光明香色等事，皆堕邪见，失心狂乱。
167 经云：“若见诸相非相，即见如来。”

八万四千种情境，
全由心所产生出来。
心净有如虚空，
八万四千种烦恼便脱离身心。
The myriad situations varying in appearance come from the mind.
Once the mind is pure and empty, the myriad sufferings leave you alone.
凡夫跟圣人，
最大的不同是什么?
What's the principal difference between the mortal and the enlightened?
凡夫活着时害怕死亡，
吃饱后忧愁肚子饿，
这都是大迷惑。
When the mortal are alive, they worry about death. When they're full, they worry about hunger. Theirs is the Great Uncertainty.
圣人的心不思虑过去，
不企盼未来，无恋当下现前，
念念都在道上。
But the enlightened don't think about the past. And they don't worry about the future. Nor do they cling to the present. And from one moment to another, they follow the Way.
如果不能领悟这个大道理，
应及早求得这天地宇宙中的至善。
If you haven't awakened to this great truth, you should conduct virtuous deeds as soon as possible,

168 八万四千法门，尽由一心而起。若心相内净，犹如虚空，即出离身心内，八万四千烦恼为病本也。

169 凡夫当生忧死，饱临愁肌，皆名大惑。所以圣人不制心于前和其后，无恋当今，念念归道。

170 若未悟此大理者，即须早求人天之善，无令两失。

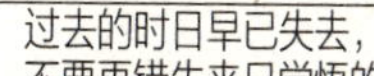

过去的时日早已失去，
不要再错失来日觉悟的契机。
To make you become at least a human or heavenly being in your next lifetime. Do not lose both of them [the great truth and the virtuous fruits produced from your virtuous deeds].

哇！师父讲得太好了！
Wow! What you've said is great!

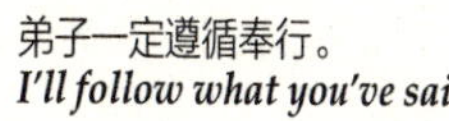

弟子一定遵循奉行。
I'll follow what you've said.

于是达摩唱夜坐偈说：
一更端坐结跏趺，
怡神寂照泯同虚。
Bodhidharma chanted an evening gatha:
At the first watch, I sit crosslegged.
My mind is pure and empty.

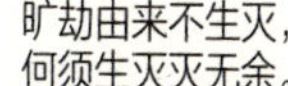

旷劫由来不生灭，
何须生灭灭无余。
There's neither birth nor death through the kalpas.
So why am I bothered about the Wheel of Birth and Death?

一切诸法皆如幻，
本性自空那用除。
All the dharmas are illusions.
Only the nature of emptiness remains.
若识心性非形象，
湛然不动自真如。
Leave all forms and appearances aside.
Be faithful to your nature of emptiness.
二更凝神转明净，
不起忆想同真性。
At the second watch, I feel more focused and clear in mind, pushing trivial thoughts aside.
森罗万象并归空，
更执有空还是病。
The universal nature is emptiness.
But it's wrong even to cling to emptiness.

诸法本自非空有，
凡夫妄想论邪正。
Dharmas are neither of emptiness nor non-emptiness. It's wrong to debate on it.
正
邪
若能不二其居怀，
谁道即凡非是圣。
All the things are empty in essence.
The ordinary and the enlightened are the same in nature.
三更心净等虚空，
遍满十方无不通。
At the third watch, my mind remains pure and tranquil, with all the directions in the universe in my mind.
山河石壁无能障，
恒沙世界在其中。
My mind flies over rivers and cliffs. The entire universe sits in it.

若能无念即真求，
更若有求还不识。
An empty mind is ultimately true. A mind slightly tainted is caught up in delusion.
世界本性真如性，
亦无无性即含融。
See the world as it is. Emptiness is the original nature.
非但诸佛能如此，
有情之类并皆同。
It holds true for Buddhas and all the living creatures in the world.
四更无灭亦无生，
量与虚空法界平。
At the fourth watch, I see neither birth nor death. Everything is empty in essence.

无去无来无起灭，
非有非无非暗明。
There's neither birth nor death. There's neither existence nor non-existance or intelligence or ignorance.
不起诸见如来见，
无名可名真佛名。
With an empty mind, one sees the Buddha. Without a name, one finds the true name of Buddha.
唯有悟者应能识，
未会众生由若盲。
Only the enlightened understands this. The ordinary are simply blinded.
五更般若照无边，
不起一念历三千。
At the fifth watch, I sit in the light of wisdom. In my empty mind, I see the entire universe.

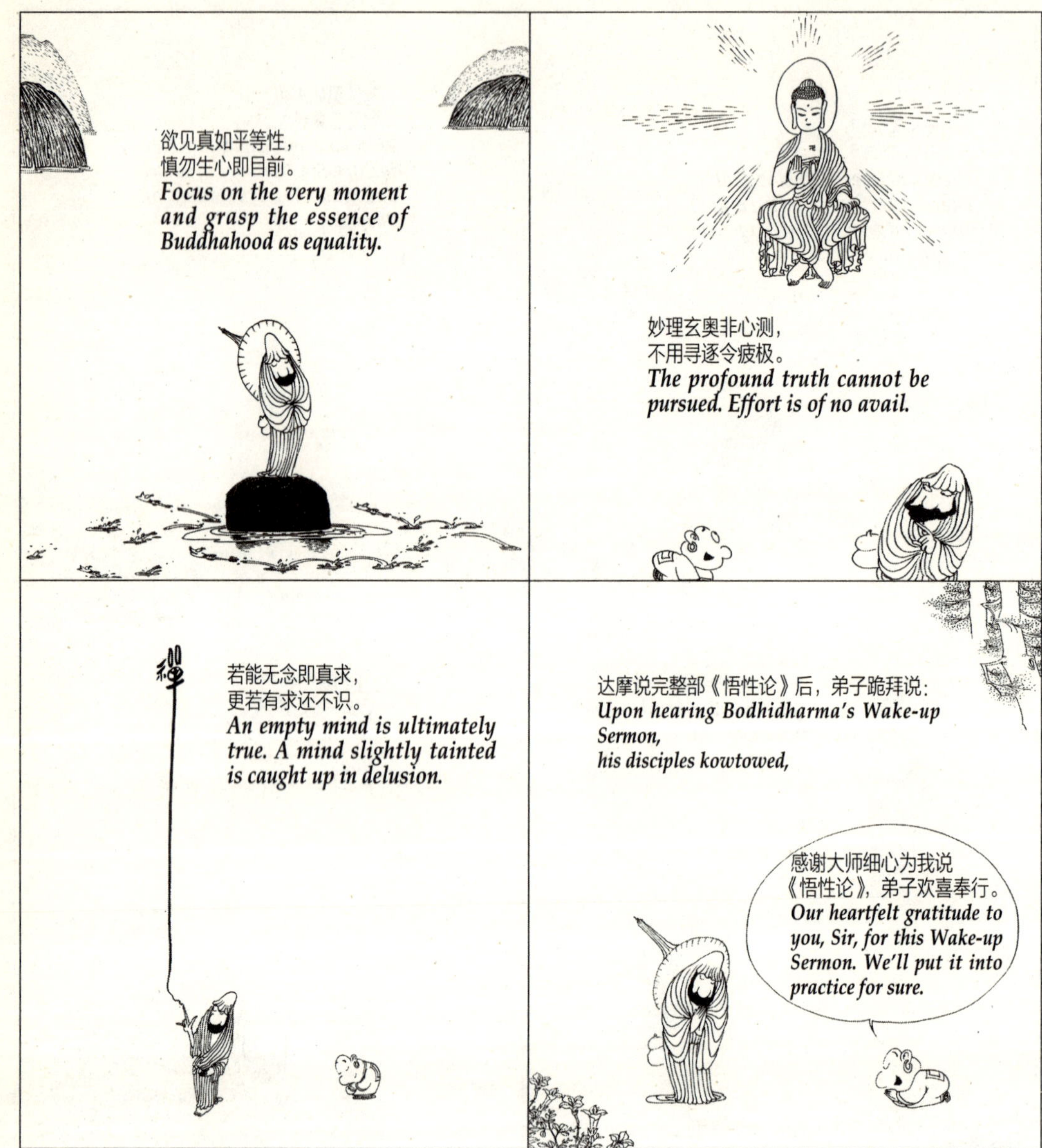
欲见真如平等性，
慎勿生心即目前。
Focus on the very moment and grasp the essence of Buddhahood as equality.
妙理玄奥非心测，
不用寻逐令疲极。
The profound truth cannot be pursued. Effort is of no avail.
禪
若能无念即真求，
更若有求还不识。
An empty mind is ultimately true. A mind slightly tainted is caught up in delusion.
达摩说完整部《悟性论》后，弟子跪拜说：
Upon hearing Bodhidharma's Wake-up Sermon,
his disciples kowtowed,
感谢大师细心为我说《悟性论》，弟子欢喜奉行。
Our heartfelt gratitude to you, Sir, for this Wake-up Sermon. We'll put it into practice for sure.

达摩观心论

Breakthrough Sermon

前　言
Prologe

佛学大辞典说："《破相论》又名《观心论》，一共有十四问。前半段十问（1980个字），内容全为观心之法，以观心一法总摄诸法；而后半段四问（3083个字），内容为破除信佛表面形式的持斋、烧香、点灯、散花、拜佛、浴佛、绕塔经行等世间迷惑。"我认为这其实是两本书，因此我们把本书前后两段分成观心论与破相论两部分。

As the Great Dictionary of Buddhism puts it, "There are 14 inquiries in Formality Refuting Sermon, a.k.a. Breakthrough Sermon. The first 10 inquiries (1,980 characters) talk about beholding the mind as the most essential method. The last four inquiries (3,083 characters) deal with how to break down the formalities such as keeping vegetarian fast, burning incense, lighting lamps, scattering flowers, worshipping the Buddha, bathing the Buddha and walking around a pagoda, as all those formalities are seen as delusionary things." Personally, I think the two parts are like two separate books. I'd like to make the first 10 inquiries into "Breakthrough Sermon" and the last four into "Formality Refuting Sermon".

第一问 观心法门
Inquiry I The method of beholding the mind
弟子问达摩："如果有人想学佛法，修什么法门最简便？"
A disciple asked, "If someone is determined to attain enlightenment, what is the most essential method he can practice?"
达摩回答：
"修观心法门最简便。"
Bodhidharma answered,
"The most essential method is beholding the mind."
为什么？
Why?
观心法门涵盖一切诸法，
也最容易学。
The method includes all other methods
and is the easiest one.

1 问曰："若复有人，志求佛道者，当修何法，最为省要？"答曰："唯观心一法。"

2 总摄诸法，最为省要。

第二问　一法能摄诸法
Inquiry II A method that includes all other methods

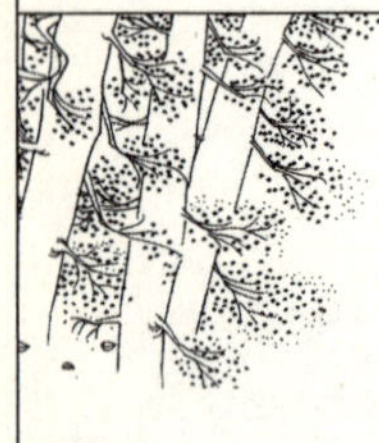

弟子问达摩：
“只有一门观心法，如何能涵盖诸法？”
A disciple asked, "But how can one method include all the others?"

心是万法根本，
一切诸法唯心所生，
如果能了解心，
则万法皆备。
The mind is the root from which all things grow. If you can understand the mind, everything else is in your hand.

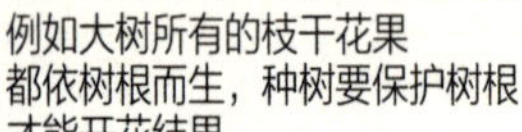
例如大树所有的枝干花果
都依树根而生，种树要保护树根，
才能开花结果。
It's like the root of a tree. All a tree's fruit and flowers, branches and leaves rely on its root. If you nourish its root, a tree thrives.

砍树时截去树根，
则大树和枝干花果必死。
If you cut its root, it dies.

3　问曰：“何一法能摄诸法？”答曰：“心者万法之根本，一切诸法唯心所生；若能了心，则万法俱备。”

4　犹如大树，所有枝条，及诸花果，皆悉依根。栽树者，存根而始生子；伐树者，去根而必死。

首先要了解自己的心，
Those who understand the mind
之后才开始修行，
则会简单又容易有成就。
Attain enlightenment with minimal effort.
如果不明了自己的心便开始修道，
费力又产生不了效果。
Those who don't understand the mind practice in vain.
但每个人的际遇
有好坏顺逆啊！
But conditions in life vary for different people. Some enjoy favorable conditions, while others suffer from unfavorable ones.
一切情境好坏善恶，
都是由我们自己的心所造，
Everything good or bad comes from your own mind.
要安顿自己的身心，往心外寻觅，
将会一无所获。
Try to reach an inner peace. You'll achieve nothing, when you try to find something beyond the mind.

5 若了心修道，则省力而易成；不了心而修道，则费功而无益。

6 故知一切善恶皆由自心。心外别求，终无是处。

第三问　了见自心
Inquiry III To see your mind
弟子问：
“如何观心才能参透呢？”
A disciple asked,
“What shall I do to attain enlightenment by beholding my mind?”
大菩萨修行波罗蜜多时，
明了四大五蕴本性空寂无我。
When a great bodhisattva delves deeply into perfect wisdom, he realizes that the Four Elements and Five Aggregates are all empty in essence.
观见一切现象都是自心造作，
这个造作的心有两种。
And he realizes that the activity of his mind has two aspects.
是哪两种？
What are they?
一是清净心，
二是污染心。
Being pure and impure.

7　问曰：“云何观心称之为了？”答曰：“菩萨摩诃萨，行深般若波罗蜜多时，了四大五阴本空无我；了见自心起用，有二种差别。”

8　问：“云何为二？”答：“一者净心，二者染心。”

这两种心本来就有，人行为处世时，
清净心与污染心轮流交互出现。
By their very nature, these two mental states are always present. They alternate as cause or effect depending on conditions.
什么是清净心？
What is the pure mind?
乐于一切善因，
就是清净心。
The pure mind delights in good will and deeds.
什么是污染心？
What is the impure mind?
常思维恶业，
就是污染心。
The impure mind thinks of evil karma.
心清净不受污染，他就是圣人，
能脱离一切诸苦，证悟涅槃之乐。
Those untainted with impurity attain enlightenment. They get released from suffering and experience the bliss of nirvana.

9 此二种心，法界自然，本来俱有；虽假缘合，互相因待。

10 净心恒乐善因，染体常思恶业。

11 若不受所染，则称之为圣，遂能远离诸苦，证涅槃乐。

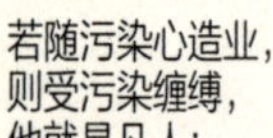

若随污染心造业，
则受污染缠缚，
他就是凡人；
All others, trapped in the impure mind and entangled by their own karma, are the ordinary.

将沉沦三界，
受尽种种痛苦烦恼。
They drift through the three realms and suffer countless afflictions.

为什么呢？
Why?

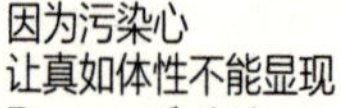

因为污染心
让真如体性不能显现。
Because their impure mind obscures their true self.

十地经

《十地经》说：
众生身中有金刚佛性，
As the Ten Stages Sutra put it, One finds in his mortal body the indestructible Buddha-nature.

犹如日轮，
体明圆满，
广大无边。
Like the sun, its light pervades the boundless universe.

12 若随染心造业，受其缠覆，则名之为凡，沉沦三界，受种种苦。

13 问：“何以故？”答：“由彼染心，障真如体故。”

14《十地经》云：“众生身中有金刚佛性，犹如日轮，体明圆满，广大无边。”

只为五阴重云所覆，
如瓶内灯光不能显现。
But once veiled by the dark clouds of the Five Aggregates, it's like the light inside a vat, hidden from view.
《涅槃经》说：
“一切众生都有佛性，
但被无明所覆不得解脱。”
As the Nirvana Sutra put it,
"All mortals have the Buddha-nature.
But it's covered and hidden in ignorance. And mortals cannot be released from suffering."

15 只为五阴重云所覆，如瓶内灯光不能显现。又《涅槃经》云：“一切众生，悉有佛性，无明覆故，不得解脱。”

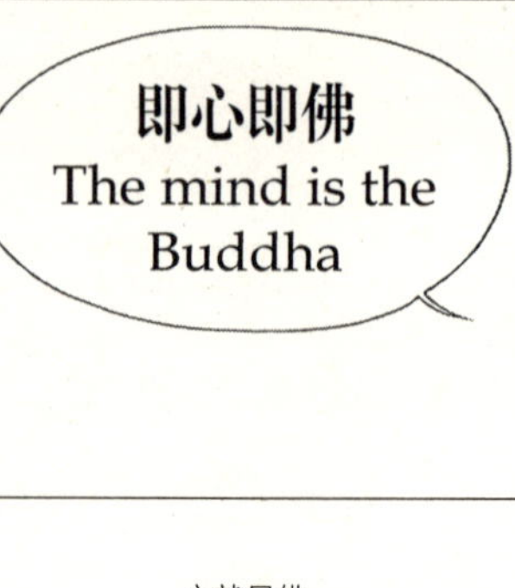
即心即佛
The mind is the Buddha

佛是什么？
What is Buddhahood?

心就是佛，
佛就是自心觉悟。
The mind is the Buddha. Buddhahood means enlightenment.

佛性是什么？
What is the Buddha-nature?

佛性就是觉性；
能自觉觉他。
Our Buddha-nature lies in awareness, including self awareness and awareness of others.

如何才是解脱？
What is liberation?

!

明了觉性智慧，
就是解脱。
Liberation means coming to know the wisdom of awareness.

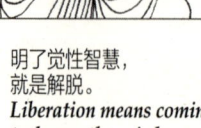

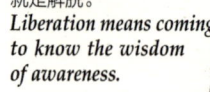

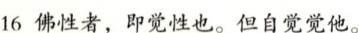

16 佛性者，即觉性也。但自觉觉他。

17 觉知明了，则名解脱。

一切诸善，
以什么为根？
What lies at the root of all good?
以觉性为根。
觉性能显现一切功德树，
生涅槃果。
All good has awareness at its root. And from this root of awareness grows the tree of all virtues, bearing the fruit of nirvana.
由于了解心识作用，
而称之为观心法。
Beholding the mind means coming to understand what the mind is capable of.
如何修行观心法门？
Then how to put the method of beholding the mind into practice?
观心有如父母照顾自己的孩子，
时时刻刻守望护着婴儿。
It's in the same way parents take care of their kids, safeguarding the kids all the time.
心如同无知的婴儿一样，
随心所欲住于染心，
用正思维规范心，
让心回归本然。
The mind is somehow like an innocent baby. Without regulation, it would fall into evil. With good instructions, it would find the right way and return to its original nature.

18 故知一切诸善，以觉为根。

19 因其觉根，遂能显现诸功德树。涅槃之果，因此而成。如是观心，可名为了。

20 观心，看护自心如父母看护婴儿，时时刻刻守望着他，心如无知的婴儿一般，随心所欲。住于染心，则用正思维规范他，让他还归本然。

第四问　无明以三毒为根
Inquiry IV Ignorance has the three poisons at its root

真如佛性一切功德，
都是以觉性为根，
不知道无明之心以什么为根？
You say that our true Buddha-nature and all virtues have awareness at the root. But what is the root of ignorance?

无明之心有八万四千烦恼情欲，
又有如同恒河沙数这么多的恶，
无明之心以三毒为根本。
The ignorant mind, with its infinite afflictions, passions and evils, as innumerable as the grains of sand in the Ganges, is rooted in the three poisons.

什么是三毒？
What are the three poisons?

贪、嗔、痴，就是三毒。
三毒心具有一切诸恶。
Greed, anger and delusion. The poisoned mind itself includes countless evils.

21　问："上说真如佛性，一切功德，因觉为根，未审无明之心，以何为根？"答："无明之心，虽有八万四千烦恼情欲，及恒河沙众恶，皆因三毒，以为根本。"

22　其三毒者，贪嗔痴是也。

23　此三毒心，自能具足一切诸恶。

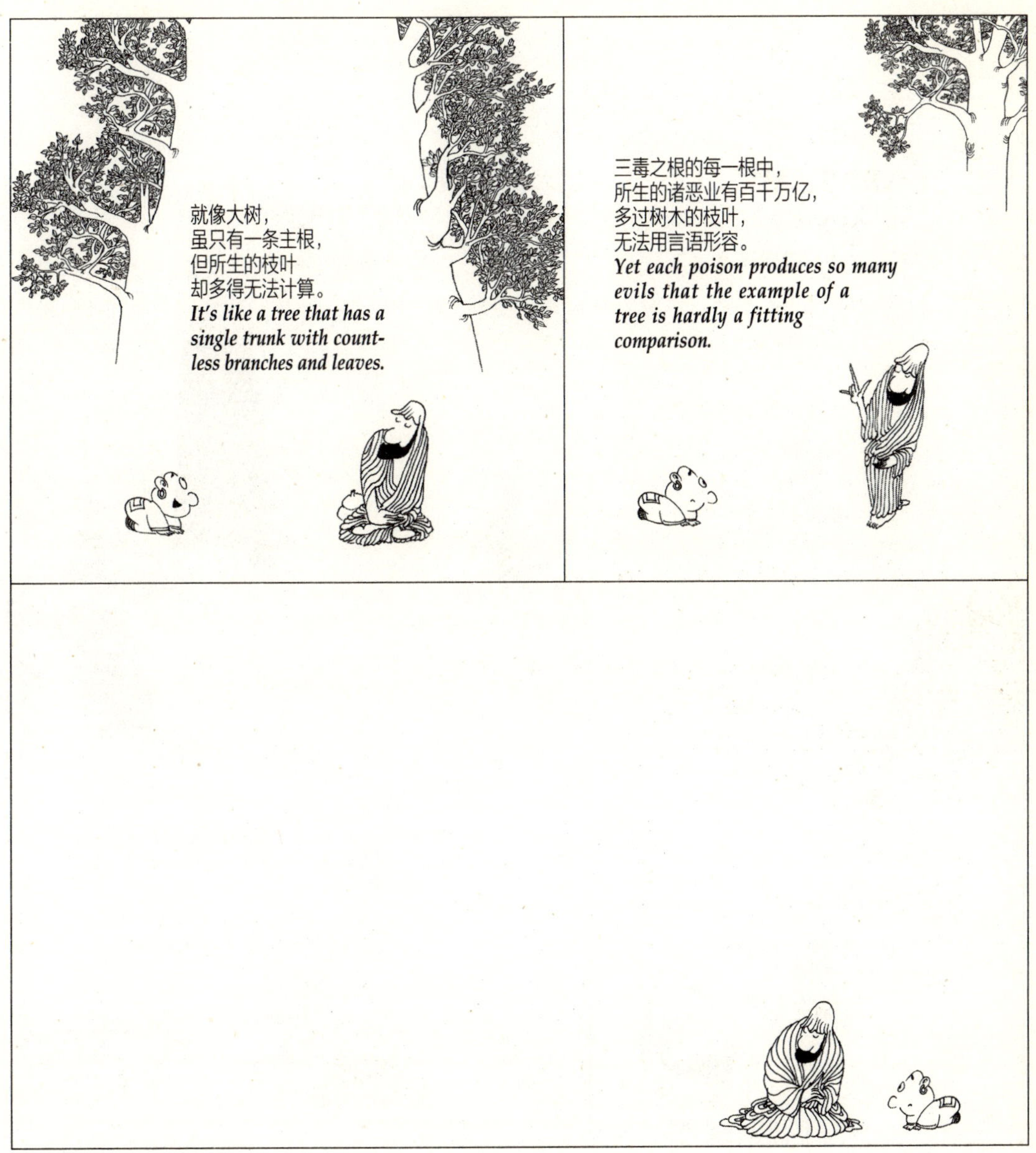
就像大树，
虽只有一条主根，
但所生的枝叶
却多得无法计算。
It's like a tree that has a single trunk with countless branches and leaves.
三毒之根的每一根中，
所生的诸恶业有百千万亿，
多过树木的枝叶，
无法用言语形容。
Yet each poison produces so many evils that the example of a tree is hardly a fitting comparison.

24 犹如大树，根虽是一，所生枝叶，其数无边。

25 彼三毒根，一一根中，生诸恶业百千万亿，倍过于前，不可为喻。

六识即六贼
Six kinds of consciousness or thieves
三毒心存在我们的本心内，
应现出来的就是六根，
六根又名六贼，也就是六识。
The three poisons are represented in our six sense organs as six kinds of consciousness or six thieves.
什么是六识？
What are six kinds of consciousness?
六识是我们的
眼、耳、鼻、舌、身、意，
They refer to eyes, ears, nose, tongue, body and mind.
相对心外的
色、声、香、味、触、法六尘。
Correspondingly we have six dusts outside, namely form, sound, smell, taste, tactile sensation and dharma.

26 如是三毒心，于本体中，应现六根，亦名六贼，即六识也。

为何又称为六贼？
But why are they called six thieves then?
六识出入于诸根之间，
贪着种种境界，能造作种种恶业。
They're called six thieves, as they are generated by six sense organs, get lost in sensations and create all sorts of evil karma.
泯灭我们内心的真如体性，
所以称它为六贼。
They eliminate the Buddha-nature in our mind.
一切众生受三毒六贼惑乱，
身心沉沦生死轮回于六趣，
受尽一切痛苦烦恼。
And because mortals are misled in body and mind by these three poisons and six thieves, they get lost in birth and death, wander through the Wheel of Six Destinies and suffer countless afflictions.
有如江河源起于细泉小溪，
虽然开始只是涓涓细流，
慢慢汇流壮大，形成波涛万里。
These afflictions are like rivers that surge for a thousand miles because of the constant inflow of small springs.

27 由此六识，出入诸根，贪着万境，能成恶业，障真如体，故名六贼。

28 一切众生，由此三毒六贼，惑乱身心，沉没生死，轮回六趣，受诸苦恼。

29 犹如江河，因小泉源，涓流不绝，乃能弥漫，波涛万里。

如果有人截断源头，
波涛流水便消失了。
But if someone cuts off their source, rivers dry up.
求解脱之道的修行者，
如果能将三毒转化为三聚净戒，
将六贼转化为六波罗蜜，
那么他将永远脱离一切苦海。
And if someone who seeks liberation can turn the three poisons into the three sets of precepts and the six thieves into the six paramitas, he rids himself of afflictions once and for all.

30 若复有人断其本源，即众流皆息。

31 求解脱者，能转三毒为三聚净戒，转六贼为六波罗蜜，自然永离一切苦海。

第五问 无心即出三界
Inquiry V The empty mind leads you out of the three realms
六趣三界广大无边，
如果只学观心，
如何能避免无穷之苦？
But the three realms and the six destinies are infinitely vast. How can we escape the endless afflictions only by beholding the mind?
三界业报唯心所生，
如果能达到本来无心，
即使在三界中也等于出三界。
The karma of the three realms comes from the mind alone. If your mind remains empty and pure, it's then beyond the three realms it seems to be in.
什么是三界？
What are the three realms?
贪、嗔、痴三毒，
就是三界。
The three realms correspond to the three poisons of greed, anger and delusion.

32 问："六趣三界广大无边，若唯观心，何由免无穷之苦？"答："三界业报，唯心所生；本若无心，于三界中，即出三界。"

33 其三界者，即三毒也。

贪、嗔、痴分成哪三界?
What do they correspond to then?
贪是欲界,
嗔是色界,
痴是无色界。
Greed is the Desire Realm, anger the Form Realm and delusion the Formless Realm.
因此称之为三界。
Collectively, they are called the three realms.

34 贪为欲界，嗔为色界，痴为无色界，故名三界。

第六问 迷心堕六趣
Inquiry VI The blind mind leads you to the six destinies
三毒所造之业轻重不同，
所受的果报也不同，分归六处。
As the karma created by the poisons can be gentle or heavy, the three realms are further divided into six divisions known as the six destinies.
哪六处？
What are they?
六处就是六趣：
一天、二人、三修罗、
四饿鬼、五畜生、六地狱。
The six divisions are referred to the six destinies, namely heaven, human, asura, demon, animal and hell.
天
人
修罗
饿鬼
畜生
地狱
依轻重不同果报，
如何分归六趣？
And how does the karma of these six differ?
众生不知正法，以迷心修持善法，
脱离不了三界，因此往生三轻趣。
Mortals who don't understand the true dharma and blindly perform good deeds are born into the three higher destinies within the three realms.

35 由此三毒，造业轻重，受报不同，分归六处。故名六趣。

36 问："云何轻重分之为六？" 答："众生不了正因，迷心修善，未免三界，生三轻趣。"

什么是三轻趣?
And what are these three higher destinies?

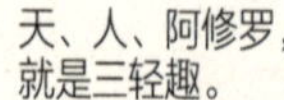
天、人、阿修罗，
就是三轻趣。
They are heaven, human and asura.

什么众生
往生天趣?
Who are born into heaven?

执迷修持十善法，妄求自我快乐，
不能脱离贪界，往生于天趣。
Those who blindly perform the ten good deeds and foolishly seek happiness are born into heaven in the realm of greed.

什么众生
往生人趣?
Who are born into human?

执迷修持五戒，
心生爱恨;
Those who blindly observe the five precepts and foolishly indulge in love and hate.

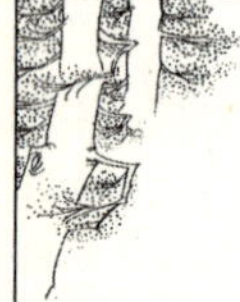

不能脱离嗔界，
往生于人趣。
are born into human in the realm of anger.

什么众生
往生阿修罗趣?
Who are born into asura?

37 问："云何三轻趣？"

38 所谓迷修十善，妄求快乐，未免贪界，生于天趣。

39 迷持五戒，妄起爱憎，未免嗔界，生于人趣。

执迷修持有为法，追求自己的福祉，
不能脱离痴界，往生阿修罗趣。
And those who blindly cling to the phenomenal world, believe in false doctrines and pray for blessings are born into asura in the realm of delusion.
这三种就是三轻趣。
而放纵三毒心，
造作各种恶者，
堕入三重趣。
These are the three higher destinies. Those who adhere stubbornly to poisoned thoughts and evil deeds are born into three lower destinies.
什么是三重趣?
And what are the three lower destinies?
恶鬼、地狱、畜生，
就是三重趣。
They are demon, animal and hell.
贪业重的人，堕入恶鬼趣。
嗔业重的人，堕入地狱趣。
痴业重的人，堕入畜生趣。
Those with the heaviest karma from greed fall into demon. Those with the heaviest karma from anger fall into hell. And those with the heaviest karma from delusion fall into animal.
!

40 迷执有为，信邪求福，未免痴界，生阿修罗趣。如是三类，名三轻趣。

41 答："所谓纵三毒心，唯造恶业，堕三重趣。"问："云何三重趣？"

42 贪业重者，堕恶鬼趣；嗔业重者，堕地狱趣；痴业重者，堕畜生趣。

这就是三重趣，
加上前面的三轻趣，
就是六趣。
These three lower destinies together with
the aforementioned three higher destinies
are collectively called the six destinies.

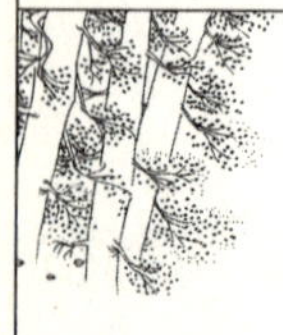

一切苦由心所生，只要能护守自己的心，
远离一切邪恶，三界六趣轮回之苦自然消灭，得到解脱。
From this you should realize that all karma, painful or otherwise,
comes from your own mind. If you can just concentrate your mind
and transcend its falsehood and evil, the suffering of the three
realms and six destinies will naturally disappear. And once free
from suffering, you reach liberation.

43 如是三重，通前三轻，遂成六趣。

44 故知一切苦业，由自心生，但能摄心，离诸邪恶，三界六趣轮回之苦，自然消灭，即得解脱。

第七问 制三毒即名解脱
Inquiry VII Liberation means to overcome the three poisons

佛陀说：
“我于三大阿僧祇劫，
经历无量的勤苦，
方成佛道。”
But the Buddha said,
“Only after undergoing innumerable hardships for three asamkhyas kalpas did I achieve enlightenment.”

为何你现在说只要观心，
降伏三毒就能得解脱？
Why do you now say that liberation can be achieved simply by beholding the mind and overcoming the three poisons?

佛陀所说的是事实。
The words of the Buddha are true.

阿僧祇劫就是三毒心，
梵语阿僧祇的意思是大到不可数。
But the three asankhya kalpas refer to the three poisoned states of mind. What we call asamkhyas in Sanskrit you call countless.

45 问：“如佛所说，我于三大阿僧祇劫，无量勤苦，方成佛道。云何今说，唯只观心，而制三毒，即名解脱？”答：“佛所说言，无虚妄也。”

46 阿僧祇劫者，即三毒心也。胡言阿僧祇，汉名不可数。

三毒心中的恶念，
多得有如恒河沙数，
每一念就是一劫，
所以称之为三大阿僧祇。
Within these three poisoned states of mind there are countless evil thoughts. And every thought lasts a kalpa. Such infinity is what the Buddha meant by the three asamkhyas kalpas.
真如本性被三毒心所覆盖，
如果不能降服三大恒河沙数
的毒恶心，怎么能解脱呢？
Once the three poisons obscure your true self and nature, how can you be liberated until you overcome those countless evil thoughts?

47 此三毒心，于中有恒沙恶念，于一一念中，皆为一劫；如是恒沙不可数也，故言三大阿僧祇。真如之性，既被三毒之所覆盖，若不超彼三大恒沙毒恶之心，云何名为解脱？

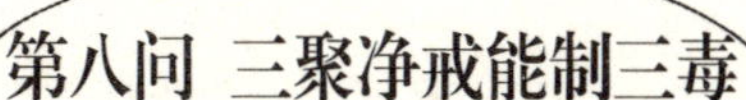
第八问 三聚净戒能制三毒
Inquiry VIII The three
sets of precepts overcome
the three poisons

如何转三毒心
为三解脱?
How to transform the three
poisons into liberation?

转贪、嗔、痴变成戒、定、慧，就是得度三大阿僧祇劫。
People who can transform greed, anger and delusion
into morality, meditation and wisdom are said to
pass through the three asamkhyas kalpas.

末世众生愚痴钝根，
不了解如来三大阿僧祇的秘密。
But people of this final age are too ignorant to
understand what the Tathagata really meant by
the three asamkhyas kalpas.

错把三大阿僧祇劫当成佛陀的世间劫数，
这种说法岂不是误人修行，退转菩提道吗?
They say enlightenment is only achieved after endless kalpas
and thereby mislead disciples to retreat onto the Bodhi Path.

48 今若能转贪嗔痴等三毒心。为三解脱，是则名为得度三大阿僧祇劫。

49 末世众生愚痴钝根，不解如来三大阿僧祇秘密之说，遂言成佛尘劫，斯岂不疑误行人退菩提道?

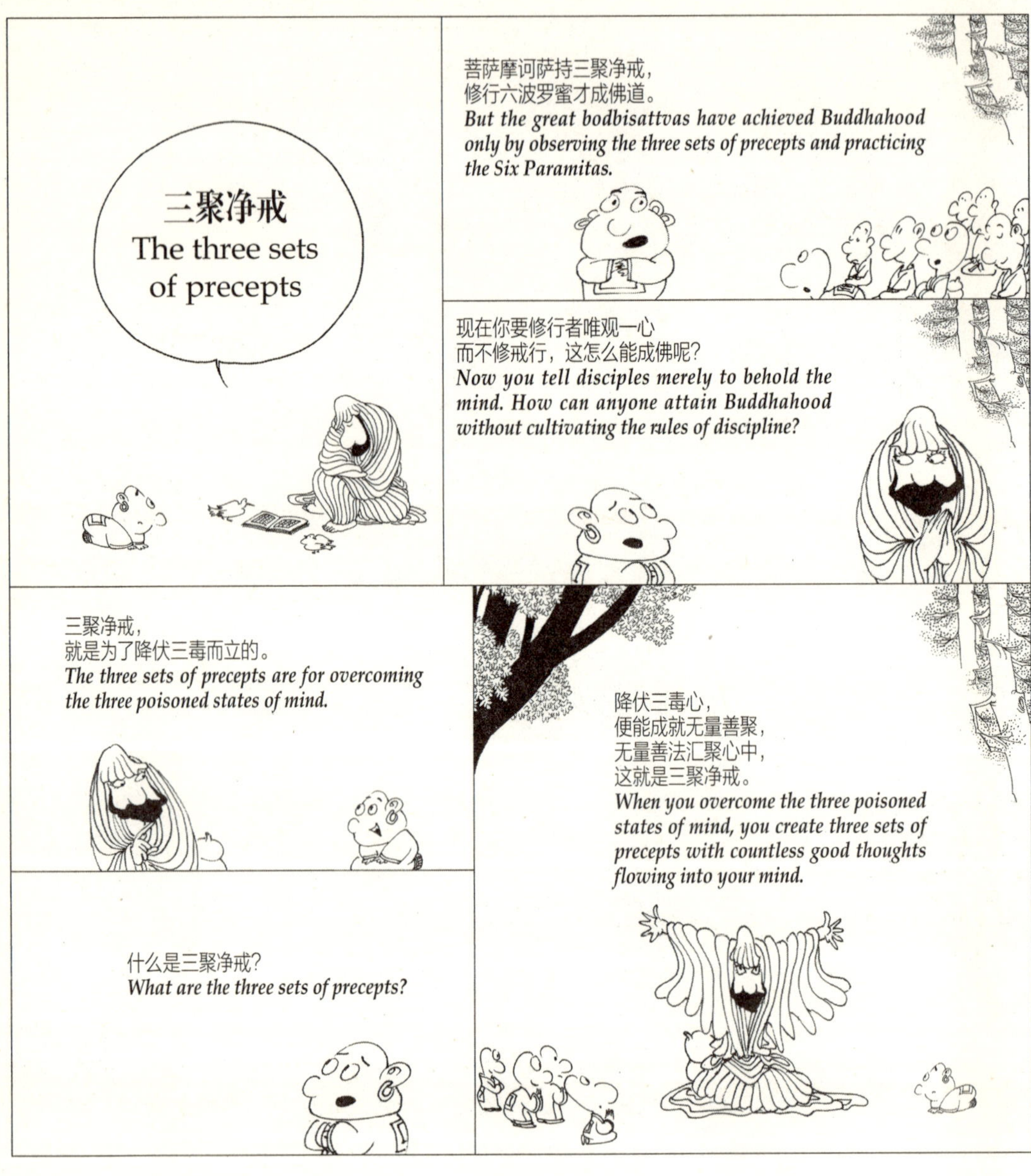
三聚净戒
The three sets of precepts
菩萨摩诃萨持三聚净戒，
修行六波罗蜜才成佛道。
But the great bodbisattvas have achieved Buddhahood only by observing the three sets of precepts and practicing the Six Paramitas.
现在你要修行者唯观一心
而不修戒行，这怎么能成佛呢？
Now you tell disciples merely to behold the mind. How can anyone attain Buddhahood without cultivating the rules of discipline?
什么是三聚净戒？
What are the three sets of precepts?
三聚净戒，
就是为了降伏三毒而立的。
The three sets of precepts are for overcoming the three poisoned states of mind.
降伏三毒心，
便能成就无量善聚，
无量善法汇聚心中，
这就是三聚净戒。
When you overcome the three poisoned states of mind, you create three sets of precepts with countless good thoughts flowing into your mind.

50 问："菩萨摩诃萨由持三聚净戒，行六波罗蜜，方成佛道；今令学者唯只观心，不修戒行，云何成佛？"答："三聚净戒者，即制三毒心也。"

51 制三毒，成无量善聚。无量善法普会于心，故名三聚净戒。

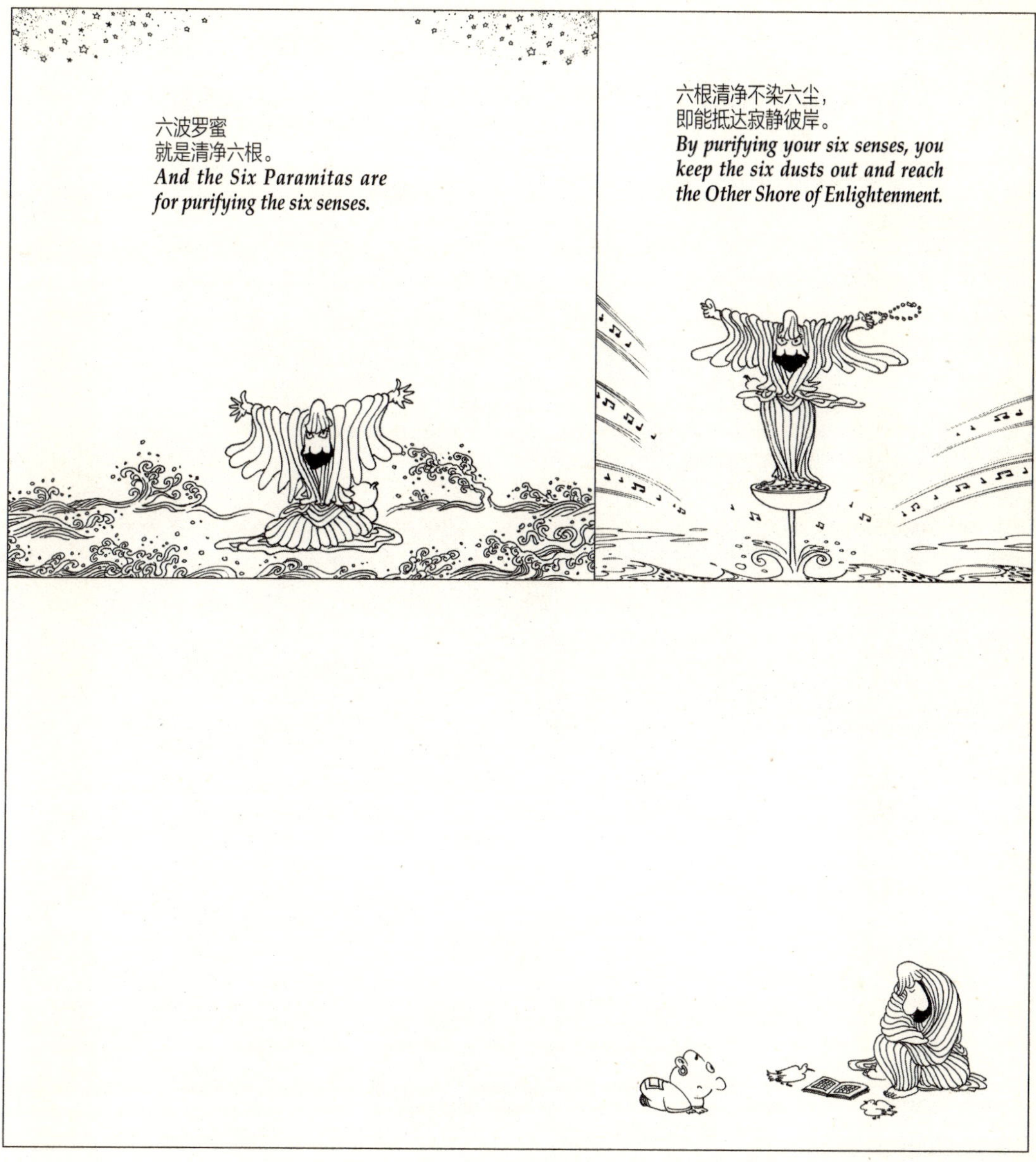
六波罗蜜
就是清净六根。
And the Six Paramitas are
for purifying the six senses.
六根清净不染六尘，
即能抵达寂静彼岸。
By purifying your six senses, you
keep the six dusts out and reach
the Other Shore of Enlightenment.

52 六波罗蜜者，即净六根也。

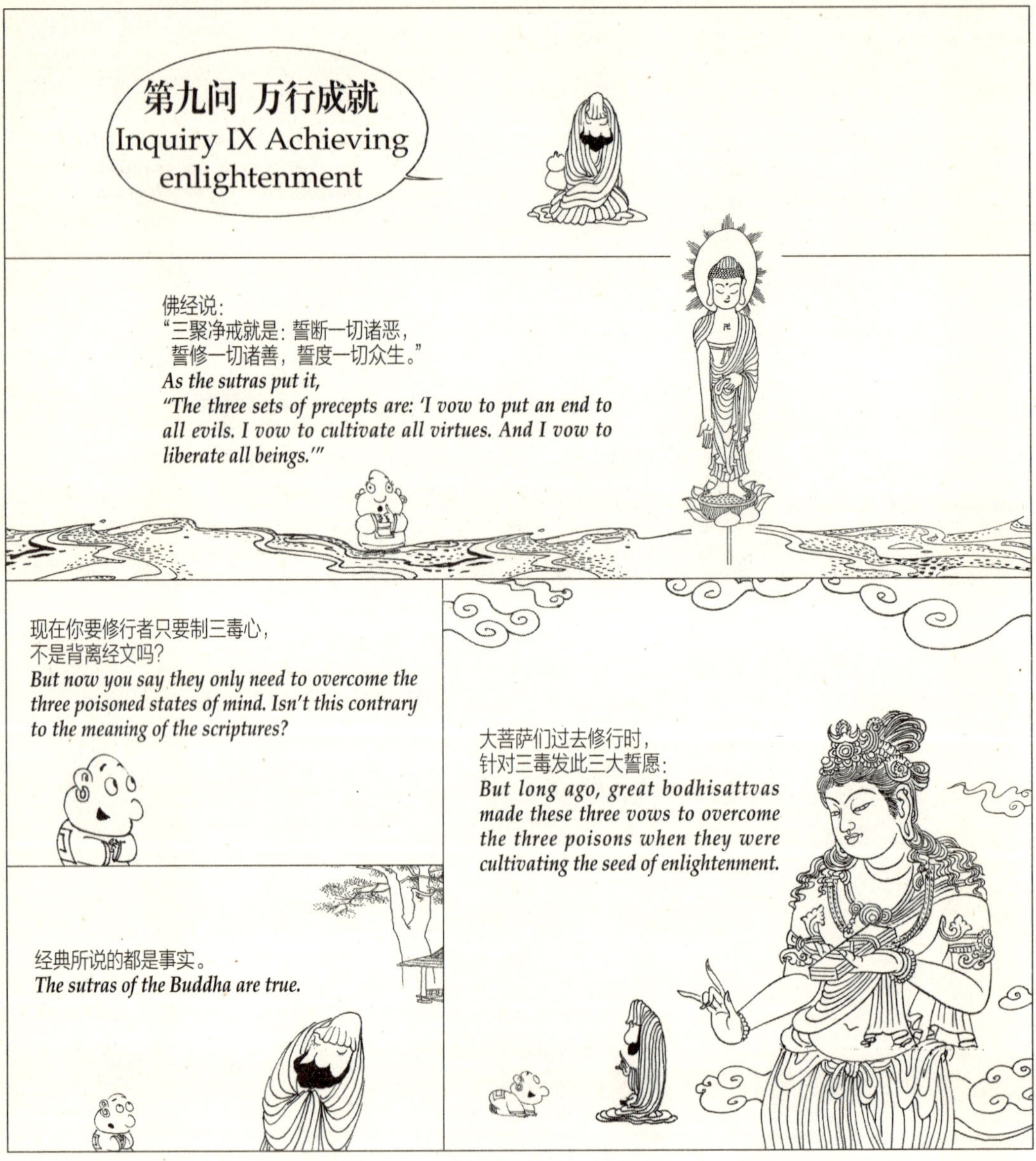

第九问　万行成就
Inquiry IX Achieving enlightenment
佛经说：
“三聚净戒就是：誓断一切诸恶，誓修一切诸善，誓度一切众生。”
As the sutras put it,
“The three sets of precepts are: ‘I vow to put an end to all evils. I vow to cultivate all virtues. And I vow to liberate all beings.’”
现在你要修行者只要制三毒心，不是背离经文吗？
But now you say they only need to overcome the three poisoned states of mind. Isn't this contrary to the meaning of the scriptures?
经典所说的都是事实。
The sutras of the Buddha are true.
大菩萨们过去修行时，针对三毒发此三大誓愿：
But long ago, great bodhisattvas made these three vows to overcome the three poisons when they were cultivating the seed of enlightenment.

53 问：“如经所说；三聚净戒者，誓断一切恶，誓修一切善，誓度一切众生。今者唯言制三毒心，岂不文义有乖也？”答：“佛所说经，是真实语。”

54 菩萨摩诃萨，于过去因中修行时，为对三毒，发三誓愿。

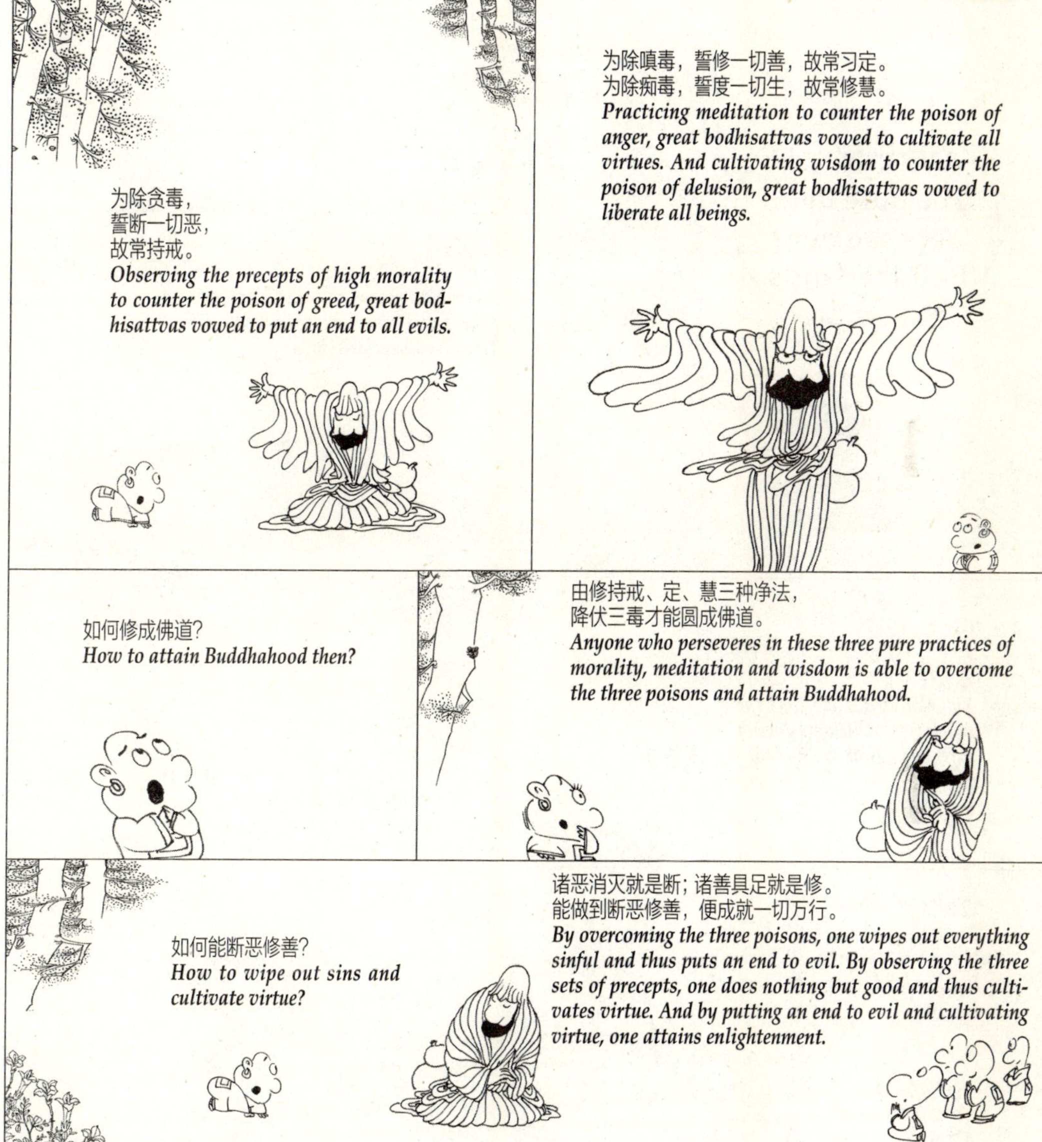
为除贪毒，
誓断一切恶，
故常持戒。
Observing the precepts of high morality to counter the poison of greed, great bodhisattvas vowed to put an end to all evils.
为除嗔毒，誓修一切善，故常习定。
为除痴毒，誓度一切生，故常修慧。
Practicing meditation to counter the poison of anger, great bodhisattvas vowed to cultivate all virtues. And cultivating wisdom to counter the poison of delusion, great bodhisattvas vowed to liberate all beings.
如何修成佛道?
How to attain Buddhahood then?
由修持戒、定、慧三种净法，
降伏三毒才能圆成佛道。
Anyone who perseveres in these three pure practices of morality, meditation and wisdom is able to overcome the three poisons and attain Buddhahood.
如何能断恶修善?
How to wipe out sins and cultivate virtue?
诸恶消灭就是断；诸善具足就是修。
能做到断恶修善，便成就一切万行。
By overcoming the three poisons, one wipes out everything sinful and thus puts an end to evil. By observing the three sets of precepts, one does nothing but good and thus cultivates virtue. And by putting an end to evil and cultivating virtue, one attains enlightenment.

55 誓断一切恶。故常持戒，对于贪毒；誓修一切善，故常习定，对于嗔毒；誓度一切众生，故常修慧，对于痴毒。

56 由持如是戒定慧等三种净法故，能超彼三毒成佛道也。

57 诸恶消灭，名之为断；诸善具足，名之为修；以能断恶修善，则万行成就。

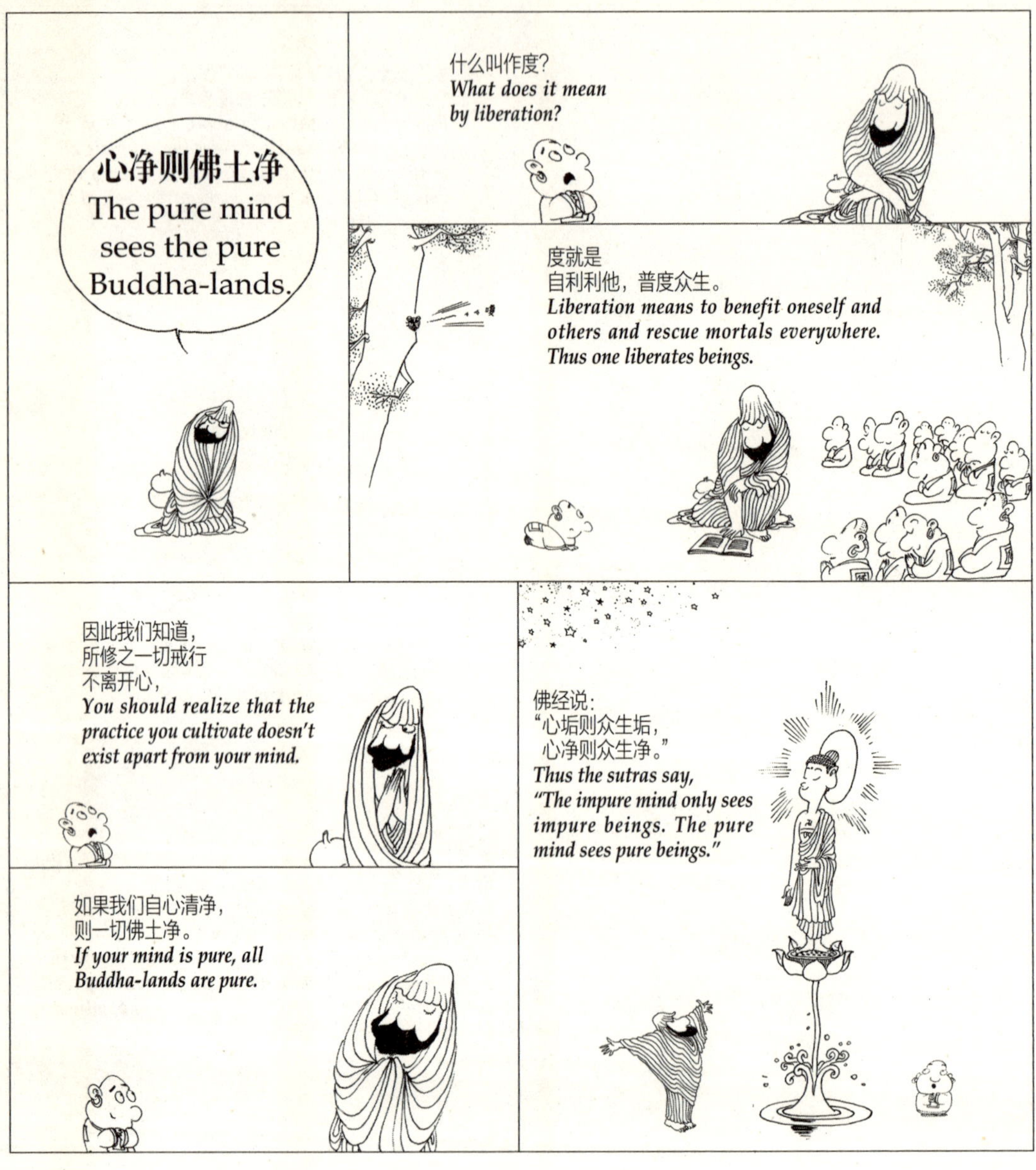
心净则佛土净
The pure mind sees the pure Buddha-lands.
什么叫作度?
What does it mean by liberation?
度就是
自利利他，普度众生。
Liberation means to benefit oneself and others and rescue mortals everywhere. Thus one liberates beings.
因此我们知道，
所修之一切戒行
不离开心，
You should realize that the practice you cultivate doesn't exist apart from your mind.
如果我们自心清净，
则一切佛土净。
If your mind is pure, all Buddha-lands are pure.
佛经说：
"心垢则众生垢，
心净则众生净。"
Thus the sutras say,
"The impure mind only sees impure beings. The pure mind sees pure beings."

58 自他俱利，普济群生，名之为度。

59 故知所修戒行不离于心，若自心清净，则一切佛土皆悉清净。

60 故经云："心垢则众生垢，心净则众生净。"

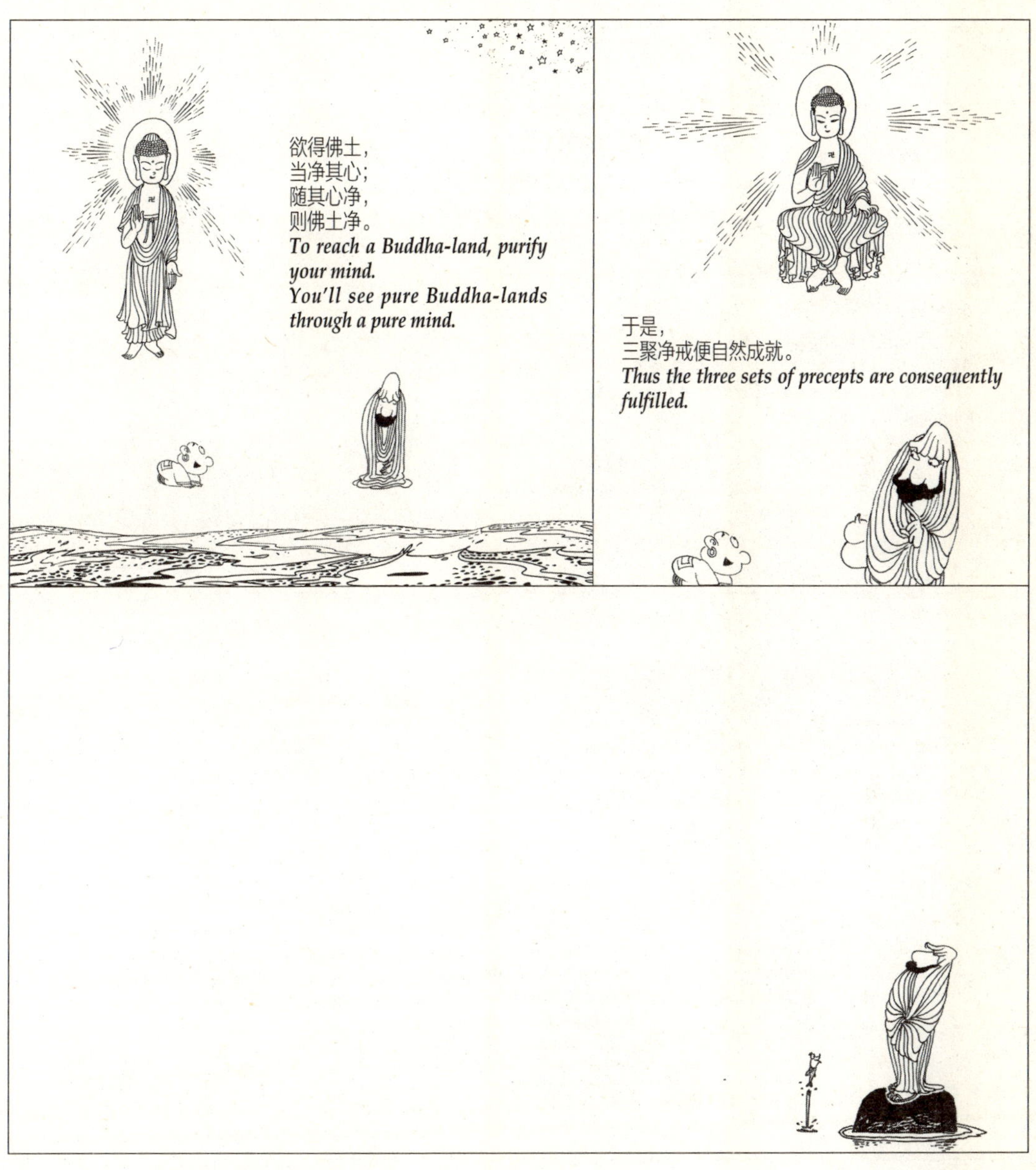
欲得佛土，
当净其心；
随其心净，
则佛土净。
To reach a Buddha-land, purify your mind.
You'll see pure Buddha-lands through a pure mind.
于是，
三聚净戒便自然成就。
Thus the three sets of precepts are consequently fulfilled.

61 欲得佛土，当净其心；随其心净，则佛土净。三聚净戒，自然成就。

第十问 以六度净六根
Inquiry X Purifying your six senses with the Six Ferries
佛经说：
“六波罗蜜也称为六度。”
As the sutras put it,
“The Six Paramitas are alternatively known as the Six Ferries.”
布施
持戒
忍辱
精进
禅定
智慧
现在你说六根清净就是六波罗蜜，
Now you say the Six Paramitas refer to the purification of the six senses.
这又怎么解释？
What do you mean by this?
想要修行六度，必须先清净六根、降伏六贼。
To cultivate the Six Paramitas, you've first of all to purify your six senses and tame the Six Thieves.

62 问曰：“如经所说，六波罗蜜者，亦名六度。所谓布施、持戒、忍辱、精进、禅定、智慧。今言六根清净，名波罗蜜者，何为通会？”答：“欲修六度，当净六根，降六贼。”

六度的真义是什么？
And why are they called the Six Ferries?
六度就是运载，
六波罗蜜喻若船筏。
The Six Paramitas are transports.
能运众生抵达寂静彼岸，
故名六度。
Like boats or rafts, they transport all the living beings to the Other Shore of Perfect Wisdom. Hence they're called the Six Ferries.
什么是布施？
What does charity mean?
舍离眼贼，
舍离一切色境，
名为布施。
Casting out the delusion from eyes by abandoning the visual world is charity.
什么是持戒？
What does morality mean?
禁制耳贼，
声尘不令放逸，
名为持戒。
Keeping out the delusion from ears by not listening to sound is morality.

63 又六度者，其义如何？六度者运也。六波罗蜜喻若船筏，能运众生，达于彼岸，故名六度。

64 能舍眼贼，离诸色境，名为布施。

65 能禁耳贼，于彼声尘，不令纵逸，名为持戒。

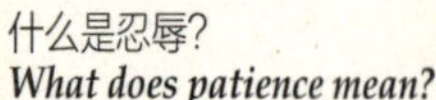

什么是忍辱?
What does patience mean?

降伏鼻贼，香臭平等自在，
调和柔顺，名为忍辱。
Humbling the delusion from the nose by
equating smells as neutral is patience.

什么是精进?
What does devotion mean?
制约舌贼，一切诸味无贪，
赞叹颂咏，名为精进。
Controlling the delusion from the tongue by
conquering desires to taste, praise or explain is
devotion.

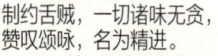

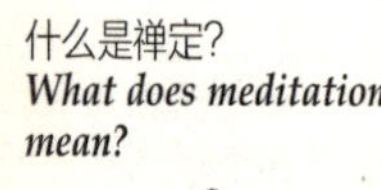

什么是禅定?
What does meditation
mean?

降伏身贼，一切所触之欲，
湛然不动，名为禅定。
Quelling the delusion from the body by
remaining unmoved by tactile sensations
is meditation.

66 能伏鼻贼，等诸香臭，自在调柔，名为忍辱。
67 能制舌贼，不贪诸味，赞咏讲说，名为精进。
68 能降身贼，于诸触欲，湛然不动，名为禅定。

什么是智慧?
What does wisdom mean?
调御意贼，不随顺于无明，
常修觉慧，名为智慧。
Taming the delusion from the mind by
not yielding to ignorance but exploring
the potential of awareness is wisdom.
达摩说:
“修行佛道众生，如果能确实做到布施、
持戒、忍辱、精进、禅定、智慧六波罗蜜，
不假时日便能抵达寂静彼岸。”
Bodhidharma said,
“Those who practice Buddharma may reach the Other Shore of Perfect
Wisdom over time, once they could truly practice the Six Paramitas of
charity, morality, patience, devotion, meditation and wisdom.”

69 能调意贼，不顺无明，常修觉慧，名为智慧。

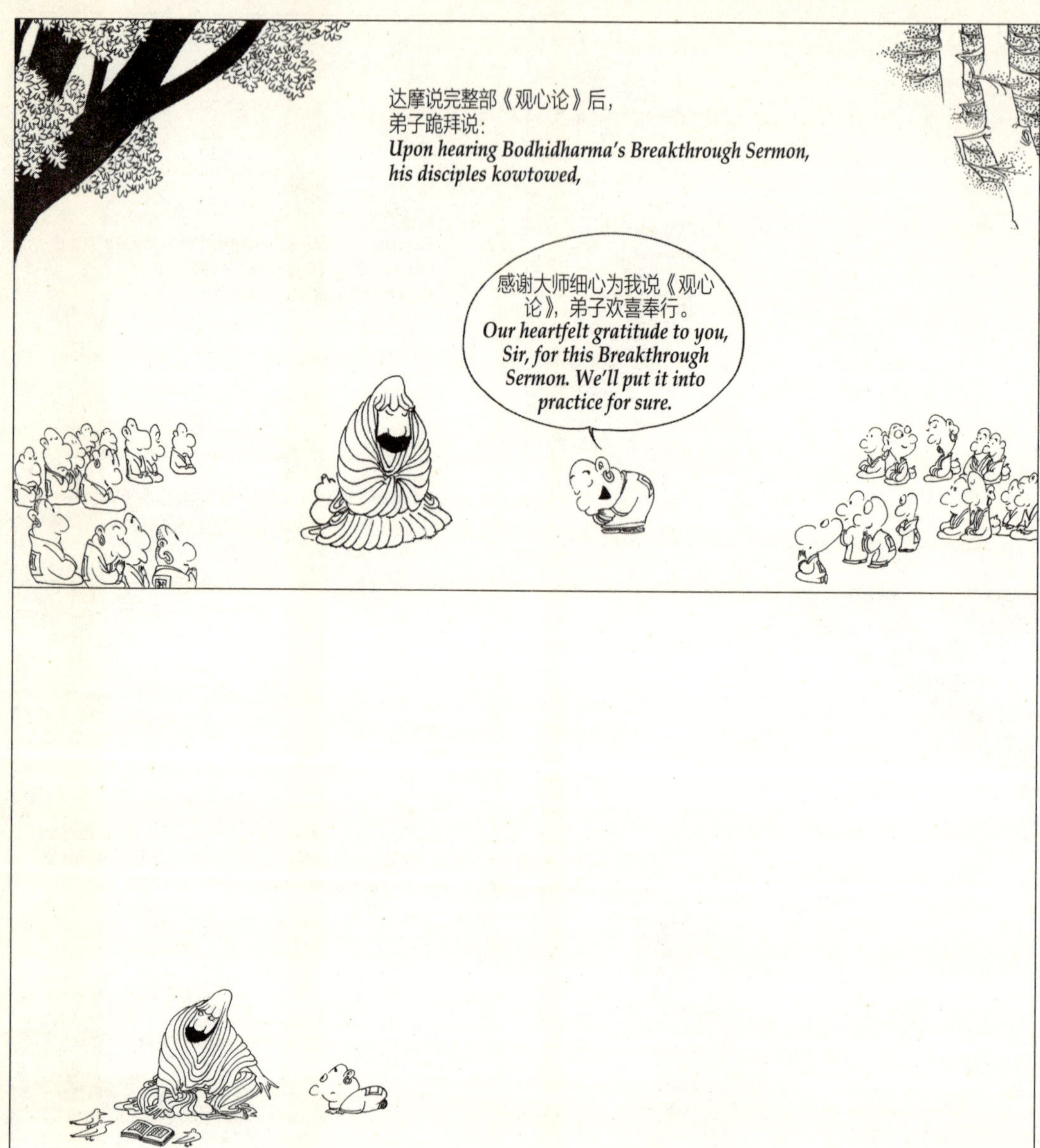
达摩说完整部《观心论》后，
弟子跪拜说：
Upon hearing Bodhidharma's Breakthrough Sermon, his disciples kowtowed,
感谢大师细心为我说《观心论》，弟子欢喜奉行。
Our heartfelt gratitude to you, Sir, for this Breakthrough Sermon. We'll put it into practice for sure.

达摩破相论

Formality Refuting Sermon

前　言
Prologue

《破相论》与《二入四行论》、《悟性论》、《血脉论》合称《达摩四论》，而《达摩四论》加上《心经颂》、《安心法门》合为少室六门集。

《破相论》一共有四问，与天台智者大师的《观心论》三十六问的最后四问，无论标题和内容几乎完全相同，两篇经的文字数也差不多。智者大师（538—597）活跃的年代与达摩相去不远，此书内容到底是谁引用谁？则留待后世学者们去研究分解。

Formality Refuting Sermon, Two Entrances and Four Practices, Wake-up Sermon and Bloodstream Sermon are collectively known as Bodhidharma's Four Sermons. These four plus Heart Sutra and Dharma Teaching of Pacifying the Mind are together called the Six Works of Shaoshi. The four inquries of Formality Refuting Sermon are almost identical to the last four of the 36 inquiries in Sramana Zhiyi's Introspection Sermon in both titles and content. The two parts are roughly the same even in the number of characters. Sramana Zhiyi (538-597) of the Tiantai Sect was active in a period roughly the same as Bodhidharma was. Then it remains for further study and analysis which of the two was the original one.

第一问
观心得解脱
Inquiry I Liberation from beholding the mind
佛经
弟子问达摩：
“佛经说释迦牟尼如来，身为菩萨时，曾食用三斗六升乳糜，方成佛道。”
A disciple asked,
“According to the sutras, when Sakyamuni was still a bodhisattva, he consumed three bowls of milk and six ladles of gruel prior to attaining Buddhahood.”
达摩回答：
“佛经所言，确实没错。”
Bodhidharma answered,
“What you read in the sutras is absolutely true.”
佛陀的确是喝牛奶之后，才开悟成佛。
That is how the Buddha attained enlightenment. He had to drink milk before he could attain Buddhahood.
但牛奶有两种，佛陀所喝的不是世间不净之乳，而是真如清净法乳。
But there are two kinds of milk. That which Sakyamuni drank wasn't the ordinary impure milk, but Pure Dharma-milk.
!

1 问：“经云‘释迦如来，为菩萨时，曾饮三斗六升乳糜，方成佛道’。先因饮乳，后证佛果，岂唯观心得解脱乎？”答：“诚如所言，无虚妄也。”

2 必因食乳，然始成佛。言食乳者，有二种，佛所食者，非是世间不净之乳，乃是真如清净法乳也。

三斗六升乳糜
指的是什么?
What are the three bowls of
milk and six ladles of gruel?
三斗指三聚净戒,
六升指六波罗蜜。
The three bowls were the three
sets of precepts. And the six
ladles were the Six Paramitas.
要先行三聚净戒
和六波罗蜜之后,
才能开悟成佛。
When Sakyamuni attained enlightenment and Buddhahood, it was because
he had drunk this Pure Dharma-milk.
如果说佛陀所喝的是
世间和合不净牛的膻腥之乳,
那岂不是在谤佛吗?
To say that the Buddha drank the
worldly concoction of impure and
smelly cow's milk is a sort of slander.
真如者,已经是金刚
不坏的无漏法身,
永离世间一切诸苦。
难道还需世间不净
之乳来充饥解渴吗?
The Buddha has an indestructible body and remains
forever free of the worldly afflictions.
Why would he need impure milk to satisfy his hunger
or thirst?

3　三斗者,三聚净戒;六升者,六波罗蜜。

4　成佛道时,由食如是清净法乳,方证佛果。

5　若言如来食于世间和合不净之牛膻腥乳,岂不谤误之甚乎?

6　真如者,自是金刚不坏,无漏法身,永离世间一切诸苦;岂须如是不净之乳,以充饥渴。

真如是什么
What is the ultimate truth?
宇宙万物的真实本质，即是真如。
The true nature of the universe is the ultimate truth.
什么是真如?
What is the ultimate truth?
开悟的佛陀已悟得真如法性，所以也称真如。
The enlightened Buddhas are also called this way, as they have attained the ultimate truth.
!
佛经所说的牛，指的是什么?
What is the cow talked about in the sutras?
并不是指生活于高原或湿地的世间之牛。
This cow lives neither in the highlands nor the lowlands.

7 如经所说，其牛不在高原，不在下湿，不食谷麦糠麸，不与特牛同群。

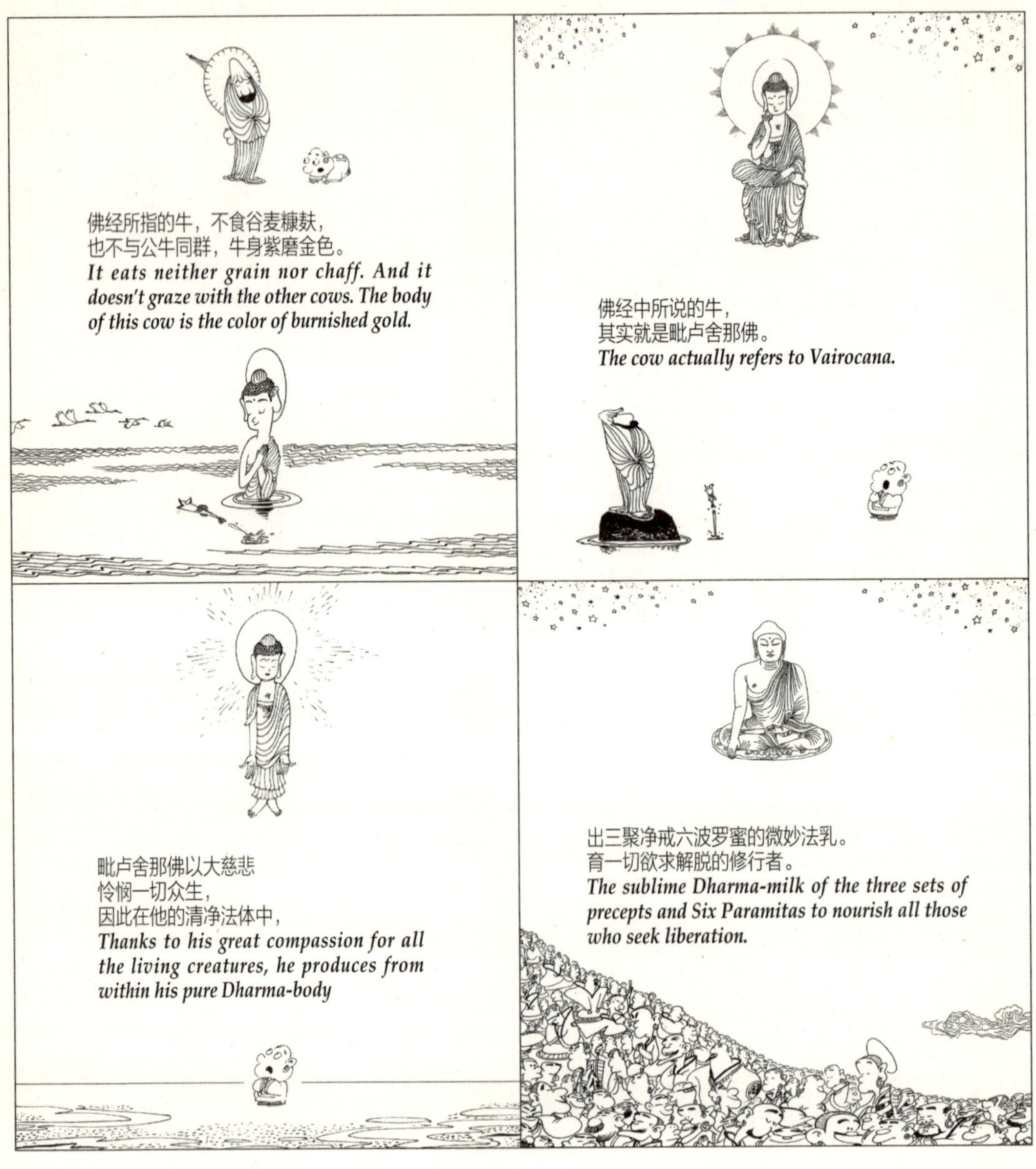
佛经所指的牛，不食谷麦糠麸，
也不与公牛同群，牛身紫磨金色。
It eats neither grain nor chaff. And it doesn't graze with the other cows. The body of this cow is the color of burnished gold.
佛经中所说的牛，
其实就是毗卢舍那佛。
The cow actually refers to Vairocana.
毗卢舍那佛以大慈悲
怜悯一切众生，
因此在他的清净法体中，
Thanks to his great compassion for all the living creatures, he produces from within his pure Dharma-body
出三聚净戒六波罗蜜的微妙法乳。
育一切欲求解脱的修行者。
The sublime Dharma-milk of the three sets of precepts and Six Paramitas to nourish all those who seek liberation.

8　其牛身作紫磨金色。

9　言牛者，毗卢舍那佛也。以大慈悲，怜愍一切，故于清净法体中，出如是三聚净戒、六波罗蜜微妙法乳，育一切求解脱者。

光明遍照
The omni-
present light
什么是毗卢舍那佛?
What is Vairocana?
毗卢舍那佛是
佛陀的法身,
Vairocana is the truth
body of the Buddha.
是光明遍照的意思 。
He embodies the omnipresent light.
毗卢舍那佛的微妙法乳,
是清净牛的清净乳,
不但佛陀喝了能成道,
The pure milk of such a truly pure cow
not only enabled "the Buddha to achieve
Buddhahood".
一切众生如果喝了微妙法乳,
也一样能得阿耨多罗三藐三菩提。
It also enables any living creature that drinks it
to attain unexcelled and complete enlightenment.

10 如是真净之牛，清净之乳，非但如来饮之成道，一切众生若能饮者，皆得阿耨多罗三藐三菩提。

第二问
假有为喻无为
Inquiry II Doing nothing remains the right way

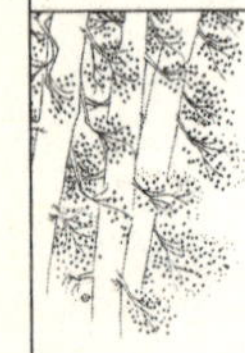

佛经说："佛令众生修造伽蓝，
铸写形像，烧香、散花、燃长明灯。"
As the sutras put it,"The Buddha asks mortals they can achieve enlightenment by performing such meritorious works as building monasteries, casting statues, burning incense, scattering flowers and lighting ever-burning lamps,

"昼夜六时，绕塔经行，
持斋礼拜，种种功德皆能圆成佛道。"
Purifying the six senses all the time, walking around pagodas, observing vegetarian fast and worshipping Buddha."

佛陀说经有无量方便，
以一切众生钝根狭劣，
The sutras of the Buddha contain countless metaphors. However, mortals have shallow minds.

不能领悟深义，所以假借
有为法来隐喻无为法。
They don't grasp the essence of the Buddharma. Therefore, the Buddha has to use the tangible to represent the sublime.

11 问："经中所说'佛令众生修造伽蓝，铸写形像，烧香、散花、燃灯、昼夜六时，绕塔行道，持斋礼拜，种种功德皆成佛道。'"

12 答："佛所说经，有无量方便，以一切众生钝根狭劣，不悟甚深之义，所以假有为，喻无为。"

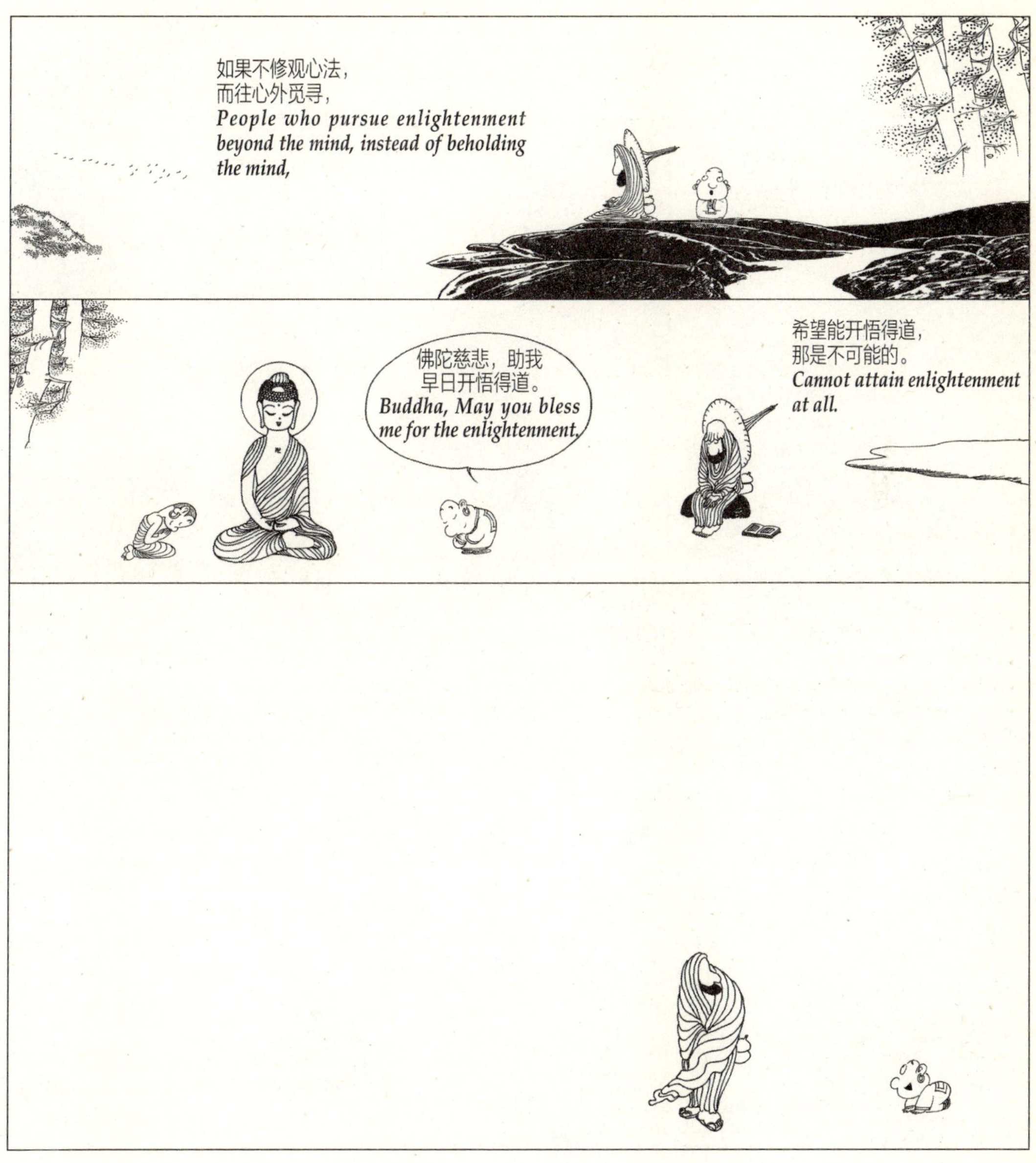
如果不修观心法，
而往心外觅寻，
People who pursue enlightenment beyond the mind, instead of beholding the mind,
佛陀慈悲，助我早日开悟得道。
Buddha, May you bless me for the enlightenment.
希望能开悟得道，
那是不可能的。
Cannot attain enlightenment at all.

13 若复不修内行，唯只外求，希望获福，无有是处。

常净六根
With the six senses purified
佛经所说的伽蓝，
隐喻什么？
What does a monastery truly mean?
伽蓝是梵文，
中文就是清净之地。
What you call a monastery, we call a sangbarama, a place of purity.
伽蓝也是佛寺的守护神，
负责保卫寺院。
The term also refers to the guardian gods of a monastery.
如果能舍除三毒，
清净六根，
身心湛然，内外清净，
就是修伽蓝。
Whoever denies entry to the three poisons and keeps his six senses pure, his body untained and his mind resting on the inner peace, builds a monastery.

14 言伽蓝者：西国梵语，此土翻为清净地也。

15 若永除三毒，常净六根，身心湛然，内外清净，是名修伽蓝。

铸写佛陀形像，
隐喻什么？
What does casting statues truly mean?
如来真容妙相，岂是金铜造像或笔墨所能描绘出来的呢？
The Buddha's sublime form can't be represented by metal statues or illustrated on paper.
铸写佛陀形像，
隐喻修行众生应遵循
佛陀求道之路觉行。
Casting statues refers to all practices cultivated by those who seek enlightenment.
求解脱的修行者，应以身为炉，
以法为火，以智慧为巧匠，
以三聚净戒、六波罗蜜为模。
Those who seek enlightenment should take their bodies as the furnace, the Dharma as the fire, wisdom as the craftsmanship, and the three sets of precepts and Six Paramitas as the mold.
熔炼身中真如佛性，入一切戒律之模具中，依教奉行一无漏缺，自然能成就真容之像。
They smelt and refine the true Buddha-nature within themselves and pour it into the mold formed by the rules of discipline. Acting in perfect accordance with the Buddha's teaching, they naturally create a perfect likeness.

16 铸写形像者：即是一切众生求佛道也；所为修诸觉行，仿像如来真容妙相，岂是铸写金铜之所作乎？

17 是故求解脱者，以身为炉，以法为火，以智慧为巧匠，三聚净戒、六波罗蜜以为模样；熔炼身中真如佛性，遍入一切戒律模中，如教奉行，一无漏缺，自然成就真容之像。

究竟常住微妙色身，
不是有为败坏之法。
The eternal, sublime body isn't subject
to conditions or decay.
如果修行者不了解铸造
描绘如来真容的真实隐喻，
凭什么会有功德呢？
Those who don't understand the
true meaning of this term cannot
create or be rewarded with merits.
烧香隐喻什么？
What does burning incense
truly mean?
烧香并不是烧世间有相之香，
而是烧无为正法之香。
The incense doesn't refer to the
material incense, but the intangible
incense of the Dharma.
正法之香能熏除所有的臭秽，
令无明恶业全部消灭。
It drives away filth, ignorance
and evil deeds with its perfume.

18 所谓究竟常住微妙色身，非是有为败坏之法。若人求道，不解如是铸写真容，凭何辄言功德？

19 又烧香者：亦非世间有相之香，乃是无为正法之香也；熏诸臭秽、无明、恶业，悉令消灭。

正法之香，
共有五种：
一者戒香：
能断诸恶，
能修诸善。
There are five kinds of such Dharma-incense. The first is the incense of morality, which eliminates evils and cultivates virtue.
二者定香：
深信大乘，
心无退转。
The second is the incense of meditation, which means the deep faith in the Mahayana with unwavering resolve.
三者慧香：
常于身心之内，
自在观察。
The third is the incense of wisdom, which refers to introspection, inside and out.
四者解脱香：
能断一切
无明结缚。
The fourth is the incense of liberation, which severs the bonds of ignorance.

20　正法香者，其有五种：一者戒香，所谓能断诸恶，能修诸善；二者定香，所谓深信大乘，心无退转；三者慧香，所谓常于身心，内自观察；四者解脱香，所谓能断一切无明结缚。

五者解脱知见香：
能观照常明，
通达无碍。
The fifth is the incense of perfect knowledge,
which means being always aware and nowhere obstructed.
这五种香是
最上之香，
世间无物能
与之相比。
These five are the most precious kinds of incense and far superior to anything the world has to offer.
佛陀在世时，令弟子们以智慧火
燃烧这五种宝香供养十方诸佛。
When the Buddha was in the world, he told his disciples to light these five kinds of precious incense with the fire of wisdom as an offering to the Buddhas of the ten directions.
现今众生，不了解佛陀真实本义，
以世俗之香敬佛。
But people today don't understand the Buddha's real meaning. They pay homage to the Buddha by offering him the worldly incense.

21 五者解脱知见香，所谓观照常明，通达无碍。

22 如是五种香，名为最上之香，世间无比。佛在世日，令诸弟子，以智慧火，烧如是无价珍香，供养十方诸佛。今时众生不解如来真实之义，唯将外火。

烧香敬佛可以
得福报吗?
Can anyone win the blessing from the Buddha by burning incense?
燃烧世间沉香、檀香,
是障碍之香,
They use an ordinary flame to light the worldly material incense of eaglewood or sandalwood that is the incense of sin.
希望由此获得福报,
会有可能吗?
In the meantime, they pray for some future blessing that never comes.

23 烧世间沉檀熏陆、质碍之香，希望福报，云何可得乎？

散花功德
Scattering flowers
散花的意思
也是这样吗?
Does it hold true for scattering flowers?
散花，就是演说
佛陀所说的正法。
Scattering flowres refers to elaborating on the Dharma
散佛法功德花，
助有情众生修行，
散真如性花，普施庄严。
And scattering flowers of virtue, in order to benefit others and glorify the true self.
此功德花是佛所赞叹的，
此花永远常住，永不凋谢。
These flowers of virtue are those praised by the Buddha. They last forever and never fade.

24 又散花者，义亦如是。所谓演说正法。

25 诸功德花，饶益有情，散沾一切；于真如性，普施庄严。此功德花，佛所赞叹，究竟常住，无凋落期。

如果有人能散此功德花，
所得福报无以计量。
And whoever scatters such flowers
reaps infinite blessings.
如果说佛陀令众生
摘集美丽的花朵散花，
You're terribly wrong to think that
the Buddha meant for people to harm
plants by cutting off their flowers.
这种损害花草的行为，
不可能是佛陀的本意。
How could the Buddha encourage
people to commit such a thing as
to harm flowers?
为什么呢？
Why?
持净戒的修行者，
无害于天地森罗万象。
Those who observe the precepts don't
injure any of the myriad life forms in
heaven or on earth.

26 若复有人，散如是花，获福无量。

27 若言如来令众生，剪截缯彩，伤损草木，以为散花，无有是处。

28 问："所以者何？"持净戒者，于诸天地，森罗万象。

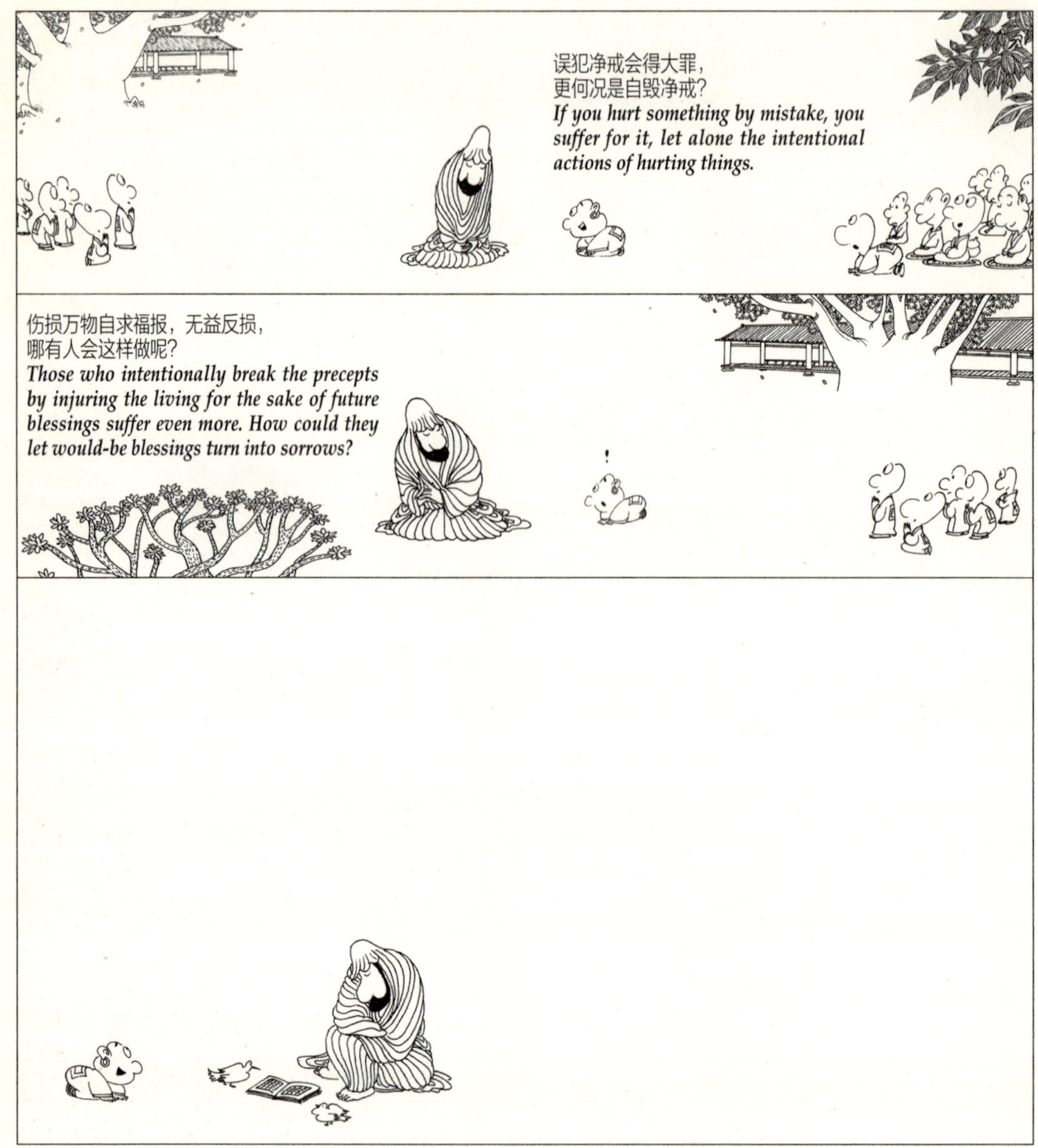
误犯净戒会得大罪，
更何况是自毁净戒？
If you hurt something by mistake, you suffer for it, let alone the intentional actions of hurting things.
伤损万物自求福报，无益反损，
哪有人会这样做呢？
Those who intentionally break the precepts by injuring the living for the sake of future blessings suffer even more. How could they let would-be blessings turn into sorrows?
!

29 不令触犯，伤损万物求于福报，欲益反损，岂有是乎？

一灯燃百千灯
One lamp to light many others
长明灯隐喻什么？
What does the ever-burning lamp mean?
长明灯就是正觉心！
修行者点燃内心
的黎明比喻为灯。
The ever-burning lamp represents the awakened heart. Practitioners illuminates the dawn before enlightenment of their mind.
因此一切求解脱的修行者，以身为灯台，以心为灯炷，
Those who seek liberation see their body as the lamp, their mind as its wick,
一切戒行为添灯油，
以智慧比喻灯火。
The precepts as its oil and the power of wisdom as its flame.

30 又长明灯者：即正觉心也，觉之明了，喻之为灯。

31 是故一切求解脱者，身为灯台，心为灯炷，增诸戒行，以为添油；智慧明达，喻如灯火。

常燃这个真正的觉悟灯，
能照亮一切无明痴暗。
By lighting this lamp of perfect awareness, they dispel all ignorance and delusion.
能以此法轮转相开示，
以一盏灯点燃百千灯，
灯灯无尽，因此称之为长明灯。
And by passing this Dharma on to others, they're able to use one lamp to light thousands of lamps. And because these lamps likewise light countless other lamps, their light lasts forever, thus the name the ever-burning lamp.
过去有佛名为燃灯，就是这个意思。
Long ago, there was a Buddha named Dipamkara, or literally the Lamplighter. This was the meaning of his name.
愚痴众生，不能体会如来方便之说，依虚妄为行执着有为法，
But the deluded don't understand the metaphors of the Buddha. Instead, they persist in delusions and cling to the tangible.
点燃世间酥油灯，以照亮空室，
宣称这是依教而行，岂不荒谬？
They light butter lamps only to illuminate empty rooms, claiming that they're following the Buddha's instructions. How foolish and absurd they are!

32　常燃如是真正觉灯，照破一切无明痴暗，能以此法，转相开示，即是一灯燃百千灯，灯灯无尽，故号长明。

33　过去有佛，名曰燃灯，义亦如是。愚痴众生，不会如来方便之说，专行虚妄，执着有为，遂燃世间酥油之灯，以照空室，乃称依教，岂不谬乎！

为什么呢?
Why?
佛陀眉间白毫一毫放光，能照亮一万八千世界，
The light glitters from one curl between the Buddha's brows can illuminate countless worlds.
这岂是酥油灯能做到?稍作思考就知道不可能。
A butter lamp is no match. Or do you think otherwise?
什么是六时行道?
What does purifying the six senses all the time mean?
守护六根，时时刻刻常行佛道。
It tells to guard your six sense organs from outside delusions and put the Buddharma into practice all the time.
修一切觉悟行，调伏六根长时不舍，就是六时行道。
Never lose control over the six senses is what it means.
绕塔经行，隐喻什么?
What does walking around pagodas mean?

34 问:“所以者何?”佛放眉间一毫相光，上能照万八千世界，岂假如是酥油之灯，以为利益?审察斯理，应不然乎!

35 又六时行道者:所谓六根之中，于一切时，常行佛道，修诸觉行，调伏六根，长时不舍，名为六时行道。

塔，隐喻
修行者的身。
A pagoda is your
body and mind.
过去的觉悟者们都是
修行此道，直到涅槃。
The enlightened in the past followed
this path to nirvana.
应该让觉慧巡绕于身心，
心中念念不停，就称为绕塔。
When your awareness circles your
body and mind without stopping, this
is called walking around a pagoda.
当今世人不会此理，
不向内观心，却往外追寻，
而对身心造成障碍。
But people today don't understand
what this means. Instead of looking
inside, they insist on pursuing outside.
This brings them nothing but delusions.
绕世间塔经行，日夜疾走，
徒劳无功，对于真性一点利益也无。
They have their physical bodies to walk around
physical pagodas. And they keep at it day and night,
wearing themselves out in vain and coming no closer
to their true self.

36 绕塔行道者：塔是身心也。

37 当令觉慧巡绕身心，念念不停，名为绕塔。过去诸圣，皆行此道，得至涅槃。

38 今时世人，不会此理，曾不内行，唯执外求，将质碍身。绕世间塔，日夜走骤，徒自疲劳，而于真性，一无利益。

持斋者必须体会
佛陀的真意，
The same holds true for observing a fast.
如果不能理解，
持斋只是徒劳无功。
It's useless unless you understand what this really means.
持斋的真意
是什么？
What does observing a fast mean?
持就是护，
就是于诸戒行，
如法护持。
And to observe means to uphold, to uphold the rules of discipline according to the Dharma.
斋就是齐，
就是齐正身心，
不令散乱。
Fast means to regulate, to regulate your body and mind, so that they're not distracted or disturbed.

39 又持斋者：当须会意，不达斯理，徒尔虚功。

40 持者护也，所谓于诸戒行，如法护持。斋者齐也，所谓齐正身心，不令散乱。

必须做到
外禁六情、
内制三毒，
Fasting means guarding against the six attractions on the outside and overcoming the three poisons on the inside
殷勤觉察，
清净身心，
明了此义，
就是持斋。
And striving through introspection to purify your body and mind.

41 必须外禁六情，内制三毒，殷勤觉察、清净身心。了如是义，名为持斋。

五种斋食
Five kinds of fasting food
斋食有哪几种?
What does fasting food include?
有五种斋食。
Fasting includes five kinds of food.
哪五种?
What are they?
一法喜食、二禅悦食、三念食、四愿食、五解脱食。
They are delight in the Dharma, harmony of body and mind, invocation, resolution and liberation.
什么是法喜食?
What is delight in the Dharma?
依持正法,
欢喜奉行,
就是法喜食。
This is the delight that comes from acting in accordance with the Dharma.

42 又持斋者，食有五种。

43 一者法喜食，所谓依持正法，欢喜奉行。

什么是禅悦食?
What is harmony in meditation?
内外寂静，
身心悦乐，
就是禅悦食。
This is the harmony of body and mind with peace inside and tranquil outside.
什么是念食?
What is invocation?
常念诸佛，
心口相应，
就是念食。
This is the invocation of Buddhas with both your month and your mind.
什么是愿食?
What is resolution?
行住坐卧，常求善愿，就是愿食。
This is the resolution to pursue virtue whether you're walking, standing, sitting or lying down.
!
什么是解脱食?
What is liberation?
心常清净，
不染俗尘，
就是解脱食。
This is the liberation of your mind from worldly contamination.

44 二者禅悦食，所谓内外澄寂，身心悦乐。

45 三者念食，所谓常念诸佛，心口相应。

46 四者愿食，所谓行住坐卧，常求善愿。

47 五者解脱食，所谓心常清净，不染俗尘。

修这五种
就是持斋?
Are these five the fasting food?
修持这五种食,
才称之为持斋。
These five are the foods of fasting.
如果有人不修行这五种净食
而自称持斋,则是错得离谱。
Unless a person has these five,
he's wrong to think he's fasting.
只断除世间无明之食,
便误以为是经文所说
的持斋,就是破斋。
You actually break the fasting,
once you mistakenly hold it for
stopping intaking the prohibited
food.
如果连斋都破了,
还说什么得福报呢?
And once you break it, you
reap no blessing from it.

48 此五种食,名为斋食。持斋之食有五种。若复有人,不食如是五种净食,自言持斋,无有是处。

49 唯断于无明之食,辄作解者,名为破斋。若亦有破,云何获福?

世间迷惑者悟不出这道理，
身心放逸，造作一切恶行。
The world is full of deluded people who don't see this. They indulge their body and mind in all manner of evil.
酒
酒
恣意放纵贪欲，
不生惭愧。
They give free rein to their passions and have no shame.
虽然断除荤食，
自以为是持斋，
还是一无是处。
And when they stop eating ordinary food, they call it fasting. How absurd!

50 世有迷人，不悟斯理，身心放逸，皆为诸恶；贪欲恣情，不生惭愧，唯断外食，自为持斋，必无是处。

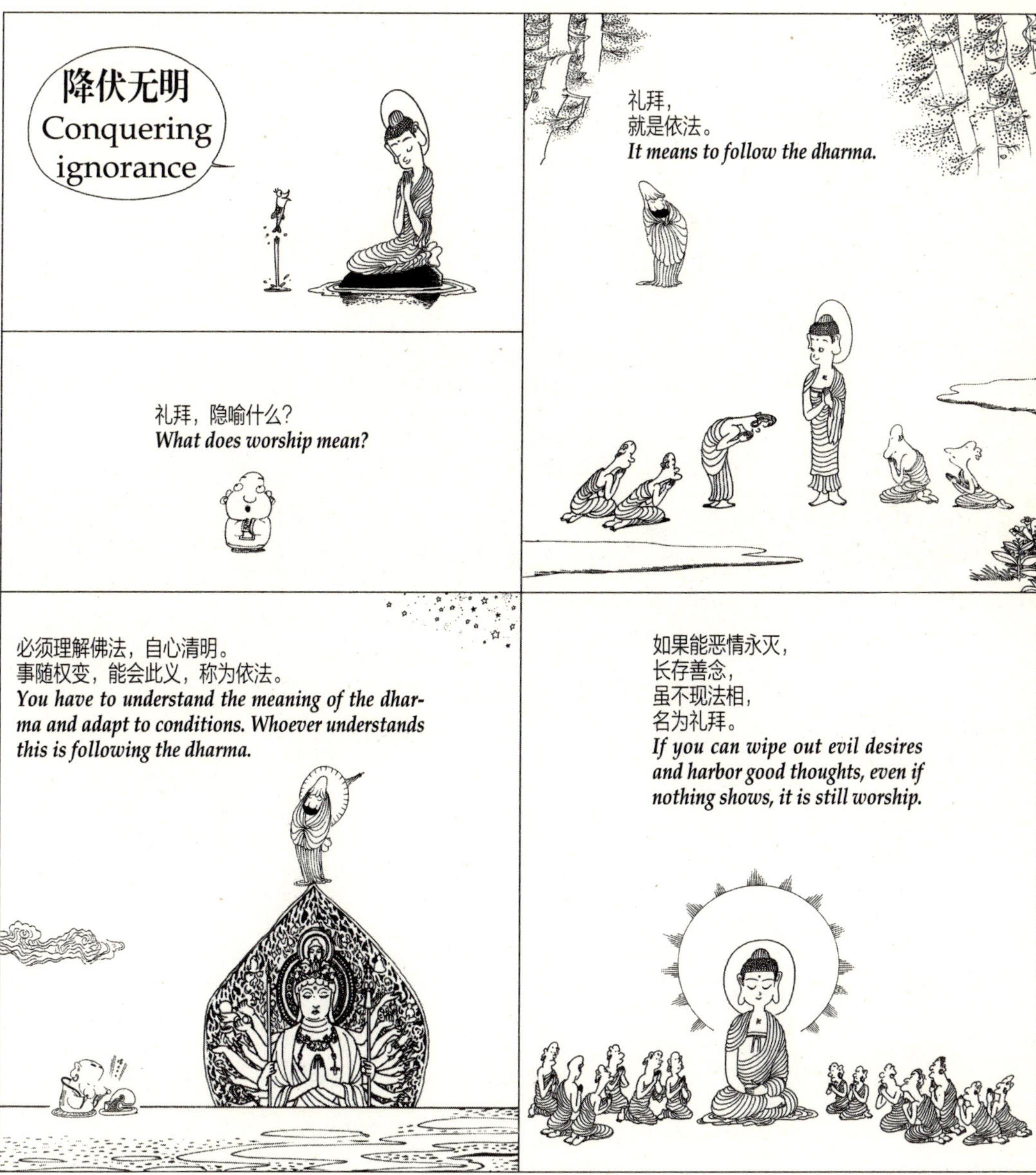
降伏无明
Conquering ignorance
礼拜，
就是依法。
It means to follow the dharma.
礼拜，隐喻什么？
What does worship mean?
必须理解佛法，自心清明。
事随权变，能会此义，称为依法。
You have to understand the meaning of the dharma and adapt to conditions. Whoever understands this is following the dharma.
如果能恶情永灭，
长存善念，
虽不现法相，
名为礼拜。
If you can wipe out evil desires and harbor good thoughts, even if nothing shows, it is still worship.

51 又礼拜者：当如法也。

52 必须理体内明，事随权变，会如是义，乃名依法。

53 夫礼者敬也；拜者伏也；所谓恭敬真性，屈伏无明，名为礼拜。

佛陀为了让世俗者表达谦下心，
也接受众生礼拜。
The Buddha wanted worldly people to think of worship as expressing humility and subduing the mind.
礼拜必须屈身，心明而恭敬，
觉外明内，自性与佛法相应。
So he told them to prostrate their bodies, show their reverence, let the external express the internal and harmonize essence and form.
如果不依法而行，执取外求，放纵贪痴，常造恶业。
Those who fail to cultivate the inner peace, but only concentrate
instead on the outward expression, never stop indulging in greed, delusion and evil while exhausting themselves to no avail.
外即空劳身相，现虚假形貌，面对圣人不自惭，面对凡夫狂妄。
They may deceive others with postures and act shamelessly before the enlightened and arrogantly before the ordinary.
这样做无法避免轮回，
还妄想成就功德？
But they'll never escape the Wheel, much less achieve any merit.
!

54　若能恶情永灭，善念恒存，虽不现相，名为礼拜；其相即法相也。世尊欲令世俗表谦下心，亦为礼拜；

55　故须屈伏外身，示内恭敬。觉外明内，性相相应。

56　若复不行理法，唯执外求，内则放纵贪痴，常为恶业；外即空劳身相，诈现威仪；无惭于圣，徒诳于凡，不免轮回，岂成功德？

第三问
以七事喻七法
Inquiry III The seven everyday things to represent the seven practices
《温室经》说：
“洗浴众僧，获福无量。”
As the Bathhouse Sutra put it,
“Through the bathing of Buddhist monks, people receive limitless blessings.”
温室经
帮众僧洗浴，功德无量，
观心法门也可以吗？
How does this relate to beholding the mind?
佛陀说洗浴众僧，
不是真指世间的洗浴。
Here, the bathing of monks doesn't refer to the washing of anything tangible.
佛陀曾为诸弟子开示《温室经》，
受持洗浴之法。
When the Buddha preached the Bathhouse Sutra, he wanted his disciples to remember the dharma of washing.
假借世间事物比喻真实宗旨，
隐喻七事供养的功德。
So he used an everyday concern to convey his real meaning, which he couched in his explanation of merit from seven offerings.

57 问：“如《温室经》说‘洗浴众僧，获福无量’。此则凭于事法，功德始成，若为观心，可相应否？”答：“洗浴众僧者，非世间有为事也。”

58 世尊曾为诸弟子说《温室经》，欲令受持洗浴之法；故假世事，比喻真宗，隐说七事供养功德。

是哪七事？
What are they?
一净水、二燃火、三澡豆、四杨枝、五净灰、六酥膏、七内衣。
Of these seven, the first is clear water, the second fire, the third soap, the fourth willow catkins, the fifth rubbing ashes, the sixth ointment and the seventh the undergarment.
佛陀以这七事比喻七法。
He used these seven to represent seven dharmas.
一切众生依此七法沐浴庄严，即能除毒心、无明、垢秽。
Anyone who follows these seven ways will eliminate the poisoned mind, ignorance and filth.
!
比喻哪七法？
What are those seven dharmas?
一净戒、二智慧、三分别、四真实、五正信、六柔和、七惭愧。
Morality, wisdom, separation, honesty, true faith, patience and shame.
什么是净戒？
What does morality mean?
洗净诸非，有如净水洗诸垢，就是净戒。
It tells people to wash away excess, just as water washes away dirt.

59 其七事云何？一者净水，二者烧火，三者澡豆，四者杨枝，五者净灰，六者酥膏，七者内衣。

60 以此七事喻于七法，一切众生由此七法。沐浴庄严，能除毒心、无明、垢秽。

61 其七法者：一者谓净戒洗荡愆非，犹如净水濯诸尘垢。

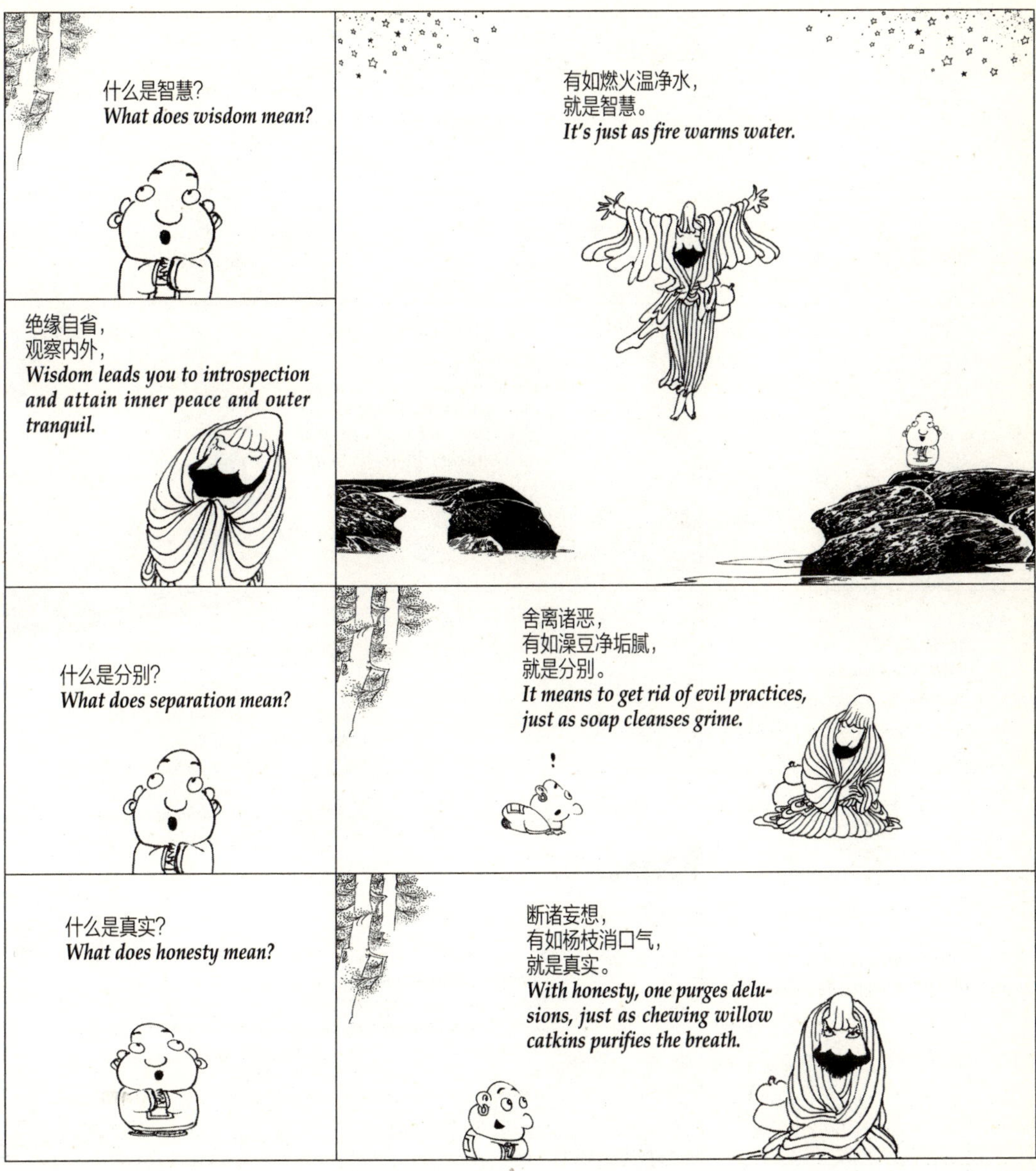
什么是智慧?
What does wisdom mean?
有如燃火温净水，
就是智慧。
It's just as fire warms water.
绝缘自省，
观察内外，
Wisdom leads you to introspection and attain inner peace and outer tranquil.
什么是分别?
What does separation mean?
舍离诸恶，
有如澡豆净垢腻，
就是分别。
It means to get rid of evil practices, just as soap cleanses grime.
!
什么是真实?
What does honesty mean?
断诸妄想，
有如杨枝消口气，
就是真实。
With honesty, one purges delusions, just as chewing willow catkins purifies the breath.

62 二者智慧观察内外，犹如燃火能温净水。

63 三者分别简弃诸恶，犹如澡豆能净垢腻。

64 四者真实断诸妄想，犹如杨枝能净口气。

什么是正信?
What does true faith mean?
决定无疑，
有如净灰摩身障，
就是正信。
The true faith helps remove all doubts, just as rubbing ashes applied on the body prevents illnesses.
什么是柔和?
What does patience mean?
忍辱甘受，
有如酥膏润皮肤，
就是柔和。
With patience, one stands humiliation and disgrace, just as ointment softens the skin.
什么是惭愧?
What does shame mean?
悔诸恶业，
有如内衣遮丑体，
就是惭愧。
One with the sense of shame redresses evil deeds, just as the undergarment covers up an ugly body.
以上是佛经所说
七法的秘密义，
These seven represent the real meaning of the sutra.
是佛陀为大乘
利根修行者所说。
When he talked about this sutra, the Buddha was talking to far-sighted Mahayana followers,

65 五者正信：决定无疑，犹如净灰摩身障风。

66 六者柔和：忍辱、甘受，犹如酥膏通润皮肤。

67 七者惭愧：悔诸恶业，犹如内衣遮丑行体。

68 如上七法，是经中秘密之义。皆是为诸大乘利根者说。

不是小智下劣的
凡夫所能理解，
Instead of narrow-minded ordinary people of dim vision.
真是听不懂……
I can't get it...
所以现在的人也
无法领悟。
It's not surprising that people nowadays don't understand it.
还是不懂啊……
I can't get it...

69 非为小智下劣凡夫，所以今人无能解悟。

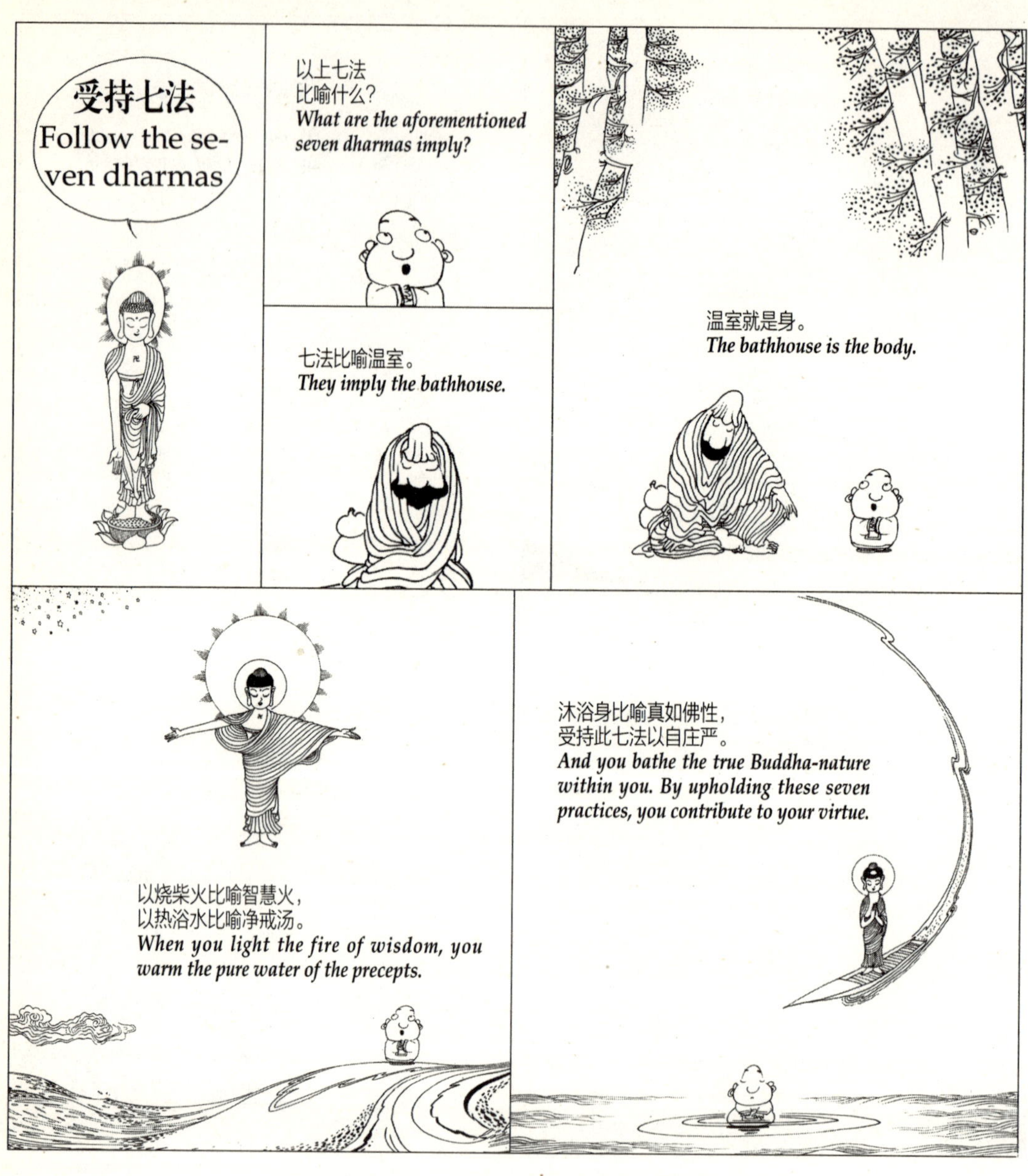

受持七法
Follow the seven dharmas
以上七法
比喻什么？
What are the aforementioned seven dharmas imply?
七法比喻温室。
They imply the bathhouse.
温室就是身。
The bathhouse is the body.
以烧柴火比喻智慧火，
以热浴水比喻净戒汤。
When you light the fire of wisdom, you warm the pure water of the precepts.
沐浴身比喻真如佛性，
受持此七法以自庄严。
And you bathe the true Buddha-nature within you. By upholding these seven practices, you contribute to your virtue.

70 其温室者，即身是也。

71 所以燃智慧火，温净戒汤，沐浴身中真如佛性，受持七法，以自庄严。

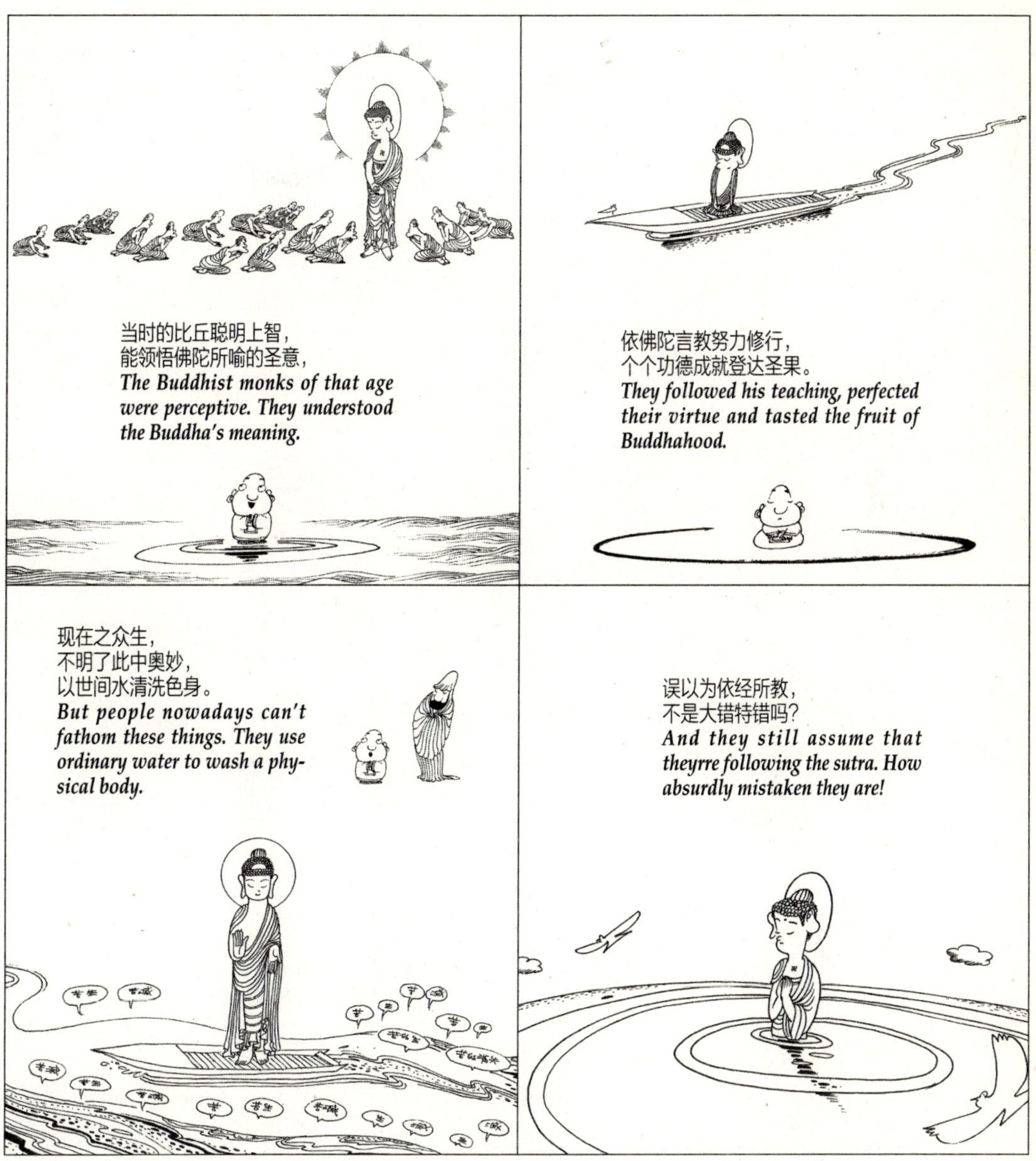
当时的比丘聪明上智，
能领悟佛陀所喻的圣意，
The Buddhist monks of that age were perceptive. They understood the Buddha's meaning.
依佛陀言教努力修行，
个个功德成就登达圣果。
They followed his teaching, perfected their virtue and tasted the fruit of Buddhahood.
现在之众生，
不明了此中奥妙，
以世间水清洗色身。
But people nowadays can't fathom these things. They use ordinary water to wash a physical body.
误以为依经所教，
不是大错特错吗？
And they still assume that theyrre following the sutra. How absurdly mistaken they are!

72 当日比丘，聪明上智，皆悟圣意，如说修行，功德成就，俱登圣果。

73 今时众生。莫测其事，将世间水洗质碍身，自谓依经，岂非误也？

真如佛性并非
世间有形色身，
烦恼尘垢本来无相，
Our true Buddha-nature has no shape.
And the dust of affliction has no form.
岂能用世间之水
清洗无为之身？
当然无法办到。
How can people use ordinary water to
wash an intangible body? It won't work.
!
清洗色身能得干净，
有如清洗万丈深渊。
Wash a physical body is right like something
that you try to cleanse a bottomless chasm.
得等清水注满深渊，
方得干净。
It won't be cleaned until it is
filled with crystal-clear water.

74 且真如佛性，非是凡形；烦恼尘垢，本来无相；岂可将质碍水，洗无为身？事不相应。

75 若洗此身求于净者，犹如洗堑，堑尽方净。

由此证明清洗
色身并非佛说。
Thus, it is not the Buddha's mea-
ning to wach a physical body.
只是以世间沐浴隐喻真实宗旨，
解说七事的供养功德。
The Buddha only tried to explain
the seven practices of offering by
borrowing the term of bathing.

76 以此验之，明知洗外，非佛说也。

第四问 念在心不在言
Inquiry IV Invoking with your mind ins-tead of words
佛经说：
The sutras say,
“至心念佛，必能往生西方净土。”
“Someone who wholeheartedly invokes the Buddha is sure to be reborn in the Western Paradise.”
佛经
如果只要念佛就能成佛，
何必以观心法门求解脱？
Since this leads to Buddhahood, why seek liberation in beholding the mind?
念佛必须正念，
明了义理为正，
不明义理为邪；
If you're going to invoke the Buddha, you have to do it right. It's right to grasp the essence of Buddharma. It's wrong to do it without knowing the essence.
正念必得往生，
邪念怎能达到
如此境界呢？
Unless you understand what invoking means, you'll do it wrong. And if you do it wrong, you go nowhere.

77 问：“如经说言：‘至心念佛，必得往生西方净土。’以此一门即应成佛，何假观心？求于解脱。”

78 答：“夫念佛者，当须正念，了义为正，不了义为邪。正念必得往生，邪念云何达彼哉？”

佛就是自心觉悟，
察觉身心不令生起恶念。
Buddhahood means self-awareness, the awareness of your body and mind that prevents evil from arising in either.
念就是忆想，忆持戒行不忘精进。
能明了此义，就是念。
And to invoke means to call to mind, to call constantly to mind the rules of discipline and to follow them with all your might. This is what's meant by invoking.
忆想
Call to mind
念在于心，不在于言。
以筌求鱼，得鱼忘筌。
Invoking is done with thought, instead of words. If you use a trap to catch fish, once you succeed, you can forget the trap.
以言求意，得意忘言。
以佛求心，得心忘佛。
这才是念佛之名。
And if you use words to find meaning, once you find it, you can forget words. If you try to see your mind with help of Buddha, once you see it, you can forget the Buddha. That's the right way to invoke the Buddha's name.

79 佛者觉也；所谓觉察身心，勿令起恶。念者忆也；所谓忆持戒行，不忘精进。了如是义，名之为念。
80 故知念在于心，不在于言。因筌求鱼，得鱼忘筌；因言求意，得意忘言。既称念佛之名。

念佛之道，
如果心无实，
只是口诵空名。
To invoke the Buddha's name, you have to understand the dharma of invoking. If it's not present in your mind, your mouth chants an empty name.
三毒内臻，
人我填臆，
将无明心。
As long as you're troubled by the three poisons or by thoughts of yourself, your deluded mind will keep you from seeing the Buddha.
禅
向心外求佛，
枉费功夫。
有如诵与念，
义理悬殊。
It's only a waste to seek Buddhahood outside your mind.
Chanting and invoking are worlds apart.
诵与念，有何差别？
What's the difference?
在口唱颂，就称为诵；
在心默想，就称为念。
Chanting is done with the mouth.
Invoking is done with the mind.

81 须知念佛之道。若心无实，口诵空名，三毒内臻，人我填臆，将无明心。

82 向外求佛，徒尔虚功。且如诵之与念，义理悬殊。

83 在口曰诵，在心曰念。

念从心起，
名为觉行之门；
诵在口中，
即是音声之相。
As invoking comes from the mind, it's called the door to awareness. Chanting is centered in the mouth and appears as sound.
执外求理，
终究一无是处。
If you cling to appearances while searching for meaning, you won't find a single thing.

84 故知念从心起，名为觉行之门；诵在口中，即是音声之相。执外求理，终无是处。

心是涅槃门
The mind is the door to nirvana
心是成佛的法门吗？
Is the mind the door to Buddhahood?
涅槃常乐由真心所生，
The eternal bliss of nirvana comes from the mind at rest.
三界轮回从心中生起。
Rebirth in the three realms also comes from the mind.
心
Mind
心是开悟得道成佛的门户！
The mind is the door to enlightenment and Buddhahood!
心是自在解脱的关键。
The mind is the door to freedom and liberation.

85 涅槃常乐，由真心生；三界轮回，亦从心起。心是出世之门户，心是解脱之关津。

已知门户，
要进入有何困难？
Those who know where the door stands may find no difficulty in reaching it.
已知关键，
还担心通不过吗？
Those who know where the ford lies may worry nothing about crossing it.
环顾今时浅识，
只知道在事物表相用功。
The people I meet nowadays are shallow in mind. They think of merit as something that has form.
浪费财宝，多伤水陆，
妄造许多佛像、佛塔，白费功夫。
They squander their wealth and slay creatures from land and sea. They foolishly concern themselves with erecting statues and pagodas. But what they do is nothing more than a mere waster.

86 知门户者，岂虑难入？知关津者，何忧不达？

87 窃见今时浅识，唯知事相为功，广费财宝，多伤水陆；妄营像塔，虚役人夫。

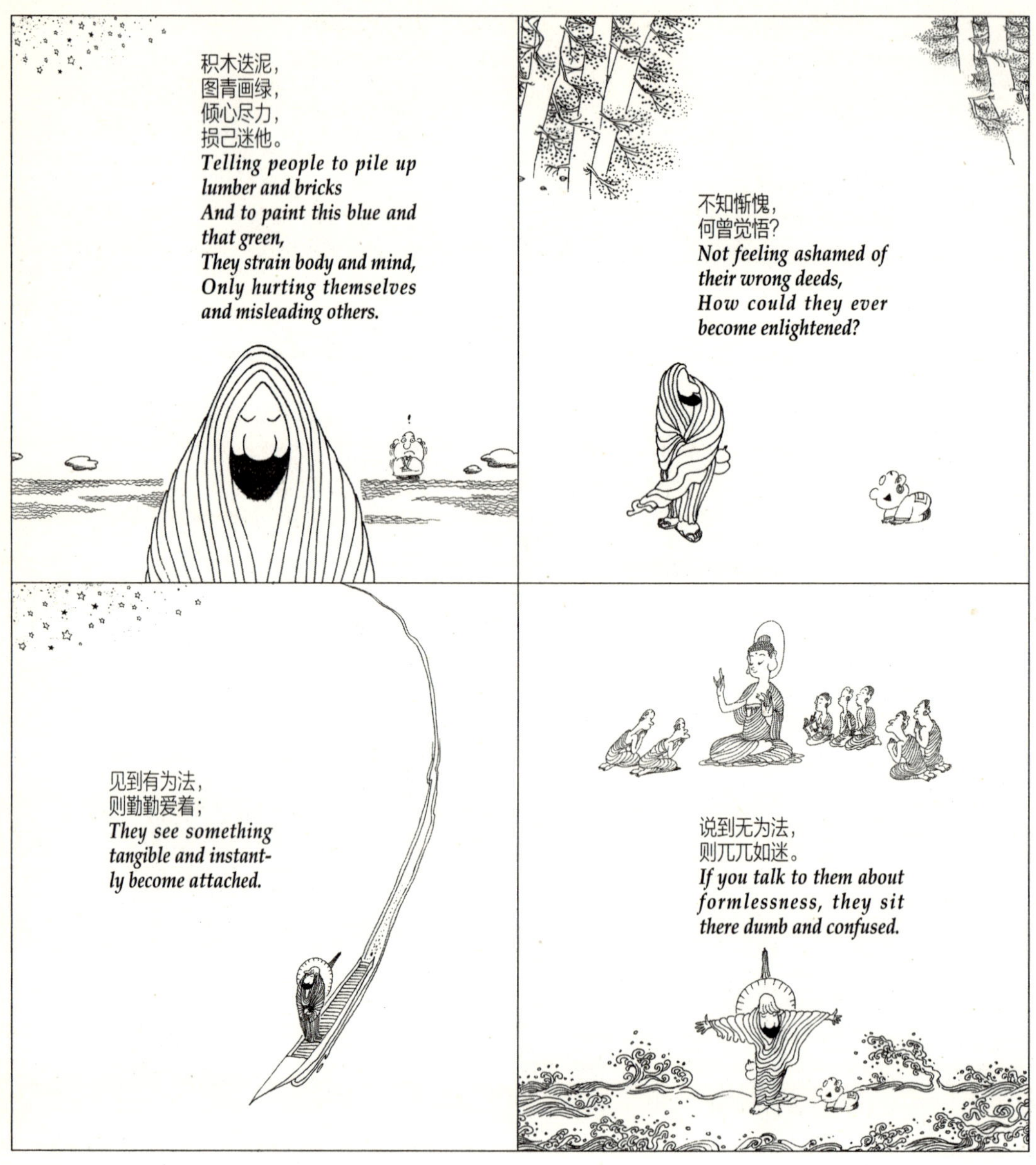
积木迭泥，
图青画绿，
倾心尽力，
损己迷他。
Telling people to pile up lumber and bricks
And to paint this blue and that green,
They strain body and mind,
Only hurting themselves and misleading others.
不知惭愧，
何曾觉悟？
Not feeling ashamed of their wrong deeds,
How could they ever become enlightened?
见到有为法，
则勤勤爱着；
They see something tangible and instantly become attached.
说到无为法，
则兀兀如迷。
If you talk to them about formlessness, they sit there dumb and confused.

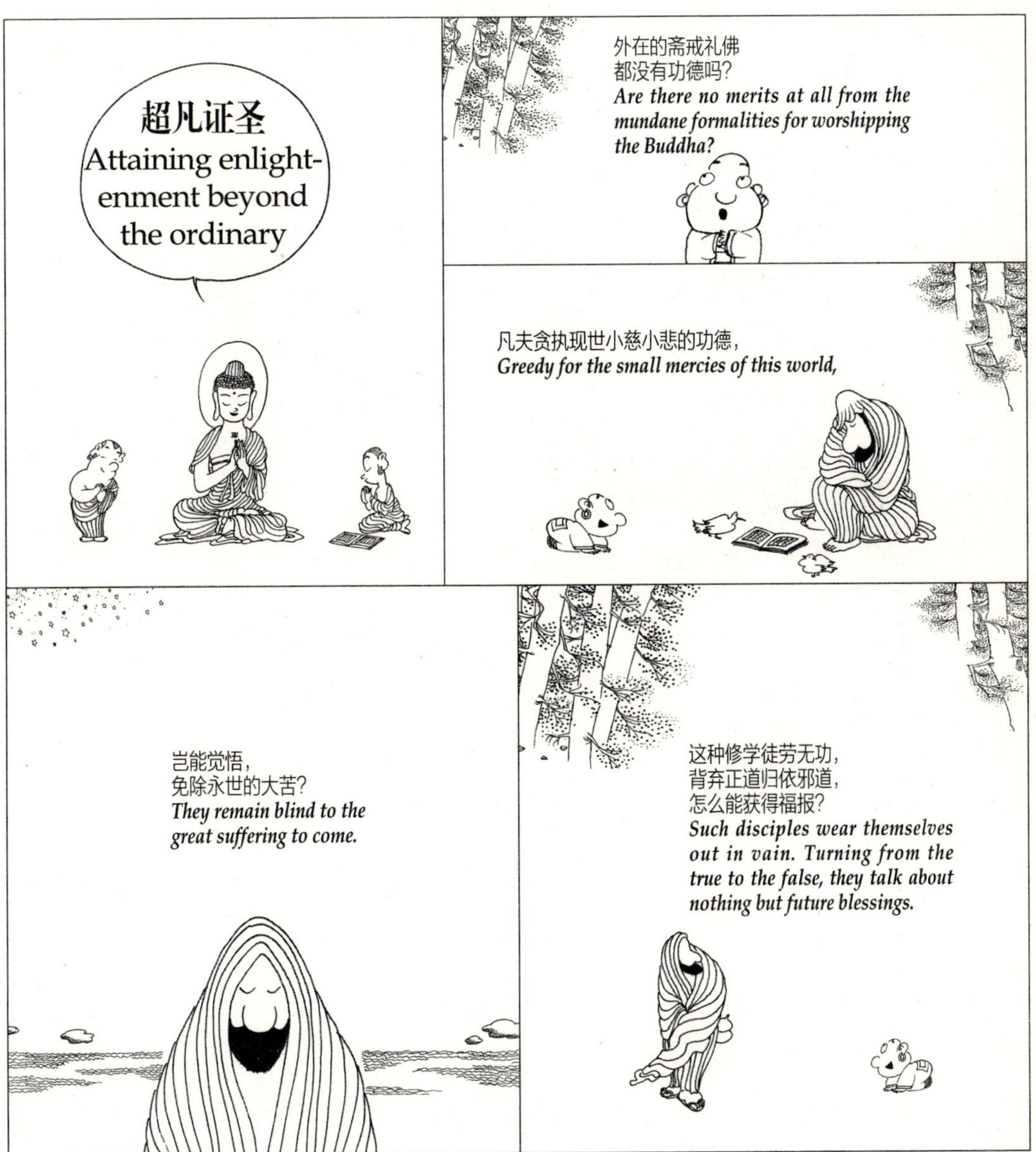
超凡证圣
Attaining enlightenment beyond the ordinary
外在的斋戒礼佛
都没有功德吗?
Are there no merits at all from the mundane formalities for worshipping the Buddha?
凡夫贪执现世小慈小悲的功德,
Greedy for the small mercies of this world,
岂能觉悟,
免除永世的大苦?
They remain blind to the great suffering to come.
这种修学徒劳无功,
背弃正道归依邪道,
怎么能获得福报?
Such disciples wear themselves out in vain. Turning from the true to the false, they talk about nothing but future blessings.

88 且贪现世之小慈，岂觉当来之大苦？此之修学，徒自疲劳，背正归邪，诳言获福。

正确修行观心法，
内观自心，
消除无明，
外观色尘，
If you can simply focus on your mind's Inner Light and behold its outer illumination of ignorance,
让贪、嗔、痴
三毒永远消逝。
You'll dispel the three poisons once and for all.
心

89 但能摄心内照，觉观外明；绝三毒，永使消亡。

心心是佛
The mind is the Buddha
修道成佛要花多长时间?
How will it take to attain enlightenment and Buddhahood?
见性即能成佛，就在当下现前。
One attains enlightenment and Buddhahood at the very moment, once he sees his mind and nature.
守护眼、耳、鼻、舌、身、意六根以避六贼，心不受侵扰自然清净。
He keeps the inner peace in his untained mind by safeguarding the six senses of eyes, ears, nose, tongue, body and mind off the delusions from the Six Thieves.
便能得恒河沙功德，种种庄严无数法门，一一成就超凡证圣。
Then without effort, he gains possession of an infinite number of virtues, perfections and doors to the truth.

90 闭六贼，不令侵扰，自然恒沙功德，种种庄严；无数法门，一一成就，超凡证圣。

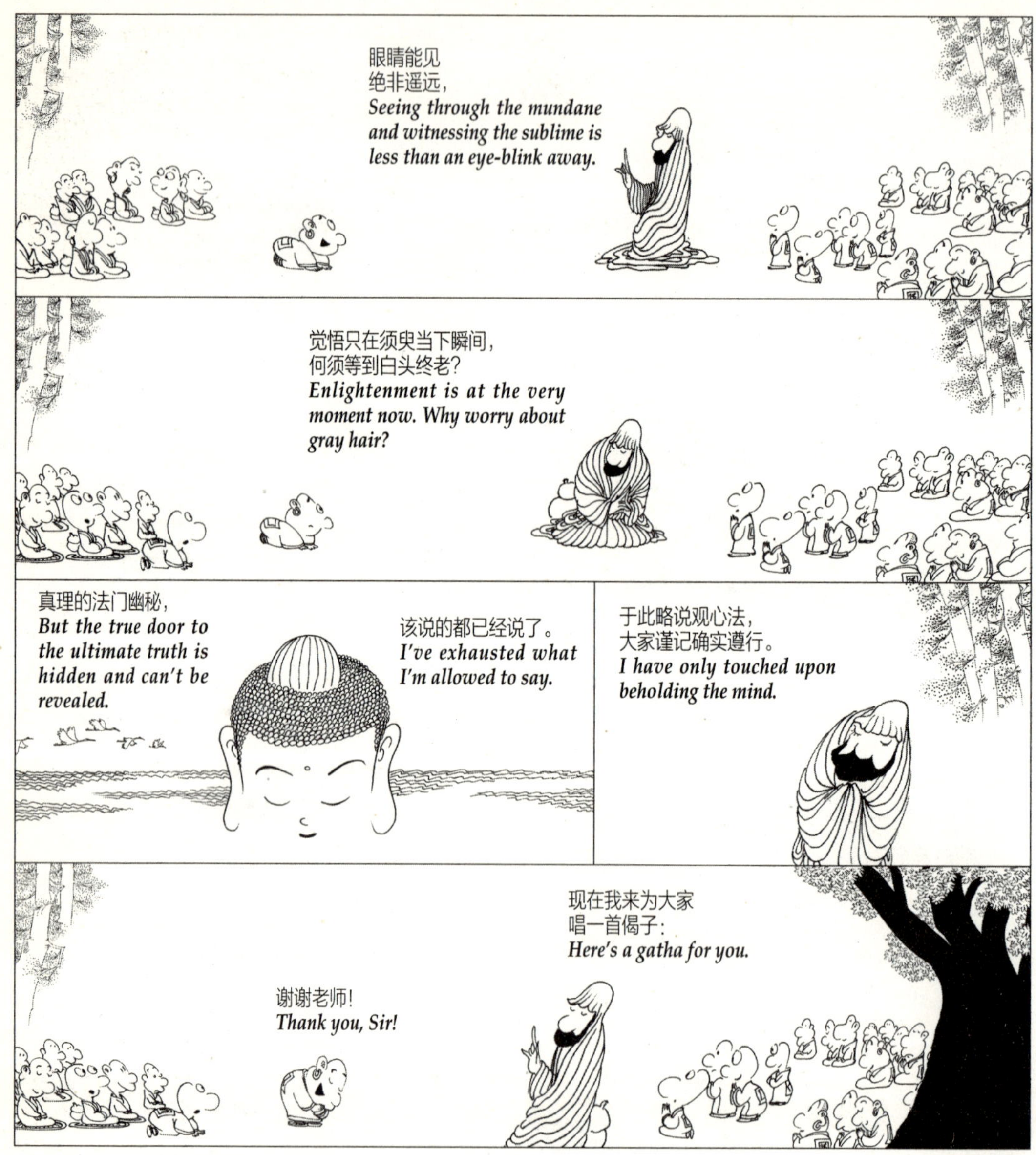
眼睛能见
绝非遥远，
Seeing through the mundane and witnessing the sublime is less than an eye-blink away.
觉悟只在须臾当下瞬间，
何须等到白头终老？
Enlightenment is at the very moment now. Why worry about gray hair?
真理的法门幽秘，
But the true door to the ultimate truth is hidden and can't be revealed.
该说的都已经说了。
I've exhausted what I'm allowed to say.
于此略说观心法，
大家谨记确实遵行。
I have only touched upon beholding the mind.
现在我来为大家
唱一首偈子：
Here's a gatha for you.
谢谢老师！
Thank you, Sir!

91 目击非遥。悟在须臾，何烦皓首？

92 真门幽秘，宁可具陈？略述观。

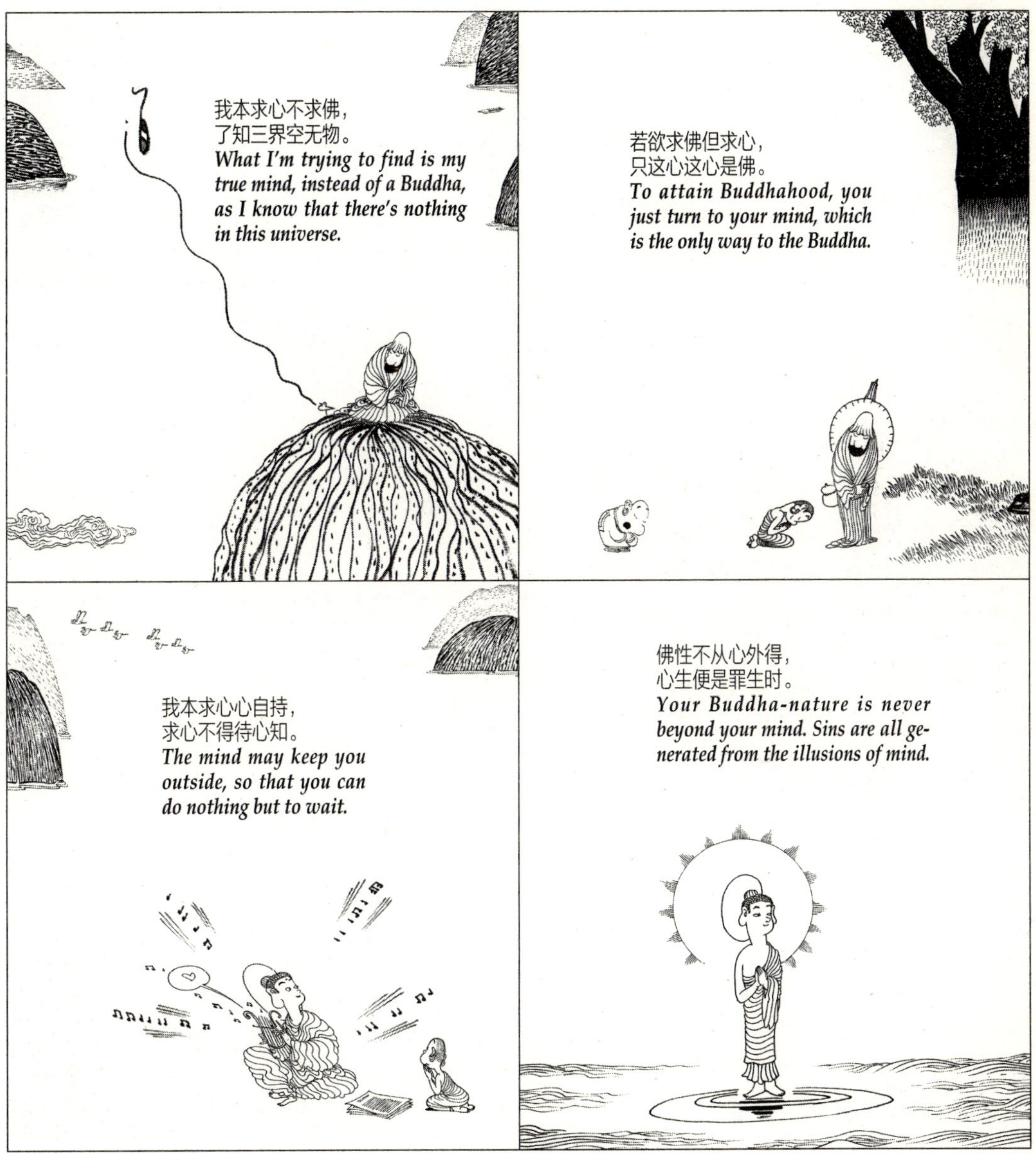
我本求心不求佛，
了知三界空无物。
What I'm trying to find is my true mind, instead of a Buddha, as I know that there's nothing in this universe.
若欲求佛但求心，
只这心这心是佛。
To attain Buddhahood, you just turn to your mind, which is the only way to the Buddha.
我本求心心自持，
求心不得待心知。
The mind may keep you outside, so that you can do nothing but to wait.
佛性不从心外得，
心生便是罪生时。
Your Buddha-nature is never beyond your mind. Sins are all generated from the illusions of mind.

达摩说完整部《破相论》
之后，弟子跪拜说：
Upon hearing Bodhidharma's Formality Refuting Sermon, his disciples kowtowed,
感谢大师细心为我说《破相论》，
弟子欢喜奉行。
Our heartfelt gratitude to you, Sir, for this Formality Refuting Sermon. We'll put it into practice for sure.

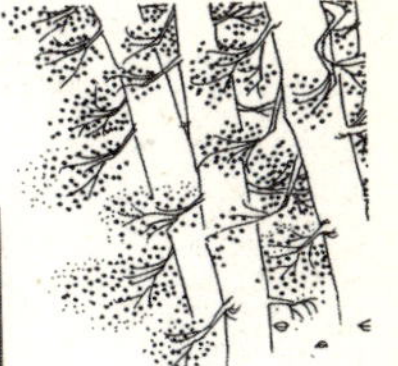

达摩安心法门

Dharma Teaching of Pacifying the Mind

迷悟之间
Between delusion and enlightenment
学僧问达摩：
“什么是迷？ 什么是悟？”
A disciple asked,
“What is delusion? And what is enlightenment?”
达摩回答：
“迷时人逐法，解时法逐人。”
Bodhidharma answered,
“The deluded depend on the dharam. The dharma depends on the enlightened.”
“解时识摄色，迷时色摄识。”
“Consciousness reigns over forms in enlightenment. Forms reign over consciousness in delusion.”
WISDOM

1　迷时人逐法，解时法逐人。

2　解时识摄色，迷时色摄识。

怎么说?
What does that mean?
如果我们面对现前情境时，
用心去分别计较好坏，
便处在梦觉之中。
One feels as if he were in a dream, once he fusses about the conditions he's in, be it favorable or unfavorable.
如能看清自心本应寂静不动，
面对情境时不起心动念，
One may see into the essence of his mind as being emptiness and treat the conditions as they are, without a single thought arising.
这就叫作正觉。
This person then has acquired awakening or enlightenment.
什么是自心现量?
What is self-dimension?
把变化情境当成不存在的，
那也是我们的心自己的想法。
Every change appearing in front of us is generated from our mind.
面对任何际遇时也是如此，
是真实存在或是不实的，
都是我们的自心作用。
Every condition, favorable or unfavorable and existing or non-existing, is also generated from our mind.
什么是解脱?
What is liberation?

3 但有心分别计较自心现量者，悉皆是梦；若识心寂灭，无一切念处，是名正觉。

4 问："云何自心现量？"答："见一切法有，有不自有，自心计作有。"

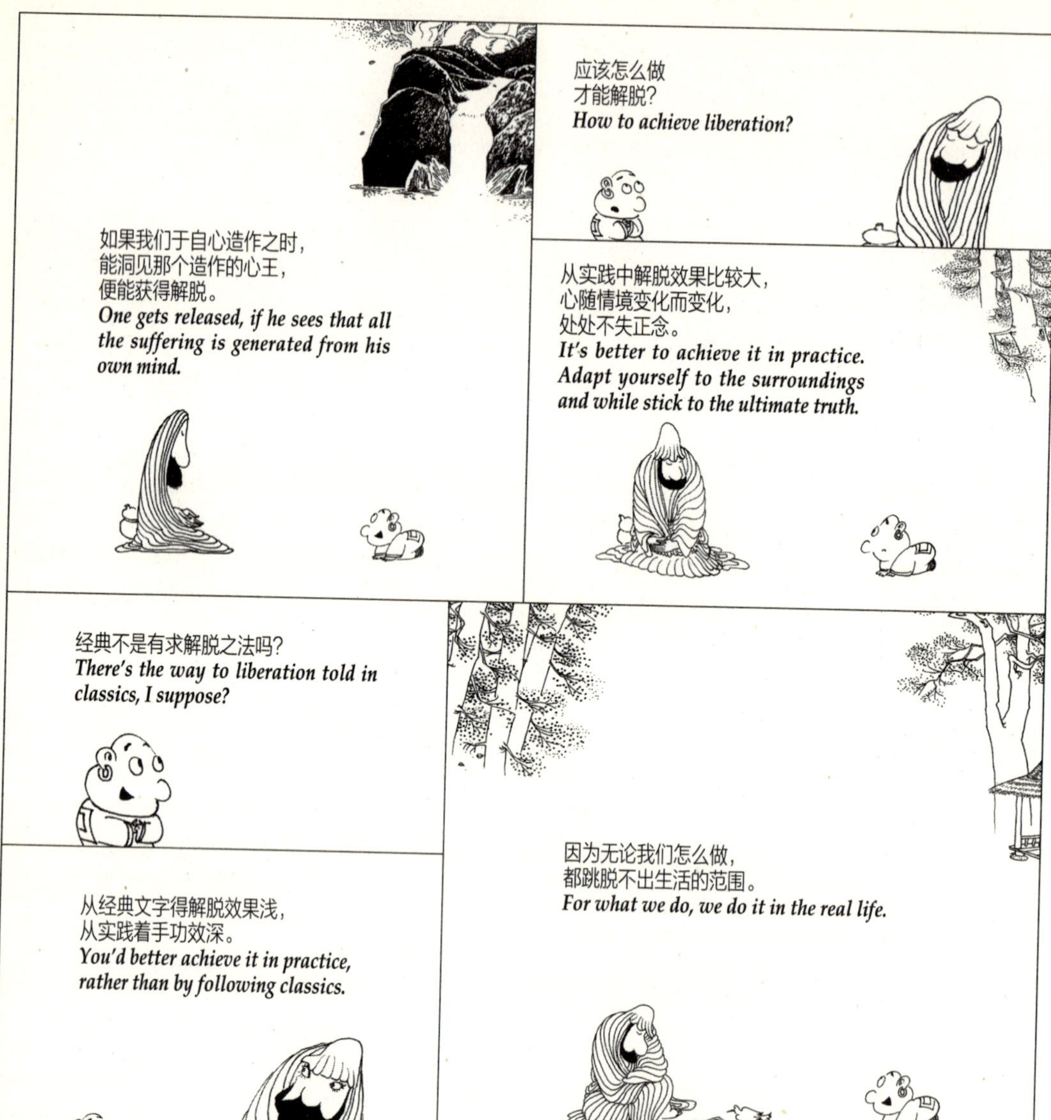
如果我们于自心造作之时，
能洞见那个造作的心王，
便能获得解脱。
One gets released, if he sees that all the suffering is generated from his own mind.
应该怎么做
才能解脱？
How to achieve liberation?
从实践中解脱效果比较大，
心随情境变化而变化，
处处不失正念。
It's better to achieve it in practice. Adapt yourself to the surroundings and while stick to the ultimate truth.
经典不是有求解脱之法吗？
There's the way to liberation told in classics, I suppose?
从经典文字得解脱效果浅，
从实践着手功效深。
You'd better achieve it in practice, rather than by following classics.
因为无论我们怎么做，
都跳脱不出生活的范围。
For what we do, we do it in the real life.

5　又若人造一切罪，自见己之法王，即得解脱。

6　若从事上得解者气力壮，从事中见法者，即处处不失念；

7　从文字解者气力弱，即事即法者深。从汝种种运为跳踉颠蹶，悉不出法界。

心体即法界
The mind is the realm of the ultimate truth.
如何悟通生命的实相?
How to see into the truth of life?
如果想从法界进入法界，就是笨人。
我们的心造作一切时，都离不开法界心。
Only a fool dreams to enter the realm of the ultimate truth by way of the dharma. Your mind never stands alone outside that realm whenever a thought arises.
为什么呢?
Why?
因为心本身
就在法界之内。
As your mind is in the realm of the ultimate truth.

8 若以法界入法界，即是痴人；凡有施为，皆不出法界心。

9 问："何以故？" 答："心体是法界故。"

什么是法界?
What is the realm of the ultimate truth?

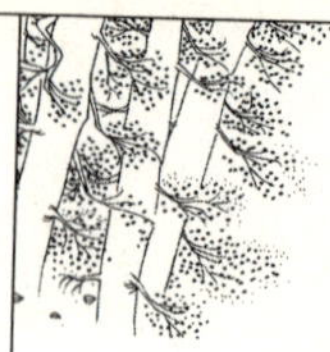

一切世间万物
的真如实相,
就是法界。
The original nature of all the living creatures is the realm of the ultimate truth.

一切现前情境
就是法界。
What appears in front of us is the realm of the ultimate truth.

至人无我见
A perfect man isn't caught in the idea of self.
世人有种种学问，
为什么不能得道呢？
Why cannot the ordinary find the Way, even if they're knowledgeable?
因为他有自我，
所以无法得道。
Because they're caught in the idea of self.
有我
就无法见道？
They cannot see the Way the, can they?
至人能达到：
逢苦不忧、遇乐不喜。
是由于他没有自我。
A perfect man remains calm in happiness and suffering, as he isn't caught in the idea of self.
遇乐不喜
逢苦不忧
Remain calm in happiness and suffering.

10 问："世间人种种学问，云何不得道？" 答："由见己故，所以不得道。"

11 己者我也。至人逢苦不忧，遇乐不喜，由不见己故。

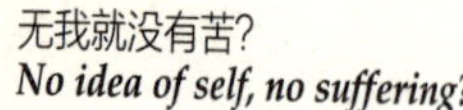

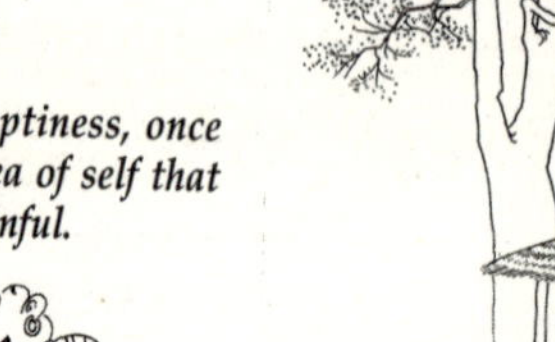
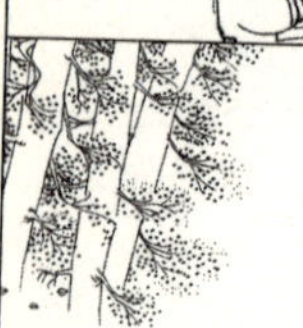
无我就没有苦？
No idea of self, no suffering?
没有一个察觉苦乐的我存在，
因此能达至空无。
You reach the realm of emptiness, once you're released from the idea of self that makes you feel happy or painful.
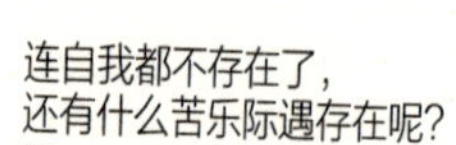

连自我都不存在了，
还有什么苦乐际遇存在呢？
How could the feelings of happiness and suffering exist, since there's no such a thing like self?

如果诸法皆空，
还有谁需要修道呢？
Will be practices necessary, once all the dharmas become empty in essence?
无人存在，
当然不需要修道。
There's nobody in existence. Naturally, there's no need of practices.

不修行可以成道吗？
Can a person find the Way without practices?

12 所以不知苦乐，由亡己故，得至虚无；己尚自亡，更有何物而不亡也？

13 问："说法既空，阿谁修道？"答："有阿谁须修道？若无阿谁，即不须修道。"

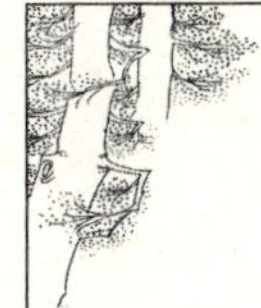

如果没有自我存在，
面对任何情境时便没有好坏顺逆。
Without the idea of self, there's no discrimination of conditions, be it favorable or unfavorable.

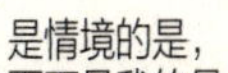
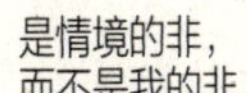

是情境的是，
而不是我的是；
It may be a favorable condition. But it has nothing to do with me.

是情境的非，
而不是我的非。
It may be an unfavorable condition. But it has nothing to do with me.

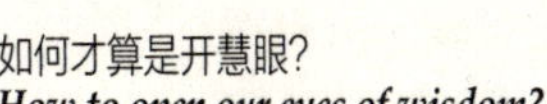
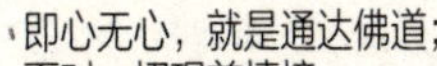

如何才算是开慧眼？
How to open our eyes of wisdom?

即心无心，就是通达佛道；
面对一切现前情境，
不心生好坏见解，就是达道。
You attain Buddhahood, once you see your mind as a thing of emptiness. You find the Way, once you see the conditions as they are, without imposing your judgements.

于任何当下，
能如实知其本源，
就是此人开慧眼。
Anyone who sees the things in front of him as they are at any moment has his eyes of wisdom opened.

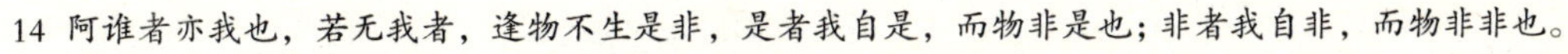

14 阿谁者亦我也，若无我者，逢物不生是非，是者我自是，而物非是也；非者我自非，而物非非也。

15 即心无心，是为通达佛道；即物不起见，是名达道。逢物直达，知其本源，此人慧眼开。

当下即生命实相
The truth of life lies in the very present moment.
什么才是生命的真如实相?
What is the ultimate truth of life?
任何当下现前，就是一生的时间薄片。
The very present moment is a slice of the entire lifetime.
把所有当下相加，即是自己整体一生。
Add them up, you get your life.
因此所有的当下，才是生命的实相。
The truth of life lies in the very present moment.
面对当下现前，应怎么做才对?
How to deal with the very present moment?

智者无我，
他随着情境变化而变化，
面对任何际遇时，
没有好坏顺逆分别。
The wise have no such an idea of self. A wise man adapts himself to the ever-changing conditions and sees them as they are, without discriminating them as being good or bad.
愚人期待世界依自己
所期待的方向发展，
于是便有际遇顺逆取舍。
A fool expects in vain to have the things develop as he expected. Thus he has a discriminative view of conditions.
如何才算是见道?
What is to find the Way?
面对际遇时不见际遇，
就是见道。
One finds the Way, once he sees the vicissitudes of life as nothing.
如何才算是行道?
What is to follow the Way?
心不造作任何妄想，
就是行道。
One follows the Way, once no delusions arise from his mind.
如何才算是见佛?
What is to see the Buddha?

16 智者任物不任己，即无取舍违顺；愚人任己不任物，即有取舍违顺。

17 不见一物，名为见道。

18 不行一物，名为行道。

心面对任何变化情境，
都不安住，无所造作，
就是见佛。
One sees the Buddha, once his mind remain undisturbed by whatever he sees and experiences.
面对情境时看到好、坏、顺、逆，
就看到烦恼痛苦。
One is plagued with suffering and affliction, once he treats the conditions as being good, bad, favorable or unfavorable.
自心取舍际遇善恶差别，
便立即堕入地狱。
One falls into the hell, once he holds a discriminative view of what he sees and experiences.

19 即一切处无处，即作处无作处；无作法即见佛。

20 若见相时，即一切处见鬼；取相故，堕地狱。

心非色非有
The mind is the formless non-existance.
观察自心不使妄动，
必能得解脱。
You attain liberation through introspection and by reining it from delusions.
如何安住自己的心？
How to tranquillize our mind?
如果心生忆想分别，
即受炙热烈火焚烧。
这就是“现见生死相”。
Your mind suffers on fire, once a delusion arises. That's what we call "birth and death in your eyes".
五蕴炙热
The fire of the Five Aggregates
若见法界性，
就是“涅槃性”。
One achieves nirvana, once he sees the realm of the truth of life.

21 观法故，得解脱；若见忆想分别，即受镬汤炉炭等事，现见生死相。

22 若见法界性，即涅槃性。

没有忆想分别，
就是“法界性”。
One achieves the realm of the truth of life, once he has no discriminations to what he sees and experiences.
那么心到底是什么？
What is the mind indeed?
心非色，
故非有；
The mind is the formless non-existance.
用而不废，
故非无。
The mind is in existence, as it's always in work.
心用而常空，
故非有；
The mind is the empty non-existance.
空而常用，
故非无。
The mind is in existence, as it's always in work, essentially being empty, though.

23 无忆相分别，即是法界性。

24 心非色，故非有；用而不废，故非无；又用而常空，故非有；空而常用，故非无。

附录　达摩无心论

Appendix No Mind Sermon

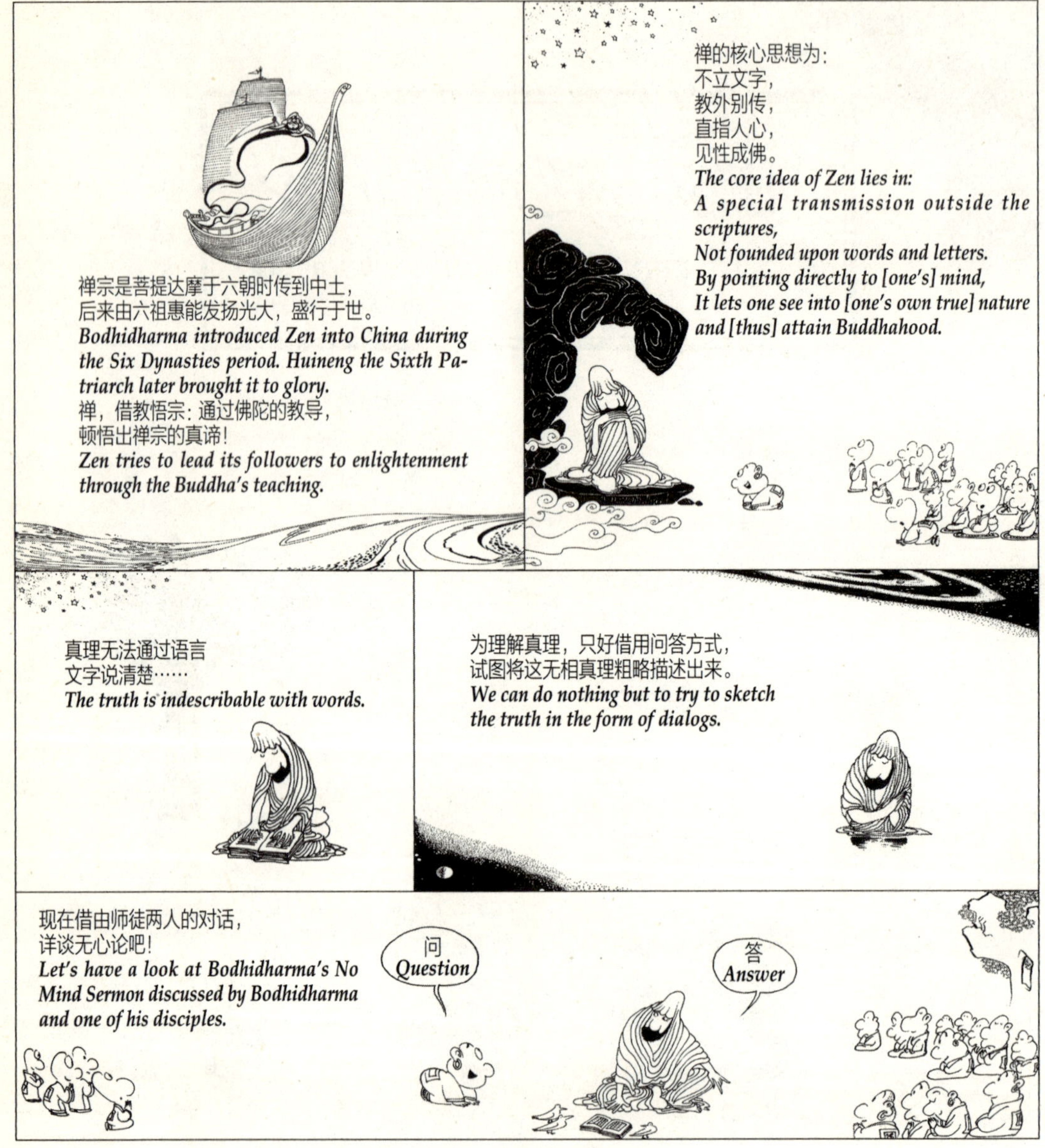
禅宗是菩提达摩于六朝时传到中土，
后来由六祖惠能发扬光大，盛行于世。
Bodhidharma introduced Zen into China during the Six Dynasties period. Huineng the Sixth Patriarch later brought it to glory.
禅，借教悟宗：通过佛陀的教导，
顿悟出禅宗的真谛！
Zen tries to lead its followers to enlightenment through the Buddha's teaching.
禅的核心思想为：
不立文字，
教外别传，
直指人心，
见性成佛。
The core idea of Zen lies in:
A special transmission outside the scriptures,
Not founded upon words and letters.
By pointing directly to [one's] mind,
It lets one see into [one's own true] nature and [thus] attain Buddhahood.
真理无法通过语言
文字说清楚……
The truth is indescribable with words.
为理解真理，只好借用问答方式，
试图将这无相真理粗略描述出来。
We can do nothing but to try to sketch the truth in the form of dialogs.
现在借由师徒两人的对话，
详谈无心论吧！
Let's have a look at Bodhidharma's No Mind Sermon discussed by Bodhidharma and one of his disciples.
问
Question
答
Answer

1　夫至理无言。要假言而显理。大道无相。为接粗而见形。今且假立二人共谈无心之论矣。

无心能见闻觉知
Seeing, hearing and feeling without mind

弟子问达摩：
“到底是有心，还是无心？”
The disciple asked,
“Does the mind exist or not?”

达摩回答：
“无心。”
Bodhidharma answered,
“There's no mind.”

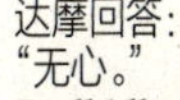

既然是无心，
那么由谁来见闻觉知？
是谁知无心？
Then how can we see, hear and feel, since there's no mind? And how can we say that there's no mind, since there's no mind?

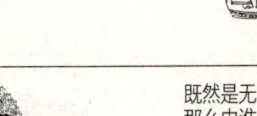

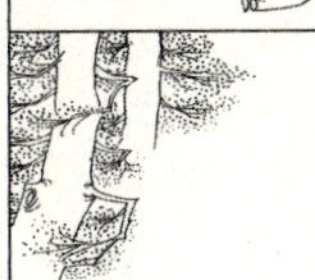

无心能见闻觉知，
无心能知无心。
We see, hear and feel without mind. Without mind, we know that there's no mind.

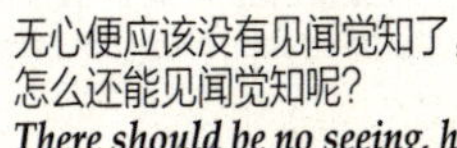

无心便应该没有见闻觉知了，
怎么还能见闻觉知呢？
There should be no seeing, hearing or feeling, once there's no mind. How can we still do those things?

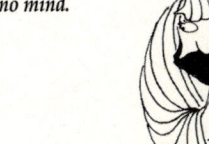

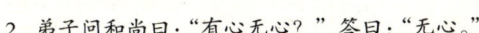

2　弟子问和尚曰：“有心无心？”答曰：“无心。”

3　问曰：“既云无心。谁能见闻觉知。谁知无心。”答曰：“还是无心既见闻觉知。还是无心能知无心。”

4　问曰：“既若无心。即合无有见闻觉知。云何得有见闻觉知。”

虽是无心，
但还是能见闻觉知。
We can, even without mind.
能见闻觉知，
怎能称为无心？
How?
见闻觉知本身就是无心，
此外再也没另一个无心存在。
Such a thing as seeing, hearing or feeling itself is no-mind. There's nothing like that beyond.
怕你不了解这个道理，
现在详细为你解说，好让你能明白。
I'll elaborate on it, for your understanding.
如果我们面对现前情境时，
没有我存在，让见闻觉知
只是纯粹的见闻觉知。
Suppose that you see, hear and feel without the idea of self and let seeing, hearing and feeling as they are.
于是便能达到
见而无见、
闻而无闻、
觉而无觉、
知而无知的境界。
In this way, you are capable of seeing while not seeing, hearing while not hearing, feeling while not feeling and knowing while not knowing.

5　答曰："我虽无心能见能闻能觉能知。"

6　问曰："既能见闻觉知。即是有心。那得称无。"和尚曰："只是见闻觉知。即是无心。何处更离见闻觉知别有无心。我今恐汝不解。一一为汝解说。令汝得悟真理。"

7　假如见终日见由为无见，见亦无心；闻终日闻由为无闻，闻亦无心；觉终日觉由为无觉，觉亦无心；知终日知由为无知，知亦无心终日造作，作亦作亦无作，作亦无心。故云见闻觉知总是无心。

这就是以无心见闻觉知，
因此见闻觉知即是无心。
That's seeing, hearing and feeling without mind and vice versa.
如何能了知无心呢?
How to come to the understanding of no mind?
你仔细推求看看，
心是什么形状?
能掌握得到吗?
Think it over. Do you know the exact shape of your mind?
心在体内?
心在体外?
心在内外之间?
Is it inside your body? Outside yourbody? Or in-between?
内、中、外三处都找不到啊。
It is nowhere there.
翻遍宇宙天地一切处，
求觅不可得，
就知道确实是无心。
So we know that there's no mind, as we cannot locate it in the universe.

8　问曰：“若为能得知是无心？”答曰：“汝但仔细推求看，心作何相貌，其心复可得，是心不是心。”

9　为复在内，为复在外，为复在中间。如是三处推求觅心，了不可得，乃至于一切处求觅亦不可得，当知即是无心。

生死不断
Wheel of Birth and Death

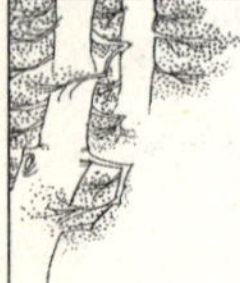

既然一切处都无心，
便应该没有罪业和福报了。
为何众生还轮回于痛苦烦恼？
There should be neither sins nor merits, since there's no mind. Then why the living creatures suffer from the Wheel of Birth and Death?

因为众生迷妄，
于无心中妄生心。
Deluded as they are, they have delusions arise from the no-mind.

造作种种我执妄想，
因此轮回于痛苦烦恼。
Confined in their delusions, they cannot escape the Wheel.

例如有人在黑暗中看见木头人，
误以为是鬼，看见绳子误以为是蛇，
便心生恐惧。
For instance, one is shrouded with fear when he mistakes in dark a wood puppet for a ghost or a rope for a snake.

10 问曰："和尚既云一切处总是无心，即合无有罪福，何故众生轮回六趣生死不断？"答曰："众生迷妄，于无心中而妄生心，造作种种业妄执为有，足可致使轮回六趣生死不断。"

11 譬有人于暗中见机为鬼见绳为蛇便生恐怖。

众生也是如此，
在无心中妄执有心，
So it is true in the living creatures.
They are plagued with delusions
arising from the no-mind.
E=MC²
而造作种种业，
于是便产生痛苦烦恼。
Then they are plagued with suffering
generated from their karma.
苦
如果众生能得大善知识的教导，
学习坐禅觉悟无心法门，
They need to follow the instructions by
great Buddhist gurus and learn about meditation to pacify the mind.
WISDOM
一切业障尽灭，
一切痛苦轮回便消失了。
Then the karma is put to an
end and the Wheel disappears.

12 众生妄执亦复如是。于无心中妄执有心造种种业，而实无不轮回六趣。

13 如是众生若遇大善知识教令坐禅觉悟无心，一切业障尽皆消灭生死即断。

有如阳光照射黑暗，
黑暗立刻化为光明。
It's like the darkness that recedes
in front of the sunshine.
如果了悟无心，
一切罪业尽灭
也像如此。
The karma is put to an end,
once you come to understand
there's no mind.

14 譬如暗中日光一照而暗皆尽。若悟无心，一切罪灭亦复如是。

菩提与烦恼
Bodhi and affliction
众生的言行和快乐痛苦，
确定都是无心吗？
There's no mind, whatever the living creatures say and do or whatever they feel, happy or painful, isn't it?
的确是无心！
众生迷妄执着有一个自我造作的心，
才会有痛苦烦恼产生。
Indeed! They are plagued with suffering and affliction, because they are deluded by the mind blinded with delusions.
若能了知无心，一切的痛苦烦恼立刻便消失了。
因此如来为执着有心的众生说有生死。
One is released from suffering and affliction, once he's come to understand there's no mind. That's why the Buddha talks about birth and death for those deluded living creatures.
菩提是相对烦恼得名，
Bodhi is named so, as there's affliction.
涅槃是相对生死得名，
名相是相对的。
Nirvana is named so, as there's birth and death.
Names and forms are relative concepts.

15　问曰："弟子愚昧心犹未了审。一切处六根所用者应答曰语种种施为烦恼菩提生死涅槃定无心否？"答曰："定是无心。只为众生妄执有心即有一切烦恼生死菩提涅槃。"

16　若觉无心即无一切烦恼生死涅槃，是故如来为有心者说有生死。菩提对烦恼得名，涅槃者对生死得名，此皆对治之法。

无心无烦恼
No mind, no affliction
如果我们无心可得，
烦恼菩提也不可得。
Neither affliction nor bodhi is attainable, once there's no mind to attain.
也没有所谓的生死涅槃了。
There's no birth, death or nirvana to attain, either.
菩提涅槃既然都不可得，
为何过去诸佛都得菩提？
But how could the Buddhas in the past attain bodhi, if neither bodhi nor nirvana is attainable?
这是用世俗语言来表达，
说是得菩提涅槃。
To attain bodhi and nirvana—it's only what we put it in secular words.
以最高真理的角度而言，
一切皆无可得。
From the angle of the supreme and ultimate truth, however, nothing is attainable.

17 若无心可得，即烦恼菩提亦不可得，乃至生死涅槃亦不可得。

18 问曰："菩提涅槃既不可得，过去诸佛皆得菩提，此谓可乎？"答曰："但以世谛文字之言得，于真谛实无可得。"

维摩经
所以《维摩经》说：
“菩提者不可以身得，不可以心得。”
So the Vimalakirti Sutra says,
“Bodhi is unattainable, physically or spiritually.”
金刚经
《金刚经》也说：“无有少法可得。”
诸佛如来知道一切法不可得，
故而得之。
And the Diamond Sutra also says,
“There's no attainable dharma at all.”
The Buddhas only attained the Buddharma, because they knew in heart that there's no attainable dharma at all.

19 故《维摩经》云：“菩提者，不可以身得，不可以心得。”又《金刚经》云：“无有少法可得。”诸佛如来但以不可得而得。

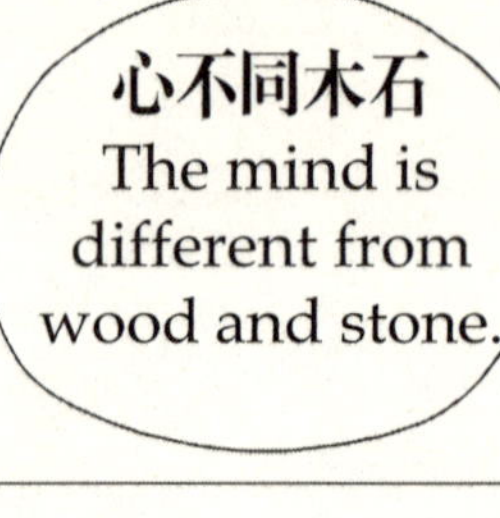
心不同木石
The mind is different from wood and stone.

一切处都无心，木石也无心。
有情众生岂不跟木石一样？
There's no mind. Wood and stone have no mind, too. The living creatures are the same as sentimentless substances like wood and stone, aren't they?

我所说的无心，
不同于木石的无心。
No, they are different.

为什么无心
不同于木石？
Why's that?

例如天鼓虽然无心，
但能发出种种妙音教化众生。
For example, a heaven drum produces beautiful sounds to lead the living creatures to enlightenment, even if it has no mind.

20 问曰："和尚既云于一切处尽皆无心。木石亦无心，岂不同于木石乎？"答曰："而我无心心不同木石。"

21 问："何以故？"答："譬如天鼓。虽复无心，自然出种种妙法教化众生。"

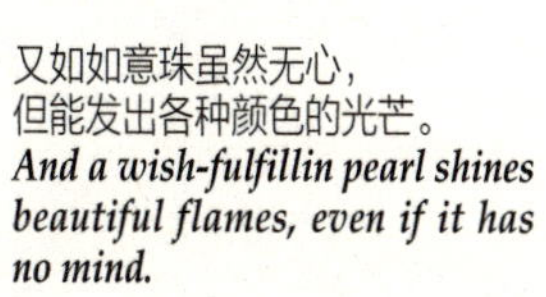

又如如意珠虽然无心，
但能发出各种颜色的光芒。
And a wish-fulfillin pearl shines beautiful flames, even if it has no mind.

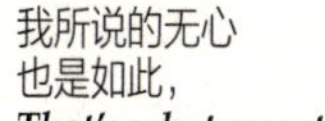

我所说的无心
也是如此，
That's what meant by me.

虽然无心但能善巧地觉悟诸法实相，
具般若智能，自在应用无碍。
One may come to see into the ultimate essence of dharmas and possess and use the supreme wisdom, even if he has no mind.

宝积经

所以《宝积经》说：
"以无心意而现行，
岂同木石乎？"
Ratnakuta Sutra put it this way,
"Without mind, one may still follow the Way.
How could he be the same as wood and stone?"

无心即是真心！
真如自性者即是
没有虚妄的心。
No mind is the true mind!
Anyone who has attained Buddhahood is free from the deluded mind.

22 又如如意珠，虽复无心自然能作种种变现。

23 而我无心亦复如是。虽复无心善能觉了诸法实相，具真般若三身自在应用无妨。

24 故《宝积经》云："以无心意而现行，岂同木石乎？"夫无心者即真心也，真心者即无心也。

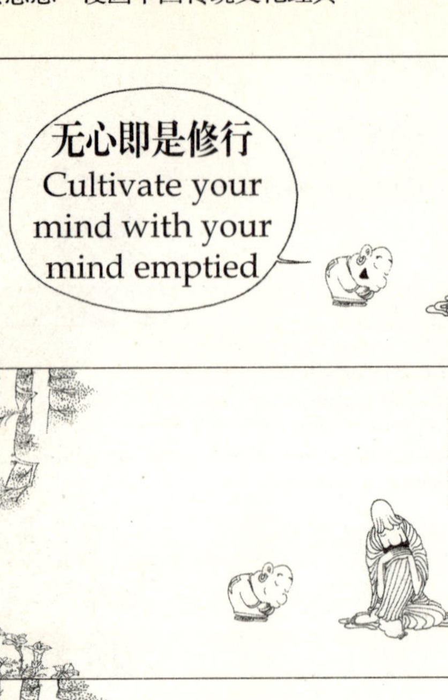
无心即是修行
Cultivate your mind with your mind emptied

心要怎么修行？
How to cultivate our mind?

于眼前情境觉知无心即是修行，此外再也没有别的修行了。
See what you see as it is. That's the right way to cultivate. Beyond it, there's nothing more.

因此面对任何情境时令心寂灭，即是无心。
Tranquillize your mind, whatever the situation is. That's what meant by me as no mind.

这时弟子忽然大悟。
The disciple came to a full understanding all of a sudden.

WISDOM
现在我已经知道，心外无物、物外无心，言行举止都得自在。
I feel at ease now, as I've grasped the essence of what meant by there's nothing beyond your mind and there's no mind beyond things.

断尽一切疑惑，我的心再也没有挂虑疑惑障碍。
With all the doubts removed, my mind is free from worries, doubts and obstacles.

25 问曰："今于心中作若为修行？"答曰："但于一切事上觉了。无心即是修行，更不别有修行，故知无心即一切，寂灭即无心也。"

26 弟子于是忽然大悟，始知心外无物物外无心，举止动用皆得自在，断诸疑网更无挂碍。

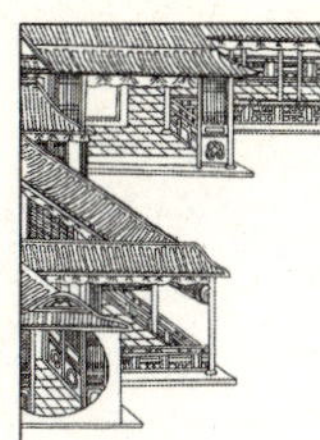

于是立即站起来向达摩作礼，
并作了一首无心颂：
心神向寂，
无色无形，
睹之不见，
听之无声。

The disciple then stood up, saluting Bodhidharma, and chanted an ode:
The mind is in essence empty,
Formless and shapeless.
It is invisible.
It is inaudible.

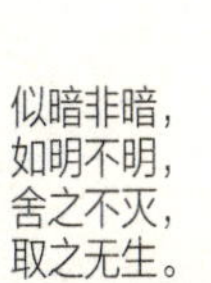

似暗非暗，
如明不明，
舍之不灭，
取之无生。

It is not that dark.
It is not that bright.
It remains the same, despite being abandoned.
It remains the same, despite being adopted.

大即廓周法界，
小即毛竭不停，
烦恼混之不浊，
涅槃澄之不清。

It is as vast as covering the realm of truth.
It is as tiny as hairs and downs.
Suffering is not as that chaotic as we thought.
Nirvana is not as that crystal-clear as we thought.

真如本无分别，
能辨有情无情，
收之一切不立，
散之普遍含灵。

The Buddha-nature is in everybody.
It tells mercy from the merciless.
With it covered, nothing is true.
With it uncovered, all gets enlightened.

27 即起作礼。而铭无心，乃为颂曰。

妙神非知所测，
正觉绝于修行，
灭则不见其坏，
生则不见其成。
The Utlitimate Way is indescribable.
The truth disappears where intentional practice arises.
Without birth, there's no death.
大道寂号无相，
万象窈号无名，
如斯运用自在，
总是无心之精。
The Great Way is formless in essence.
All the things are nameless in nature.
Bear it in mind and you'll be at ease.
That's the essence of what's called no mind.
WISDOM
无心般若
The supreme wisdom of being no mind
在所有的般若法之中，
无心般若是最上乘的佛法。
Being no mind is the supreme wisdom of all.
无心无意
No mind or intention
无心无意无受行的心，
能摧伏外道。
One conquers the false, once he has no mind, intention or suffering.

28 和尚又告曰：诸般若中以无心般若而为最上。故《维摩经》云："以无心意无受行，而悉摧伏外道。"

若知无心可得，
法即不可得，
罪福也不可得，
生死涅槃也不可得。
Since no mind is attainable, the dharma, sins and blessings, as well as nirvana are all unattainable.
一切都不可得，
连不可得之念也不可得。
Nothing is attainable, even the idea of being unattainable.
于是达摩作了一首偈颂：
昔日迷时为有心，
尔时悟罢了无心。
Bodhidharma chanted a gatha:
Focusing too much on your mind, you're deluded.
Without mind, you get enlightened.
虽复无心能照用，
照用常寂即如如。
Without mind, it still illuminates.
Without illumination, it is Buddhahood.

29 又《法鼓经》云："若知无心可得，法即不可得，罪福亦不可得，生死涅槃亦不可得，乃至一切尽不可得，不可得亦不可得。"

30 乃为颂曰："昔日迷时为有心，尔时悟罢了无心。虽复无心能照用，照用常寂即如如。"

达摩又作了一首颂:
无心无照亦无用,
无照无用即无为,
此是如来真法界,
不同菩萨为辟支。
Bodhidharma chanted another gatha:
No mind, no illumination and no function.
No illumination or function, there's no action.
That's the realm of the Buddha.
Bodhisattvas are only pratyekas.
以上所说的无心,
就是无妄想相的心啊!
No mind actually refers to
no-mind with delusions.

31 重曰:"无心无照亦无用,无照无用即无为。此是如来真法界,不同菩萨为辟支。"

32 所言无心者,即无妄相心也。

妄有入无
From delusions to emptiness
太者广大无边，
上者至高无上。
广大至高的妙理就是太上。
Tai means being boundless vast.
Shang means being supreme.
Taishang then refers to the Supreme Truth.
什么叫作太上？
What does taishang mean?
所以说太上是
“四通八达无所不至”。
That's why taishang is
“something omnipresent”.
欲界、色界、无色界三界，虽有延康福寿，
但终究会沉沦于痛苦轮回，不能说是太上。
The three realms, be it the Desire Realm, the Form Realm or the Formless Realm, always fall into the Wheel and suffering, despite various happiness and blessings. They are not taishang.

33 又问：“何名为太上？”答曰：“太者大也，上者高也，穷高之妙理，故云太上也。又太者通泰之位也。”

34 三界之天虽有延康之寿福尽是故，终轮回六趣，未足为太。

十住菩萨虽已出离痛苦烦恼，
但尚未完全通达妙理，
因此不能称之为太上。
The bodhisattvas of the ten abiding are released from suffering and affliction. However, they are still way from grasping the essence of the Supreme Truth, thus cannot be called taishang.

十住菩萨的十住是什么？
What are the ten abidings then?

菩萨修行之过程分为五十二阶位，
其中第十一至二十阶位称为十住。
The 11th-20th stages of the 52 stages of the bodhisattva are the ten abidings.

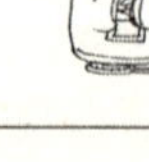
是哪十住？
What are they?

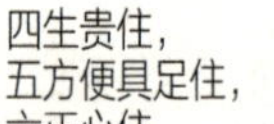
一初发心住，
二治地住，
三修行住，
The first is the abiding of awakening operation.
The second is the abiding of nurturing.
The third is the abiding of practice.

四生贵住，
五方便具足住，
六正心住，
The fourth is the abiding of producing virtues.
The fifth is the abiding of being replete with expedient means.
The sixth is the abiding of correct mind.

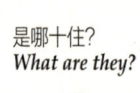

35　十住菩萨虽出离生死，而妙理未极，亦未为太。

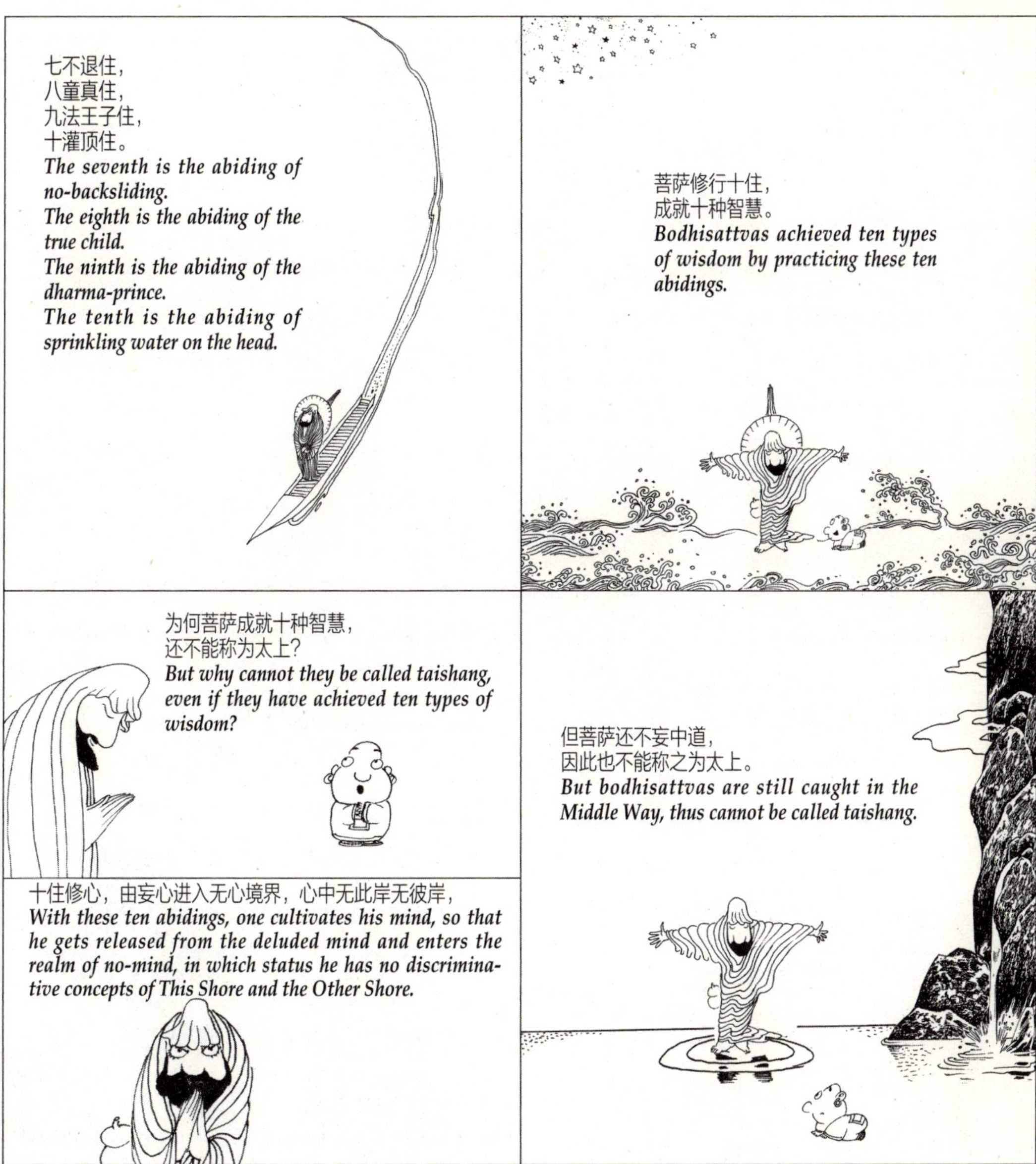
七不退住，
八童真住，
九法王子住，
十灌顶住。
The seventh is the abiding of no-backsliding.
The eighth is the abiding of the true child.
The ninth is the abiding of the dharma-prince.
The tenth is the abiding of sprinkling water on the head.
菩萨修行十住，
成就十种智慧。
Bodhisattvas achieved ten types of wisdom by practicing these ten abidings.
为何菩萨成就十种智慧，
还不能称为太上？
But why cannot they be called taishang, even if they have achieved ten types of wisdom?
但菩萨还不妄中道，
因此也不能称之为太上。
But bodhisattvas are still caught in the Middle Way, thus cannot be called taishang.
十住修心，由妄心进入无心境界，心中无此岸无彼岸，
With these ten abidings, one cultivates his mind, so that he gets released from the deluded mind and enters the realm of no-mind, in which status he has no discriminative concepts of This Shore and the Other Shore.

36 十住修心妄有入无，无其无有双遣不妄中道，亦未为太。

即使菩萨修行达到无前、
无后、无中间的妙觉境界，
Bodhisattvas may achieve the
Supreme Realm of being without
the past, present or middle.
但还不能空掉妙觉境界，
因此也不能称为太上。
But they cannot see the Supreme
Realm as emptiness. So they
cannot be called taishang.
菩萨应如何修行，
才能达到妄心永远止息？
What should bodhisattvas do to
tranquillize their deluded minds?
妙觉无所存、无所思，
乃至无思无虑，
那么妄心便永远止息。
In the Supreme Realm there is no
existence, no thought and no worry,
so that the deluded mind dies.
如果菩萨能空掉妙觉境界，
便能达至佛道至极。
They can attain Buddhahood when
see the Supreme Realm as emptiness.

37 又忘中道三处都尽，位皆妙觉。菩萨虽遣三处，不能无其所妙，亦未为太。

38 又忘其妙则佛道至极，则无所存。无存思则无思虑，兼妄心智永息。

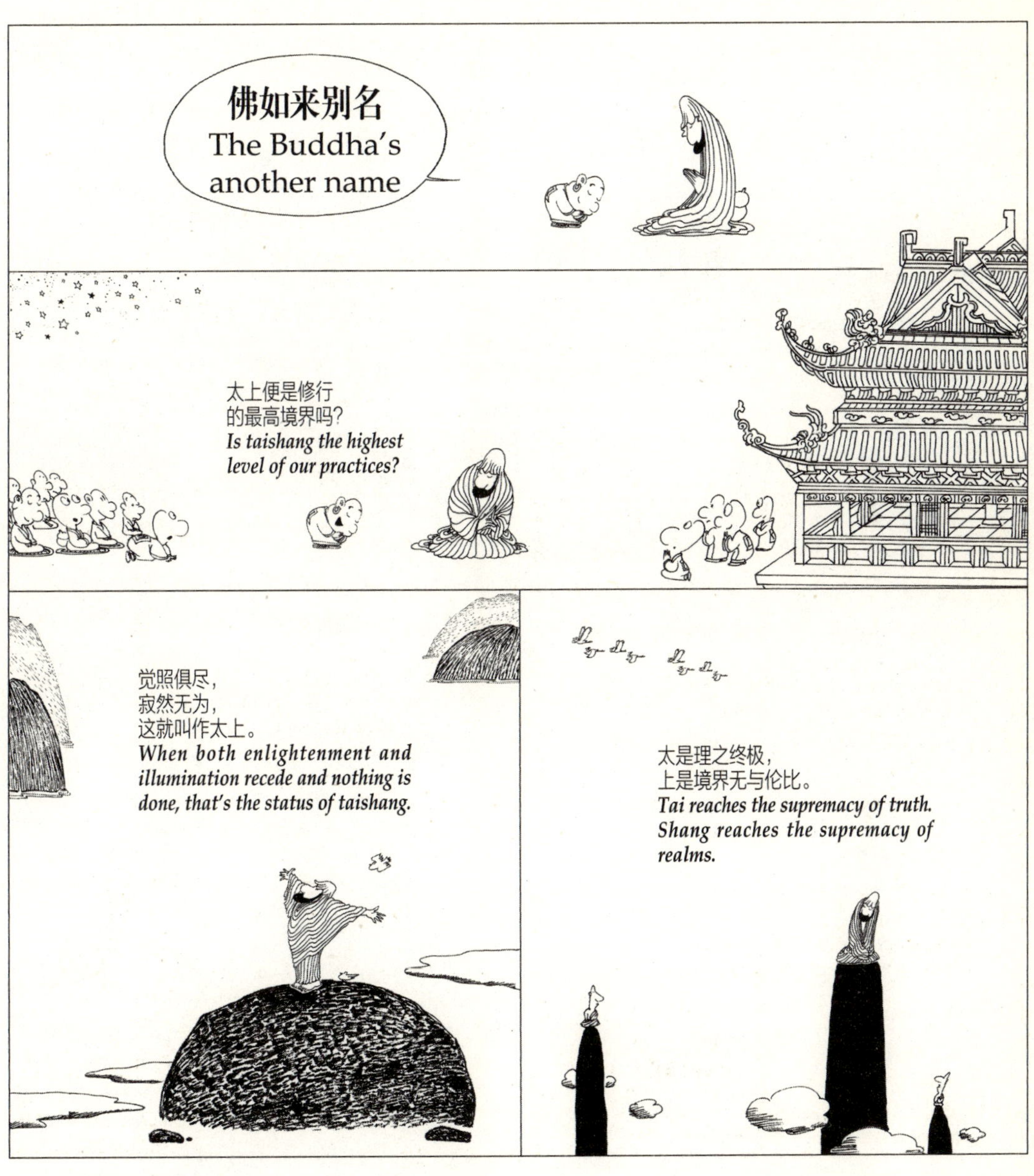
佛如来别名
The Buddha's another name
太上便是修行的最高境界吗？
Is taishang the highest level of our practices?
觉照俱尽，寂然无为，这就叫作太上。
When both enlightenment and illumination recede and nothing is done, that's the status of taishang.
太是理之终极，上是境界无与伦比。
Tai reaches the supremacy of truth. Shang reaches the supremacy of realms.

39 觉照俱尽，寂然无为，此名为太也。

40 太是理极之义，上是无等色。

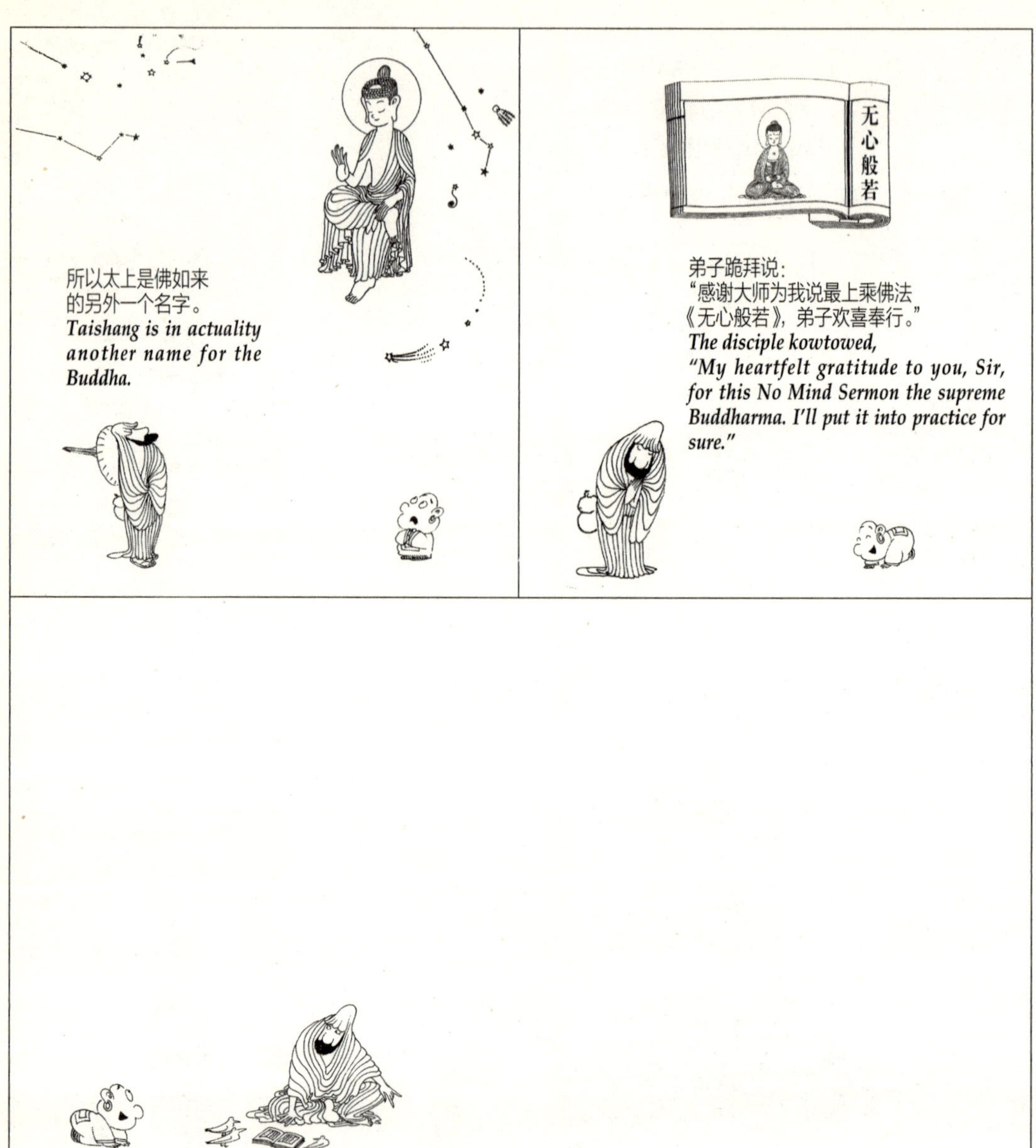
所以太上是佛如来
的另外一个名字。
Taishang is in actuality another name for the Buddha.
无心般若
弟子跪拜说：
"感谢大师为我说最上乘佛法
《无心般若》，弟子欢喜奉行。"
The disciple kowtowed,
"My heartfelt gratitude to you, Sir, for this No Mind Sermon the supreme Buddharma. I'll put it into practice for sure."

41 故云："太上。"即佛如来之别名也。